Gaelen Foley is the *New York Times* bestselling author of rich, bold historical romances set in the glittering world of Regency England and the Napoleonic Wars. Her books are available in twelve languages around the world, and have won numerous awards, including the Romantic Times Reviewers' Choice Award for Best Historical Adventure.

Gaelen holds a BA in English literature with a minor in philosophy and it was while studying the Romantic poets, such as Wordsworth, Byron and Keats, that she first fell in love with the Regency period in which her novels are set. After college, she dedicated herself completely to her artistic pursuits, spending five and a half years moonlighting as a waitress to keep her days free for writing and honing her craft.

Gaelen lives near Pittsburgh with her college-sweetheart husband, Eric, and a mischievous bichon frise called Bingley. She is hard at work on her next book.

To find out more about Gaelen's books visit her website at www.gaelenfoley.com

My Ruthless Prince

THE INFERNO CLUB

GAELEN FOLEY

piatkus

PIATKUS

First published in the US in 2012 by Avon Books,
An Imprint of HarperCollins Publishers, New York
First published in Great Britain as a paperback original in 2012 by Piatkus
By arrangement with Avon

A CIP catalogue record for this book
is available from the British Library.

ISBN 978-0-7499-5741-4

Printed and bound in Great Britain by
Clays Ltd, St Ives plc

Papers used by Piatkus are from well-managed forests
and other resposible sources.

MIX
Paper from
responsible sources
FSC® C104740

Piatkus
An imprint of
Little, Brown Book Group
100 Victoria Embankment
London EC4Y 0DY

An Hachette UK Company
www.hachette.co.uk

www.piatkus.co.uk

I did not die, and I was not alive;
think for yourself, if you have any wit,
what I became, deprived of life and death.
                    —Dante's *Inferno*, Canto XXXIV, ll. 25-27

Chapter 1

The Bavarian Alps, 1816

*W*hen another bullet whizzed past her shoulder, she whirled behind the nearest towering tree.

You're as mad as he is, coming here! she thought. But what choice had she had? She was the last friend he had left in the world, and if she didn't help him, nobody would.

All around her, the Alpine forest rang with shots and the angry, shouted orders of the black-clad guards who had come pouring out of Waldfort Castle the moment she had been spotted. Her back to the tree trunk, chest heaving, Emily Harper waited for her next chance to run.

She had been tracking her quarry for weeks from a wary distance, but when he had arrived, disappearing into the ominous mountaintop fortress, there was nothing she had been able to do but sneak through the woods and try to glimpse him, try to figure out how to lure him away.

But then one of the sentries had noticed her, and her efforts to rescue Drake had been cut short.

Now! Lunging into motion, she darted down the deer path once again, her brown woolen cloak flowing out behind her, her bow and quiver of arrows bumping at her back with every stride.

Golden shafts of sunlight pierced the forest's verdant gloom ahead like angels' lances, showing her the way. Her practiced gaze scanned for each next step over the rough, angled ground. The slope was sharp—she nearly slid—but turned slightly, dropping in an agile skid, then she leaped off the thick, gnarled root of a tree that gripped a boulder like a bony hand, and raced on.

They were gaining on her.

The wild drumming of her pulse throbbed in her ears, but her footsteps fell silently over the thick bed of pine needles that softened the forest floor.

She had not stopped to count how many of the foreign mercenaries were chasing her, some on foot, some on horseback.

Some with dogs.

But if there was any doubt that the elite Promethean cabal was real, the presence of their security detail was awfully convincing.

As soon as her presence had been detected, their security forces had come pouring out from behind the walls of the remote Bavarian castle where a secret gathering of some the richest and most powerful men in Europe was under way.

If they were not up to something nefarious, then why did they need all the armed guards keeping people away?

Emily did not personally care what twisted new schemes of tyranny the highborn occult conspirators were dreaming up in their endless hunt for power. She had come for just one reason: to bring Drake home.

He did not belong here, no matter what he said, and even if these hired thugs drove her all the way back down the mountain, she vowed to herself she would merely climb it again. She refused to quit, refused to give up on him. Her beloved lunatic needed her— whether he knew it or not. Whatever it took, she was not leaving without him. He had not abandoned her in her darkest hour, and the time had come to return the favor.

Drake was in more trouble than he knew. Never mind his enemies—now even his friends wanted to kill him.

"Dort! Dort ist er!"

"Là-bas!"

Hang it. A scowl flicked over her face as another bullet flew above her head, biting into the bark of the tree ahead.

They had seen her.

With an angry glance over her shoulder, she dodged behind an ancient elm to the side of the path ahead, shrugging her bow off her shoulder. Her hands smoothly nocked an arrow, as if with a will of their own.

As she waited for her moment, her memory was filled with images of the hours-long games of hide-and-seek she and Drake used to play as children on his family's estate.

They had run like wild savages through the forested park of Westwood Manor back at home: the earl's rambunctious heir and the woodsman's untamed daughter.

Such grand rivalries had driven them to compete, trying brashly to outbrave each other in their little shared adventures, their feats of derring-do, swinging from trees, using fallen logs as bridges over the fairly deep ravine where the stream ran through the earl's sprawling acreage. Who could skip a stone better, who could throw a stick farther, like a spear. They set traps for rabbits, but then were too tenderhearted to hand their prizes over to Cook. They had let the coneys go and had whiled away many a summer afternoon catching frogs.

But then, the Seeker had come, that towering, taciturn Scot called Virgil, and Drake had been chosen for the Order of St. Michael the Archangel. His parents had agreed to this secret duty laid upon his bloodlines centuries ago by the Crusader knights in his ancestry. With their blessing, he soon had gone away to that mysterious military-style school in Scotland, bragging to her that one day, he would become the Order's greatest warrior.

She had kicked him in the shins for his boasting at the time, then had wept her heart out when the next day came, and there had been no one to play with except for the odd collection of hurt wild animals she had nursed back to health and gradually turned into pets.

In time she got used to being alone, while Drake grew steadily toward his goal. Soon, the rowdy, black-haired boy had become a breathtakingly handsome young man, who was no longer allowed to tell her where he went each time the Order sent him out on one of those long, dangerous missions.

And then, last year, on one of the darkest days of her life, they got word from the Order that he had disappeared.

Emily pressed her back against the wide trunk of the tree, listening to her pursuers advancing.

Maybe I should let them catch me.

They would take her into the castle, closer to Drake. But she dismissed the thought in the next heartbeat.

Too risky. She was not a lady, and angry enemy males like these were known to make rough use of lowborn women.

She would gladly give her life for Drake, but no Promethean dog would ever take her honor.

As her pursuers advanced, coming closer through the trees, Emily shot her arrow well beyond them into the woods: misdirection.

Immediately, they raced off in reaction to the sound. She nocked another arrow and fired a second for good measure. The guards rushed off to track down the source of the noise. As soon as they left, she slung her bow over her shoulder again and sped off in the other direction.

Ahead, the sunlight glittered on the rushing mountain stream where she had filled her canteen earlier. She bounded from rock to rock to get across it, but when she suddenly heard more men coming, she knew the time had come to hide.

Her gaze homed in on a low miniature cave, a mere hollow between the layers of rock, likely a fox's den. Sizing it up, she saw she was slight enough of build to fit in the narrow opening—and she was desperate enough to try it.

Quick as a cat, she ran to the narrow bank of the crystal stream. It was only a strip of muddy earth and a few piled boulders before it angled up into the steep rock face that bracketed the noisy little waterfall on both sides.

Emily climbed. Her heart was pounding, but she

was somehow keeping fear at bay. Still, dying in these woods so far from home was a greater possibility than she cared to admit, and the prospect of being caught and used for cruel sport by foreign mercenaries was not much better.

Pulling herself up to the edge of the little cave, she peered into it. No one was home, thankfully, but the rounded indentation in the dirt confirmed that it had once been some animal's dwelling place.

Emily vaulted up the rock face and rolled into the den, concealed by darkness. She pulled her cloak around her; its brownish gray hue blended into the stone.

"He came this way, *Capitaine!*"

She smirked to herself in her hiding place. Of course, they would assume they were following a man, whether or not they had glimpsed her boyish garb. But it was just as well, for it meant they had not got a clear look at her face.

"Keep moving!" a strong, English voice replied.

Emily's eyes widened and she caught her breath; she knew that deep, slightly scratchy voice like the sound of her own heartbeat.

"Go that way," Drake added, repeating the command in French and German to the others. "I'll check over here."

He had to know. He had to know it was she. Surely, he had sensed her in his soul through the almost mystical bond they had shared since childhood.

Heart pounding, she bit her lip against a crazed smile at his nearness. At last! *This* was what she had been praying for, one chance to talk to him.

To bring him back to his senses. To coax him home like one of her wounded wild animals. He did not know what he was doing, coming here.

She waited for the other men to leave, joy and relief

welling up in her even though the last time she had seen Drake, the blackguard had put a knife to her throat and used her as a hostage so he could escape.

Of course, he'd never hurt her, she assured herself.

No matter how much the Prometheans might have scarred his body and damaged his mind, even blacking out much of his memory with their abuses during the months they had kept him in that dungeon—no matter how much their evil might have changed him—he was still Drake.

And in her heart, he was still her best friend, even though it was foolish to think so since he was an earl, and she was nobody in particular.

She could hear the others retreating into the woods to continue the hunt for the intruder. Nearby, there was no sound above the rapid babbling of the mountain brook. Not even the birds called, frightened away by the gunfire.

She stayed motionless for a long moment . . . until she heard his voice, quiet and grim. "Tell me, please, dear God, tell me it isn't you in there."

Emily slowly pulled the edge of her cloak down from her face. At first, from her vantage point, she could only see the lower half of his muscular body.

The long, loose black coat. Well-worn black leather breeches. Black knee boots.

Hoping he would not be angry, she whisked her cloak back and rolled out of her hiding place, peeking out to make extra sure the others were gone, and then dropping lightly from the fox's den to the narrow bank below.

She grinned at him and tossed her long hair over her shoulders. "Surprise."

From the other side of the stream, Drake pinned her in a cold, unsmiling stare.

Her saucy grin faded as she watched his angular face pale with dread, possibly fury at the sight of her.

Shaking his head in disbelief, not uttering a word, the tall, black-haired demigod of a man scanned her from head to toe, making sure she was not hurt.

She did the same to him as she warily approached, relieved to find no new injuries on his tall, formidable body. In his eyes, however, she saw the same fractured intensity blazing in their coal black depths.

It was then that she knew that as mad as it was of her to come here, she had done the right thing.

He was not even close to being all right.

God, it pained her, that lost look in his soulful eyes after all he had been through. Clearly, he did not understand the consequences of his actions. What did he think he was doing? The Prometheans could not possibly trust him. They would kill him, and if they did not, now the Order would.

His brother warriors now viewed him as a traitor.

She took another step toward him, holding his gaze. "How are you? Are you all right?" she murmured.

With a cold smile, he did not answer the question.

But Emily did not take offense any more than she had the time that falcon with the broken wing had bitten her finger. Drake needed help, and that was why she was here.

Holding his gaze, she approached, though it made her heart hurt whenever she looked into his eyes and read the pain left behind by what these Promethean bastards had done to him. His time in their captivity had turned him into a remote, brooding stranger whose very presence seethed with silent hatred and rage—a man who had once been a practical joker.

As a lad, he'd been fond of pulling pranks. In his twenties, he'd been a fun-loving rogue with the unfortunate habit of singing rude tavern songs at the top of his lungs when he was drunk, laughing off the attentions of all those horrid painted women, high and low, who fawned on him and called him "Westie," short for his title, Earl of Westwood. In his thirties, he was still just as beautiful on the outside. He had always been so beautiful . . . but inside, she knew the torturers had wrecked him. Destroyed his once-contagious charm, his fiery lust for life. Now she seemed to be the only one who could reach him because of their history together.

He trusted her.

After months of beatings and interrogations, the Order had pulled whatever necessary strings they could to get their agent back. Drake had been returned to them in such a damaged state that it had unsettled them all. He'd attacked his former teammates like a wild man, not recognizing them, thinking everyone wanted to kill him. Begging them not to put him in a cage, ranting that he had to get back to James. The old man was in danger, he had said over and over again. Instead of paying attention to any of this, his saddened friends had brought him home so he could mend.

It still filled Emily with rage to think of how thin he'd been when she had first seen him, how he had jumped at the slightest noise.

Whatever his captors had done to scramble his wits, he'd had no recognition of his own mother or the country estate where he'd grown up.

The only thing he had remembered . . . was her.

While Lord Rotherstone, one of his closest friends in the Order, had guarded him at Westwood Manor, Emily had thrown herself into the task of healing her beloved childhood companion.

They had been making fine progress after a few

weeks. She had slowly, gently, quietly, begun to lead him out of the dark storm he lived in. She had even claimed the victory of seeing him wake up one morning having slept the whole night through.

He seemed to be doing so well after a time that the last thing she had expected was for Drake to take matters into his own hands, escaping by taking her hostage, all so that he could return to his precious James and those who had abused him.

In the face of all evidence to the contrary, Emily still could not bring herself to believe that Drake had turned traitor. It was impossible.

No, she had an awful feeling that his real motive for coming back was to try to get revenge.

Which just went to show how unstable he still was.

The Order had been battling the vile Prometheans for centuries. One man was not about to take down the whole organization alone. *Mad or sane, though*, she thought, *leave it to Drake to try.*

Whatever he had up his sleeve, clearly, he had not figured *her* into his plans.

"What the hell are you doing here?" he demanded in a low, taut voice as she ventured another step toward him.

"Aren't you happy to see me?" she attempted in an airy tone.

He looked at her in exasperation. "Not in the least."

"You know why I'm here, Drake," she chided softly, willing patience. "I've come to take you home."

He closed his eyes. Lowered his head. And scratched his eyebrow. Which did not bode well.

Then he flicked his jet-black eyes open again and glared at her. "Get the hell out of here. Now."

"No."

"I appreciate the gesture, Em, but you made the trip

in vain. I'm staying here, and you are going home. Go on. Climb back into that cave and hide until we've pulled back to the castle. I'll cover for you."

"No! I'm not going anywhere without you! Do you think I came six hundred miles for nothing?" She glanced into the woods to make sure the others were not returning.

But she warned herself not to lose sight of the fact that she was dealing with a dangerous man who was no longer quite the master of his faculties. If she pushed him too hard, there was no telling what he might do.

She reached out her hand to him. "Come with me, Drake. Escape with me now, before they come back. I'll take care of you."

"Oh, Emily," he whispered with a fleeting, anguished wince.

"I already lost you once. I can't go through that again."

"They will kill you," he whispered. "They will kill us both."

"Not if we move right now. We can still get away. You know we can, you and I, together. These woods. It'll be just like old times. Let me take care of you, sweeting. You are confused. I know you don't want to be here."

He shook his head, turning away from her in agitation. "Why don't you ever listen? I can't believe you're here. I told you I have to do this!"

"But you don't. Whatever you think you're trying to do here, you're only going to get yourself killed. I can't allow that, Drake. You've bitten off more than you can chew this time, and you need to come home. Whatever James might have told you, this is *not* where you belong."

"You're the one who doesn't belong here!" he shot back in a fierce whisper, taking a large step closer.

"How could you put yourself at risk this way?—and you say I'm the one that's mad!"

"Drake, denying what you've been through is not going to help you get better. You're not well! You need time to heal. Just be patient. You will get back to your full strength in time, then maybe—"

"I am back to my full strength," he growled.

"Physically, perhaps. But we both know you're not ready inside for any sort of mission. Come home with me. You've got to let me help you. You know you can trust me. Please, Drake. Let's escape now before they come back."

"No."

She paused, taking a new strategy. "So, you want to send me back six hundred miles all by myself?" she asked, for she could be as ruthless as he when the occasion called. "You know how dangerous it is in these forests. Wolves. Bears. Men."

He narrowed his eyes at her, well aware of what she was attempting.

He had killed the last man who had threatened her.

"You'd have me travel back through three war-torn countries alone? I'm out of money. I don't speak the language."

"It's a wonder you made it this far alive," he muttered. "You've never even been outside the shire."

"I followed you," she said simply, shrugging. "You and James. I thought you almost spotted me a few times."

He lowered his gaze. "I thought I was imagining it." Then he shook his head at her. "Why did you do this to me?"

"Not to you. For you. Because you need me." She took his hand in hers and pulled. "Come on, we'll talk later. We need to go right now."

He remained planted though his fingers lightly encircled hers. "I'm sorry, Emily. No."

"Drake, you're not an agent anymore!" she whispered in exasperation. "The Order fears you have betrayed them!"

"Maybe I have. Did you ever think of that?"

"Don't be absurd. If you turn yourself in, I know it'll be all right. I'll vouch for you. We'll go to them together and explain that you just made a mistake, you erred in judgment, thinking you could come here and take them down alone—"

"I did not make a mistake," he answered darkly.

Just then, the sound of male voices nearing through the woods made Emily suck in her breath.

"Come on, Drake! Please!"

"No! I am not going with you. Now get back in that bloody cave and hide right now—"

"Enough," she cut him off, resorting to her pistol.

He arched a brow as she drew her gun and aimed it at him.

"Let's go, now."

"What, you're taking me captive?"

"Come on, you idiot!" she pleaded.

He let out a low, cynical laugh. "Pull the trigger, please." He parted the neck of his shirt, presenting the top of his chest. "You might as well. I'd rather you do it than anyone else."

She glowered at him for calling her bluff, but grabbed him by his shirt with her other hand, prepared to drag him physically back to England if she had to. "I've had it with you. Come on, now!" she ordered, taking him captive at gunpoint. "Don't give me any trouble. Walk!"

He was laughing at her.

"You're coming with me. Blast it, Drake, I am trying to save you here!"

"What makes you think I have any desire to be saved?" He grasped her wrist where her hand clutched his shirt. "Let go of me, Emily." He looked deep into her eyes and repeated in a meaningful whisper: *"Let me go."*

"No," she breathed, staring into his eyes as she shook her head. "Never."

"I already told you it's too late for me. I know what I'm doing, Emily. Now, go. You've got to do this for me. Nothing's worth it if you should die."

Her eyes welled with tears.

"Don't cry." He touched her face wistfully. "Don't make a sound. Just go back to that cave and stay out of sight. They're coming. Go on, now. I'll get them out of here. Wait till we're gone, then you run like hell down this mountain and go home. You've got to trust me. Tell the same to Max."

Emily refused to move. "It'll never be home again," she choked out. "I can't leave you here to die."

He looked over his shoulder. "If you don't run, you're going to die with me. Is that what you want?"

"Maybe. It's better than going back alone."

He looked taken aback at her answer, but she held his stare in defiance. Did the idiot still not know how she felt about him?

"You have no idea of what you've yourself gotten into," he uttered.

"I don't care, I can't let them hurt you again!"

"Damn it! I'm going to wring your neck for this," he muttered, then suddenly grabbed her by her wrist and yanked her to him, taking the pistol out of her hand and tucking it into the back of his waist. A second before the Promethean guards rushed into the clearing by the stream, Drake did something he had never done before.

Something that shocked her to the marrow.

He caught her up in his arms and kissed her, claiming her mouth with unabashed, lusty intent.

She was too shocked at first even to react. After all, his mother had made it very clear to her years ago, when Emily was as an awkward fifteen-year-old, that this must never happen, or her father would be sacked.

She had done her best since then not even to let girlish daydreams of kissing him play across her mind.

Not that her efforts had always been successful.

She was old enough to know now that she wanted him and to sense that he had often stayed away precisely because he thought about it, too.

But none of her daydreams had ever pictured their first kiss happening like this, with a dozen Promethean guards rushing into the clearing and surrounding them.

Terror mingled with intoxication: Both made her knees weak. She clutched his broad shoulders to keep from falling over, tentatively following his lead.

Drake ignored the men completely and went on kissing her, his tongue in her mouth, his fingers sensuously clutching her hips while the men jeered and shouted in surprise to find them thus.

When he finally ended the brash, rather rude kiss and released her, Emily saw stars.

"False alarm, boys," he drawled at last, sounding slightly breathless. He licked his lips and hungrily held her stunned gaze—though she noted his exasperation with her still simmering in the midnight depths of his eyes.

She could not look away, quite shocked at him and at the potent mix of fear and want pounding in her blood.

"What's this?" one of the guards demanded in English.

"This?" Drake cast the man one of his old, devilish grins. "*This* is my girl."

"Your girl?" they exclaimed in skeptical surprise.

"Aye. You boys nearly shot my favorite little servant wench. I'd have been *very* cross if any of you had so much as scratched her pretty bottom." He slapped her on the arse, and Emily gasped outright.

The men exchanged wry, humorous glances.

"Your servant, *Capitaine*?" a leathery Frenchman questioned, as though not quite buying it.

"Oh, yes. She's quite devoted to my comforts," Drake said slowly, with an innuendo that roused their laughter. "Aren't you, love?"

Emily could not manage an answer at first, blushing and tongue-tied. She knew she had better play along but was completely out of sorts and rather mortified.

Above all, she was stung by his insulting choice of terms for her—a servant wench, indeed?

The difference in their stations had long been a sore spot for her, as he knew full well, since that was obviously what had made his parents deem her unworthy of their splendid son. His pointed reminder of it now just went to show how furious he was at her for coming here. She quite believed His Lordship had just put her in her place.

Ungrateful villain.

"I had a feeling she might follow me. We've been doing this for years, haven't we, sweeting? Ever since she was old enough to know what to do with a man. But alas, she got addicted," he drawled, staring into her eyes. "Every time I try to set her aside, she just keeps showing up again."

"Hmmph," said Emily, lifting her chin, half-amused, half-outraged at his braggadocio, and well aware there was a grain of truth in it.

Indignation at his sly goading helped her find her spunk again. Very well, she could play along as brazenly as he if it meant the difference between life and death.

"If I'm the only one addicted, then why do you keeping sending for me—milord?" she countered with an arch look.

"Good question," he murmured, staring at her in lusty approval. "You are my dirty little secret, aren't you?"

That's what your mother's afraid of. She grasped the lapel of his black coat and moved closer to him. "We both know you need someone lookin' after you."

"And we both know what *you* need, as well," he replied with an extremely wicked smile. When he ran his hands down her waist to her hips, she could not hold back a gasp; her eyes glazed over slightly.

She cursed herself for the haze of desire he cast over her, for her beloved spy was only putting on a show to deceive the others. *Don't get so excited,* she told herself. This was just a ruse.

After all, it had long been established that the wild rogue Inferno Club member Lord Westwood would happily dally with any woman in England.

Except for her.

She huffed and looked away, blushing. Half of her wanted to throttle him for thwarting her perfectly sensible plan to get him out of here, while the other half wanted these onlookers to leave so the two of them could finish the game they had just started, right here on the soft forest floor.

Her pulse raced as he held her against his muscled body. No wonder the men appeared to believe their charade.

She could feel Drake's heart pounding in response

to her, as well, and the thickening swell of his nether regions against her navel.

"I was beginning to think he didn't like women," one of the soldiers muttered.

"No, he just likes the wrong women," Emily tossed out with a cheeky sideward glance. "Mind your own business, anyway. I didn't come here for you."

"Oho! She told *you*!"

The men guffawed at her impertinence.

"I wish," another opined under his breath.

She dismissed them with a queenly toss of her head while Drake watched her with a serene smile. She returned her full attention to him, running her hand up his chest in playful chiding. "As for you, sir, if you didn't want me to come, you should've been more convincing in your good-bye. It was quite halfhearted, as I recall."

Drake laughed softly and captured her chin, lifting her face to his. "Well, you're here now, you cheeky little minx, so you might as well come in. I'm sure I can find a few uses for you when I get off duty."

"What do you mean to do with her, *Capitaine*?" the weathered fellow clipped out in a businesslike tone.

"Good God, Jacques, use your imagination," he retorted with a scoff. "And you call yourself a Frenchman."

The others laughed.

"That's not what I meant, as you well know," Jacques answered impatiently. "What is Falkirk going to say about this?"

Drake shrugged, sliding his arm more snugly around Emily's waist as he inspected her curves at closer range. "Nothing, likely. Whatever modest amenities I require for my personal comfort are of no interest to the Council."

"Well, you had better ask him. He's the one who pays us, not you."

"True. But I'm the one who hired you sorry bastards. And I can get rid of you just as easily, don't forget it. Falkirk would not have made me the head of his security if he did not trust my discretion. Besides, she won't be any trouble, will you, sugarplum?" With an indulgent half smile, he tapped her fondly on the nose. "You promise to be a good girl for me?"

Emily managed an obliging smile, but the look in her eyes was a glare. *Now you're pushing your luck.* "Aye, milord."

"See? She's very obedient." He was deliberately goading her.

Just you wait.

"She'll stay out of the way, so don't you mind her. She'll share my room," Drake added. "That way she'll be close to hand whenever I have need of her."

Her pulse raced at the heated promise in his eyes.

But then, one of the younger soldiers made the mistake of an ill-timed jest. "Eh, I have a few tasks in mind the chit could do for me when you're done with her, *Capitaine*."

"*Ja*, why don't you pass her around when you're through?" a tall, strapping German rumbled with a grin.

All humor vanishing, Drake slowly turned to the mercenaries, his stare icy. "What did you say?"

The feckless French lad started to repeat himself, but the older, leathery Jacques held up his arm. "Shut up, Gustave."

Gustave looked confused. "What? Ah, come, she's just a servant."

"*My* servant. My property." Drake said something to

them in French that immediately silenced their jokes and wilted their wolfish grins.

Emily did not understand the words, but Drake's murderous snarl was that of the pack's dominant male warning his underlings away from a choice piece of meat. His tone of voice matched the bristling tension in his body, and his hand drifted down to the weapon at his side, as if he was quite prepared to back up the verbal rebuke with any degree of violence necessary.

She had also tensed, rather frightened. She lowered her head.

"*Comprenez?*" he barked.

The men mumbled in assent, shrinking from the challenge.

"Good." He returned to English so she could understand, too, and kept his arm around her shoulders, a visible declaration of his protection—and apparent ownership. "Then let's get back to the castle. Return to your posts and stay alert. Next time, it might not be a false alarm."

The chastened men mumbled agreement, following the second-in-command, Jacques, out of the grove.

Furtively, Emily sent her fierce protector an anxious glance. He was still in a bristling stance as he watched them walk ahead, indeed, he was watching their every move.

When he relaxed slightly, he looked down at her with an inquiry in his dark eyes. *You all right?*

She nodded, but then glanced toward the fortress in distress. *To the castle, really? Must we?*

You only have yourself to thank, his dark smirk replied, but his eyes were grim. "Come on." He kept his arm draped across her shoulders, emphasizing his proprietary claim on her to the other soldiers, who caught up with them as they came back out onto the dusty mountain road.

Glancing around at all the armed mercenaries cowering from Drake, Emily saw no choice but to go along with the charade. He was clearly all that stood between her and an unspeakable fate.

Perhaps you should have thought of that earlier, she chided herself, her emotions in an angry tumult at this unexpected turn of events. She was furious at him for thwarting her rescue plan, and, besides that, her pride still smarted from his rude reminder of her lower status.

Well, she might be a servant, but she was nobody's "wench." How depressing, that after a lifetime's daydreams, her idol had only kissed her at last for the sake of a ruse.

Her frustration climbed with every step they took up the winding road toward the Promethean stronghold. *Blast it, this was not supposed to happen!* She had not tracked him for hundreds of miles and crossed the Alps to join the madman in whatever game he was playing.

If it was a game.

A chill ran down her spine at the darkest possibility, the one she'd been refusing to consider.

Maybe he *hadn't* come for revenge.

Dread gripped her at the thought, but could it be possible that old James Falkirk really *had* succeeded in turning him, as Drake's fellow agents feared?

After all the years that Drake had devoted himself to the Order, it seemed completely counter to reason. But the mind was a mysterious thing, and for a time, the wounded Earl of Westwood had forgotten everything, even who he was.

If the Prometheans could do *that* to him, why *couldn't*

they persuade him to renounce his old life and join their dark cult?

Maybe the months of torture had broken him so deeply inside that the Drake she knew and loved was truly gone, replaced by someone else, as he had tried to warn her back in England. A mindless slave with all the lethal skills of a top Order agent. Someone willing to do the enemy's bidding without hesitation.

Someone evil.

Emily looked askance at him . . . and wondered.

Very much on guard, Emily determined to keep her eyes open and her mouth shut until she had a better idea of what was going on around here, and where Drake's loyalties actually lay at the moment.

Waldfort Castle loomed ahead, its stone bulk rising through the trees. Its mighty footprint in the mountainous terrain formed an uneven quadrangle with pointed turrets at the irregular corners.

Dark gray roofs topped timeworn walls hewn from rugged, golden brown stone. It had a center tower that was square-shaped halfway up its length, but a second cylindrical layer on top of it extended even farther skyward. The keep's many narrow mullioned windows glittered in the sun.

Below the castle, green woods embraced the walls; behind it, white mountains, and above it, blue skies. It did not look at all like a place where sinister things could happen.

But looks could be deceiving.

As they approached the gatehouse, Emily noted the
coat of arms engraved atop the barrel vault at the entrance to the bristling fortress. The hairs on her nape
stood on end when she saw the torch symbol in the
center of the crest—a favorite insignia of the Prometheans, as Drake had told her long ago.

Her heart thumped as she walked by his side under
the spiked portcullis and through the opening in the
castle's massive outer shield wall.

Once inside the fortifications, they passed through a
smaller gate in yet another defensive wall.

Emily held her head high though her stomach was in
knots. Drake's presence beside her helped her keep up
a confident façade, but at the moment, even he seemed
like a stranger. Maybe all this had been a very bad
idea. But it was far too late to turn back as she was
escorted into an arcaded courtyard at the heart of the
mighty keep.

Drake kept a steadying hand on the small of her
back. But with the other guards around them, he still
avoided eye contact with her, staring straight ahead,
his chin high. Something about the set of his broad
shoulders warned her he was prepared to fight if it
came to it. *God.* The last thing he needed for the sake
of his dubious sanity was to engage in more violence.
In the heart of the Promethean stronghold, however,
with guards on every side of them, she realized that
what he had said earlier was true—one wrong move,
and they both could die.

What on earth was he thinking, coming into the
lion's den like this? Why would they even accept him?

How far had he gone to win their trust?

"This way," he urged her, escorting her across the
inner courtyard, a steadying hand pressed against her
back.

Most of the guards parted ways with them there, splitting up to return to their various posts. Jacques and two others escorted them into the castle proper.

As soon as they stepped inside, Emily faltered, taken aback by a sudden indescribable sensation—a wordless, welling dread—as if she had just walked through an invisible wall of evil upon entering this place.

Gooseflesh rose on her arms at the eerie atmosphere inside the castle, the strange, faint odor on the air.

The smell of death, corruption . . .

"Come along," Drake murmured.

If he noticed her instinctual revulsion, like a horse balking before a road where danger lurked that the rider could not see, he gave no sign.

She told herself she was being silly. The sudden drop in temperature was merely the result of their having passed into the cooler shadow of the building.

Yet the kindly German peasants in the outlying farms had warned her not to come here when she had stopped to buy supplies and ask for information. She had only picked up a few basic words in their tongue along the way, but from their gestures, their hasty signs of the Cross, and the grim shaking of their heads, she gathered that the locals considered Waldfort Castle cursed. *"Nein, fraulein.* Do not go there. *Sehr gefährlich."*

Very dangerous.

But for her loyalty to Drake, here she was. She took a deep breath, squared her shoulders, and walked in.

On the ground floor, the first area they entered was the Guards' Hall, a vast, vaulted dining room, long and narrow, with giant fireplaces on both ends; it had a stone floor, whitewashed walls, and massive columns joined by Gothic arches. There was not much furniture, just a long, dark table with plain wooden chairs around it.

They marched through it and out the other side, entering a more richly adorned corridor.

Suddenly, a white door opened ahead.

From between the two guards ahead of her, Emily spied a lean, distinguished gentleman, who appeared to be in his sixties, emerging from the room. He pulled the door shut quietly behind him and came toward them, slight of build and elegantly dressed, with patrician features and a shock of pewter hair. Yet as he approached, Emily was struck by the thought that there was something oddly reptilian about his bony face and cold, gray eyes.

"Did you capture the intruder?" he asked Drake at once. As soon as he spoke, she recognized him as a fellow Englishman by the touch of Yorkshire in his accent. "Was it someone from the Order?" he added.

"Er, not exactly, sir." Drake nodded wryly to the guards to step aside.

They parted, revealing Emily in their midst.

"Well." As the old man's shrewd, penetrating gaze narrowed in on her, Emily realized this was the infamous James Falkirk.

Drake's supposed savior.

The Promethean magnate was the one who had finally ordered Drake freed from the dungeons, not out of any particular concern for his well-being, of course, but merely as a change in tactics, since the brutal daily beatings weren't producing the desired results.

When the others had failed to break the captured agent through cruelty, Falkirk had hoped to manipulate Drake through kindness instead, promising him protection from the torturers, winning his trust, all in an effort to turn him to the dark side.

Emily was not sure if she should regard the old man with gratitude or an even deeper hatred. True, Falkirk had probably saved his life, but Drake's confusion about whose side he was on at present—his loss, essentially, of himself—was due to this old schemer and his mind games.

Falkirk's cold stare probed her. "And who might this be?"

Drake cleared his throat slightly. "This is the girl I told you about, sir."

Falkirk arched a silvery brow at him. "Indeed?" He dismissed Jacques and the others with a glance.

They bowed briefly and retreated, leaving the three of them alone. Emily waited tensely, ready to follow Drake's lead, as before.

"Do you remember in London, sir, when we were confronted outside the Pulteney Hotel? She was the one who threw the rock at that Order agent who held us at gunpoint and tried to stop us from escaping."

"Ah, yes, your little servant girl." Falkirk turned back to stare at Emily in amazement. "You mean to say this slip of a girl followed you all the way from London?"

Emily pressed her lips together. She did not like being discussed like a piece of furniture.

"Even when we were young, her survival skills were impressive, sir. Her father was the woodsman at my estate. He taught her how to track animals, how to live off the land. That's how she found us."

"All the way from England . . . for love of you?" Falkirk chuckled softly as he scanned her in surprise. "It's a long way to go for a man you can't have, my dear."

His words were so casually cruel, he might as well have run her through. She dropped her gaze with a barely concealed wince. "I know my place, sir. I cannot help the way I feel. Besides, he needs me."

Drake cleared his throat slightly, studying the floor.

"When I was not yet twenty, the owner of a neighboring estate tried to rape the girl. I killed him to protect her. She's been devoted to me ever since."

"Hmm." Falkirk nodded slowly.

Emily stared at the ground, shocked to her core that he had just told Falkirk that.

But it seemed the old man would not be satisfied by anything less than the truth. "I see. So, you love him, do you?"

Emily lifted her chin and met his stare in shock.

Falkirk waited.

She could not bear to glance at Drake. "Yes, sir."

"And does he love you?"

"No, sir. That would not be fitting," she said barely audibly.

"But you share his bed?" He folded his arms across his chest, studying her.

Emily cringed at his interrogation, momentarily tongue-tied, for Drake had never touched her until moments ago, down in the forest. But this was the story they were telling, and the tension she felt emanating from his big body reminded her to stick to it. "Rich girls can afford to keep their morals, I suppose," she forced out obliquely.

Falkirk smiled at last in cynical approval. "That they can," he said indulgently, apparently quite entertained. "What is your name, then?"

"Emily Harper, sir."

"Hmm. Well, you've proved yourself to me already, as I recall. Back in London, it was you who allowed us to get away when that Order agent had us at gunpoint."

"He was going to kill my lord," she murmured with a nod at Drake.

"So, you saved him, and that allowed him to save me, in turn," Falkirk said. "I'm in your debt."

Emily bowed her head.

The old man appeared to accept their explanation for her arrival. Drake spoke up to make sure of it. "I hope you do not mind, sir. I did not foresee her following me, but it isn't safe to send her back alone."

"No, of course not." He shrugged. "You are entitled to a servant if you wish. I'm just a bit puzzled, is all." Falkirk studied him, intrigued. "We offered you a woman before, a thorough voluptuary, but you wanted no part of her or her courtesan's tricks."

Drake dropped his gaze. "No, sir."

"Now I see why. A proper whore isn't quite to your taste. You prefer something a little more . . . innocent. Really, Westwood, dallying with the servants," the old man murmured in amusement, baiting him like a soft-voiced Satan. "I wouldn't have taken you for the type."

Drake smiled almost intimately at him. "We all have our vices, sir. Besides, she's not as innocent as she looks."

Falkirk's lips twisted. "Very well, then. If you are sure she can be trusted. The stakes couldn't be higher, as you know."

"Absolutely."

"Well, have at it, then, if that is your preference. She is pretty enough, I'll grant you that. Fetching creature, underneath all that dust. Clean yourself up, girl. And then look after my head of security well. You may be just what he needs."

"With pleasure, milord." Emily moved closer to Drake.

Falkirk looked warily from one to the other, then dismissed them both with a nod, returning to the room from which he'd come. When the door opened, she glimpsed a richly decorated dining room; a number of older gentlemen were sitting around the table though no food was served.

Some sort of meeting appeared to be in progress.

Then the door closed, and Drake touched her elbow, nodding to her with a cautioning look to go with him.

Emily followed, letting out a low sigh of relief that at least they had cleared that hurdle.

They walked on, but her mind replayed the scene she had just witnessed. Now that she had seen Drake and Falkirk together, she was even more confused about what was going on. Obviously, Falkirk had saved Drake's life by getting him out of the dungeon, but the Order knew that Drake had saved Falkirk's life, in turn.

As the second most powerful of all the Prometheans, James Falkirk had many enemies; but he was a scholar, not a warrior, and in the increasing frailty of his years, he had to rely on younger men for his security.

That was where Drake came in.

After Falkirk had removed the broken Order agent from the dungeon, Drake had become so gratefully devoted to him that, with his warrior skills, he had ended up saving Falkirk's neck on numerous occasions.

An odd bond seemed to have formed between them over the past year or so that all of this had been going on.

Frankly, Emily was amazed at how much influence Drake now seemed to have over the old schemer. Falkirk certainly appeared to trust him. Maybe they really were that close.

Or maybe Drake had played a few mind games of his own on his supposed master.

She could not wait until they were alone so she could ask him about that, and a great deal more.

Going deeper into the castle, she saw that while the Guards' Hall had been left very much in its rugged medieval state, the main floor and the owners' residential quarters had been luxuriously refurbished in the flowery rococo style of the previous century.

They passed grand saloons full of gilding and candy-colored pastels, claw-footed furniture with velvet upholstery, ornate chandeliers, and gleaming white chimneypieces. But the opulence of the State Rooms only sharpened her sense of something evil dwelling within.

At the end of the central hallway, Drake led her up a grand staircase. They bypassed the second and third floors, but on the fourth, they left the stairs and proceeded down a simple hallway where the décor once more abandoned Baroque profusion in favor of the older, plainer style: strong, rustic, German simplicity.

Drake led her down the corridor, then stopped before one of the rounded wooden doors, of which there were many, placed at regular intervals. She watched his face uncertainly, but he avoided her gaze as he took a key out of his black waistcoat pocket.

He unlocked the door and opened it, revealing a simple, square box of a chamber. He nodded to her to go in ahead of him.

Emily stepped into his spartan quarters, looking all around her. The chamber had a low ceiling with a few exposed, heavy, dark beams and creamy walls of wavy plaster.

To the right of the door was a small fireplace. To the left, a washstand with an old, rust-tainted mirror above it. There were no windows in the chamber, but a small balcony opened off the opposite wall. Drake had left the little balcony doors wide open to admit the light and the fresh mountain air, and the Alpine view beyond was spectacular. Emily was drawn toward it, but then she stopped, noticing his crisply made bed in the corner.

One bed.

With a slight gulp, she turned and looked at him.

He leaned against the open door, watching her in his room with a hooded gaze, his arms folded across his chest.

"You can put your things over there." He nodded toward the wall, where his extra coat and a few shirts hung on clothing pegs.

She nodded, acutely aware of his silent reproach as she walked across the small faded oval of a braided cottage rug and went to lean her bag against the wall.

"Well, then. Make yourself at home," he concluded with a trace of sarcasm in his voice. "You heard James. Stay in this room and keep out of trouble, if that's possible for you. I've got to get back to my post."

She turned to him as she took off her cloak. "You're leaving already?"

"I'm not on holiday, Miss Harper."

"Miss Harper?" She stared at him in irked bewilderment as she draped her cloak over her arm. "What's wrong with you?"

His only response was an icy glare.

She realized he was as angry at her for coming as she was at him for refusing to escape.

A stalemate.

She threw her cloak angrily on his bed. "Well, why don't you get it off your chest?" she flung out.

He shut the door, unable to resist, it seemed. "What the hell do you want me to say?" he whispered harshly. "You had no business coming here!"

"You think I wanted to?" she whispered back. "I risked my life to come here for you—and this is my thanks?"

"I told you not to follow me. Damn it, I knew you were going to do this."

"Oh, sorry. Why don't you just put a knife to my throat again, you madman?"

He narrowed his eyes. "I apologized for that."

"Well, I'm sorry that you're so unhappy to see me, but I'm here now, so what are we going to do?"

He shook his head wearily. "I haven't the slightest idea."

Emily searched his face. "At least tell me if you got your memory back. You had that headache for three days the last time I saw you. Remember the poultice I made for you? The sage tea? When we walked in the forest at your estate, it was all starting to come back to you."

He just looked at her, more stubborn than a whole team of mules.

Emily wanted to throttle him. "All right, I understand, you're angry! Believe me, but I had no choice. I had to come and warn you. You *do* realize the Order is authorized to kill you? That agent in London, he would've shot you if not for my good aim!"

She had thrown a potato at the agent from her bag of supplies for the journey. A rock would have been more convenient, but he was an Order agent. She hadn't wanted to hurt him, just to give Drake a chance to get away.

Drake was shaking his head at her. "It was Jordan, Emily. I've known him forever. He wouldn't have shot me."

"He had a pistol aimed right between your eyes!"

"Never mind that. Listen to me." He grasped her shoulders, leaning down a bit to glower in her face. "Right now you need to forget ever seeing him or Rotherstone or any of those men. Forget their names. I mean it. You must wipe them from your mind. Anything I ever told you about the Order or the Prometheans, erase it from your memory right this moment. You know nothing. Understand?"

"I know nothing," she repeated with a nod.

"I was a fool ever to have told you about any of it."

"You were a boy," she said softly, gazing at him. "You were excited about your great *destiny*."

The reminder seemed to pain him.

"You needn't worry," she added. "I've never told a soul."

"Good. Because if the people here thought they could get any information out of you, they would—" He stopped himself with a shaken look, released her, and turned away. "But I'd kill you myself before I'd let them take you down there," he whispered.

She froze, her gaze suddenly riveted on his back. "Down where?"

"Never mind. Just stay in this room, keep your head down, and don't talk to anyone. It'll all be over soon."

"What do you mean?"

"Don't worry about it," he mumbled. "I have to go."

Frightened, she followed him toward the door. "Drake—wait."

He paused, regarding her from the corner of his eye. "What?"

She stepped in front of him so he couldn't escape and stared into his eyes. "Tell me the real reason you came here."

He almost, but not quite smiled. "It's none of your business."

"Why did you escape from Lord Rotherstone and return to James? Please."

He just stared at her in mute defiance, his jet-black eyes guarding inscrutable secrets.

"You cannot have chosen the Prometheans over the Order!" she whispered.

"Can't I?"

She shook her head slowly, holding his stormy stare. "No. I'll never believe that. Never you. The Order has been your whole life. You cannot have turned against your brother agents and Virgil. You came here to get revenge, didn't you?" she challenged him in a barely audible tone.

He held her gaze for a long moment. "Life is pain, Emily. The Prometheans understand that."

"No." She shook her head in refusal of his stark words. "Life is beauty and light, Drake. Look out there. The trees, the mountains, the sky." She touched his cheek tenderly. "You mustn't give up. You've known hatred and suffering as few men have, but there is also love, and goodness."

He flicked an indifferent glance toward the balcony, as she had suggested, then he looked at her again, cynically, indeed, almost coldly, with pity. And he cupped her cheek, in turn.

For a moment, he gazed at her lips, as though remembering their kiss of a short while ago.

Emily wanted another.

"May you always keep your delusions, my darling," he whispered. "They might have survived if you had not come here."

He started to move past her, but she scowled and stopped him, laying a stubborn hand on his chest and capturing his gaze.

Then she tried bluffing the truth out of him. "I know the real reason you're here. Say whatever you like. But Drake, it's madness. There are too many of them, even for you."

"Do you think I care what happens to me?" he breathed.

"No, but I do. I'm not going to let you die."

"You don't have a choice." He thrust her aside, reaching for the door handle, as if he could not get out of the room fast enough.

Emily turned, impassioned. "That's what you really came here to do, isn't it? To die?" she demanded, her voice trembling. "And to take as many of them down with you as possible."

One hand on the handle, he let out a low, world-weary laugh. "What, a suicide mission?"

She nodded.

"You still think I'm some sort of hero."

"I know you are," she said at once from the bottom of her heart.

"What a fool you are," he murmured slowly, staring at her. "My blind, beautiful, little fool."

Her face fell, but his hardened as he glanced over his shoulder at her one last time. "Stay out of my way," he ordered. Then he pulled the door shut behind him.

Chapter

3

 rake paused outside the door, but although his heart was pounding, he refused to give an inch to emotion.

He could not afford to.

He locked her in, put the key back in his pocket, and strove to ignore the panic throbbing in his temples. He could not think of anything worse than Emily's showing up here. She had no idea what she'd gotten into.

How on earth she had made it so far alive, he could scarcely fathom; but, of course, the rural setting would have worked in her favor. The woodsman's daughter could defend herself expertly in the world of nature.

When it came to the world of men, however, no.

She had no concept whatsoever of the evil that he faced in this place. She had never been exposed to anything of its kind. Nor should she.

He stared at the door. He could feel her on the other side of it, but he backed away, shaking his head slightly.

She spoke of the beauty of trees and sky, hills and

light, unaware that she herself was the most beautiful thing in the world, at least to him.

He shut his eyes. Hating her for loving him. Hating himself for the kind of kiss he had taken from her for the first time their lips had ever touched and the degrading words he had spoken over her.

But degradation, using a woman, was all the people here could understand.

He had to get her out of here.

As soon as it was safe.

He'd find a way.

Steely-eyed, he pivoted on his heel and marched down the corridor. Still, his awareness of her clung to him like a playful spirit haunting him every second, teasing him with those unearthly violet eyes. Trying to lure him back toward treacherous things like life and joy and all that pointless rot he had long since given up on. But did she truly think they had ever been apart?

Did she not know she had been with him all the time in that unspeakable cell, the memory of her sweetness the one slender ribbon tying him to whatever had once been good in him long after pain and instinct had turned him into a demon? The one thing that had stopped him from becoming something far more monstrous than any Promethean.

Like some silent, healing angel come to comfort him, she had returned to him after every beating, every cut, every broken bone. She could not touch him, but the thought of her had been enough to keep him alive, the bright memory of the sun on her hair, those freckles whose arrangement he knew as well as the constellations.

The torturers had caused his mind to swallow up many of the details of his old life as a warrior for the Order of St. Michael the Archangel. But even they had never succeeded in making him forget the reason *why* he fought.

Because of Emily, and everything she stood for to him.

When he thought of home, he did not think of the mansion, or his parents, or the lordly stables that were the envy of the shire. He thought of the woodsman's daughter, roaming the hunting grounds of Westwood Park, wild and free, innocent as some ethereal woodland nymph, untouched by the corruption of the world.

That was how Drake had wanted, needed her to stay, always. But it was too late. Her blind devotion to him had drawn her there. And after the way the Prometheans' evil had infected him, he had a terrible cold feeling in his gut that he would be her downfall.

She had to go. Soon. He could not be distracted by her. He despised and feared how deeply he was drawn to her. It could get him killed in this place.

He might, by some miracle, still be able to save her life—he had to, or his whole existence would have been in vain. But he already knew that when it came to the crystalline innocence of her heart, it was only a matter of time before it shattered. She would look into the face of evil here, and she would never be the same.

God knew, he was not.

He suppressed a shudder and hurried down the stairs, jogging down the white marble spiral. With a grim set to his jaw, he walked toward the dining room where the Council was in session, still utterly refusing to think of the last time he had been a guest at Waldfort Castle.

He had not stayed on the fourth floor then but in the dark place, far down below. He swept its memory out of his mind once again and kept his face coldly expressionless but for the trace of suffering that never quite left his eyes.

Approaching the dining room where James had called the meeting, he knew full well that behind that door was a roomful of murderers, every one of them. If he had not penetrated their organization so deeply, perhaps he never would have believed it. Like the rest of the world, he'd have been deceived by their façade of quiet banality.

How polite the gentlemen could be, taking tea in aristocratic drawing rooms, playing chess at White's or other clubs for the well-connected, strolling on a Sunday afternoon with their already-tainted grandchildren. But there was another side to them, a terrible secret at the core of who they were.

Their elegant friends and royal connections would have been horrified to witness their warped ceremonies, like the one in which Drake had forced himself to participate recently. The black candles, the hooded robes, the weird ancient chants full of blasphemies, the blood that ran from the slit throats of sacrificed animals and dripped from the places where they pierced themselves to glorify the cruel images they worshipped.

Their strange system of belief was based on occult scrolls of the Magi found by Crusader knights in a desert cave hundreds of years ago. They had blended it over the centuries with many other sources of hidden ancient knowledge, but essentially, their creed placed them at the center of the universe and rejected all authority in life and on earth except their own.

To them, Prometheus, the Titan of Greek myth who had given fire to humanity, and Lucifer, the lightbearer, had become one and the same. But in their view, Satan was not the monstrous enemy of God and man but a rebel prince, wronged, powerful, and heroic.

The Prometheans' willingness to pursue their goals in a manner worthy of the Father of Lies made it difficult for the Order, constrained by the knight's code of conduct, to defeat them.

But Drake was no longer, technically, a knight of the Order. His hands were no longer tied by these noble ideals.

The time had come to fight fire with fire.

He had come to destroy the destroyers, deceive the deceivers, to infiltrate the infiltrators, and to murder the murderers. To fight evil with pure, black evil. He no longer cared what lines he crossed, for he had nothing left to lose.

At least, not until Emily showed up.

But she wouldn't be there long. He would not allow it, for he understood the danger she was in. The very innocence that made her so powerful, such a treasure to him, was the very thing that could sentence her to her doom.

The Prometheans hated goodness wherever it appeared. They could not stand to be around it. They were fascinated by it, but every instinct they possessed urged them to destroy it. If they were to realize that the virginal young beauty was much more to him than some servile sexual plaything, he shuddered to think what they might do to her.

Get this over with. Letting himself quietly into the room, Drake returned to his post behind James's chair.

The old man sat at the head of the table, for it was he who had called this secret summit of the leaders.

Count Septimus Glasse, the owner of the castle, a fiery, bearded German, eyed Drake warily as he took his place. "The security breach has been handled?"

"Yes, my lord. It was of no consequence, merely a servant," he added, bowing his head in deference.

"*Your* servant, we hear."

"Yes, sir."

"That is rather peculiar."

Drake just looked at him.

"James, are you quite certain we can trust your head of security?" asked the olive-skinned cardinal, their robed representative in Rome. "After all, he was once numbered among the enemy."

"Drake is one of us now, Antonio," he replied. "He has proved his loyalty by saving my life on numerous occasions. Surely it cannot seem such a shock to you that even a former agent of the Order could finally come to see that it is our vision that is best for Mankind, not theirs. Besides, gentlemen," James added in mild amusement, "there is no greater zealot than a convert. Go on, Drake. Tell them of our creed."

"With pleasure, sir." He stood square, his hands loosely clasped behind his back, his chin high. "Mankind is base and savage, my lords, barbarous, stupid, and cruel. For his own good, he must be tamed, managed, by those who have humbly sought and acquired the true enlightenment. If man will not submit to reason or just authority from the enlightened, then his will must be broken first, through force."

The Austrian general who served as corrupt advisor to the Habsburgs gave a low laugh. "Couldn't have said it better myself."

James smiled with pride in his student. "Go on, m'boy. What of God?" he encouraged him.

"If the vile creature, man, is indeed made in the image of God, then this is a childish, tyrannical deity to whom no man of reason owes his allegiance," Drake replied. "If God exists at all, he is our enemy, for it was he who gave us life, and life is only pain. All else is delusion."

"You speak of the subject of pain with some authority, monsieur," said the suave French duke, swirling the brandy in his snifter.

The Prometheans had situated him well, anticipating the chance of Napoleon's downfall. The French duke had gone into exile with King Louis as a loyal friend during Napoleon's reign, but now that the Little Emperor was jailed at Elba, the Prometheans had already planted their man close to the Bourbon throne.

"Yes, Your Grace," Drake answered his question in a low, dull monotone. "This technique was how I came to understand the truth myself."

"Tell me—" Septimus Glasse spoke up again. "Do you resent your treatment at our hands, Englishman?"

"No, sir, I am grateful. Now the rest of my life won't be wasted in the folly of the Order's lies and illusions. Better to suffer and see the truth than to remain blind."

"Indeed," the cardinal murmured. "I imagine that with all the weapons training the Order must have given you, you would be very good at making more converts for us."

"Yes, sir, I believe so. If I am found worthy of that privilege."

"What about your previous life as an agent of the enemy?" the Austrian general pursued.

"I remember very little about it, sir."

"And what he has remembered, he has entrusted to me," James replied, "to be used at my discretion, at the appropriate time."

Glasse shrugged. "Obviously, he is a valuable asset."

James nodded. "His perspective will be crucial in our quest to defeat the Order once and for all."

"Unless all this is a trick," the Russian novelist chimed in. The highborn writer's books and plays had enchanted the young, impressionable Czar.

"I am not that brave, sir." Drake gazed at him, allowing the fashionable leader of Russian intellectual circles to stare into his eyes, as if to probe his motives for himself, boring into his very soul.

"You see?" James murmured proudly at length. "I told you, my friends, it would be a waste to kill him, that I could bring him round. Drake is on the true path now. Besides, if my bodyguard has proved his loyalty to me, then nobody else has cause to question him."

"Very well, old friend," Glasse murmured to James. "If you are satisfied, then so are we, of course."

The cardinal shrugged in agreement. "Better he should be for us than against us."

"Precisely."

"So, tell us, Falkirk, why have you called this gathering of the Council?" the Austrian general inquired. "You indicated it was a matter of the utmost consequence."

"Ah, but we are missing someone," the French duke interjected with a faint, sly smile.

"Indeed," James answered with a low laugh. "No doubt you all are wondering why Malcolm isn't here." James looked around at them for a long moment.

Meanwhile, ever so subtly, Drake's hand moved closer to the hilt of his weapon. If any man objected to James's scheme, he was ready.

"The truth is," James admitted, glancing around at him, "our dear leader Malcolm wasn't invited. I didn't feel he was ready to see the wonder that I have called you together to show you, my friends. Drake—the box, please."

Drake stepped back, turned around, and retrieved the ancient kingwood case from where it sat on the nearby sideboard.

He brought it over and set it on the table, then glanced at James in question. The old man nodded, and Drake dutifully opened the box.

James stood, tilting the box so that the others could see inside. "Behold, gentlemen. The lost scrolls of Valerian the Alchemist, the greatest of our forefathers."

"The Alchemist's Scrolls!" the men exclaimed, rising from their seats to lean closer, staring at the yellowed medieval documents.

"Are these truly the authentic—?"

"But where on earth did you find them?"

"It's a treasure trove . . . is there anything in these scrolls to help us now?"

"Much." James looked around soberly at them, and the men settled back in their seats, amazed. "Gentlemen, allow me to be blunt. The current head of the Council has failed us. Badly. We must face the facts.

"Malcolm pays no more than lip service to the old gods. He thinks the dark wisdom is no more than fairy tales. He mocks the princes of the air and the unseen powers of this world, the very forces that sustained Valerian and have inspired our forefathers since the Middle Ages."

James planted his hands on the table and looked around at them. "If our so-called leader were truly one of us, we would not have met with our recent bitter failure. Look at the priceless opportunity he let slip through our fingers.

"Napoleon's empire gave us our greatest opportunity since Charlemagne to bring all the peoples of Europe together as one. Think of the chance that is gone. One language, one currency, no more wars, no more hunger. Who can say? In time, we might have extended our rule across the Mediterranean to overtake the Ottoman Empire, and across the water, as well, to the Americas.

"For decades we worked, spent untold fortunes inserting our loyal believers into every royal court, patiently, carefully, waiting for our moment. And then it came. In the person of the brilliant Napoleon Bonaparte, that muse of fire, a perfect tool wrought for us by the hands of the gods.

"We were useful to him, but he was even more useful to us without even knowing it. We just let him keep on conquering countries, aiding him where we could, and kept on putting our people into high places throughout his ever-growing empire. He had no son. That meant we only had to wait for him to die. Then all that he had built, the whole globe, perhaps, would have fallen naturally, easily into our hands like a ripe plum.

"What step did we overlook?" James asked them in cold anger. "Nothing. What price did we shrink to pay to bring about our vision on earth? We gave our all, down to the last drop of blood of that which was most precious to us. We were so close! But it all crumbled. Why? Why, I ask you?" he demanded.

"Eh, because of the Order," the Frenchman murmured.

"No. It would be nice to think so," James shot back, "but the fault, I'm afraid, lies closer to home. The enemy could not have vanquished us if we had not chosen a leader who makes a mockery of the gods. This feckless fool Malcolm threw away the chance to establish our dream of a new order in the world merely to fulfill his own greed."

"These are dangerous words, James," Septimus warned fondly.

"Yet I must speak them, if our brotherhood is ever to rise again. These are the facts. Napoleon is fallen. Our chance is lost. It will not come again in our lifetimes, perhaps not for a century or more—and the fault must be laid at Malcolm's feet. But still he remains as head of the Council? How can this be?"

They were silent, mulling his points.

James shook his head. "I can no longer be silent. Not after all the blood we shed, the risks we took. The sacrifices that every one of us made," he reminded them bitterly as he scanned their faces.

The Promethean leaders dropped their gazes, lowering their heads with pained expressions as James gazed at each one.

"We *gave* as Malcolm never did. You know what my words signify," he added darkly. "No wonder it all came to naught. Our very leader refused the gods their sacrifice. We parted with what we loved and watched Niall grow up from a spoiled boy into a dangerous and ill-tempered man.

"The truth is," James continued, "Malcolm's had us all, in his game. He thinks himself above our rules and our 'strange ways,' though they served our ancestors since the Crusades. No, he's much too modern for all of that 'medieval rubbish,'" James said bitterly. "But now look at what his cleverness has brought us. Failure. Destruction."

He shrugged. "We're the ones who chose him for our leader. A man without vision. A man who believes in nothing. I hate to say it, but I fear we got what we deserve."

"He's right," the novelist spoke up. "We have brought this on ourselves."

James sent him a nod of appreciation for the support. "If Malcolm Banks remains in power, in my view, we might as well give up. His foolish decisions as head of the Council have handed us defeat when victory was in our grasp. He has proved he does not deserve to sit in the principal chair. Removing him is our only hope." He looked around at them.

"Believe me, brothers, our chance will come again,

one day. We may not be alive to see it; it may take two hundred years. But the discovery of the Alchemist's Scrolls after all the centuries they were lost is a sign from our dark Father not to be discouraged, not to give up the fight. With the hidden knowledge that Valerian has passed down in these writings, mark my words, we shall rise again to raise the torch of truth for a whole new generation. But first, the one responsible for our failure must be punished. Now is the time to strike."

"Why now?" the Austrian asked.

"Malcolm's faction is weakened at the moment," James replied. "You may have heard that his pet assassin, Dresden Bloodwell, was killed in London by an Order agent a few weeks ago."

"What of Malcolm's son?"

"Yes, where is Niall?"

"Funny you should ask." James cast Drake a knowing smile. "Gentlemen, it may startle to you to hear the most unsettling piece of news. Malcolm sent his son to kill me while I was in London."

"*What?*"

"To kill you?" they exclaimed, predictably outraged.

"You, James? But you're one of our most revered leaders!"

"Obviously, he sees him as a threat," the Russian murmured.

James hesitated with a grim look. "The truth is, I don't believe he meant to stop with me. It appears Malcolm no longer wishes to answer to the Council. I daresay he's decided he can get along without us."

"What exactly do you mean?" the French duke demanded.

"I'm saying Malcolm seeks to rule alone—he and his son. And he's soon going to come after us if we don't eliminate him first."

"Would he really take it so far?" the cardinal murmured into the ominous hush that had fallen over the room.

"Why not? He's got nothing left to lose." James shrugged. "He knows we no longer trust him after his failure as our leader. The attack on me was only the beginning. Once I was out of the way, I am certain he planned to send Niall and his thugs after the rest of you."

The room went silent as the members of the Council pondered these disturbing revelations.

"Don't forget, at the last meeting of the Council," James reminded them, "Malcolm tried to make one of us the scapegoat for his incompetence. Remember? He ordered Niall to garrote Rupert Tavistock right in front of us. Surely you knew it was intended as a warning to us all."

The field marshal shook his head, marveling. "I can't believe he sent his son to kill you."

"Fortunately, Drake was on hand to protect me," James replied.

"So—" The Frenchman leaned closer. "Is Niall dead?"

"No," James answered judiciously. "He was captured by the Order. Suffice it to say that Niall will not be a problem anymore. I doubt any of us will ever hear from Junior again."

Most of them seemed pleased at this news though a few looked slightly shaken by it all.

"Does Malcolm know the Order has his son?" the cardinal inquired.

"I don't believe so. But it won't be long before he starts wondering why he hasn't heard from him, and why Niall hasn't returned from London. That is why I called this gathering on such short notice, and I appreciate you all making it here so quickly. I hope it wasn't too inconvenient. Septimus was kind enough to offer his hospitality here at Waldfort, and the location seemed central enough for everyone to reach with relative ease."

Glasse gestured politely in welcome.

"So, here we are," James said, planting his hands on the table before him, "and time is of the essence. We must decide what we intend to do, and if we are going to act, we must move quickly in order to take Malcolm by surprise. I would not give him time to marshal his forces against us. At the moment, he has not yet realized anything's wrong, but I doubt we have more than a fortnight."

"So, let us take a vote, then, and be done with it," Glasse spoke up impatiently. "Those in favor of keeping Malcolm as head of the Council, say aye."

The chamber was perfectly silent.

"Those opposed to his continued leadership?"

Hands lifted all around the table.

It was unanimous.

"Very well, then," James said grimly. "Malcolm is hereby deposed as head of the Council. We will begin considering our plans on how to move against him at once—"

"But who will take the role of our new leader in the meanwhile?" Glasse interrupted.

Drake was well aware that Falkirk and his old friend, their host, the German count, had arranged in advance between themselves for this question to be asked at the crucial moment. "Someone has got to take responsibility as the next head of the Council," Glasse added.

They all looked at James.

"It must be you, James, yes," several of them murmured.

"Me, my lords?" He seemed genuinely shocked, but of course, this had been their plan from the start.

"Let us vote again," Glasse urged, rising from his chair, the first to lift his hand. "Those in favor of James Falkirk as the next head of the Council?"

"Aye!" the others agreed before he had even finished speaking the words.

James appeared overwhelmed. "I do not seek this, my brothers."

"That is why you are the perfect antidote to Malcolm's self-interest," the cardinal assured him.

The old man shook his head. "I don't know what to say, gentlemen. I am just an old scholar."

"Say that you accept," the Russian author answered with a smile.

"Well, of course, I will serve in whatever capacity is required," he said modestly.

"Everyone knows you, James. Everyone trusts you. You have given us all your wise counsel at one point or another over the years. If Malcolm had listened to you in the first place, the outcome with Napoleon might have been very different."

James appeared to restrain deep emotion. "Truly, I am honored by your faith in me, and I swear to you on my life that I will uphold the creed and do my best to bring about the goals our forefathers laid out so long ago."

"So, where do we begin?" the French duke asked, as James sank back down into his seat.

"Well," James said with a wise, old, grandfatherly sigh followed by a thoughtful pause. "It seems to me that we need to make a fresh start, clean the slate. A new beginning before we set out on the next leg of our long journey through the ages. The Order decimated our ranks during the fall of Napoleon, and those who are left are deeply dispirited." He pulled the box with the scrolls closer. "I say we gather them all here together and give them something to restore their flagging faith."

"Like what?" the Russian asked.

James caressed the kingwood case fondly. "While I was studying the Alchemist's Scrolls, I came across a magnificent ceremony, lost to us all these centuries . . . a ritual of renewal that Valerian carefully laid out for a time of defeat such as the one we now face. You know the persecution our forefathers faced back in his day."

"Yes."

"He called it the ritual of rebirth, to be held at the lunar eclipse."

"So, that's why you wanted us to come now," the Frenchman murmured with a rueful smile. "There is an eclipse of the moon in about a fortnight, isn't there?"

James nodded with an enigmatic smile. "The past must be purged, the darkness fully embraced before the light can break again. After all we've been through—let us call it what it is, utter defeat—this is the perfect opportunity to bring our scattered remnants back together, all our poor wavering believers, and fill them up again with fire.

"If ever we have needed to come together, renew our vows to the dark Father, and offer sacrifice as we invoke his help and favor, that time is now," James finished.

"What sacrifice does this ritual require?" the cardinal murmured while the others nodded in agreement.

James glanced at him, silent for a moment. "Only the very highest is acceptable for this ceremony. It calls for the blood of a virgin, pure of heart."

Nothing the Prometheans did could surprise Drake anymore, but the words struck him with horror like a knife in the gut.

Emily's innocent smile flashed across his mind.

The answer, meanwhile, had drawn the French duke's cynicism. "Eh, are there any of those left on the earth, I wonder?"

"There would be if you had not seduced them all," the Russian jested.

"Never fear, my brothers." James shut the box of scrolls with a serene smile. "The Dark Father will provide. And when such blood has flowed, and our strength is renewed, then we shall set out to rebuild, just as we always have. The Order defeated us last time, but now we have a secret weapon against them, as well," James said, with a nod over his shoulder at Drake. "In the meanwhile, we must send for all our believers so they can get here in time for the eclipse. Also, I will begin preparing a contingent to go and deal with Malcolm."

The men were quiet, absorbing all this.

"At least the Scot's greed has left our coffers full," James added dryly. "We'll need all our gold to re-establish our influence in the royal courts. Duping kings is easy enough—inbred fools—but wooing courtiers and bribing politicians, that, my friends, can get expensive."

They laughed at his jest, then Glasse proposed a toast to the new head of the Promethean Council. James accepted their homage with a modest nod.

Drake, meanwhile, had tensed, a sickening knot in his stomach and only one thought on his mind.

Thank God he'd had the foresight to create the impression from the start that the untouched Emily was nothing but his own little whore.

Chapter 4

*A*fter cleaning herself up, as James Falkirk had haughtily suggested, from her weeks of hiking through the Alps, Emily washed her clothes in the washbasin, made herself busy oiling her boots, sharpening her knife, checking the string on her bow, and then, when there was nothing left to do, pacing back and forth across Drake's room, beginning to feel rather like a caged animal.

None of this was supposed to happen. Drake was *supposed* to have come to his senses and fled this place with her. Instead, she was stuck here with him, and she still wasn't even sure if he was mad or sane.

His words from earlier today still chilled her. *Life is pain.* That did not bode well at all!

If he was here on a suicide mission, then she had to stop him. But how? He wouldn't even tell her whose side he was on.

She was beginning to feel very fortunate that she'd had the foresight to write to Lord Rotherstone after tracking Drake northward from the Bavarian capital of Munich and before returning to try to rescue him.

She had agonized over whether to take the risk, but now was very glad she had sent off that courier from the quaint German city though it had cost her the rest of her money.

There were no guarantees her message would actually make it to Drake's old friend and fellow agent back in London, nor could she say how long it might take to reach the marquess.

Nor could she predict the Order's reaction with any certainty once they received the news.

Her choice to give Drake's former colleagues this information could cost her dearly if things continued going as wrong as they had earlier in the day.

After all, Drake was now officially considered an agent who had gone rogue.

His brother warriors had instructions to shoot him on sight before he revealed Order secrets to the Prometheans.

But Emily had to believe that loyalty would at least compel them to give Drake a chance to explain himself before they sought to put him down like a rabid wolf.

After all, they had been friends since they were boys.

Back in England, she had seen firsthand how much Max, Lord Rotherstone, had cared for his damaged friend, and how like a brother he had tried to help Drake regain his memory.

Whatever commands they had received from their superiors, Emily did not believe his brother warriors could bring themselves to pull the trigger on one of their own. Surely his friends could not give up on him any more than she could. And when Drake told them he had come for revenge, they would understand.

Maybe they would even arrive in time to help.

Now, however, she was beginning to have doubts.

If Drake was here for revenge on these fiends, then why wouldn't he just admit it?

Didn't he trust her to keep his secrets?

Or was she merely deceiving herself, refusing to face what was right in front of her—that Drake had indeed forsaken all sanity to embrace their twisted creed? Was he good or evil? Had he become a true Promethean?

Emily needed answers, the sooner the better.

So, naturally . . . she searched his chamber while he was gone, hunting for any clues that might reveal his true motives.

She went through his belongings, opening the same drawers from which she had borrowed one of his shirts, sifting through his clothes and shoes, his extensive collection of weapons and his personal arsenal of ammunition, looking for anything he might have hidden in the room that could give her a clue to what was going on in his head.

But the canny ex–Order agent had covered his tracks too well, leaving her no way either to confirm or deny her fears. She read every page of his barely legible notes in the small logbook he kept regarding his activities as James's head of security.

This was how she learned that Drake had hired the majority of those black-clad guards in Paris, on behalf of James. They were a mercenary band of battle-hardened veterans of Napoleon's army, from a mixed regiment made up of men from different areas where conscripts had been demanded as the emperor's due. Most were French, but some were German, some Italian. One was Belgian.

Now they fought for hire, and the older one, Jacques, had been their sergeant.

Emily put his notes away in frustration, unsure if

Drake was still the person she had known and loved since childhood or if he had resigned himself to darkness.

After all he had been through, she could not have blamed him, in a sense. But if he *had* started dabbling in evil, what did that mean for her, sharing this small chamber with him?

Night was already falling as she hastily put away his things after all her snooping. She lit two candles in the room, beginning to wonder if she had made a serious miscalculation in coming there.

Then her thoughts were interrupted as the low, metallic scrape of the iron door latch heralded his return.

Still unsure if he was altogether friend or foe, she was torn between relief and trepidation when the door opened and he came in, tall, dark, and dangerous.

Much too dangerous if he had ill intent.

He did not smile at her as he closed the door behind him, carrying a tray of food with a covered dish and a tankard of ale. When his glance flicked over her with a startled smolder in his eyes, she folded her arms across her chest nervously.

Keeping her distance, she watched him cross to the chest of drawers, where he set down the tray.

"What's that?" she asked, following him at a wary distance.

"Your supper."

"Oh. That's all for me?" She offered a cautious smile. "What about you?"

"I ate already in the Guards' Hall."

"Oh." She ventured over to him by the chest of drawers, peering into the pewter tankard of good German ale he had brought her, then peeking under the lid keeping her plate warm. "It smells good."

She suddenly noticed him eyeing her chest. She

stepped back, wide-eyed, clutching the white linen shirt against her throat.

He sent her an idle frown. "You took my last clean shirt."

"Oh. Right." She realized in nervous relief that he wasn't staring at her body. He was only staring at the shirt. "Sorry. It was all that I could find. I-I'll give it back as soon as my clothes are dry."

He shrugged and turned away. "Don't worry about it. Looks better on you than it does on me." Then he nodded toward the tray. "Eat. You must be starved."

"I am a little hungry." As he turned away, Emily removed the lid from the plate, then glanced at him in question. "What is it?"

Drake was taking off his coat. "Bavarian cuisine," he said dryly.

She furrowed her brow, studying the unfamiliar food. The plate held a pale white sausage with a blob of mustard beside it, a little pile of pickled red cabbage, and . . . "What is that?"

"Potato dumplings," he informed her in wry amusement. "Go on, you'll like it. And if you don't, too bad. It's all we've got."

She flicked her eyebrows upward briefly at his matter-of-fact tone, but broke off a piece of the potato dumpling with her fork. "So, what have you been doing all day?"

"My job."

"What's that? Protecting James?"

He nodded, unbuckling the weapons belt slung around his lean waist.

She shook her head, feigning a casual air, when in truth she was fiercely determined to draw any scrap of information out of him she could. "I can't believe you're helping them," she remarked in an idle tone.

He just looked at her.

She put the forkful of food in her mouth.

Then he dropped his gaze dismissively, hanging his gun belt on a peg and unbuttoning his waistcoat.

Emily washed down a bite of sausage with a swallow of ale. "This is good. It was kind of you to think of me."

His insolent one-shouldered shrug feigned nonchalance, but she smiled cheerfully at him when he sauntered over and borrowed a swig from the tankard after she had set it down. Then he went about his business.

Emily sampled the pickled cabbage, coaxing it onto her fork with the hunk of dark bread. "Well, you must admit, it's a little strange, an earl working as a bodyguard," she pressed him.

He eyed her warily, tossing his waistcoat over the chair. But he remained as silent as the tomb.

"Why do you care so much what happens to that old man?" she inquired.

"I told you. He saved my life."

"And you saved his, which means the debt is paid. So, why don't you tell me why you're here?"

"Mind your own business, Emily." He turned away, lifting his shirt off over his head.

Lifting the fork to her mouth, she went motionless at the sight of his muscled male beauty. His supple flesh glowed with warm vitality in the candlelight.

Emily lowered the fork again in a daze. *Egads.* She had not seen Drake without his shirt on since he'd been a skinny ten-year-old splashing about in the swimming hole.

Good Lord, he was all man now, tall and sinewy, though scarred here and there, to her dismay. Yet somehow the evidence of these old, healed injuries only emphasized the fierce power of his magnificent body, the unstoppable quality of the man.

It was useless. She could not stop staring, captivated by the sleek curve of his shoulder, the rugged bulk of his arm, the chiseled splendor of his abdomen.

He glanced over at her with a rather sardonic look as he poured some water from the pitcher into the white washbowl. "You all right?"

"Um—ahem, yes—of course," she forced out with an awkward little cough and a sudden scarlet blush. Nodding nervously, she forced herself to turn away, chagrined.

Thankfully, Drake opted to ignore her. He leaned down to splash his face. She studied him again while he was distracted, marveling that he had muscles where she didn't even know muscles could be.

By the time she heard his low sigh of weary relaxation a moment later, she had managed to regroup. She smiled faintly and, still blushing, went to hand him the towel.

He accepted it with a low, male grunt of thanks.

Now I understand how you drove all those London women mad, she thought, gazing at him as he straightened up again, drying his face and throat.

She could not tear her eyes from him, watching with a queer, ticklish pleasure in the pit of her stomach.

She thought again of his kiss that afternoon in the forest, and her rapt gaze followed Drake's hand as he ran the towel down his chest to catch a stray drip of water.

But then, as he turned toward her, she saw the marking on his chest, and her blood ran cold.

By the lantern's light, the small, round brand burned onto his powerful chest marred his Adonis-like perfection. She sensed his posture stiffen the second her gaze homed in on it, but truly, she could not believe her eyes.

Her stare flew up to his in bewilderment.

His face had become a mask of cold, hard challenge; he stared back as though daring her to question him.

Emily was too shocked to say a word.

The mark on his body matched the torch engraved on the arch outside the castle gates. The torch of the so-called Illuminated Ones. He had told her about it long ago. The Prometheans seared their true believers with what they called the Initiate's Brand.

Well, it seemed she had her answer. She could not seem to catch her breath.

He turned away while she stood there reeling.

Heart pounding, she dropped her gaze, trying to absorb what she had seen.

He pulled a dark, knitted sweater on over his head.

"Drake," she forced out at last.

"Just eat your supper," he advised her in a cool tone.

Then he grasped the single chair in the room and carried it out onto the balcony. After placing it outside, he took the extra blanket and one of the pillows from the bed.

Emily stood by, barely knowing what to say. Shaken, she sat down slowly on the edge of the bed, feeling as stunned as though someone had clubbed her on the head.

After a moment, Drake approached her slowly. With her head down, she saw his black boots halt in front of her.

"Look at me," he murmured.

She was not sure she could bear to.

He did not wait for her to lift her head, but grasped her chin none too gently and lifted her face to make her meet his gaze.

"Who else knows you're here?" he demanded in a low tone, staring shrewdly into her eyes.

Emily floundered. She suddenly did not dare confess that she had sent the letter to his former colleagues.

There was no telling how he might react.

"Does Rotherstone know where you are?" he prompted, as if he could read her mind. "Answer me."

"No," she whispered hoarsely. It might have been the first lie she had ever told him.

Meanwhile, she was acutely aware of his fingertips beneath her jaw, pressing into his skin.

"Does anyone else in the Order know where you are?" he demanded in a soft but steely voice.

She shook her head slowly.

His dark eyes probed her, but after a heartbeat, he seemed to take her at her word. He nodded, lowering his hand to his side.

Then he bent down slowly, still studying her face. "Back in London, you followed me to the Pulteney Hotel. I assume you saw my fight with Niall Banks. That red-haired man."

She nodded, her heart in her throat.

"Did the Order find Niall where I left him? What happened after my carriage pulled away?"

Emily swallowed hard. "I saw Lord Rotherstone and Virgil and the others take that red-haired man into custody. He came out screaming when they emerged from the hotel. I think you dislocated his shoulder."

The trace of a cruel half smile curved his lips. "Pity. What else?"

She shook her head, lifting her shoulders. "They drove away. Then I followed you."

His gaze softened slightly as he stared at her. "Stop looking at me like you're terrified of me. I'm not going to hurt you."

"You've taken their mark," she forced out in a strangled voice, nodding at his chest though it was covered now by his jersey. "The Initiate's Brand. I saw it."

He nodded once, holding her stare defiantly.

She couldn't believe it. "Did they do that to you against your will?"

"I cannot say that they did."

"Oh, Drake." She covered her mouth with her hand to stifle a sob, tears rushing into her eyes.

Some of the fire retreated from his eyes, but he shook his head ever so slightly. "It's not worth crying over."

No, Drake, it's a tragedy. She turned away, unable to look at him, in her sheer confusion and disappointment. It was true. The Drake she knew and loved was gone.

The Prometheans had won. He bore the proof on his body that he was now a traitor to everything he had once held dear. And when his friends arrived, they would have to kill him.

She would not stand in their way.

She brushed off his hand when he tried to cup her cheek.

Studying her, he offered no tender word of solace, no reassurance. "Good night." He straightened up to his full height and prowled off toward the balcony. "Leave these doors unlocked. I'll have to leave early. I'm back on duty at dawn." He took one of his pistols with him and went out to sleep on the balcony.

No word in any of the languages Drake spoke could have expressed his disgusted, miserable fury at the success of his deception as he dragged himself outside and dropped heavily into the chair he had brought out.

Through the balcony doors, he could still hear Emily crying softly as he set the gun down nearby within easy reach. He pulled the blanket over himself, propped his feet up on the balcony railing, and stared across the forest treetops at the white half-moon.

Half in darkness, half in light.

Rather like himself.

Bloody hell. Drake rubbed his eye sockets with one hand, trying to drown out the sound of Emily's little sobs.

But he had to hold the line. Though her tears wrenched him, he could not risk letting her see behind his mask as a Promethean convert.

If he told her the truth, she'd never be able to lie well enough to fool James. Chances were, she would unwittingly give away the game, and they'd both be dead.

True, Drake had come back to the castle on what was likely a suicide mission, but he did not intend to die until he had also made sure that his enemies would join him.

Things were moving in the right direction. The meeting had yielded an encouraging development. James would be sending for all the Prometheans still left out there to come to the castle. He could kill them all together. At this point, it was only a matter of figuring out how.

In the meanwhile, lying to Emily was for the best.

Perhaps doing so would help to inspire her to leave. He wanted her out of here, but he could not get rid of her without her cooperation. The sort of escape he could provide for her would require her to run on her own two feet and use her woodland skills to hide and flee.

Attached to him as she was, he had known he might need some useful means to drive her away. Letting her believe he was evil was as good a ploy as he was likely to find.

Drake sighed, resting his head back against the chair.

It was not very comfortable, but she was welcome to take the bed. He didn't sleep much, anyway.

Presently, as he closed his eyes, he could still see her in crisp detail in his mind, his oversized shirt draping her petite frame.

When he had stepped into the room earlier, bringing her dinner, he had been stunned at the delicious prospect of her in his room, all clean and warm and tousled, as if she had spent the day lounging in his bed.

She had almost caught him looking her over, from her dainty bare feet all the way up to her cascade of long, golden brown hair, flowing past her delicate shoulders.

His shirt hung to midthigh on her, and when she had turned away, his glazed stare had raked her slim, smooth legs and the alluring curve where the fabric loosely skimmed her firm derriere.

Then she had turned to face him again, pushing up the long sleeves. Though she had fastened the buttons at the neck, the deep V of the shirt still exposed the full, silky run of the white valley between her breasts.

At the sight of that lovely valley, he had felt his blood heat up with real, hot, needy desire for the first time in two years. He could not stop thinking about the way she had tasted when he had kissed her earlier in the forest.

And he pondered the interesting knowledge that it had not bothered him to do so.

Once upon a time, he had been a lover of legendary prowess. But ever since his sojourn in the dungeon, he could hardly stand for anyone to touch him, even by accident.

He felt very different after that kiss this afternoon, however. He had liked it a great deal. In truth, he'd been shocked at how quickly, how fiercely his body had responded to her. Savoring the thought of her scantily clad figure, he suddenly looked down at himself in surprise.

All his musings on Emily's many enticements had started getting him hard.

He reached under the blanket in astonishment and grasped himself.

"Damn," he whispered, surprised but pleased.

He hadn't had one like that since before he'd been captured.

Indeed, he had not lain with a woman in two years, and frankly, had lost all interest in sex—at least, it would seem, until today.

Considering he had lost his mind and his memory for a while due to his ordeals, losing his potency as a man had seemed to him the least of his problems.

It had comforted him slightly to know that at least his many malfunctions weren't his fault. Everything had worked perfectly before the torturers had got hold of him.

Afterward, however, well, he had more or less concluded it was all over for him where women were concerned.

Back in London, James had hired that whore to pleasure him, but the experience had only traumatized him further. Her too-aggressive touch had nearly made him retch; all he had been able to feel toward the high-priced harlot was revulsion and disgust. It had been a humiliating episode, but Drake had put it out of his mind because the bleak truth was, he didn't really care anymore about sex or women or anything. All that mattered was killing Prometheans.

He had all but accepted the fact that his once-splendid manhood, which had brought delight to so many was defunct, a poor fallen soldier who would not rise again.

But lo and behold, he had discovered that he was wrong. He held hard evidence to the contrary in his hand. He gave it a welcome-back squeeze through his trousers: aye, a full-fledged and extremely needy erection.

Well! It would seem his ol' fella had come raging back to life on account of the lovely Emily.

Rather delighted by this surprising upward turn of events, he removed his hand from his crotch. Even his own touch felt wonderful after all that time, but he didn't dare push his luck.

It occurred to him that this unforeseen and still tentative, instantaneous, nay, magical repair to his member could be of use if he could not get Emily to leave. If it was her virginity that could put her in danger from the Prometheans, perhaps they could do something about that, the two of them—only as a last resort, of course.

He had been warned since boyhood in the most dire terms not to touch her, that if he misbehaved where his whimsical little playmate was concerned, her father would be dismissed from his post, and both Jack Harper and his violet-eyed daughter would be sent packing.

Drake had obeyed his parents in this, all the more so when he grew old enough to understand the duty of a gentleman not to molest the females under his employ.

Nor had he ever wanted to behave in a way that made Emily lose respect for him or cease to trust him. Quite in contrast to his many casual bed partners, she had become a necessity to him over the years, one of the few constant pillars of his life. She was always there for him to go home to whenever his work for the Order started steering him into a dark place in his head. She never had to say much. Just being around her soothing, quiet simplicity helped him sort things out in his own mind.

So deeply was it ingrained in him to treat her as chastely as a brother that he barely dared allow himself to imagine what it would be like to make love to her.

Still, if it came to a question of keeping her safe from these bastards and their sick hunt for a virgin sacrifice, perhaps there was something the two of them could do about that.

The easiest way to guard her from the threat would be to make their ruse a reality. He could seduce her . . .

His cock was alive and well, indeed, throbbing at the possibility. Drake slowly turned and peered over his shoulder into the room through the open balcony doors. Emily lay curled up on the edge of his bed, staring into the small fire she had built in the hearth before his arrival.

His pulse pounded. He did not want her to cry. He did not want her to be sad or to doubt him or to see him as a traitor. Her opinion of him was one of the last things he still cared about in life. The temptation was strong.

How easy it would be to go back in there and comfort her. Tell her it would be all right. She would believe him. She always did. He could touch her at last, and let her take him into her exquisite arms. Lay her down.

He knew in his blood she wanted him, too.

Then they could have what they both had longed for and fantasized over and totally pretended to ignore for so long, playing innocent, as if they were not in love, no matter who forbade it. At last, they could become lovers.

Drake stared at the curve of her hip, his chest rising and falling with each deep breath in the hunger that gripped him. His blood was on fire.

Yes, why not? he thought with a hard swallow, his pulse racing.

But then came the grim reminder from his worldly, warrior half. *Because you're going to die,* it said. *Remember what you're here for. She's already lost you once.*

You've already put her through enough.

Well, that put rather a damper on his enthusiasm.

He let out a cynical sigh and looked forward again at the mountains and the moon.

He stared at the dark landscape for a long moment, recalling her silly attempt to convince him earlier today that life was worth living because of some picturesque scenery, trees and whatnot, as if he gave a damn.

He shook his head to himself wryly. *Beautiful little fool.*

But . . . perhaps the Alpine view wasn't half-bad, he conceded with a faint, begrudging smile.

There was something far more beautiful to gaze at inside the room, in his opinion. But gazing would only lead to touching and get him in trouble.

Drake shut his eyes with the trace of a smile still on his lips. Feeling more like himself than he had in two years, he did his best to go to sleep.

He had no intention of admitting it, but damned if a part of him wasn't glad she was there.

Chapter
5

London

A thick fog blanketed London that night as the ornate black carriage rolled up to Dante House.

The Tudor mansion on the Thames looked even more sinister with the vaporous night air swirling around its turrets. Max St. Albans, the Marquess of Rotherstone, alighted at once from his town coach, not waiting for his footman, and marched through the forbidding wrought-iron gates to the front door of the Inferno Club.

The brass knocker in the shape of a medieval scholar made after a portrait of the poet Dante seemed to smirk at him as he rapped forcefully.

The butler, Gray, admitted him in short order. Max shooed away the giant guard dogs, who gave him a clamorous welcome.

"Virgil?" he clipped out.

"Downstairs, my lord. The others have also arrived."

"Good." Max gave Gray his opera coat, for he had been sitting in the theatre box with his lady when the messenger had brought him this most consequential communiqué.

At last, they had word of Drake.

He had sent word around at once, calling the others together immediately to discuss what to do, and he now headed down to the Pit to join them.

He paid no mind to the florid excess of the décor with its crimson walls and heavily carved wood; Dante House had been deliberately fashioned to look like some lavish bordello or gaming house in keeping with the Inferno Club's scandalous reputation.

This façade, of course, helped to keep the decent world away. The Prometheans in particular would not have ventured near it, taking such care as they did to appear as upstanding pillars of Society.

Stepping into the dusty music room, Max crossed to the harpsichord. He glanced over his shoulder out of habit, then played the few notes that triggered the bookcase to turn away from the wall.

Gears and mechanisms based on simple clockwork science creaked beneath the floorboards. The bookcase popped away from the wall, revealing the opening.

He walked over silently and opened it like a door, stepping into the dark labyrinth hidden inside the walls. He pulled it shut behind him and made his way down to the Order's covert lair hewn into the limestone beneath Dante House, their headquarters, affectionately known to all their London agents as the Pit.

He found his team and their handler, Virgil, already waiting for him when he arrived, the torchlight flickering on the clammy, cavelike walls.

They sat at the rough wooden table where they had planned many a mission. Rohan Kilburn, the Duke of Warrington, was wiping a smudge off the gleaming blade of his knife, while Jordan Lennox, the Earl of Falconridge, was scanning the advertisements in the evening newspaper for any coded messages that someone might have been trying to send.

Sebastian, Viscount Beauchamp, the Earl of Lockwood's heir, had also joined them. The younger agent was drumming his fingers restlessly on the table, annoying Virgil.

The taciturn old Highlander had recruited all of them ages ago and had long served as the head of the Order in London. The men all looked over as Max jumped down lightly off the ladder.

"There he is," Beauchamp murmured.

"Max," Jordan greeted, while Rohan merely nodded.

"Thanks for getting here so quickly," he said as he tossed his cloak aside and joined them.

"What's all this about?" Jordan asked.

Max reached into his breast pocket and pulled out the folded piece of paper. "I've just received a letter from Drake's little friend."

"The gamekeeper's daughter?" Rohan echoed in surprise.

Max nodded. "Emily Harper. They're in Germany."

"What, she followed him?"

He nodded wryly, and every man there reacted with the same astonishment Max had felt when the courier had brought it to him.

"How on earth . . . does she even speak German?"

"She barely speaks at all," Max said. "A woman of few words."

"Now there's a rarity," Beau muttered.

"Well, she's discreet. Which is why I reckon Drake

trusted her years ago with information he never should've shared."

"Shite," Rohan muttered.

"Exactly," Max replied. He hesitated. "It would seem Drake is now officially James Falkirk's head of security."

Virgil cursed, got up from the table, and walked away.

They all stared after him for a second, then Beau turned to Max with a dark look. "So, where exactly are they? Did she give specifics?"

"Waldfort Castle in the Bavarian Alps. It's north of Munich. She says various men have been arriving. It sounds to me like Falkirk has called a number of the leaders together to meet there. Now we know why Drake took off."

"Not necessarily," Jordan cautioned.

"When do we leave?" Rohan asked bluntly.

"Wait a second," Jordan insisted. "What makes you think this girl can really be trusted? As much as it chagrins me to remind you of the incident, now that you've just barely let me live it down, none of *you* got hit in the head with a potato by this charming little miss. I did."

Rohan laughed aloud. The other two couldn't help smiling. Virgil merely frowned over his shoulder, arms folded across his chest.

"The girl's got damned fine aim, I'll give her that," Jordan muttered. "But one thing only drives her: Whatever helps Drake. Why would she tell us where he is when she knows what we intend?"

"He's right, it could be a trap," Beau agreed, but Max scoffed, shaking his head.

Max threw the paper down. "Read it. She's begging for his life. That's why she wrote it. She says she's gone to bring him back. Only, at this point, she's not sure she'll be able to do it by herself."

"But she helped him escape," Jordan said skeptically. "You told us at the time that you thought she might have even been in on that whole charade of Drake's putting a knife to her throat and taking her hostage. That's how he made you back off."

Max shrugged. "I considered the possibility that she might be in on it, but she was genuinely devastated after he escaped."

"Devastated enough to go after him," Rohan agreed. "I wonder if Kate would do that for me."

Beau smirked at him.

"This girl is no actress," Max said grimly. "She struck me as the sort who can barely tell a lie."

"Oh, that'll really help if the Prometheans get a chance to question her," Beau muttered.

"So, what do you want to do?" Jordan asked.

Max shrugged. "We've got to go get him."

Rohan nodded in agreement. "We'll just make sure we're ready for whatever we might find."

"Virgil, what do you think?" Max asked.

The Highlander walked back slowly to the table. "Jordan makes a good point. This could be an ambush. Either way, leaving Drake out there is not an option we can entertain. He can identify all of you, and if he has turned traitor as a result of all he's been through, the consequences could be disastrous."

"Don't forget, Falkirk has the Alchemist's Scrolls now," Jordan reminded them. "That's sure to impress the rest of the Council. We've known for some time he's been trying to find a way to overthrow Malcolm. James could seek to use these scrolls as a tool to rally supporters against your brother." He directed his words to Virgil, for it was no small irony that the head of the Order and the head of the Promethean Council were brothers.

With very bad blood between them.

Max nodded, meanwhile, resting his hands on the table. "If this girl's letter is in earnest, as I believe it to be, not a trap, this does present us with a profound opportunity. Not just to recover Drake but to wipe out the whole Council with one blow where they are gathered."

"I say we'd better get to Munich. Fast," Rohan murmured.

"It'll take time. The Alps are not exactly easy terrain," Beau remarked.

"They didn't seem to pose much of a problem for our little tracker," Max said with a wry half smile.

"She must have an impressive set of survival skills," Jordan agreed with a nod. "Lucky for us that Drake chose the woodsman's daughter for his dalliance rather than the chambermaid."

"Actually, he never touched her. It was obvious," Max said with a wave of his hand. "Chit's as pure as the Alpine snow."

"Then God help her if the Prometheans catch her," Jordan murmured.

"Drake will protect her."

"If he's turned?"

"He could never turn that evil. He'd feed us to the wolves before he would ever betray her," Max said. "You saw how he was with us—"

"Like a rabid dog," Beau agreed.

"But she had him eating out of her hand."

"Maybe she's right," Jordan said with a shrug, directing his comment to Virgil. "Maybe he can be saved."

"Don't get sentimental," Rohan said flatly. "*I* can still pull the trigger if you two can't. I just need your orders." Rohan also looked at Virgil in question.

The tall, brawny Scotsman, his wild red hair shot through with gray, considered his response for a long moment before speaking. "You're going to have to assess the situation when you get there and deal with him accordingly. It's impossible to say from the distance if he is with us or against us. He could have done all this as a ruse."

"Then why would he not contact us?" Jordan argued. "Why wouldn't he include us?"

"Maybe he thinks he can handle it on his own. I know a few agents who've acted likewise on occasion." Virgil raised an eyebrow in particular at Rohan. "However," Virgil continued, "if you catch up to them and find that he has truly joined their side, he must be sacrificed. And the girl, as well, if she tries to get in the way. She already knows too much."

Rohan flinched ever so slightly and laid his knife down on the table. As their team's most expert killer, he knew Virgil was speaking to him. "Yes, sir," he promised quietly.

As chilled as Max was by their handler's reply, he knew the Highlander was right. Drake was, at best, playing a role as a Promethean. But it would be foolish to place too much faith in his mental state.

Max had seen for himself how confused his boyhood friend had become after months of torture in a Promethean dungeon. Drake had not given up their names through all that time, but that was because his mind had shut down, his memory splitting off from itself, as it were, so that he was no longer *able* to tell the enemy what he knew.

At the moment, they had no way of knowing if his return to Falkirk was an act of genius or lunacy.

"For myself, I find it hard to imagine that Drake would ever betray us. He told them nothing even under torture," Max reminded them. "I know this man. I cannot think he'd do it."

"Well, Falconridge will make the call once you arrive," Virgil instructed. "Whether Drake lives or dies."

"Me?" Jordan exclaimed. "Why is it always me?"

"You're the most objective. The best observer," Virgil answered. "Max wants him spared for loyalty's sake and Rohan wants him put down to protect the Order. I can always count on you to weigh both sides, lad." The old man slapped him fondly on the shoulder.

"Sir, maybe Niall knows something about this castle. The layout, anything that could help us get inside."

Virgil nodded. "I will talk to him."

The agents exchanged a grim glance. It was Beau who spoke up. "With all due respect, sir, hasn't the time has come for stronger measures than just talk? You've been 'talking' to Niall ever since he was captured weeks ago, and it's yielded next to nothing—"

"Mind your tongue!" Virgil scolded, smacking the young agent in the back of the head. "How dare you?"

"You're coddling him!"

"Sir, we all can see the prisoner knows more than he is telling." Jordan spoke us with all his gentlemanly tact.

"Perhaps you'd let *us* question your, er, nephew before we go."

"Aye, I can make him talk."

"No," Virgil shot back.

"Stop protecting him!" Rohan warned. "Whatever he is to you, he's still an enemy!"

"Sir, he is an asset like any other," Max said calmly, knowing that if Virgil and Warrington started, they would never get out of here. They were more like father and son than Virgil had ever been with Niall.

"I will question him myself!" their handler boomed, outshouting Rohan when he started to protest, holding a finger in his face. "I was interrogating prisoners since before you were born, you coxcomb! Now, stay out of it and go make your preparations for the mission!"

Rohan let it go with a large, disgruntled sigh.

The men exchanged ominous looks.

"I'll arrange for the boat to take you across the Channel. Kiss your wives good-bye," Virgil grumbled in a cynical tone. "You leave at dawn."

"Yes, sir," Jordan murmured.

As they got up from the table, Max heard Beau attempt to placate the old man.

"I meant no disrespect, sir. I just want you to be careful. Blood is not always thicker than water."

"Get out of here," the Highlander muttered, waving him off in what passed for Virgil as gruff affection.

Beau turned, met Max's wry glance, and discreetly shrugged. Then the agents returned to the upper regions of the house and set off to gather supplies and put their affairs in order for the mission.

Virgil let out a long, weary exhalation after his boys had gone. He shook his head to himself at their warnings about Niall.

To be sure, these men were more like sons to him than the younger copy of himself locked in the nearby cell, who stared at him with such hatred like some cursed, malevolent mirror every time he went in to try to talk to him.

He knew they only nagged him out of concern, and that, indeed, they had a point. By all rights, he *should* be using harsher measures to force Niall to talk, but even Virgil, old, battle-hardened warhorse that he was, could not bring himself to do it.

The deep decades-old heartbreak that he had buried

within himself had now resurfaced, skewing his view of this situation more than he was ready to admit.

It wasn't Niall's fault that he had been turned into a Promethean.

Thirty years earlier, Malcolm's hatred had driven him to kidnap Virgil's betrothed and marry her himself, virtually holding her hostage as a way to tie Virgil's hands against bringing the full force of the Order against his Promethean cell.

What Malcolm hadn't known was that Virgil had already lain with Catherine, not long after the traditional Scottish handfasting ceremony betrothing them. They hadn't been able to resist each other, and Virgil's honest intentions toward the bonny lass were clear. As a result, she was already pregnant as their wedding date approached.

So, when Malcolm, along with his henchmen, had abducted her out of her parents' home, he had taken both Virgil's intended wife and unborn child away from him.

When he first learned it, he had lost his mind in such a fit of Highland fury that it had taken three of his fellow agents to hold him back, at least long enough to get control of himself and begin to consider a rational plan.

His first concern was for her safety. And that was ultimately what had defeated him.

Every time he had planned or set out on a rescue operation in the ensuing years, he had called it off at the last minute, knowing that Malcolm would not hesitate to kill both Catherine and the baby boy who eventually was born. Virgil had not been head of the London station at that time but a field agent. One of his teammates, in fact, had been Rohan's father, the previous Duke of Warrington. His fellow fighters had urged him to let them conduct a raid. If he was too close to it, his friends would do it for him and get his family back.

But Virgil did not dare. He knew his brother all too well. The up-and-coming Promethean leader would cut their throats before the Order agents had even gained the building. Any attempt at rescue would only bring them death. So, for their own safety, he had let his brother keep them . . . as hostages.

All that had happened long ago, though such wounds never healed.

Catherine had not long survived her forced marriage to Malcolm, murdered, he had heard, during an attempt to escape with the baby.

Once she was dead, Malcolm had kept the boy and raised him as his own.

Virgil had never expected to get his now-grown son back in his custody. He had Drake to thank for that.

Perhaps this Emily Harper and he had something in common, Virgil mused. For as much as the girl refused to give up on Westwood, Virgil felt the same toward his long-lost son.

Of course, it was rather awkward, because Niall had been brought up to believe that Malcolm was his sire and that Virgil was his hated uncle.

Virgil had told Niall the whole difficult story a few weeks ago, but his son refused to believe it, despite their obvious physical similarities.

He did not remember his mother but seemed to consider Malcolm not just his father but his closest friend.

Virgil had never been so jealous in his life. But he refused to blame the lad. He'd come around in time.

He had to believe that.

He had never stopped loving his son from afar though they were strangers. It wasn't Niall's fault, after all, that Malcolm had warped his mind with all that occult Promethean filth. Virgil clung to his faith that Niall could still be saved.

After all, if James Falkirk could undo Drake's Order training and turn him into a Promethean, then surely, Virgil could do the opposite, he reasoned. He could win Niall over for the Order.

That was why he had gone easy on him. He had to show his son there was another way than the Promethean creed of force and pain and cruelty and "might makes right."

He was sure that if he could just break through the hatred Niall had been taught from his cradle, then his splendid grown son would begin to feel the bond between them. Somehow, he had to win Niall's trust.

Hoping that something might coax the lad to share some information about this Waldfort Castle in Bavaria, he rang for Niall's supper from the kitchens; Gray soon sent it down to the Pit on the dumbwaiter.

Virgil picked up the tray and carried it down the tunnel roughly hewn into the rock.

There were several of these subterranean passageways connecting the various functional sections of the Pit. This one led from the agents' meeting chamber to an underground cavern divided into three holding cells.

Only one was occupied at present.

Behind the bars of the middle cell, Niall Banks had been the Order's guest for a month and a half, ever since the night they had found him beaten to a pulp on the floor of the Pulteney Hotel—Drake's handiwork. By now, his dislocated shoulder had pretty much healed after Virgil had returned it to its socket.

As Virgil arrived in the torchlit hollow of the Order's in-house jail, bringing the prisoner his supper, he remained on his guard, still uncertain how sophisticated Niall's training had been.

He dared not underestimate him, but to his expert eye, with years of evaluating the countless warriors and agents he had trained from boyhood, Virgil detected a hint of spoiled, civilian softness in Niall Banks, though the red-haired man was a giant, like many of their Highland blood.

Faced with Niall's flat stare, Virgil hid the surge of fatherly pride to behold the braw specimen that he and Catherine had produced. He himself was six-foot-three, but Niall had even an inch or two on him. The lad must have weighed about eighteen stone. Massive. Even more heavily muscled than Virgil had been at Niall's age, in his prime.

They looked so much alike that surely Niall perceived the truth, Virgil thought, unless he was being willfully blind. Malcolm was only five-foot-ten with blond, spiky hair and ice blue eyes.

But Niall refused to accept the news of who his real father was because he did not want it to be true. What he wanted was to become the next head of the Prometheans, following Malcolm.

Niall had apparently been groomed since boyhood for this eventual post, and with all the cult's delusions of grandeur, fully expected to rule the world one day, if even from the shadows, as was the Promethean way.

Well, thought Virgil, ignoring the fact that he was making excuses for him again, the truth about who had sired him was a lot for the lad to take in.

He ignored the knowledge, as well, that a man of thirty could hardly be called a lad. Most of all, he ignored the murderous hatred in Niall's eyes.

He could not bear for Niall to hate him. Losing his

son had been bad enough, but to be despised on top of that was worse.

Treasuring the chance to take care of his son as he had not been allowed to during Niall's boyhood, Virgil carried in the covered tray of food. He went and set it on the high table pushed up against the wall across from the cells, out of the prisoner's reach.

Niall got up from his cot and sauntered toward the bars.

"I brought your supper," he told him gruffly.

"Well, give it to me, then."

"If you want this food, I need some information."

"Oh, really?" Niall replied with a mocking smile.

Virgil rested his hands on his waist, keeping a wary distance. "What do you know about Waldfort Castle?"

"Why?" he countered.

"Just answer the question. Who owns it, and how do we get in?"

"Go to Hell," Niall said.

Virgil took a step closer, restraining an impulse of fatherly discipline that made him want to take Niall out to the proverbial woodshed. "My agents want your blood," he said. "I cannot continue to hold them in check unless you give me something."

Niall stared at him for a long moment. "The owner is Count Septimus Glasse. He's the head of operations for all the German principalities."

"There. Was that so hard?"

"Can I have my bloody food now, or is starving me for information part of what you consider being a good father?"

"How do my men get in?"

"How should I know? I've never been there. I don't know!" he reiterated at Virgil's look of doubt.

Virgil suppressed a sigh, feeling old. Reluctantly, he

took the tray over to the cell. Niall approached on the other side of the bars. Virgil took the lid off the tray, made sure there were no utensils for Niall's use as weapons, and that the plate was tin, not glass, which could be broken and used as a blade.

Satisfied that there was nothing on the tray but food, he slid it into the short, horizontal opening in the bars fashioned for that purpose.

Niall took the tray with a nod of thanks, but as Virgil turned away, Niall suddenly cast the tray aside and grabbed Virgil from behind, snaking his arm through the bars and throwing it around Virgil's neck. He pulled him back against the bars with a crash.

Aghast, Virgil struggled to tear away the massive arm cutting off his air.

"You think you're my father?" Niall snarled in his ear. "Do you think I give a shit if you are? I'll kill you just the same." His choke hold tightened.

Virgil clawed at the giant arm around his neck. "Don't—do this! You are my son!"

The chokehold tightened. "No, I'm not. You're nothing to me."

They were the last words Virgil heard.

Niall's heart pounded. He refused to think about what he was doing but just held on.

When the old man stopped struggling and slumped, Niall used all his strength to hold the body up with one arm while he reached his other hand into Virgil's coat pocket and searched for the keys that were kept there. He'd made a mental note of that detail weeks ago but had bided his time since then, waiting for the proper moment.

Listening intently a while ago, he had heard the agents leave. He had to get out of here before they came back.

His fingers suddenly grasped the keys. He shoved the body away from the cell door.

Virgil's corpse dropped to the ground.

Niall did his best to still the shaking of his hands and unlocked his cell, triumph throbbing in his veins as he slid the door open.

He helped himself to his uncle's weapons, then checked his pulse, making sure the man was dead. A part of his mind or soul was screaming at what he had just done, but he did not stop to think.

All that mattered was escape.

Not that he was afraid of them. How weak they were! He still couldn't believe he hadn't been tortured. But it seemed old Virgil had no stomach for such work.

God knew the man had been foolishly easy to lie to, for Niall *had* been to Waldfort Castle once before, about two years ago. That was where he had first met the black-haired lunatic who had dislocated his shoulder, James's so-called bodyguard. If he ever crossed paths with that bastard again, he would finish him off.

The pistol he took from Virgil's body was loaded; Niall checked it to be sure, then stole the old man's knife, tucking the large, sheathed blade through his belt as he crept down the tunnel.

As he approached the meeting room, he listened intently for any telltale sound that one of the Order's agents might still be in the next chamber. He could hardly hear above the pounding of his heart; but if they had wanted his blood before, they'd stop at nothing now to snuff him out for what he had just done.

He did not intend to give them the chance.

He paused and listened hard at the edge of the tunnel, but there was only silence. Pistol in hand, he glanced around the rough-hewn wall of the tunnel into the adjacent chamber.

Empty.

He stepped into it the torchlit chamber, searching for a way out, but what he saw made him pause. He scanned the chamber, fascinated.

Damn. The Order's inner sanctum.

As Niall crept across the meeting room, he wondered if this was what he might have been a part of if Virgil's claim about being his father were true.

Might he have ended up as an agent of the Order rather than the heir apparent of the Prometheans?

He studied the room in mingled amazement and disgust.

A white Maltese cross hung on rusted chains from the ceiling of the cavern. A table with a lantern on it sat in the middle. An ancient Byzantine mosaic of the Archangel Michael was embedded in the floor.

Niall was tempted to piss on it, but there was no time for churlish tricks. He crossed to the table and quickly riffled through the maps and papers strewn on it. *What are the bastards up to?*

He glanced nervously over his shoulder, but then his gaze was captured by a letter on the table.

He picked it up, his eyes narrowing as he read it. *Well, well, James. My father will hear about this.*

Traitor!

He slipped it into his breast pocket, but he wasted no more time seeking an exit. There were a couple of ladders leading up into the house, but Niall had often heard the guard dogs barking from above. They'd tear him apart. He had to find another way out.

He tried a tunnel that led off the main chamber, unsure of where it might lead. But a cold smile crossed his face when it brought him to a small dock with three rowboats tied to it.

He rushed to crank open the river gate that separated the Order's private dock from the Thames, under the overhanging eaves of the house.

Within moments, Niall was rowing out into the river under cover of night, turning the boat to coast swiftly along with the current.

He cast a grim look over his shoulder at the back of the mysterious house where he had been kept. It was receding fast, along with the lights of London.

Good-bye, Uncle. Niall refused to heed the doubts gnawing at his soul. Being captured had been nothing but a temporary inconvenience, but he was none the worse for wear thanks to his captor's foolish sentimentality.

Indeed, his captivity had paid off, for now he knew exactly where Falkirk had gone.

Waldfort Castle.

Niall had to get back to his father. Warn Malcolm about James Falkirk's little meeting.

There could be no doubt as to its purpose.

Falkirk had called the others together in secret to scheme against Father and him.

Niall had to hope there was still time to bring the situation under control.

In the meanwhile, he rowed harder to gain as much of a lead as possible on the Order agents who were sure to come after him like the hounds of Hell.

He smiled coldly to himself, wishing he could have seen their faces when they came back and found their handler dead.

Chapter

6

Bavaria

Comfrey to speed the healing of wounds.
Blessed thistle to restore the patient's loss of appetite.
Feverwort to break the hold of ague.
Coltsfoot and bloodroot for a cough.
Beggar's buttons to ease pains of the joints.
Marshmallow root for a queasy stomach . . .

Fragments of memory wove themselves into a fitful dream as Emily slept alone in Drake's bed . . . for he was not the only one who had ever fallen into a dark place.

One afternoon when she was seventeen, she had gone collecting herbs to keep her apothecary jars well supplied. Bark, roots, berries, and flowers, weeds, worts, and sedges, each had its own medicinal purpose, and she had crossed the Westwood acreage on the hunt, rambling through wood, marsh, and meadow, gathering the plants to be dried for diverse uses.

She knew to watch her step for poachers' traps, but she was unconcerned, having helped Papa set most of them herself. Beyond that, she had sensed no danger, upon reaching the edge of the Westwood property. Indeed, she had felt no more than idle surprise when the sound of hoofbeats came thundering over the rolling green meadows of the adjoining estate.

She straightened up with her herb basket in hand as she spotted Mr. Lamont exercising his fine bay hunter. The London dandy had his beaver hat cocked at a dashing angle, the tails of his impeccable riding coat flapping over the gelding's haunches.

The Thoroughbred impressed her with its gliding liquid canter. The haughty London rakehell did not.

Well, our neighbor's back. The absentee landlord only came from London twice a year to make sure his tenants were paying their rents. It kept him in funds for the gaming tables, she supposed.

Drake had invited him over once for port when both landowners had happened to be at home, and that was when he'd first caught sight of Emily.

She clutched the handle of her basket harder and edged back toward the cover of the trees as he reined in before her.

"Well, hullo there!" he hailed her, sweeping off his fashionable hat.

She bowed her head and sketched a humble curtsy. "How do you do, sir," she mumbled.

While his tall blood horse pawed the turf, he had perused her with a grin from ear to ear, perusing her with an idle stare. "Well, how perfectly charming! A little country maiden and her basket—like you just stepped out of a Wordsworth poem. I fear I'm quite enchanted. Please, refresh my memory, darling. Who are you, exactly?"

She awkwardly informed him who she was.

"Oh, right! Jack Harper's little girl. All grown-up now, or nearly so. How is your father, child?"

"I'm afraid he hasn't been well, sir. It's his back. I'm collecting some herbs to help him."

"You must allow me to assist," he announced, and he swung down from his horse, not waiting for her permission.

Emily wished he would go away, but who was she to say such a thing to a wealthy gentleman?

With no real choice about his company, she let him tag along for a bit while she plucked a few linden flowers.

He stared at her, inhaling one of the blooms. "You've grown into a very lovely girl, Miss Harper." She had pulled away when he had followed his compliment with a light touch of her cheek.

She had stepped back with a warning stare. "Excuse me, sir. I must get back to my father."

"What's your hurry?" Still smiling, he had captured her wrist.

Something in his eyes had begun to make Emily very nervous.

"Don't be shy, my dear. What beautiful eyes you have. Has anyone ever told you that? The color's splendid. I shall have my tailor make me a waistcoat in just that shade." He ignored her resistance and pulled her closer, pretending to inspect her eyes.

Her heart pounding with rising fear, Emily did her best to hide her distaste. "Thank you, sir, but I have to get back to the house."

"Stay." He paused, holding her in a frank stare. "I'll make it worth your while."

Her eyes widened in confusion.

"Come, little country maiden, let me teach you a few of the pleasures we know in Town."

"Let go of me!"

"Spirited filly!" He laughed when she tried to knee him in the groin. "Easy now. Just relax," he ordered as he yanked her against his body. "Don't be coy. I won't do anything you don't like. I'm told I'm quite good at this, actually—"

"If you do not let go of me this instant, I shall tell Lord Seaton that you attacked me." Drake had been known by that courtesy title while his father was alive. "He'll put a bullet in you if you touch me!"

"And why is that?" A flicker of uncertainty passed behind his leering eyes, but a mocking half smile curved his thin lips. "Has Seaton already broken you in to the saddle? Good, then I'm sure he won't mind sharing. We both know he's in Town at the moment."

"He'll be here in a trice if I call for him," she warned.

"Oh, really? And what are you? Whatever he's promised you, I assure you, it was a lie. He's got even more women in London than I do. Oh, you didn't know that? Well, you might as well take my offer. I'm afraid you're nothing to him but a little country sport."

Emily hit him on the head with her basket and pulled away with all her strength, then ran.

"Come back here, girl! I did not dismiss you!"

Terrified, she glanced over her shoulder and saw him chasing her. Her heart in her throat, she fled him, bewildered by his lewd actions and hurt by his spiteful words. She was not as familiar with this section of the property, however, and as she pounded through the woods, perhaps she was distracted by the pang of knowing that what he had said was at least partly true.

Drake was always in London; he seemed to have forgotten all about her. But this was no time to pout over how her childhood friend seemed to have abandoned her.

All of a sudden, she stepped on something that crunched.

Her foot smashed through the layer of loose dirt and scattered leaves, and the next thing she knew her body followed; she screamed as she fell through the rotting boards concealing an old, abandoned well.

She seemed to fall for ages down the pitch-black shaft, but landed with a jolt, crying out on impact as she slammed down to the bottom. Her right foot touched down first, instantly breaking her ankle; she was hurled against the packed-earthen wall, banging the back of her head, jamming her elbow and biting the inside of her lip so hard it bled.

Then she fell silent, her breath coming in short, terrified gasps. For one woozy-headed moment, she struggled to make sure she was alive, that nothing had impaled her. Her ribs felt bruised, but she could move her hands and arms; she wiped the blood off the corner of her lips, and concluded that her ankle had got the worst of it.

The blinding pain made her eyes smart with tears. But she was more furious than scared.

She gritted her teeth against the pain and looked up slowly to where Mr. Lamont had come to stand at the edge of the well. His face was as white as a sheet.

"Go and get my father," Emily ordered in as forceful a tone as she could muster. "I'm hurt. Tell him to bring rope. And a doctor."

She heard Mr. Lamont curse to himself. He backed away from the edge of the abandoned well.

"Mr. Lamont? Mr. Lamont!"

He did not reappear.

To Emily's horror, it dawned on her that this coward was willing to leave her to die out here, merely to hide the fact of what he had done.

If she was dead—disappeared—then she'd never be able to tell anyone that he had tried to rape her.

She had nothing to eat or even to drink with her; there was no water in the well. She had no cloak to keep her warm for the next three nights while despair set in that no one was ever going to find her in this lonely tomb.

Why, Papa and she knew these woods as well as anyone, and neither of them had even been aware that this ancient, dried-out well was there.

After the first day had passed, Emily had the sense and skill and the raw temerity to set her own broken ankle, shoving the bone back where it belonged, only to faint with pain.

When she had come to, she had torn off part of her dress and wrapped the wound.

But by the time Drake's face appeared days later at the jagged edge of the broken boards many feet above her, she was only semiconscious.

Up in the woods, her father tied the rope around a nearby tree and steadied it as Drake climbed down into the pit with her. He took her in his arms and brushed her tangled hair out of her eyes as he whispered questions, trying to learn the extent of the damage.

At once, he had restored her with water from his canteen. Before long, he had tied the rope around them both and held on to her as her father and a crowd of the other servants who had joined the search assisted in pulling them up. She had blinked her eyes against the light as she rejoined the land of the living . . .

And she did so now, the shroud of sleep dissolving.

When she slowly opened her eyes to the new day, she found Drake staring at her, just like he had all those years ago.

With the memory of his rescue so fresh in her mind,

as if it had happened yesterday, she moved abruptly to embrace him. She threw her arms around his neck.

The motion took him off guard. He did not have time to push her away. He accepted her hug, gingerly returning it though he seemed bemused.

Emily squeezed her eyes shut as she clung to him, her heart still pounding from the unsettling dream.

"Well, good morning to you, too," Drake mumbled.

When Emily recollected the particulars of last night, namely that he had become a Promethean, she released him from her embrace, warily pulling back.

"You all right?"

She nodded, easing back onto her elbows. "What were you doing, watching me sleep?"

He held her gaze with a faint, reluctant half smile. "I was just waiting for you to wake up."

"Why?"

"So I could thank you."

"For what?" she asked in surprise.

He shrugged. "For what you tried to do for me, by coming here. Don't think I don't appreciate it. Pound for pound, you're the bravest soul I know, my girl. Always were."

"Well, coming from you, I'll take that as a compliment," she responded, pleased. "But if you really want to thank me, you can start by giving me a proper answer. Did you get your memory back or not, yes or no?"

"More or less. Not everything, but enough."

"I knew it! Was it during that monstrous three-day headache you had in England?"

He searched her eyes with a guarded stare, then nodded. "It all started coming back to me then."

"So you are you again."

"Whatever that means." He looked away with a sardonic lift of his eyebrows. "I have to go. I'm on duty in a quarter hour."

Emily sat up in his bed, stretching a bit, while Drake rose from the stool where he'd been sitting beside her and went to buckle on his weapons belt.

A glance toward the balcony revealed the predawn gray hanging over the thick forest, a slowly paling sky above the mountains' pearly peaks.

"I'll send up breakfast for you when I go down," he told her. "I'll be busy for most of the day."

"I hope you weren't too cold sleeping outside last night? It really wasn't necessary—"

"It was fine," he cut her off.

She got up, still clad in his shirt, and pushed up the long sleeves as she followed him, barefooted, toward the door. "So, I won't see much of you today, then?"

"No." His glance skimmed over her, then he sternly looked away.

Emily let out a sigh, dragging her hand through her hair. "Lord, how am I to occupy myself?" she muttered. "You can't keep me locked up in here all day. I'll go mad."

"Well, you're supposed to be my servant. You could always see to the tasks that need doing around here."

"Like what?"

"Those dishes from last night have to go back down to the kitchen. The hearth needs sweeping. My shirts could use a washing in the stream."

She slanted him a skeptical look.

He shrugged again and smiled. "Or you can sit around here and stare at the walls if you prefer."

She snorted. "I don't prefer."

"Good. Then have it all done when I get back."

"I beg your pardon!"

"I'm only teasing."

She snorted and folded her arms across her chest.

"Watch yourself," he warned in a softer tone. "You're free to go about your tasks inside the castle, but don't trust anyone. Don't talk to anyone unless you're spoken to directly. Keep your eyes down. Do your work and keep to yourself. And Emily?"

"Yes, Drake?" She rested her shoulder against the wall, leaning closer to him. His magnetism drew her irresistibly.

"Don't go prying anywhere," he warned.

"Who, me?"

"I'm serious. Stay out of mischief for both our sakes. One more thing," he added, pausing with one hand on the door.

"What's that?"

"Don't forget, they think we are lovers."

"Would it were so," she whispered daringly. The words slipped out before she could check them.

His dark eyes narrowed in speculation. "Don't start something you're not prepared to finish."

"You started it. Yesterday. You're the one who kissed me."

Gazing roguishly into her eyes, he leaned closer until his lips hovered half an inch from hers. "But, my dear, that was only for a ruse."

"Do you kiss differently in earnest?"

"You tell me," he whispered, and he pressed his lips to hers, driving her body back against the wall, his hand resting on her waist.

Emily met his kiss in trembling enthusiasm, curling her hands over his shoulders, her heart pounding.

But Drake stopped himself a moment later, his chest heaving. "Careful what you wish for," he warned in a sensuous murmur. His gaze dipped to her moistened lips before he turned and left the room.

She closed her eyes, breathlessly leaning her head back against the wall after he had gone.

Lord, didn't that man know she'd have walked through fire for him?

Lunatic, Promethean, or not.

London

The dogs of Dante House were howling.

Virgil's body had been discovered some hours before, but as accustomed as they were to death, every agent there was in a state of shock, silent with fury.

The man who had been like a father to them, their mentor and trainer, had been cut down, and none of them had been on hand to help him.

The rage, the grief, the hunger for revenge drove them onto the schooner that had been waiting for their departure to the Continent. With few words, Rotherstone's team parted ways with Beauchamp, who stayed behind to handle the aftermath of what was sure to come.

Officials would ask questions, to say nothing of the Elders of the Order up in Scotland. The shock of Virgil's death would be felt as far away as Moscow, and in every European capital in between, where an active cell of the Order had been established.

Beau had hurried them off, knowing Niall already had a lead of at least six hours. He assured them he would see to the burial of their beloved Highlander and that they would have a proper memorial service for him once his killer had been dealt with.

At present, they could not afford to let the trail go cold. Just as Virgil had taught them, they thrust their own feelings aside and got on with the job. It was what the old man would have wanted.

And so that morning, as planned, Max, Jordan, and Rohan set sail down the Thames, on the hunt for Niall Banks. Finding Drake was just as important as it had been last night, but the wound of Virgil's murder was too fresh for them to think of anything other than making their handler's treacherous offspring pay.

They had found Emily's letter missing and knew that Niall must have taken it.

Once he read it, he would certainly realize what her news about James's secret meeting signified. That meant Niall, too, would head for Waldfort Castle in order to stomp out Falkirk's conspiracy against Malcolm.

The agents did not intend to let him get that far, however. They stood at the bow of the schooner as the sun inched over the horizon at their backs, separate and silent, each alone with his own thoughts, each seething stare scanning the river and shoreline, on the watch, each one's hand in easy reach of his weapon. In short, they wanted blood.

If Niall had the cunning to trick a seasoned knight of the Order like Virgil Banks into making such a fatal mistake as turning his back on him and letting his guard down, then the bastard was smart enough, thought Max, to know he would not live long.

Indeed, miles ahead, where the river met the coast, Niall glanced nervously over his shoulder as he paid for a ticket aboard a packet ship to Calais from the English coast.

Petty crime was not his style, but he had resorted to robbing a shopkeeper at the point of a blade shortly after abandoning the rowboat by the river's edge.

He did not have time for more caution. He was well aware that any number of Order agents would soon be on his heels. He had only a few hours' lead on them, and he knew he would be hunted like a fox. The packet ship could not get under way fast enough for him.

When at last it pulled up anchor and lumbered away from the English coast, rocking its way out into the wind-tossed Channel, only then did he exhale.

He kept a distance from the other passengers but slumped on one of the benches belowdecks and told himself the nausea he was experiencing was merely due to seasickness.

The one thing he tried not to contemplate was the sickening truth that he feared he knew deep down in his bones.

The proof was in the mirror.

He was fairly sure he had just murdered his own father, and that was something.

Even for him.

Chapter
7

Bavaria

Later that day, Emily knelt on a rock by the stream outside the castle walls, her hands stung by the icy water of the brook as she wrung out another of Drake's shirts.

She was fairly sure that, aside from keeping up their charade of master and servant, the scoundrel had given her these menial tasks to ding her pride and try to goad her into wanting to leave.

But his little scheme wasn't going to work. She refused to be driven off, especially after that kiss.

Her heart still sang, knowing *that* one, at least, had not been for show. She had been waiting for her too-noble Order knight to do that for years.

It had been worth the wait.

More importantly, his first true kiss renewed her determination to take him home, despite the Initiate's Brand on his chest.

He did not know her at all if he thought she would be giving up so easily. True, the mark on his chest showed how fierce the battle to save him might become, but at least they were together, and, by God, she had only just begun to fight.

How could she do otherwise when that unpleasant dream about the Lamont debacle had recalled in sharp detail what Drake had done for her?

He had literally saved her life.

Lack of water had nearly put an end to her existence though it was ironic that her prison was at the bottom of a well. One that had run dry.

Drake had come storming home within hours of receiving word of her disappearance. He had torn Westwood Park apart to find her, and once he had her safely in his arms, lifting her limp body from the hole, he had not left her side. He had waited until she was well enough to tell him what had happened.

After questioning her and drying her few tears, Drake, unlike his mother, did not question her veracity, but had stalked off to the neighboring estate, issued his challenge to a duel, and promptly at dawn the next morning, had put her attacker in his grave.

No more girls would be assaulted by Mr. Lamont.

With a history like that between them, the errant Earl of Westwood was not a madman but a fool if he thought he could drive her away with the supposed insult of a few menial tasks.

She relished the thought of vexing him by refusing to take offense. After all, she had never been afraid of a little hard work.

Indeed, she was glad to have something to do. It was better than sitting inside, locked in his room.

Washing clothes meant she could be outside, as she always preferred, drinking in the fresh, pine-scented air and the majestic beauty of the surrounding Alps.

She finishing squeezing the water out of his large black shirt, untwisting it from the ropelike coil she had made to squeeze out the excess water. She shook it out, then carried it over to the temporary clothesline she had strung between two trees and draped it over the rope.

Planting her hands in the small of her back, she stretched a bit, tipping her head back to let the sun warm her face. When she opened her eyes again, her gaze fell once more on the mouth of the trail that opened nearby, leading off into the woods.

An easy escape by that route beckoned, but she ignored the lure of freedom so close at hand.

Wryly, she gathered it was no accident that Drake had sent her to the stream to do her task. He probably meant for her to slip away at once. But she wasn't leaving alone, any more than he would have left her down in that hole once he had found her.

Then she glanced up at the mighty castle, still unsure of what dangerous game he was playing.

By the time she finished the laundry, hung their things on the clothesline to dry, and went back inside, she had worked up an appetite from the very physical labor.

With a twinge in her back and her stomach rumbling, she wondered if she would be given a midday meal. Service of the day's early dinner appeared to be under way in the castle. She went in, doing her best to escape notice, blending into the background like any other servant.

She remembered Drake's advice about being careful and not talking to anyone, but she couldn't resist stealing a peek into the Guards' Hall, hoping to catch a glimpse of him.

Glancing around the corner amid the servants who were continually scurrying in and out of the hall, waiting on the warriors, she did not see Drake at the long banquet table. Some three dozen well-armed body-guards of the Promethean leaders were devouring huge quantities of food. They probably ate in shifts, she thought, but Drake was not among them. *I wonder where he is.*

She walked away, noticing another line of footmen, these wearing livery. They were carrying a parade of gleaming silver trays into the stately dining room that James Falkirk had stepped out of the day before.

Emily gathered that this was where the elite Promethean lords took their meals. As she watched the footmen march in, she wondered with a bit of grave-yard humor what sort of food these demons liked to eat. Roasted snake? Frog eyeballs? Stuffed raven instead of Cornish hens?

Indeed, all washed down with a nice goblet of warm human blood. Smirking at her own musings, she turned away and proceeded down to the kitchens, where she was put to work for a while, but eventually received her portion for the day.

What the satanic Promethean masters might be eating, who could say, but the servants were given dried-out, stringy pork chops left over from what the well-fed guards had not devoured the previous night, along with one cold, mushy carrot, half a turnip, and a meager hunk of slightly moldy bread for each of them.

Emily accepted her plate with as much gratitude as she could muster and headed back to Drake's room. As she neared the staircase, the sound of raucous barking arrested her attention. It was coming from one of the opulent State Rooms on the main floor.

Curious about the clamor, Emily went to peek into the gilded drawing room near the grand staircase.

To her surprise, three of the castle's enormous black guard dogs had surrounded the dainty rococo couch, barking, tails wagging, though an occasional snarl confirmed that although they were enjoying their sport, they were serious about their game.

Watching the large, powerful dogs circling the sofa, poking their heads under it, though they were too big to crawl beneath it, Emily realized they had cornered something under there. Whatever had taken shelter under the couch was doomed without a little help.

She frowned; her first unappetizing thought was of a rat. She lost all interest in her plate of food when she realized what would happen when the dogs got hold of their quarry.

It was only a matter of time before they captured it, then they would ruin the luxurious carpet tearing their prey apart.

Emily set her plate aside and went over behind the dogs, bending down to the floor to see if she could spot the trapped creature.

The dogs ignored her, absorbed in their sport, but she was suddenly startled to find a hissing, terrorized, little tabby cat doing its best to hold off the mighty dogs from every direction.

"Oh, you poor thing," she murmured. Its tiny fangs glinting, the cat was puffed up into a fur ball, but had hunkered down for the siege.

Emily tried to shoo the dogs away, but when one of them snapped at her, warning her off their sport, she jumped back, startled.

These were dangerous animals, trained to attack. She did not intend to try to stand against them. Instead, with barely a twinge of regret, she plucked the pork chop off her plate, caught the dogs' attention with a whistle, dangling it before them.

When they noticed the piece of meat she was offering, they forgot all about the cat and started toward her.

She threw the pork chop clear to the other end of the drawing room. The dogs lunged after it and proceeded to battle over it among themselves.

The cat was gone in a flash, streaking out from under the couch, a blur of gray bulleting toward the doorway and disappearing from the room.

She smiled and wiped her hands off on the dun-colored woolen skirts of her work dress, the only other set of clothes she had brought with her.

Leaving the drawing room with a certain fellow feeling for the outnumbered feline, Emily followed to see if the cat had been injured in its ordeal. If so, perhaps it would let her help. But it was naught but a flash of fur ahead, diving down the backstairs at the far end of the hallway.

She followed, calling softly to it, but the panicked tabby raced on.

I wonder where that leads, she thought, pausing as she reached the top of the dark stone stairs, down which the cat had vanished. Maybe it had kittens down there somewhere, for it was that time of year.

She bit her lip, glancing over her shoulder, with Drake's warning not to go exploring the castle ringing in her ears.

Of course, if she had listened to him, she wouldn't even be there. Her mind made up to at least have a look, she glided silently down the stairs.

They turned, then came to an odd, stone room with octagonal walls and only one narrow window. There was a thick wooden door reinforced with iron on the other side of the room; it was open a few inches.

It was the only place the cat could have gone.

Once more, Emily followed, half-intrigued, half-uneasy. She hauled the heavy door open wider and stepped through into darkness; then she pulled it back to the same position in which she had found it before proceeding down the next set of stone-carved steps.

The atmosphere grew cold and clammy. It was not the sort of warm, cozy place where any sensible cat would want to drop her litter, but Emily was much too curious to turn back.

Deeper and deeper the stairs led down into the bowels of the castle. She wished she had grabbed some source of light, but her eyes adjusted to the indigo shadows, and she pressed on.

The weight of stone above, the darkness palpable, the smell of stale air, mold, and earth, and the ancient sense of age made her feel like she was entering a crypt. Every step down was like walking back in time to a lost age hundreds of years ago, when Waldfort's foundations had first been laid.

When she came to the bottom of the stairs, she stopped, staring ahead uneasily.

A few, narrow defensive windows high above let in just enough light to sketch the shapes of mighty columns reaching up into elegant vaulted arches.

What is this place?

Some kind of old cistern?

Cautiously, she walked on. To her right, the great stone blocks of the castle's foundations bore the scars of ancient battles. Burn marks. The limestone was pitted and scored in places where various missiles had struck it over the centuries. She could almost hear the ghostly echo of embattled knights in chain mail ducking away from the incoming fire of catapults.

Then she halted once again, staring ahead at the row

of cells she spotted lining the aisle on both sides of her. The hairs on the back of her neck stood on end; gooseflesh rose on her arms as she realized that it was definitely not the castle's cistern.

No, she was standing in the dungeon.

The first cell she peered into had a heap of ancient human bones littering the corner. Emily swallowed hard, her heart pounding.

Everything in her wanted to run away, but she could not. To think, Drake had been kept prisoner somewhere in a place like this . . .

Her throat tightened. The eeriness was almost more than she could bear, but she found herself compelled to go a little farther, just to look around.

All the cells were empty, thankfully.

She had forgotten all about the cat in the meanwhile, but she saw it then, sitting rather contentedly in a chink in a crumbling section of the wall that appeared to have suffered from decades of water damage. Chunks of stone or perhaps cement were missing, and since the dungeon sat beneath ground level, that must have made it convenient for the cat to come and go as it pleased, with naught but an easy climb.

Drake's words about not going around snooping were a faint memory by now. Emily told herself she would leave in a moment, but first, she wanted to see what was in the odd chamber straight ahead.

At the end of the corridor lined by cells, an open door beckoned into a dark stone room. She approached it, trembling with mingled repugnance and fascination. She stopped a few feet from the open door, not daring to go closer.

There was just enough light to reveal the sinister outlines of medieval instruments of torture.

She recoiled from the sight of an iron chair in the

center of the room with built-in manacles and leg irons. That did not look medieval.

No. It looked much newer.

How horrible. Was it possible that Drake had endured such fiendish devices when he had been captured? The thought turned the blood in her veins to ice. The vaulted space beneath the castle was so silent—but to her the air seemed thick with the screams of prisoners once trapped inside the walls.

Backing away from the unspeakable chamber, she whirled around and ran, fleeing back up the stairs.

Reaching the heavy wooden door at the top of the stairs, she found it still cracked, just as she had left it. She listened for anyone else's presence before stealthily reemerging into the empty, octagonal anteroom.

She shut the dungeon door behind her all the way.

That cat should stay out, where the dogs can't get her, she thought in shaky anger and lingering dread.

Crossing the octagonal room, she mounted the next set of stairs, taking care not to let anyone notice her coming up from the stairwell when she reached the hallway above.

Upon reentering the rococo main floor of the castle, she put her head down, as Drake had advised, and hurried back toward his room. When she passed two of the foreign bodyguards, the men eyed her rather like the dogs had eyed the pork chop.

She kept her distance, skittering along the edge of the wall as the cat had done. With her pulse thudding in her arteries, she sped on, but when she stepped around the corner, she nearly ran headlong into James Falkirk.

"Oh, I'm sorry, sir!"

"Miss Harper." He stopped also, rather startled at their near collision. The old man lifted his chin, studying her, his eyes narrowed in curious speculation. "You seem lost, my dear."

More than you know. She hid her surprise at his too-perceptive words. "No, sir. I-I'm finding my way round all right. I was just, um, seeing to milord's laundry."

"Ah. I trust you are settling in, then?"

"Yes, sir." She bowed her head in deference.

He had the most unsettling stare. "It was quite brave of you to come all this way for your protector. I daresay he is in need of a woman's touch."

Emily peered up through her lashes at him in trepidation.

"I do hope you are able to, ah, fix him with your skills, Miss Harper. He's been slow to heal. Not his fault, of course. He's been through considerable unpleasantness." He paused, weighing and sifting her very soul with his penetrating gaze. "This was where he was held, you know."

Emily lifted her head in shock. "Here?"

"I'm afraid so. Coming back to Waldfort, where it all happened, has been very difficult for him. But it could not be avoided." He shrugged.

Her wits were suddenly reeling at the revelation.

This castle? That dungeon?

That unspeakable torture room?

"Are you quite well, Miss Harper?" James Falkirk inquired with the tranquil air of a man who knew exactly what he was doing.

Emily could barely catch her breath. "Y-yes, sir. I-I must be on about my duties."

"Indeed."

She sketched a curtsy and turned to go, but halted, glancing back at him. "Drake told me you saved his life, sir," she forced out. "For what it's worth, you have my thanks for that—from the bottom of my heart."

"Hmm. If you would thank me, then help your master to make a full recovery, and soon. We're awfully keen for him to get his memory back. That is what would be best for Drake," he added pointedly.

She could not be certain, but his words sounded to her like a veiled threat. "I'll do my best, sir."

"Good. I'm glad we understand we each other, my dear." He nodded her dismissal with a vaguely reptilian smile. "Off you go, then."

Her heart in her throat, Emily bobbed another respectful curtsy and whisked away from the seemingly harmless old man in a state of terror and revulsion. Why, he knew just what to say to people to make them do exactly what he wanted!

She could still feel the cunning old chess player watching her in mingled suspicion and amusement as she sped off in a bit of a panic.

Nevertheless, for whatever reasons of his own, James Falkirk had given her some stunning information.

She could not have withstood her brief tour of the dungeon if she had known that was the place, the very place, that had been Drake's hell on earth.

And he was here—! Where it had all happened. Forced to face it every day. How could he bear it?

No wonder he was so angry that I came, she thought as she ran up the main staircase, taking the steps two at a time in an unladylike fashion that would have made his haughty mother cringe. Drake was afraid they both might end up down there—he just hadn't wanted to say so!

He hadn't wanted her to know the full extent of the danger she was in.

And the danger she had placed him in, as well.

And through him, all his brother agents.

Oh, what have I done?

Yes, Drake had taken the Initiate's Brand, but she still was not entirely convinced he was a real Promethean; if it was some insanely brave ruse he was playing out, if he was still the great knight of the Order that he had always been, then she was truly a serious liability for him, being there.

Lionhearted as he was, he might have withstood the torturers' worst, himself, but if they were to put *her* in that wicked chair, she did not doubt he would soon tell them whatever they wanted to know. Simply because it was so deeply ingrained in him to protect her.

Good God, she had better play her part as his servant plaything well, exactly as he had explained it to her.

Gaining the upper hallway, she hurried on, eager to reach his room so she could at least have a moment alone to collect her thoughts. At the moment, her fears continued to savage her. Of course, she had long known that the Prometheans were very dangerous people, aye, ever since Drake had first told her about them as a lad.

But seeing the evidence of their evil firsthand had suddenly made it all real to her in a way it had not entirely been before.

God, she would never forgive herself if she caused Drake to be returned to that terrible place through some mistake of hers. She did not think he could survive it.

Indeed, in that moment, she quite hoped that it *was* no ruse—that he *was* a real Promethean, just as he claimed, no longer a hero—because if he really was one of them, then at least they would not hurt him again. He might have turned evil, but at least he would be safe.

Of course, she now knew Drake had not told James

Falkirk that his memory had returned, since just a few minutes ago, the old man had encouraged her to help Drake remember. Meanwhile, however, just this morning, Drake had admitted to her, cautiously and reluctantly, that his memory *had* returned, before he had left England.

Well, she thought, rather dazed and confused. At least this showed that he still trusted her more than Falkirk.

That wasn't saying much, but it was good to know.

Reaching their chamber at last, she flung the door open, then stopped in her tracks to find Drake already there.

He was leaning over his opened cache of weapons and ammunition, retrieving a few items from the trunk, but he glanced over when she burst in.

The slight smile that greeted her and the sudden warm glow in his eyes hinted that he was still thinking about their kiss.

But then he noticed her air of distress.

"You all right?" He furrowed his brow, straightening up to his full height.

Emily opened her mouth to speak, but no words came out. She abruptly found she did not know what to say.

After what she had just learned, she was not sure she was quite ready to see him yet.

His smile vanished, and he stepped toward her with an increasing look of concern. "What's the matter?"

"Nothing," she whispered, and shut the door behind her.

"Emily." Drake studied her with a frown, resting his hands on his waist. "Did somebody bother you?"

"N-no, it's, um—" She swallowed hard and lowered her head, trying to decide if the truth or a lie was the best answer in this case.

God only knew how he would react if she told him the truth, that she now knew this was the castle where he'd been held prisoner. A bad idea, surely, to try to bring it up.

On the other hand, his trust in her was her only weapon in this fight. If she tried to lie to him, a trained spy, he'd know. And then he'd trust her less.

Casting about, she opted for a safer middle ground. "I-I just ran into Mr. Falkirk. That's all."

He took a step forward. "Did he question you?" he asked tersely.

"Not really. He asked if I was settling in."

He scanned her. "And what did you say?"

"I said yes, and I showed him I was—doing your laundry."

One eyebrow lifted. "You did my laundry?"

She nodded. "It's drying."

He stared at her. "You didn't have to do that."

"Better than being bored out of my wits."

He absorbed this, then gave her a nod as his guarded smile returned. "Well, thanks for that." Satisfied with her answer, Drake started to turn back again to his weapons case.

I can't lie to him. How could she hold the secret in?

It went against her nature and was beyond her power.

"He told me something," Emily blurted out abruptly.

"Hmm, what was that?" he asked, glancing at her with an array of guns laid out in front of him on the bed.

Emily stared at him, her heart pounding. "He told me t-this was where you were held."

He held her gaze sharply, frozen for a second, then, before her eyes, he shut down completely. "Did he, now?" he murmured as nonchalantly as if she had told him she thought it was going to rain.

Emily winced at his casual façade.

But the way his broad shoulders stiffened and his lips thinned, like an animal ready to bare its teeth, and the cool manner in which he turned back to his weapons and would no longer meet her gaze spoke volumes.

"Drake—is there anything at all that I can do?"

"Well, you've mastered the laundry. Why don't you try shining my boots."

If that was a jest, it fell utterly flat, thanks to the bitterness in his voice.

She just looked at him.

"Sorry," he mumbled, avoiding her gaze. "Do what you like. I hardly care."

She took a step toward him. "It's all right," she whispered. "I only want to help."

"Do you?" He turned and glared at her though she doubted the fury in his eyes was really aimed at her.

She nodded.

"Then never mention this to me again." He put the rest of his guns back in their case, closed the lid, and walked past her, ignoring her tender gaze as he stalked to the door.

As she turned, watching him imploringly, she could no longer hold back. "I would do anything to take this from you."

He paused at her anguished whisper, but he did not answer and did not look back. He was quiet for a moment, his hand on the door.

"I have to go," he said at length. "James needs my help with something."

"Drake." She laid her hand on his back.

He flinched. "Don't touch me."

Then he walked out.

Tears rushed into Emily's eyes. She leaned against

the wall behind her. Unfortunately, when she closed her eyes, she could only see the imaginings that now tormented her. The thought of Drake in that iron chair being brutalized, terrorized, humiliated.

Shaking, she shook her head at the image in near panic, and when she opened her eyes, she wept for what had been done to him.

What had been stolen from him.

All she wanted was to take him in her arms and swear that she would never let anyone hurt him again. But she did not have the wherewithal to make any such promise.

Her own powerlessness to help him infuriated her.

Now she saw the full extent of what she was up against, not just the demons around him, but the ones inside him, too.

And for the first time, Emily faced the black, sinister doubts that rose up before her in all their hellish fury to confront her heart, jeering at her for foolishly believing her love could ever be enough to save him.

The secret Promethean temple inside the mountain had not been used in an age, James explained. He wanted to go and make sure it was in good repair for the night of the eclipse, in two weeks' time.

Drake escorted him, as usual, riding in the carriage and keeping an eye out the window on Jacques's men, who provided the outer layer of protection for the Promethean leader, on horseback ahead and behind them.

The sturdy coach made slow progress up the bumpy, rural road; it soon narrowed to little more than a cart path. The local farmers were probably the only ones to use the road a few times a year, he thought, when warmer weather allowed them to drive their goats to higher pastures or to bring tools that they might need for mending fences up the mountain.

The landscape was even wilder than that just around the castle. Wildflowers burst out everywhere from the ground. The wind rippled through the forest. Birds flittered from tree to tree. An eagle circled overhead, and a few deer went bounding across the road.

Whenever there was a break in the trees, the towering forests dropped away to reveal blue sky and white peaks across the distant green valleys.

Drake gazed at these vistas and tried not to think about Emily.

He had no intention of ever speaking one word to her or to anyone else about what he'd experienced. He had stowed the horrible memories in a strongbox in the back of his mind and had no desire to open it again, not even a crack, not even for her.

If he did, he feared it would be like Pandora's box, and every ugly thing inside him would come flying out, beyond what she or Max or James or anyone else could have possibly imagined.

He would burn down the world.

No, it was much better to block it from his mind and carry on with the rest of his short stay on this earth.

But he wished she would not ask him any more questions, so he could just hold her. He needed her so much more than he cared to admit, more than she had any idea.

But if she insisted on asking questions, that cramped little room was going to start to feel much too small.

Just then, they hit a rut in the road that made the carriage pitch violently. James bumped into Drake, who steadied the old man. "Are you all right, sir?"

He nodded but was visibly uncomfortable. "We should be there shortly."

Drake glanced at the remote location. "Hard to believe there's a structure as large as you say somewhere close by."

James smiled. "It's just beneath our feet. Its isolation is part of what makes it preferable. We're generally left to ourselves out here." He squinted against the sunlight as he studied the nearby meadows out the carriage window. "The site was donated by one of our members a hundred years ago. Owner of a mining company. The caves you'll see were originally part of his operation. Gold, silver, coal."

"Really?" Drake said in surprise.

James nodded. "The riches of the Alps. Many minerals have been found in these mountains. When the gold and silver ran out, and the coal had been mined as deeply as his engineers were able to go, he donated the space to us. There are quartz crystals in the walls that were of no interest to him as a merchant but have long been revered by those with an interest in occult science."

"I see."

The carriage rolled to a bumpy halt. Drake glanced out the window. The mountain road had ended, but from its terminus, a footpath continued on, climbing toward the peak. When they got out of the coach, James pointed with his walking stick toward the footpath. Drake offered his arm for the old man to lean on.

They proceeded up the path.

"By the way," James murmured as he hobbled along the steep dirt path beside him, "I'd like you to lead the team who'll be sent to France to kill Malcolm. You can choose whom you want to take with you from among Jacques's men."

Drake glanced at him in surprise.

"You will do this for us?" the old man said.

"Gladly."

He nodded, satisfied. "I'll have details for you on how to penetrate his chateau in the Loire Valley. Security is very high. But if you go, even if the others are cut down, I know I can rest assured that at least you will finish the job."

"Yes, sir. Thank you."

"It won't be too long before I send you. We can't risk Malcolm's catching wind of what's occurred, or you'll never get near him."

"Just say the word."

James patted his arm in a grandfatherly fashion as he leaned on him. "Good lad. A bit of a fly in the ointment the other Council members and I have to work out first, though, before we send you off."

"What's that?"

"The bastard's hidden the Council's operating funds. He's moved the accounts around without telling anyone."

Drake snorted. "Sounds like him."

"We need to know where he's hidden the money before we dispose of him."

"I could always go and capture him, sir. Bring him here and make him talk."

James shook his head. "I had thought of that, but I'd rather not bring him here. He's ruled the Council with an iron fist for so long, I'm concerned he might intimidate the others into backing down if they have to face him in person. If they go wobbly and crawl back to him, you can imagine what that will mean for me."

"I understand, sir."

James winced, leaning harder on him, while the path ended a few yards ahead at a wall of naked rock surrounded by massive boulders and overgrown brambles. "Better to have him dispatched in France before he knows what's coming."

Drake nodded. "I agree. My only concern is who will be protecting you while I am away?"

James patted his arm fondly. "I am touched by your

concern, my boy, but I shall be quite safe once you've rid the world of Malcolm Banks. Ah, here we are! It should be . . . right through there." James pointed with his walking stick to the mounds of wild shrubbery and great stones that looked like they had been tossed there by a giant.

"I'll go and have a look." Drake left the old man to rest his bones against a large rock, jogging the rest of the way up the trail.

Cautiously stepping into a natural break in the thick screen of thorny brambles and the huge rhododendrons in bloom, he pushed the branches aside and saw the rounded entrance to a small, dark cave.

He advanced, pressing through the bushes and, walking behind them, ventured into the cave. It was quite dark but did not go very deep, perhaps ten feet, before he came to the back wall and found a smooth door of stone or some form of cement. It appeared to be no more than the place where the spent mine had been sealed, but James had said it was the entrance to the Prometheans' lair within.

Intrigued, Drake ran his hands along the cool, rectangular frame of the door, but he had no idea how to get it open. Either they would need explosives, or James had some new trick up his sleeve, as usual.

Drake went back out and called the all clear.

Jacques assisted Falkirk up to the place where Drake waited.

"We'll need light in there," the old man advised as he crossed the cave, pushing his spectacles up higher onto his nose.

The Frenchman gestured to one of his subordinates, who lit a lantern and brought it over to James. Indeed, they had been instructed to bring along an odd assortment of things in the carriage, tools for cleaning and repair, whatever might be needed for their task of putting the underground temple back in order after long disuse.

"Now, then." When James lifted the lantern before a spot on the back wall of the cave, the light played over something flat, with a dark gold hue.

James rubbed the spot with his gloved hand, and Drake moved closer, fascinated as the old man's efforts revealed a small brass plaque set into the back wall of the cave.

It had a dial in the center, which in turn was surrounded by a circle of engraved markings that James's attentions presently revealed.

"Greek letters," Drake murmured, glancing at him in question.

James cast him a smile askance with a glint of schoolboy mischief in his eyes. "Send the men out."

"Move back," Drake ordered them at once.

The others retreated, but he remained. Then James began turning the dial back and forth, pointing it to a series of letters in succession.

Some sort of code.

"It's a combination lock?" Drake exclaimed.

James chuckled. "Indeed. And now . . ." As he turned the dial to what was apparently the final letter in the code, a deep, grating rumble of stone scraping stone shook the little cave.

To Drake's amazement, the solid stone wall before them rolled aside, sending up a puff of dust. When it stopped, the hidden opening was revealed, leading into the mountain.

James smiled matter-of-factly and handed him the lantern.

Drake moved closer, thrusting the light into the pitch-black darkness beyond. He saw stairs carved into the rock wall, curving down into a vast, hollow cavern.

"That's a long way down," he commented. "Take my arm, sir. Jacques, bring up the supplies."

The hired mercenaries were peering curiously into the cave, but Jacques sent them off to fetch the necessary items. Then Drake stepped into the cave, turning back to assist the old man.

James accepted his offered forearm, but they made slow progress, climbing down the long, curving steps that had been carved right into the living rock.

The earthy smell combined with the damp chill that clung to subterranean stone, and Drake shivered with unbidden memories of the dungeon. He thrust them out of his mind, as usual, and regarded the few bats flapping through the dark vault instead.

James made a sound of discomfort, wincing.

"Mind your footing, sir," he advised, still privately marveling from some detached region of his battered psyche, that he, a former team leader for one of the Order's cells, should be helping the new head of the Promethean Council into one of the evil cult's most sacred sites.

As far as he knew, no Order agent had ever got so far inside the enemy's organization.

At least that made all that had happened to him worth it.

"What's that?" he asked, pausing and ready to reach for his weapon as the lanternlight hinted at two large, human shapes waiting at the bottom of the steps.

"That's Prometheus and his protégé," James said wryly.

"Oh." They continued, and, drawing closer, the lantern's feeble glow revealed the details of two large figures carved from stone. He could make them out better as they neared the bottom of the staircase, which the looming statues framed.

Steadying James with one arm, Drake raised the lantern to stare at the giant idol of Prometheus, with his menacing narrowed eyes and small, goatish or perhaps satanic horns; this sinister towering figure was depicted passing a torch to a smaller but still-Herculean figure of a man.

Drake and his supposed master passed under the archway formed by the statues' outstretched arms, each with a hand gripping the same handle of the torch.

Then he stepped down onto the cavern floor, helped James down, and nodded to the others, who were following them into the great chamber, bringing supplies as well as more light, both torches and lanterns.

As James bent to rub his sore knee, Jacques arrived. The French sergeant met Drake's gaze with an uneasy question in his eyes.

Drake looked back at him matter-of-factly.

Jacques dismissed his nonanswer with a very Gallic shrug, then beckoned his men on: Some of the French soldiers were making a swift sign of the Cross as they saw the place ahead.

Drake smirked. If any of them thought God heard or cared, they were deluded, but he returned his attention to the old man. James was gesturing impatiently for the lantern. "Give me that. We'll let some daylight in so we can see what we're doing."

Drake followed James over to one of the raw stone walls of the great cavern. "Here it is," James muttered, padding his brow from his exertions. "You will have to turn this crank."

"What's it do?" he responded as he stepped over to man a wood-handled crank anchored to the stone.

"You'll see." James nodded.

Drake threw his shoulder into the crank, which hadn't been touched in decades. As he worked it back and forth, chains running up from it began to grind and clank, clattering over the pulleys above.

He glanced up warily as the handle's reciprocating motion was turned into circular motion. The mechanism above began to open a round gap in the cavern's ceiling, exposing the blue sky.

Massive wooden doors reinforced with iron slowly parted and lowered inward; these widened as he worked the wooden arm. When it would go no more, he locked the handle into place and let go of it, dusting off his hands.

James was beaming. "The observatory! These mountains put us so much closer to the stars . . ."

Drake said nothing, glancing up at the sky doors overhead. A few bats swooped out, disturbed by the intrusion.

"From here, we shall have a perfect view of the lunar eclipse on the night of Valerian's ritual." James clapped him on the back and walked back toward the center of the cavern. "Now let's get this place cleaned up! There is much to be done to make everything ready."

As James hurried off to put the men to work and examine his revered Promethean temple for the ravages of time, Drake turned around and scanned the cavern by the dusty rays of light that had broken through the subterranean darkness.

The upper arches of the cave's natural roof bristled with dramatic stalactites that sparkled with quartz and dripped now and then with the water running down their tips. Quite beautiful, but the man-made features of the temple cave chilled him. Carvings crouched around the space, nightmare figures writhing in the stone, demons, idols. Gargoyles? It was hard to say. Some of the poses were obscene.

Drake sauntered toward the altar at the center of the temple. It was surrounded by a large circle engraved into the smooth stone floor. The Wheel of Time—a favorite Promethean symbol—adorned with astrological and alchemical symbols. Four freestanding pillars rising from the circle marked the cardinal directions.

James was busily snapping orders at the guards to sweep away the bat guano that soiled their sacred space.

Drake drifted closer, staring at the main structure, a sinister raised dais in the center of the Wheel of Time.

With a few steps leading up to it, the floor of the dais was about chest high on him and decorated with a pentagram. Drake somehow refrained from shaking his head.

In the center of the raised platform stood a stone altar about the length of a person. His stomach turned at the sight of leather restraints waiting to strap down the victim's hands and feet.

From the corner of his eye, he noticed James watching him intently. At once, he chased any sign of horror off his face. "What do you think?" the old man inquired.

"Beautiful," Drake replied.

James smiled in approval of his answer, then pointed to a black-painted metal door a few feet across from the bottom of the steps that led up to the dais. "Get that open for me, would you? There's a good lad. I'll need those hinges oiled. We can't have it squeaking at the most solemn moment of the ceremony. Be careful of any wild animals that might have found their way into the tunnel."

"Tunnel, sir?"

"The sacrifice is brought in through that doorway. Once you open it, you'll find a tunnel that leads to another entrance into the mountain, different from the one we used. He or she is taken into the tunnel and joins us through that door."

"I see," he forced out. He was horrified by James's cool and businesslike explanation and his utter seriousness, as if he saw nothing at all wrong with it, but Drake did not have the luxury of letting his emotions show.

He managed a nod, dropped his gaze, and did as he was told.

James stood by, watching him muscle the rusty door open, but secretly, Drake was reeling.

In a sense, he felt as though he was seeing James's true face for the first time, and he did not know what to make of it.

Nevertheless, the reality of his precarious situation struck him all over again. So he masked his shock and pulled the door open, peering into the dark tunnel, through which an unknown number of terrified victims had been brought in to face an unspeakable death.

If he had not gone mad already, this moment might well be the straw that broke the camel's back, he thought wryly.

Meanwhile, Jacques and his men were earning their unusually high wages by questioning nothing and simply following James's commands. In the presence of pure evil, they scurried about, nervously tidying the temple as if this were the most mundane of tasks.

Drake's own heart was pounding with a degree of fear he had not felt in a long time.

"Are you all right?" James murmured, studying him with a keen and penetrating eye.

"Of course, sir," Drake said with an equally businesslike nod. "What else would you have me do? Shall I have a look into the tunnel, then?" He hooked his thumb idly over his shoulder at the dark space through the door.

"Yes, make sure no wild animals have taken up residence in there. For that matter, the whole space here could use a look round."

"Very good, sir. Light?" He beckoned to the nearest Frenchman, who dutifully handed him a torch.

Drake grasped the torch in his left hand and pulled his rifle into position under his right arm, snug against his side, then he ducked through the door and advanced into what he soon realized had originally been a coal-mining tunnel.

He followed the tunnel for a few hundred yards without incident. If any small animals had ever found their way into this shelter, the spring season must have drawn them back out into the world again. At the far end of the tunnel, he encountered a heavy metal door, which he forced open.

Squinting against the light, he stepped out and turned, surveying his surroundings. He was in a meadow, a few acres away from the tree line of the woods.

The light breeze stirred his hair, and, for two seconds, he allowed the sun to warm his face. He took a deep breath.

Bracing himself to return, he slipped back into the darkness, pulled the door shut behind him, and marched back to the temple. He informed James that the tunnel was clear, then proceeded to walk the perimeter of the interior, searching every nook and cranny of the sprawling mountain cavern, on the watch for whatever he might find.

When he came to a dark alcove at the other end of

the cavern, he thrust his torch in to have a look, and to his surprise, it flared without warning.

He cursed and pulled back, taken off guard and nearly singed. He avoided dropping the torch but held it out farther from his body, wondering why it had blazed with such sudden ferocity.

As he backed out of the alcove, the flame returned to its normal height.

Drake furrowed his brow, his eyes smarting from the smoke. As his vision adjusted again after the unexpected bright burst of light, he spotted the round wooden cap on the alcove floor.

It reminded him of the boards Emily had fallen through so long ago, the ones covering up the abandoned well.

Realization dawned. The cap must cover one of the old mine shafts, he thought. More cautiously, he moved into the alcove once again, stretching out his arm and letting the torch go first.

Again, the flame flared.

Firedamp.

Obviously, the seal on the mine shaft must be leaking, he realized. The highly flammable gas could not be seen or smelled, but his torch told him loud and clear that, indeed, firedamp was in the air.

His memory was not so befuddled that he had forgotten the current science in the newspapers James made him read.

This natural gas was often found by mining operations. The leading scientists of the day were still figuring out how best to use its highly combustible vapors.

Back in England, he had seen the new gas-burning streetlamps that had recently been installed on a few of London's most notable avenues, especially those that were well trafficked at night.

But the new gaslights had a hazardous reputation.

Half the populace wouldn't go near them for fear of the explosions they caused every once in a while, sending panic in the streets.

Drake stared at the wooden cap.

At that moment, he knew exactly what he would do. The solution to all his problems flooded into his mind.

Slowly, he looked over his shoulder at the vile Promethean temple, with its grotesque statues and unspeakable stone altar. On the night of the eclipse, the great cavern would be filled with all the surviving true believers of their insidious cult . . .

Drake nonchalantly backed away from the alcove, veiling the savage triumph in his eyes.

"Find something?" James asked, turning to him curiously.

He shook his head. "All clear, sir," he answered with an odd smile.

The Prometheans worship Satan's fire, he thought. *So let them burn in it.*

Courtesy of the Inferno Club.

hat evening, Emily sat on the low stool before the hearth, idly prodding the fire with the poker and waiting for the pot to boil. Her mood of hard-won serenity had finally been achieved by her coming to a decision. A final, desperate stratagem to get Drake out of there.

Earlier that day, following the shocking discovery that Waldfort Castle was the very place Drake had been held as a prisoner, she had dried her tears at last, calmed herself, and spent the rest of the day considering what to do next.

She had to do *something*.

Mulling it over all day long, she channeled her nervous energy into the small things she could find to do for him in the meanwhile.

Some women might have considered the simple chores demeaning, but she savored the chance to do her wounded friend any small, tender service. Besides, it kept her hands busy, and it gave her time to think.

She had finished his laundry. His clothes were cleaned and either folded or ironed and tucked away in drawers or hung up on the row of wall pegs. She had dusted and swept, changed the sheets, made the bed, and plumped the pillows.

The whole room smelled of fresh mountain air and spring sunshine. For a finishing touch, the little bouquet of wildflowers she had picked to brighten his room sat in a tin cup on the chest of drawers.

Now she was heating water on the fire, but long before beginning the present task, she had made up her mind that there was only one solution.

She had to get him out of this evil place. He had no business being here. She had seen for herself that they trusted him enough that he could walk out anytime of his own free will. All they'd have to do was clear the boundaries of the property and run. The Prometheans might give chase, but between Drake's spy skills and her forest craft, they could flee them undiscovered.

All that remained was to persuade him.

Tonight she would stop at nothing to win his agreement.

Of course, it would have to be undertaken carefully.

After the way they had parted earlier, he was probably apprehensive about returning to the room.

Her first task was to show him it was all right and she was not a threat. She must give him breathing room and see that he relaxed.

The second she heard him outside the closed chamber door, her prediction about his uneasiness upon returning to the room was confirmed. It seemed to take him an awfully long time to get his key out and unlock the door.

Holding her position on the stool, she sent a knowing glance toward the door, then returned her attention to the fire, and barely looked at him when he edged in, very much on guard.

"Hullo," she said nonchalantly.

He shut the door behind him and mumbled a greeting in response. Then he glanced around, taking in all the improvements she'd made. "You've been busy," he remarked in surprise.

She smiled at him. "A bit. I'm having tea. Would you like some?"

"What kind?"

"Blackberry. I brought it in my bag from home."

"Blackberry tea from home?" he echoed as he took off his coat. "How can I pass that up?"

She just smiled and kept her distance, leaving him to make himself comfortable after a hard day's work.

"It's almost cozy in here now," he said, unbuttoning his waistcoat. He nodded at the blooms. "Nice flowers."

"Ah, dirty things in there," she instructed, pointing to the basket in the corner, which she had brought up from the ground-level laundry.

"Sorry, I'm—dusty," he said ruefully, and he added under his breath, "Been underground all day."

Hmm. She resisted the urge to ask him what that meant while he walked out to the balcony and shook the dust from his waistcoat over the railing.

Emily turned back to the fire. Before the water reached the boiling point, she pulled the pot out of the flames and used a cloth to carry it over to the washbasin on the dresser, pouring it full of warm water so he could refresh himself.

Returning from the balcony, he glanced at the warm clean water, then back at her in surprise. "Well, that was nice of you."

"I know," she said blithely. Sending him an arch

smile, she returned to put the rest of the water back on to boil while Drake took off his shirt.

She stole an eager glance at his bare, muscled back but vowed to behave and sat back down on the stool, fighting the urge to watch him washing up.

She rested her elbow on her knee and propped her chin on her fist, gazing into the cheerful flames and listening to the lonely warble of some night bird's call from beyond the open balcony doors. "Oh—" She suddenly remembered. "There's a washcloth and towel for you there, and I left you a square of the homemade soap . . ." She turned to make sure he had found the needed items, but her words trailed off as she looked at him, captivated once more by the rugged splendor of his body.

"Found it," he informed her in the midst of splashing his face and throat.

"Good," she forced out in a slightly strangled tone. The water was not the only thing hot enough to boil at the moment. She took it out of the fire and, with slightly trembling hands, poured it into the waiting teapot she had requested from the kitchens. Leaving their blackberry tea to steep and the Earl of Westwood his privacy to finish washing the rest of his delectable self as he saw fit, Emily removed to the balcony.

Out in the cool, silken darkness of the night, she leaned against the railing and stared up at the half-moon shining down on the sweeping mountain vistas, and the black velvet sky sprinkled with stars.

At length, Drake walked out and joined her. He had put on one of the soft white shirts she had cleaned for him, which was wise if he didn't want her to touch him. That beautiful sculpted chest was too much temptation.

He had poured the tea into two mugs for them, and

as he joined her, he handed her one. She smiled in thanks; he leaned against the rail beside her.

For a long moment, neither of them spoke. She hid her delight that he had joined her, but inside, was thoroughly encouraged. The cares of the day slowly faded as they stood side by side in companionable silence, soaking in the beauty of the night.

Emily was acutely aware of him beside her: tall, strong in so many ways, endlessly interesting, at least to her. Most of all, she was attuned to the ever-vigilant tension in him, thrumming slightly, as always, in his big, sinewy form.

But he took a sip of the blackberry tea from home, swallowed, and gave his approval in one of his wordless male rumbles, like a purr in his throat.

A moment after that, he let out a long sigh, and only then, did she sense him beginning to release his tension.

"So, what do you think of the Continent?" he asked her matter-of factly out of the blue.

She sent him a quick, shy smile and shrugged, delighted at his effort at making conversation. "Well, I didn't have time for the usual tourist sights."

"No?"

"It was a fast trek. Bewildering, to be honest. Why are there are so many languages and dialects?" she complained in an airy tone. "I had barely figured how to say something in one, when it changed to the next." She shook her head. "I gave up on talking to anyone but myself before we crossed the Rhine—and trying to figure the money? Ugh. I'm quite sure one of those innkeepers in France charged me a week's wages for a bowl of soup and some bread."

"Well, if he gave you the bread, it was probably worth it."

"It was good," she admitted with a smile.

Drake flashed a rather roguish grin in answer, then he took another sip of her homemade tea.

Emily could not take her eyes off him. The glow in her heart for him could have lit up the night.

If there was one good thing about being there, she thought, at least for once she had him to herself. No Lady Westwood, his mother, looking over her shoulder with suspicion. No Lord Rotherstone, all business, trying to help Drake get his memory back so the Order could find out how much, if anything, he might have told the Prometheans under torture.

At that moment, all of that was behind them. Emily noticed herself edging closer to him, seeking his body's warmth. She held herself back from caressing his shoulder, however.

His two requests this morning had been very clear. *Never mention this to me again* and *Don't touch me.*

She wrapped her hands more firmly around her warm cup of tea. "Are you going to eat in the Guards' Hall again tonight?" she inquired as the conversation lagged.

"No, I asked to have supper sent up to both of us here."

She glanced at him in surprise.

"You've been alone all day," he pointed out.

She pressed her lips together and shrugged.

He gazed at her intently before turning away to stare across the mountainside. "I want to apologize for the way I acted earlier today."

She looked at him in surprise. "There's no need."

"You were only trying to help. It's true, this is where I was held. There's nothing I could do about coming back here. James wanted it. I don't like it, but I'm all right."

She kept her eyes down. "I wasn't going to mention it."

"Well . . . thank you for understanding. Friends?"

She looked down at his offered hand in wry hesitation. "You said I wasn't to touch you."

"You can touch me now if you like."

She put her cup of tea on the railing, then turned to him, holding his gaze. "I was hoping you would say that."

When she laid her hands on his chest, he set his drink aside, as well. Emily stepped closer to him, sliding her palms slowly up toward his shoulders, lifting her head to continue staring into his dark, soulful eyes. He smiled at her ever so faintly, a hint of curiosity in his gaze as he curved his arms around her waist.

With a warm caress, she cupped her fingers around his nape and pulled him down to kiss her.

Drake's lips met hers with soft caution; she could sense his surprise at her advance—and could feel him holding himself back. But there was no need for him to.

Behind her closed eyes, all Emily wanted was to love and reassure him. Just barely parting her lips, she let him set the pace.

He tilted his head the other way and kissed her again, a warm, nuzzling caress. As his smooth lips glided back and forth lightly over hers, her toes curled.

She clung to him, weak-kneed and dizzy with delight; though she steadied herself holding on to his big shoulders, she waited breathlessly for more. With every racing heartbeat, she was barely aware of Drake stealing control of the situation from her.

He released her waist to capture her face between his hands, kissing her over and over again until she was in a trance. Her palms molded the iron contours of his arms as she slid her light hold down to his waist.

His right hand caressed her hair, his left tipping her chin upward while his tongue stroked hers. His kisses were flavored like sweet blackberry tea. He tasted of home.

And that was where she must bring him. However much she wanted him, that was the point of all this. Her final option was to lure him out of this place by offering him the pleasure of her body. If it was the only way left to save him . . .

Well, it was hardly a sacrifice, after all the years she'd been in love with him.

She played with his tongue as his kisses deepened. He drank her in like the rarest of wines. His hands began roaming over her body, tenderly stroking her neck and shoulders, tracing the lines of her arms. Growing arousal made her bold. She slipped her hands under his shirt and, touching his naked flesh for the first time, gasped in wonder at the feel of him. Caressing him was almost more than she could bear, his sleek sides, his chiseled abdomen. His body was even more beautiful to touch than to look at. Returning his kisses hungrily, she gloried in the smooth, warm velvet of his skin and went on savoring him with her fingertips. For a man who didn't want to be touched, he was now returning her caresses as hotly as he was receiving them.

Emily did not even dream of stopping him when he cupped her breasts through her gown, squeezing, groping her. She welcomed it. She had wanted it for so long.

They should have done this a long time ago if he wasn't so blasted honorable, she thought. Still kissing her in abandon, Drake maneuvered her against the railing of the balcony, backing her into the corner. She smiled playfully against his mouth, but when he pulled back a small space, glancing into her eyes to make sure this was all right, she licked her lips in silent permission for whatever he might choose.

He planted his hands on the railing on either side of her, then leaned closer, brushed the tip of his nose affectionately along her cheek and ducked his head to kiss her neck. Emily melted, bracing her elbows on the wooden rail behind her, tipping her head back as he lavished her neck and throat with his attentions. Her long hair flowed over the edge of the railing, teased by an occasional puff of wind, while the starlight sparkled on her eyelids and danced in his black hair.

The soaring height of that balcony, jutting from the side of a mountaintop castle, added to her sense of teetering on the precipice. Ah, but she had fallen for him long ago. Meanwhile, he nudged her feet apart with his toe and discreetly slipped his thigh between her legs.

Emily moaned at the pleasant friction of the contact and closed her eyes with bated breath as Drake began unfastening her bodice. "Do you know how long I've wanted you? How hard I've fought this?" he breathed at her ear while his fingers plucked at the ribbons of her gown with an expertise that those blows to the head had not removed from his memory, the once-notorious lover. "Every time they told me not to touch you, it only made me want you more."

"I wanted you, too."

"I know," he murmured with a roguish smile in his voice.

She pulled back with a playful scowl. "You *know*?"

"I could see it in your beautiful eyes." He trailed his finger down her face. "The temptation was extreme. Now you appreciate my self-discipline."

"Pshaw. I was waiting for you to kiss me."

"I was waiting, too. For the right time. Funny it should come now."

She cupped his face adoringly. "Better late than never."

He turned to press a kiss into her palm, unlaced the final ribbon, and stared deep into her eyes. "May I?"

"I'm yours," she whispered.

Like a man opening a gift he had waited his whole life to receive, Drake took a delicate hold of the fabric at her bodice and freed her breasts gently.

Then he stopped, staring at her: her chest, her body, her blowing hair. With her loosened gown falling off her shoulders and her breasts exposed to the moonlight, Emily held very still. She could almost hear his heart pounding in the silence. He shook his head, and said in a strangled tone, "You are too good for me."

"I was meant for you," she informed him softly.

He swooped down without warning and kissed her, hard. He kissed her with a searing passion that amazed her, claiming her completely, his hot mouth branding her for his own. Her senses reeling, the next thing Emily knew, he was on his knees before her, his arms wrapped around her hips, his warm, wet mouth at her breast.

She embraced him, reveling in his possession, transported by his utterly male enjoyment of her. Raking her fingers through his silky black hair, she watched him exploring, tasting both of her nipples in turn; her body was on fire, her senses set ablaze by the enthralling tug and play of his burning kisses.

She was trembling with desire, and she felt him do the same. Stroking his head, gazing at him through heavy-lidded eyes, she wondered if she would still have the strength to say no.

The time to find out was suddenly upon her all too soon.

"Let's go inside," he rasped, tearing himself away from her breasts.

The freshly made bed beckoned from just inside the room as Drake swept to his feet, towering over her again.

She blinked away the rapture of his kisses as best she could and shook her head, trying to find some way to clear the hot haze from her mind. "I want to," she confessed in a breathy whisper. "More than you know. But—"

"But what?" he whispered with a cajoling little smile so gorgeously seductive that she actually flinched and bit her lower lip.

"We can't."

"Why not?"

"Because if I lie down with you, we will make love, and I'm not making love with you until we've left this place."

He furrowed his brow and shook his head uncomprehendingly, as if he had just been woken from a dream. "What?" he murmured.

She took both of his hands in her own. "Leave with me," she whispered. "Let's go back to England or anywhere safe. Then you can have me. Anytime, any way you want."

"Is that what this is?" He stopped, pulled back, and looked at her in shock. "You're manipulating me? This whole time?"

"Desperate times, love."

"Emily!" he said, flabbergasted.

"Drake," she answered calmly.

"I trusted you! Why—?"

"Because this is insane!" she retorted.

"You should have thought of that before you followed me!"

"I followed you because I love you, Drake. That is why I'm here."

He flinched at her calm, steady declaration, then shook his head with a growl. "I don't *want* you to love me."

"It's not your choice to make." She refused to wince at his lie. He wanted, needed her love, and he knew it. There was no denying it after all that.

Surely knowing he was discovered, he turned away in seething frustration. Looking increasingly angry, he dragged his hand through his hair. "I can't believe you would play these games with me."

"It's for your own good."

"For God's sake, cover yourself," he grumbled, but she just looked at him, lifting her chin in proud defiance.

"That's my offer," she said evenly. "Anytime, any way you want me. Anywhere but here."

He snorted. "And I thought the torturers were good," he taunted, glaring at her. He helped himself to one last, insolent look at her bare breasts, then met her gaze in reproach, shaking his head at her.

He pivoted and went stalking into the chamber, grabbing his coat off the peg on his way out.

Emily jumped slightly when the door slammed.

Only after he was gone did she let out a shaky exhalation. Warding off a twinge of humiliation, she slowly pulled up her sleeves again.

Well, her bold gamble hadn't gone perhaps as well as planned, she admitted, adjusting her bodice, covering herself again. But at least now she'd got the blackguard thinking.

Patience. Give the medicine time to work.

Assuring herself he'd be back, she picked up the now-cold cup of blackberry tea and took a sip, hoping it might help to soothe her. Her stomach had knotted up a bit at his reaction, but the tea was no help.

She made a face and poured it out over the railing.

All the while, her mind revolved on Drake. Had she pushed him too far? She was aware that his whole life had become a maze of mind games, living among the Prometheans. He would not have expected it from her. But what choice had she had?

The lunatic wouldn't listen to reason.

Don't worry, she promised herself. *Falkirk's influence on him is nothing compared to yours, especially now.*

If only she could be sure.

Well, she was nowhere near giving up hope.

He would come to his senses soon. Then they could leave this place, and as soon as they reached some safe haven, then she could finish giving him his reward.

Indeed, she could hardly wait.

Smiling to herself in spite of his bluster, she languidly pushed away from the railing and went back into his room, still savoring the pleasure of what they had just shared. She was no expert on men, but, oh, yes . . . she believed he would be back.

I am not *going back in there*, Drake vowed.

He'd find somewhere else to sleep. For if he had to see her looking that beautiful one more second, playing her games with him, trying to bribe him with her body, he was going to do something rash. Maybe he should just ravish her and be done with it.

But, of course, he would never force any woman, especially Emily. That would make him no better than bloody Lamont. But a man could dream . . .

Fuming with frustration, he stalked down the corridor, still throbbing, and not from simple fury. His body was beyond indignant at the denial when heaven had been offered up to him, waved under his very nose like a silver tray arrayed with the most delectable temptations.

Who would have guessed that his little, violet-eyed Emily would turn out to be crueler than a Promethean lord?

Virginal she might be, but she was not without her wiles. That conniving minx, with her soft hair and her yielding body and her impossibly stubborn will.

Good God, he hadn't touched a woman in so long, and the truth was, he had waited for Emily Harper all his life.

Well, she had got the best of him tonight.

He was surprisingly shaken by her brash move. The one person in this place he had thought could be trusted not to play games with his mind.

Of course, he understood why she had done it. But he still couldn't go. Not when he had just figured out how to destroy them.

Brushing her angrily out his mind, or at least trying to, he took refuge in the all-male sanctuary of the Guards' Hall, where the men who were off duty congregated at their leisure. If ever there was a time for a good German beer, it was now.

Jacques and five of his men were seated at one end of the hall, while the elite personal bodyguards of a few Promethean leaders sat at the other. The latter were Drake's counterparts, serving their high-ranking foreign masters in the same capacity in which he served James.

True believers, they were sure to be present on the night of the ceremony. They would have to be factored into the equation. He kept his distance from them, pouring himself a beer from the tapped barrel by the sideboard, then walking over to Jacques's end of the hall. The French mercenaries, some smoking, some playing cards, were seated casually around the fire.

Drake noted their surprise when he joined them; he

rarely fraternized with them and only did so then because there was nowhere else to go.

For that matter, where the deuce was he to sleep tonight? He was not sure he trusted himself to go back into that room, and if he did, he was not at all sure he trusted *her* not to drive him mad.

Every man had his breaking point, and he was already walking far too close to the edge.

Joining the men, he gestured to one of the younger fellows to get out of the leather armchair where Drake wanted to sit.

He was particular about where he positioned himself in a room. He could not possibly sit with his back to the door, for example. He had to be able to see what might be coming at him. Especially with that collection of highly skilled Promethean bodyguards loitering at the other end of the vast room.

The lad launched himself out of Drake's way, and Drake settled a moment later into the chair. Then he attempted to calm his churning thoughts by simply focusing on the taste of the beer: earthy and rich, with a light foam.

Ahh.

Jacques was watching him with a curious quirk of his eyebrow.

"What?" Drake grunted.

"Is good?" the French sergeant asked wryly, nodding at his pewter tankard.

Drake conceded this with a wary nod. "Aye." Then he retreated into himself once more, but not for long.

"What the hell are you laughing at?" he asked the two fellows playing cards.

They were looking at him, saying something.

"Eh, nothing, sir."

He stared at them. "I thought so," he warned.

But Jacques smiled slyly. "*Capitaine*, we are just wondering why you are not with your servant girl? Did she tire you out already?"

The others laughed, tempting fate, but Drake decided not to take offense. Scowling, he gave them the only answer that came to him. One word: "Women."

"Aha!"

The Frenchmen laughed again more heartily, warming to their favorite topic and his rare receptivity.

"I knew it!"

"Did she throw you out already?"

He gave them a sardonic look, but did not really mind their jesting for some reason.

"Perhaps you need advice on how to handle her," one began.

And then all the helpful French fellows, ever the experts on the daughters of Eve—or so they thought proceeded—to advise him, their unromantic British blockhead.

Drake drummed his fingers slowly on the chair's arm as he listened to them, rather amused in spite of himself. He guzzled half his beer.

"Did you give her any compliments?"

"Did you make a conversation? Did you ask how is her day?"

"She's my servant," he retorted, playing along. "Why the deuce should I care how her bloody day was?"

"Oh, no, no, no! This is abominable!"

He grinned at their aghast responses to his apparent indifference to the chit, and shrugged off their advice with a nonchalant curse in their own tongue, smiling into his beer.

"No, I don't believe it," Jacques declared at last, noting the deviltry in Drake's eyes. "The *capitaine* is full of shit."

Just then, James appeared in the doorway, spotted Drake, and began walking toward him.

Drake rose slowly, but Jacques had not yet spotted the old man coming up behind him. "I think this *petite jeunne fille* means more to you than you let on, monsieur. Far more!"

"Nonsense," he replied, then he looked at James in question, praying the old man had not heard the man's remark. It was all too true. "Sir?"

"Ah, there you are. I have here your instructions on what we will need to prepare for our many colleagues' arrival."

"Yes, sir." He nodded, taking James's list, glancing at it. "I will see to it at once."

"That's all right. You may begin tomorrow," he replied in a droll tone, glancing in curious amusement from Drake to the Frenchmen. "Getting a bit of advice on the ladies?"

"Oh, yes, sir," Drake muttered wryly.

The men smiled, as did James. Perhaps the old man was bemused to find him acting for once more like a human being than some lethal automaton. Well, he had Emily to thank for it, but Drake still prayed that James had not overheard Jacques's all-too-perceptive observation.

"Good evening, gentlemen. At ease," James dismissed them.

The mercenaries resumed their places, sitting down again. James sent Drake a twinkling look of humor, then bid him good night.

He sketched a bow. "Good evening, sir."

When the old man had exited the hall, the casual atmosphere slowly returned, but Drake remained tense. Scanning the list of practicalities to be dealt with in preparation for the arrival of a hundred more Pro-

metheans and their respective entourages, he was unaware of Jacques watching him.

"Drake?" he murmured.

He looked up from the paper.

Jacques glanced over his shoulder, then leaned
closer. "What was that place today?" he whispered uneasily. "The men are asking questions. Who *are* these
people?"

Drake shook his head. "It's none of your concern."

"Come, that was a statue of the devil—"

"You accepted the contract. You took the money. No
questions. That was our deal. You don't want the answers anyway, trust me. You just do your job, and I'll
do mine."

Jacques frowned at him, uncertainty in his dark
eyes. He sat back, clearly having heard the warning in
Drake's words as well as the threat.

Perhaps Jacques had begun to sense that he and his
crew would be lucky to come out of this alive, Drake
mused, though he did not allow his grim thoughts to
show on his face. The Prometheans rarely left loose
threads hanging about for the Order to find.

Drake was fairly sure that after Jacques and his men
had served their purpose, he was going to be ordered
to poison them or some other such unpleasantness.

He took another swallow of beer, but at the reminder
of all the dark business ahead, he could not even taste
it anymore. Draining the tankard, he set it aside and
strode out of the hall without a word, without a backward glance.

Chapter
10

France

*T*he loyal Promethean agent who operated the safe house and listening post in Calais had given Niall a welcome worthy of Malcolm Banks's son and future head of the Council.

At the simple residence on a cobbled street of the quaint seaside town, the true believer had provided him with a meal and the best bed in his house, along with the use of the man's wife for the night, of which Niall had taken full advantage.

As dawn's light crept over the horizon, he was almost ready to leave. He'd been given some fresh clothes, plenty of food and water, weapons, a pair of horses, maps, and a compass, anything he might need for his trek into the Alps.

After a meal the previous night, he had finished encrypting the message for his father and handed it off to the safe-house chief, who in turn had sent off one of his most reliable couriers to hand it personally to Malcolm.

Father,

I was captured by the Order but have escaped. Falkirk is plotting against us. He has called a gathering at Count Glasse's seat, Waldfort Castle. Get there as fast as you can with as large a force as you can muster on this short notice. I will meet you there, and we'll make an example of these traitors.

N

The message was well on its way south, to Malcolm's chateau in the Loire Valley. But Niall did not intend to go there himself. There was no time. Besides, that was exactly where the Order agents would expect him to go. He had not seen them yet, but he was sure they were already on his trail.

Pulling on his coat, he thanked the agent for his assistance, ignored his groveling, and nodded slyly to the man's wife. She lowered her head, rather shamefaced after some of what he'd made her do last night.

He turned away with a smirk. Then he marched out to the horses he'd been given and made sure the fine pair were securely tethered. The journey was long and arduous, so he would alternate between them, riding one while the other served as pack animal. He checked the bedroll and saddlebags, neatly tied.

He was satisfied, as well, that his weapons would be in easy reach: a large knife at his side, two pistols in shoulder holsters, and a loaded rifle across his back.

He had to keep moving to hold on to his few hours'

lead. He did not intend to take Virgil's boys on alone if he could avoid it. He'd deal with them once he reached Waldfort Castle and joined his father, who should be bringing along a force of Promethean fighters, as Niall had advised in his note.

They could pick off the bastards following him, as well as quelling Falkirk's little insurgency. Niall was not above letting someone else do his fighting, never having been plagued with a need to be a hero.

With that, he swung up onto the horse and rode out of Calais at a gallop, heading eastward across France.

Bavaria

Emily did not know where Drake had slept. He had not returned to the room the night before, and clearly, she had lost her bet. She didn't like to lose.

By morning, she was itching with restlessness, pacing and perturbed. *Where the devil is he?*

God, I have got to get out of this room.

Determined to find out where he was hiding from her, she needed some excuse to wander round the castle, so she went to the servants' area down by the kitchens and asked if there was anything she could do to help.

Her tasks for her so-called master were already completed, she told the old housekeeper, and she couldn't just sit around staring at the walls.

The old German woman, stout, formidable, and devoted to keeping her domain in tip-top shape, was impressed with Emily's willingness and allowed her to go around tending to the candles.

So Emily went from room to room on the main floor, carrying a small folding step stool and a basket of supplies for the simple task.

She trimmed a wick here, replaced the sideboard candelabras there, and threw the spent taper stubs and clumps of wax that she collected in her basket. They would be melted down and added to the new batches of wax and tallow to be poured into candle molds and used again.

Pulling her step stool over to the wall, she tended the sconces, too, replacing the candles as needed and cleaning the soot off the glass with a rag doused in vinegar.

Back at Westwood Manor, this was work that made the housemaids groan, but Emily found the drudgery of her assignment oddly soothing. Besides, it gave the perfect opportunity to look for Drake.

She really was surprised that he hadn't come back to her. Perhaps he was embarrassed. *Perhaps he's furious at me.* It was hard to say what might happen the next time their paths crossed in the intimacy of his room.

She tamped down the gnawing worry that she might have overplayed her hand. She was not entirely convinced, after all, that he had not turned into a true Promethean.

She simply couldn't tell, and it was a hard thing to love a man who was such an accomplished liar . . .

Ah, well. She could have used a lot more illumination than what these candle stumps had to give. Wryly picking up her basket and the stool, she moved on to the next room in the rococo section of the castle.

Crossing the entrance hall to the opposite State Room, she heard the distant clash of metal on metal, faint battle sounds. They grew louder as she stepped into the gilded sitting room, where two maids were already at work, dusting the furniture and sweeping the floor.

They nodded to her when she arrived; she returned their greeting and was relieved that they seemed unperturbed by the sound. *It must be nothing.* Perhaps the guards were at practice somewhere nearby.

Not wishing to get in the maids' way, she started to leave, intent on returning later, when they were through. But one of the women said something to her in German and pointed to a door on the back wall.

Emily glanced over and saw through the bank of gothic windows a covered outdoor balcony, where, she gathered, more candles awaited her attention.

Two men loitered outside there, sheltered from the moody gray drizzle. One was smoking, the other leaning on the balcony railing as they talked.

One of the men was James Falkirk.

Instantly, Emily's guard went up. She looked uncertainly at the maid. "Should I wait?"

The woman answered, and though she probably did not understand the question in English any better than Emily could translate the German answer, her gesture, tone, and facial expression easily conveyed that it was fine for her to go and continue her task.

She got the impression that the gentlemen would not object or pay her any mind.

Emily hesitated but summoned up her courage and took the woman's word for it. She could go about her business as invisibly as any servant, she supposed, and besides, she would not mind the chance to eavesdrop on Falkirk's conversation.

She did not trust that canny old man one iota.

As she crossed to the gallery door, her heart pounding, the martial sounds grew louder. They sharpened greatly when she opened it to a damp, chilly burst of breeze.

Falkirk and the other man glanced over at her. "Why, Miss Harper," the old man greeted her with his cool, superior amusement.

Emily bobbed a curtsy like any humble maid and kept her head down. "Pardon, sir. I'm to tend the candles. Shall I come back later?"

"No, no, it's all right. Carry on." His gaze skimmed the step stool and basket she carried as she whisked past him, going obediently about her task.

Falkirk turned to his fellow conspirator and informed him in German who she was, or so she gathered.

"Ah," said the other man. He was at least a decade younger than Falkirk, with fiery dark eyes and a short black beard.

He eyed her suspiciously; Emily kept her distance. Skirting the wall behind them, she set her stool down under the first iron lantern she came to, then she stepped up on it and went about her business.

"*Spricht sie Deutsch?*" Falkirk's companion asked.

Does she speak German?

The old man shook his head. "*Nein.*"

And that was true, for that was the only part of their conversation she understood. Still, she was intelligent enough to realize they were talking about her. The other one asked some questions; James answered them, apparently informing him that she was the girl who had followed Drake.

From the skeptical tone of his voice, she got the impression the other man did not trust James's handsome head of security—and trusted *her* even less.

All the same, she pretended not to hear or notice anything as she changed out the fat, short candles inside the lantern. But she was unable to make her hands stop shaking in the proximity of such evil men.

Cleaning the lamp's glass casing with some vinegar on a rag, she noted the tone of urgency beneath their quiet exchange, but it was impossible to know the particulars of what they were saying.

Done with the first lantern, she went to the second and placed her stool beneath it, climbing up. From this vantage point, she was able to steal a glance over her shoulder at the scene below the balcony, and at last, she discovered the source of the battle sounds.

The stone balcony overlooked an enclosed courtyard where the castle guards were training and, of course, there was Drake, in the thick of the fight.

She went motionless for a moment, staring at him.

The fine rain had plastered his black hair to his head and soaked his ivory shirt so it clung to his skin; but as beautiful as he was, his onslaught against the three unlucky opponents surrounding him was downright vicious.

He swung and thrust and lunged as though he fully intended to skewer them. It did not look like practice from where she stood, at least.

When a scarlet slash bloomed across one man's arm, she shook her head in shock that they were not even using blunts on their weapons—and then she felt naïve for even thinking that they would.

The wounded man withdrew from the fight, and another grimly took his place. Drake attacked him, too.

Staring at him, the droplets of rain flying off his blade, she barely breathed, chilled by how much he was clearly enjoying the chance to batter the men into a state of cringing fear.

She had never seen him fight. She had never been allowed. Now she rather wished that she had not, considering this wild creature was her roommate.

Swallowing hard, she tore her gaze away and turned back to her chore, but the brief glimpse of his ferocity made it clear the sort of fire she had been playing with last night.

The realization shook her. If he had wanted to, he

could have easily taken what she had offered as a bribe.

It could have gone very badly if not for his discipline, his honor.

She also suddenly realized that the frustration she had whipped up in his blood last night was being vented on his opponents.

When another cry of pain from the courtyard rang out while she cleaned the second lantern's glass, she winced with a wry sense of responsibility for his wrath.

Drake had stabbed the other soldier in the leg.

Emily finished cleaning the lantern and decided to go back upstairs and fetch her bag of dried apothecary herbs. Knowing Drake's tendency to get into trouble, she had seen fit to bring it along. She would take it down to the surgeon and offer to make a poultice of comfrey.

He could apply it to his patients' wounds at the first change of bandages to ease some of the sting of their cuts and help keep their wounds from becoming infected.

Going down there would also bring her one step closer to Drake. Pleased with that prospect, she shut the little glass door of the lantern, then stepped down off the stool and picked it up to return inside. Sketching a quick curtsy in acknowledgment of the gentlemen, she walked away and got the door herself though her hands were full.

Falkirk and the stranger watched her go.

"Look at what he is capable of!" Septimus Glasse insisted. "I'm glad you are so sure of him, but you must pardon me if I do not share your confidence."

"I thought Drake laid to rest your doubts about him when he spoke to the Council about his conversion."

"The others might be satisfied, but I saw him from the start. It was my men who captured him, remember? I saw him when he was very much an Order agent, and I know firsthand how dangerous he is. It took a dozen of them to bring him down. This man fought like a demon, and yet here he is—and we are simply to accept that he is now one of us?"

"He took the Initiate's Brand," James pointed out. "That's no small thing."

"Pshaw! So we seared his body. That is nothing. You have not seen the man's tolerance for pain. I have."

James shook his head, serene, but frowning. "Septimus, my friend, you are jumping at shadows. I fear defying Malcolm has rattled your nerves."

"Or maybe you've been blinded by his pretty face?" his friend retorted with a shrewd, knowing glance.

Not that James's proclivities for handsome young men were much of a secret. Still, he was too old these days to bother with comely youths.

"His presence here could be a trap set by the Order," the German added.

"For the tenth time, Drake's loyalty is to me. He saved my life—"

"Yes, yes." He waved this off.

"The Order wants to kill *him* now even more than they want our blood!" he insisted with an impatient gesture toward the men slashing about in their brutal training. "Lord Westwood is no longer what he once was. Your torturers saw to that," he added in distaste. "Pushing him to the point of madness . . . they succeeded all too well in destroying the Order agent he used to be. But look at him now. Magnificent creature. He is like the very incarnation of our creed," he murmured, as Drake sent another opponent sprawling with a vicious kick. "He has come through the fire as few ever have and has been reborn, just as in our most sacred prayers. He has become a weapon in our hands.

"Besides," James added after a brief, reluctant pause, "there is a particular prophecy I found in Valerian's scrolls . . ."

Septimus looked at him keenly.

James was not sure how much to say. He had been shocked, himself, to find it in the Alchemist's writings.

"What sort of prophecy?" the count prompted.

"Don't tell the others. But there was a quatrain about a knight of the Order who would one day become the Prometheans' greatest leader."

The German's dark eyes widened in astonishment. He stared at James, then glanced down at Drake.

"You really think he could be the one?"

James shrugged. "Well, we don't get many converts from the Order, do we? I scarcely know what to think at this point."

Septimus fell silent for a moment, watching Drake intently, then he shook his head. "If it is fate, it will be so whether we like it or not, but I say, all the more reason to watch him with the utmost care."

"You still don't trust him."

"Of course not! I might have, once you told me that— but then this girl arrives? It's all too suspicious if you ask me. Maybe she's an Order agent!"

"Emily Harper?" James exclaimed, laughing. "Oh, my friend, you are overwrought."

"Let him prove it if he's really one of us!"

"How?" James replied. "What would satisfy you?"

"The same sacrifice we all make," Glasse replied, staring at him. "Dearest blood."

James's smile faded.

"Let him give up the girl for the night of the eclipse," he answered. "Then I will be satisfied."

James looked away, hiding a slight grimace.

He was well aware that he needed to keep his strongest allies happy. They had to be sure of him, and he had to be sure of them, in turn. He could not forge on ahead with his plans without the support and loyalty of Septimus Glasse and a few of the others.

If he refused to make his bodyguard pay the toll that every member of their brotherhood's higher echelons paid eventually, himself included, some might begin to doubt his commitment, his judgment, putting *him* at risk before his tenure as the new head of the Council had begun—and then what?

As James was even now working to overthrow Malcolm, if he didn't show he was in full control of all pertinent matters, it wouldn't be long before someone was plotting to overthrow him.

Drake's servant girl wasn't worth that risk.

Neither was Drake, for that matter, though he'd been of use.

Besides, James was not blind. He saw the tender way those two looked at each other. Drake had claimed she was no more than a plaything, but that was obviously a lie though it was a small matter, probably nothing more than male ego that made him deny his feelings for her.

Nevertheless, if the former Order agent lied about small matters, what else was he lying about? James mused. At length, he nodded, conceding to his friend's advice.

"Call the others," he murmured. "We will put the question to him. And then we will find out where his loyalty really lies."

Drake's chest still heaved as he strode back under the shelter of the colonnade, where more of the men leaned out of the rain, watching the others' progress and awaiting their turns. One of the Promethean bodyguards threw him a towel, along with an admiring remark on his performance.

Drake dried his face and nodded his thanks but walked on, hauling open the thick doors to the Hall of Arms on the ground floor. There, he picked up his canteen and took a long swig of water.

At last, he let out a large exhalation, his pulse slowing to normal.

Damn, that had felt good.

His muscles were a bit sore, but at least he had vented his frustration. A hard round of training always made him feel better. The practice helped to dissipate his seething, inexplicable emotions. Besides, it was oddly reassuring to fix his attention for a while on an area of his life where he was in full control.

Unlike last night.

He could not get the taste, the smell, the satiny texture of Emily out of his mind, but he was doing his best to ignore it. With a low sigh, he stretched his neck a bit, leaning his head from side to side and shrugging some of the tension out of his shoulders.

He took another drink; his skin was still hot from his exertions, but the rain that had soaked him began to bring a chill. He lifted his drenched shirt over his head, smirking at the distant groan of the injured man being treated by the surgeon at the other end of the hall.

Eh, you'll thank me someday.

Good old Virgil had taught them young to train in all conditions—rain, snow, blistering heat, half-light or darkness—and after a certain point, not to bother using blunts, at least on occasion. Real danger and real fear had to be created every now and then to reach the level of expertise that they would need. After all, fear did things to a man's mind in actual fighting conditions that made it useless to train when one knew it was only an exercise.

One had to learn to fight around the panicked seconds that met every human being sooner or later—the tunnel vision, a distorted sense of hearing, the fleeting clumsiness that could overtake one's usual coordination, and, if not overcome, could quickly get one killed.

If the lads got a little bloody in the meanwhile, Drake thought, they would gain some experience that might one day save their lives. Besides, the harsher forms of training would weed out the weak.

Best to know who was not built for combat before it came to the moment of do-or-die. He'd find other jobs for them.

As he pulled a fresh, dry shirt over his head, the smart ring of bootheels approached him over the cold stone. "Falkirk's asking for you, sir."

Drake cast a businesslike glance over his shoulder, still buttoning his shirt. He nodded to the guard who'd come to fetch him. "I'll be right there." Then he pulled on his black jacket, smoothed his wet hair, and straightened his weapons belt, before marching toward the interior castle doors.

He went through the heavy doors, stepping into the dim, square chamber used as a fencing studio.

"Drake. Stop right there, please."

He didn't see anyone, but he stopped and looked up. Instantly, he was on guard, not liking his position one iota.

Up on the gallery from which an audience could watch demonstrations of fine swordplay, he saw that he was surrounded by the Promethean masters, their faces cast in shadow.

His position below them in the center of the floor was absolutely open and exposed.

James rested his hands on the railing. "We have a request to make of you, Drake."

"Yes, sir, how may I be of use?" he answered, glancing around uneasily at the men above him.

He was a sitting duck here. He did not know what they wanted, but it was very clear that, one wrong word, and they could blow holes in him where he stood. He could not see weapons trained on him, but he was sure they were.

Something wasn't right.

Even the tone of James's voice sounded odd when he spoke again, cool and tense and distant. "It's about the girl," he informed him. "Emily Harper."

At once, the dark phantom of fear that Drake had trained against all morning rose at James's mention of her; but he checked himself immediately, determined to display no visible response. "Yes, sir?" he answered calmly.

"We want to know if you are ready for the next step in your initiation." Count Septimus Glasse had spoken, leaning into view at the railing above but behind Drake.

He turned, his heart pounding. But seeing the owner of Waldfort Castle, it was more difficult for him to hide his hatred. The Bavarian lord had been in command of the soldiers who had captured Drake.

And killed his team.

"The time has come to prove that you are really one of us."

Drake choked back his rage and gazed at him serenely. "What would you have me do?"

Emily descended the stone stairs to the lower regions of the castle, having fetched her herbs from Drake's chamber to give to the surgeon for the poultice.

Though she was a little reluctant to share the supplies she had brought chiefly for Drake and herself, she felt duty-bound to at least offer them, considering it was Drake who had inflicted the various nasty scratches on the other men. Why she still felt responsible for him and his actions, she barely understood.

Surely he was a grown man and knew what he was about. Nevertheless, she didn't like to see anyone suffer when she could do something about it.

As she made her way toward the Hall of Arms, she heard voices echoing to her from down the dim corridor. Her brisk walk slowed as she approached the chamber that opened off the passageway ahead.

She heard Drake's voice, strong, calm, and sure. Inevitably, she followed that beloved, familiar sound.

Yet, as she approached, she heard other voices, too, so she took care to stay out of sight, keeping to the shadows.

"How long have you known her?"

"All my life."

"And how is that?"

"Her father worked for mine," he replied.

Her eyes widened as she sidled up to the wall, listening. *They're talking about me?*

She saw him standing alone in the middle of a bare stone chamber. Whoever was asking the questions was hidden from her line of sight, as she huddled by the gothic-pillared doorway.

"So, she caught your fancy, did she?"

Drake stared upward at his unseen interrogators, his posture bristling, his hands resting tensely on his waist near his weapons. "You could say that," he replied.

Emily watched him, her heart pounding. She was not sure what was going on in there, but she could sense that he felt a threat in this situation and could hear it in his tone of voice, the note of warning, taut restraint, dark authority.

She held her breath and listened to various invisible speakers firing questions down on him.

Demands meant to shake him.

"How old were you when you first took her?"

Drake floundered, perhaps tongue-tied by the coarseness of the question. "I don't see why you need to know that."

"Surely you've nothing to hide? If she means so little, as you claim, then why won't you answer the question?"

"It's none of your business."

"Everything about our members is our business, Lord Westwood, as you know full well, and this is doubly so when it comes to you, in light of your past associations. Now, you're either one of us or you're not."

"Haven't I proved myself enough?"

"No, you have not. So I suggest you answer in full any questions you're asked—and do not attempt to lie. If you are lying, James will know."

He lowered his head. "Very well."

Emily huddled out of sight, observing from just beyond the doorway. She did not dare move for fear of being seen. "So her father worked for yours and you have known her all your life. Played together as children?"

"Yes."

"Was she your first?"

Emily stared, appalled. The cruelty of these men,

forcing him to break open the secret intimacy between them that had been his only refuge.

And hers.

But the Prometheans did not want their new recruit to have any such safe place to turn to. They wanted all his loyalty for themselves alone.

"All those years of playing together . . . you must have been quite young when you first began to notice her as a female. Was she your first?"

He stood there struggling, until someone out of sight suddenly spoke up.

"He's never touched her. Have you?"

Murmurs followed from the darkness. "What? What's this?"

"Is this true?"

"Have you lied to us about the nature of your relationship with this girl?"

"No!" Drake forced out. "Please, she is no threat to anybody here—"

"He is in love with her," the same, shrewd voice declared, the one tinged with an Italian accent.

But Emily was staring, wide-eyed, at Drake. Her entire being hung upon what answer he might give.

"Yes," another voice remarked. "I do believe our cardinal is right."

"It's obvious. Admit it, man."

He lifted his head in blazing defiance, though his voice remained stern and composed. "It is as you say."

Time stood still for Emily, hearing those words.

She wasn't sure herself if he was playing some sort of chess game with them; but if not, it must have been the strangest way that any girl had ever found out the man she loved, loved her.

"We were close—since childhood," he admitted. "But obviously, the match was not approved, by either of our families. I abided by that. I would not dishonor her."

"So you lied to us when she arrived."

"Yes. I did not want any of the men making free with her. I did not know she would follow me! She has no inkling of the danger—she knows nothing. She only came because she loves me."

Well, at least he knows that, Emily thought, her mouth gone dry as she spied on them. She was horrified that she had got Drake in trouble with these terrifying men.

Indeed, everything in her began to send a warning that she must flee immediately. If she moved right away, she could slip down to the dungeon and escape through the chink in the rock she had seen.

But she could not possibly leave Drake standing there alone to face the consequences for *her* actions. If she fled and was found to be missing, God only knew what they might to do him.

"So." Falkirk's voice reached her. "You lied when she arrived in order to protect her, but what proof do we have that you are telling the truth now?"

"Sir, I am telling you the truth."

"Oh, really?" a sharper voice taunted, another foreign accent. "Perhaps she is an agent of the enemy?"

"Emily Harper? Don't be absurd!" he retorted.

"She was shrewd enough to track you here. That is quite an uncommon skill for a mere girl."

"Her father schooled her in the woodsman's ways from an early age. Please! Listen to me! I'm sorry she intruded, but whatever her punishment, take it out on me, not on her. She has no part in any of this. Just let her leave this place—"

"Well, she can't leave now, as you know full well," Falkirk interrupted coldly. "It's her own doing, and the time has come for you to make a choice."

Drake went perfectly still.

"You are either with us or against us. The time has come to prove it. If you are really one of us, you must surrender her to our will."

Emily quaked; Drake looked equally horrified.

"What do you mean, 'surrender her'?" he uttered, his hand curling dangerously around the hilt of his sword at his side.

They were silent.

He took a step forward. "What do you want with her?" he roared. "She is an innocent!"

"As it happens, we have need of an innocent, Lord Westwood," Falkirk answered, coolly in control. "For the night of the eclipse."

"No," Drake whispered. "Not her."

"Yes. It's what we all must do. Dearest blood."

"Don't worry, she will be given sedatives to keep her peaceful. Trust me, she won't feel a thing. We are not barbarians, after all."

"James, for the love of God."

"What God, Drake?"

He fell silent.

"You would not refuse this sacrifice for the cause? She's perfect. Brave, selfless, beautiful. And a virgin, to boot, as you said you've never touched her, and it's obvious you are the only man in the world to her. Her blood will intoxicate the one we serve. What better start to our new beginning than the blood of a virgin for our lord at the ritual of the eclipse? With this gift, our future endeavors cannot fail."

Drake said nothing, did not move. She was very sure he wanted to explode, however. For her part, Emily felt ill, staring into the chamber, her very blood curdling in her veins.

"Will you give her to us? Yes or no. The time has

come to make your choice," someone informed him.

"I had a son once, Drake," Falkirk spoke up suddenly. "It's only a sacrifice if it hurts, you see."

Drake stood motionless, his face stoic, like he was made of iron, and when he spoke, his three, low-toned, simple words filled Emily with horror.

"So be it."

The ice began in the pit of her stomach and spread to every inch of her skin; she began shaking as the various men met his answer with murmurs of approval.

"Then you *are* one of us," they congratulated him.

"We'll see if he stands firm when the time comes."

"For now, he's made the right choice. Well done, Drake. It's not easy."

"You won't regret it. Once a member takes this step, there is no turning back."

"Excellent, Drake," Falkirk said at last. "I knew we could count on you."

"She will be safe until then?" he demanded.

"Absolutely. No more menial labor. She will be treated like a jewel. Send the guards after the girl," Falkirk instructed someone out of view. "Tell them I want her moved to the finest chamber we have available. That way, our brother here will not be tempted to despoil the dark father's prize."

"Don't tell her what you plan. Don't terrify her," Drake half ordered, half begged them.

"No, of course not. She'd only try to escape," Falkirk replied, his tone shockingly casual. "Post a guard outside her door to prevent it."

"Yes, sir," someone answered.

"I will guard her," Drake spoke up.

"Ah, I don't think so. You will see to your usual duties. We cannot take the chance that you might waver."

"I will not waver," he replied, but Emily was already

racing silently out of the corridor, fleeing back the way she had come, terror stamped across her face.

Her heart pounded. The darkness of this place seemed to slide against her cheeks like wraiths in a graveyard and she could barely think. *Must get out of here now. Leave my knife, bag, everything in the room. Just go.*

She took the stone stairs two at a time though her legs were shaking beneath her; she felt so weak she feared she might collapse. But somehow she kept moving, rushing back up to the main floor of the castle, her pulse roaring in her ears.

She cast a panicked glance this way and that in the central corridor. She set her sights on the set of stairs that led down to the dungeon.

She would climb through the break in the wall where the cat had escaped. From there, she'd go out to the forest and run for her life. In that moment, she could not even think of Drake. She was too much in shock at what those evil men had planned for her.

How she wished she'd listened to him. She never should have followed him.

Choking back terror, she started across the wide central hallway on the main floor of the castle, where she had gone around replacing candles. But she hadn't gone far when a voice rang out behind her.

"Miss Harper!"

Too late. She froze at the sound of Falkirk's voice, her heart in her throat. *What am I going to do?*

"A word with you, please, my dear."

Immobilized by fear, too shocked to cry, too scared to run, she could not even turn around.

Her pulse slammed as a couple of seconds ticked past. The exit she had planned to leave by was too far. She would never get there in time. Indeed, past the panic swimming through her mind, she somehow saw that her only advantage in this moment was that they didn't know she had overheard their plan.

If she could compose herself to keep up that ruse, she could probably look for a chance to slip away later. They had said, after all, that she would be safe until the night of the eclipse, whenever that was—if they were to be believed. That faint hope helped to calm her down enough to turn around, doing her best to hide her terror.

"Yes, my lord?" she forced out in a voice that was barely a whisper.

Falkirk strode toward her at the head of a quartet of guards, Drake behind them, to the side, his fiery stare fixed on her.

"My dear," said the Promethean leader, "it has come to our attention that we have been remiss in the hospitality we have shown you, or rather, the lack of it."

"Pardon, sir?" she countered meekly, frightened anew as the guards he'd brought moved into position around her, all four corners.

Drake watched them like a hawk . . .

"We were not quite, er, clear at first on your importance to our dear Lord Westwood," Falkirk continued. "We beg your pardon. I'm afraid it's all been a bit of a misunderstanding. You must let us make it up to you for this inconvenience. There is another chamber that we'd like to offer to you, one that I think you'll find far more agreeable."

"That's not necessary, I don't wish to impose—"

"No imposition, dear child. So modest. Charming creature," he remarked fondly to Drake. Then Falkirk looked at her again with his dissecting, gray-eyed stare. "Come, let us show you to your new accommodations—and no more of this servant's work

for one who is rightfully our honored guest. This way."
He swept a gallant gesture toward the marble staircase.

The guards waited for her to move.

Emily looked at Drake for instructions, but his face
was a blank. Seeing that, she was alarmed. It appeared
the whole episode had thrust him back toward the lost
state in which he had arrived at his estate weeks ago,
when Lord Rotherstone had first brought him home.

She saw she would have to be strong and managed a
stiff nod. "As you wish."

Falkirk smiled politely, turned, and led the way
toward, then up the marble staircase.

She kept her gaze down, sure that her fear would be
visible in her eyes. But as she followed him, she wondered if she had not overheard their true plans, what
she might have made of this deception!

At the top of the grand staircase, they turned in
the opposite direction from the way to Drake's room.
Unlike the simple, older style where he had been
quartered, the wing they entered must have been for
the castle owners' personal use and that of honored
guests, for it carried on the dizzying rococo theme
from below.

Reminding herself continually that her doom was
not quite imminent, Emily walked with her shoulders
squared, her chin up. Still, she thought, any young
woman would have thought it unnerving to be escorted to her chamber by half a dozen grown men—
and that, without even being aware of their sinister
intentions.

"Here we are," James said politely, opening a white
bedchamber door.

Her new cage. Emily paused, glancing into the room.
Spring sunshine beamed through the windows,

lighting up an airy, feminine space with white-and-gilt walls, a dainty floral carpet, and pink velvet curtains.

She glanced around nervously at the oil paintings in gold frames, the ornate claw-and-ball-footed furniture in fine woods with white marble tops. By the wall, draped in pink velvet to match the curtains, was a canopy bed fit for a princess.

"You will want something suitable to wear, as well, no doubt," Falkirk informed her. "If the maids can't find something proper for you in the castle, we'll send someone into the town."

"May I have my own things, as well?" she asked anxiously, already realizing it would do her no good to argue.

"I will bring your bag to you," Drake mumbled from over by the door.

"Let the servants draw Miss Harper a bath at once. Tending the candles is such a sooty job."

Emily eyed him in fear. James smiled indulgently.

"It's all right, my dear. We only wish to make you comfortable, you see? Now that we know how much you mean to Drake."

She swallowed hard. "Yes, sir."

For a fleeting instant, as he smiled at her, Emily had a glimpse of the mind games this man had played on her beloved. This smooth, smiling liar.

Taking him out of the dungeon. Pretending to be his friend.

Now he was trying to do it to her. But unlike Drake, she had never been confused about dark and light.

She knew exactly where she stood, and she held her spot firmly for the two of them, bristling with utter, steely resolve. For if there was one thing that could make her throw off any degree of fear, it was her bone-deep need to protect him. Just as he would do for her.

She knew it in her blood.

"Very well, then," Falkirk concluded, turning away, "make yourself comfortable, Miss Harper. The servants will be along shortly to attend you."

She thanked him with a ladylike nod.

The guards began filing out of her room, but Drake was the last to reach the door.

She stared imploringly at him as he sent her a piercing look over his shoulder, his expression stormy.

As they locked eyes before James ordered him out of her room, she understood the full truth about why he had not wanted her to come. This was precisely what he had feared.

She was now trapped inside his nightmare.

Chapter

11

$\mathcal{A}$s the days passed, the cult's high-ranking members, known as the Hundred, continued arriving from all over Europe, drawn by James's summons. From Naples, Paris and Madrid, from Brussels and Glasgow, Vienna and St. Petersburg, their traveling coaches with guards and outriders kept rolling in, all the occult conspirators and oligarchs with a lust for tyranny in their hearts, the castle's remote mountain setting providing them with the secrecy they required.

Drake could hardly believe he was in the thick of it, but any triumph he might have felt as an agent was overshadowed by his grim, constant worry over Emily.

They hadn't talked or been alone together since the night he had foolishly stormed out of the room, outraged by her attempt to lure him away from this place with the promise of her body. He wished to God he would have listened to her while he'd had the chance.

Instead he was up to his neck among countless circling sharks, and it was Emily's blood that chummed the water.

She had been locked away in her fine new bedchamber, kept under guard.

He had not been permitted to see her, lest he do something "rash," as James had said with a fond, chiding smile. *Sick bastard.* Drake knew now he had somehow lost sight of the old man's true evil, lulled into some degree of complacency by his amiable manner and the fact that James had once saved him from the dungeon.

That spell had been sharply broken, however. James's willingness to do such a thing to innocent Emily had pulled away the veil of what the old man truly was.

A creature without a soul.

Drake maintained his obedient façade. Although it was harder to hide his true feelings, he no longer had any qualms about including James in the massacre he had planned for the night of the eclipse.

His own, ever-hardening ruthlessness didn't bother him.

The only thing that mattered to him was Emily's safety and well-being. He would find a way to save her; no other option was possible. But he probably wouldn't come out of this alive himself, and what his death might do to her, he couldn't bear to ponder.

Whatever physical torture he had endured in the depths of Waldfort Castle was nothing compared to his inward anguish, frustration, and bewilderment over how she could have devoted herself to such a lost cause as he.

As much as he wanted to love her, it all seemed too late for that. At this point, his primary objective was simply to save her life.

His only comfort was that at least *she did not know*

the horror they had planned. He could not bear for her to know.

Hopefully, she was up there enjoying her comfortable room and fine food and the pretty gowns they had brought her, no doubt puzzled and probably bored out of her mind; but at least for the moment, he didn't have to be quite so frantic over her.

James finally gave him permission to speak to her after several days. Drake thanked him, but was wary of the old man's strange fascination with their relationship.

Emily's unselfish devotion to him, her blind faith in love, seemed to perplex old Falkirk, but then, Drake had to admit, it rather perplexed him, too.

Eager to see her and to verify for himself that she was all right, he marched into the upper hallway and informed the two guards posted there that James had given him permission to visit her for a quarter hour.

Drake hid his frustration with this absurd time limit, though, in truth, in his rakehell days back in London with the Inferno Club, this would have been enough time for him to ravish a willing lady in secret. He didn't like to rush, but sometimes the occasion called for it . . .

He reminded himself firmly these were not his intentions toward Emily as the guard knocked on the door and informed her she had a visitor.

She called at once to come in; Drake braced himself, doing his best to assume a calm, reassuring demeanor; he swiftly reviewed the lies he intended to tell her that might help allay her fears about why she had been moved and what was really going on.

Then the guard opened the door.

Drake stepped in—and his eyes widened as he came face-to-face with the refined young miss standing in the middle of the room, with her hands demurely tucked behind her back.

"Emily?" he asked in a quizzical tone, shutting the door behind him.

Egad, if he had passed her on Bond Street looking like this, he might not have even recognized her! His strange, fey, little forest girl was transformed into a delicate young lady, of whom even his mother could not have disapproved. Ribbons tamed her neatly upswept hair. Ivory lace edged the sleeves, hem, and neck of her luxurious silk day gown.

He scanned her in amazement, charmed but rather disoriented. Startled by the whole new facet of sweetness this refined presentation brought out in his dearest childhood friend, he started to grin and say something teasing—but then he noticed the expression in her wide, violet eyes, and his stomach plummeted within him.

Frozen, terrified desperation.

She knew?

"Emily?" he asked softly, taking a step toward her.

"Stop. Please, stop right there and don't come any closer," she forced out, holding a hand up as if to ward him off. "I need to know the truth."

Tears rushed into her eyes.

"I've been in this room for days trying to hold on to my faith that you're not a traitor. That you're still *you*. That you'd never let them hurt me. I so want to believe that," she whispered in a voice that shook, "but you did take their mark on your chest. You said the Prometheans understood pain. And it dawned on me that every time I've asked you if you were really with them, you never once denied it."

He stared at her, the blood draining from his face. His body went ice-cold.

"The other morning, I was bringing a poultice down to the Hall of Arms—for that man you hurt in practice," she continued. "I heard voices. Followed the sound. Drake, I overheard the whole thing. I know what they're planning to do to me. And I heard you agree to it."

Then she broke down crying.

He crossed the room to her in three swift strides and pulled her into his arms, distraught with guilt for every lie he'd told. "I'm sorry, I'm so sorry," he whispered over and over in her ear, stroking her hair, holding her up as she wept against his chest.

The terror and grief that came pouring out of her slim, shaking body melted such a thick, hardened layer of ice within him that he felt the sting of tears threatening behind his own eyes, as well. "I'll never let them hurt you. I'm still me, Emily. Please forgive me for this deception. I didn't dare tell you the truth. I didn't think you'd be able to lie to them."

She breathed his name amid her tears and wrapped her arms around his waist, sobbing with an exhaustion that he knew came from the depths of her heart. She had fought so hard for him in her way. She had come so far.

Only to wonder if he had betrayed her.

But he never would. If only he had known she was suffering! He had had no idea that she had overheard the other day's confrontation.

His conscience burned for putting her through so much pain.

It was time to make everything right. He shook his head slightly to himself as he held her in fierce tenderness. "Your first guess was right from the beginning," he breathed in her ear, knowing they must hide this conversation from the guards outside her door. "I know who I am, I got my memory back, and I came here for revenge. I mean to kill them all. And I know now how I'm going to do it, too," he whispered. "I've figured out a way."

Lifting her tear-stained face from his chest, she met his gaze with startled innocence in her reddened eyes.

He cupped her damp cheeks between his hands and with his thumb, brushed away the next tear that fell. "I didn't want you to come here," he reproached her in the gentlest of tones. "Perhaps I panicked. But there was no way that I could have told you the truth. I lied to try to keep you out of it. But I never meant to scare you, my darling. Back in England, you helped me more than you know. You gave me back my strength to continue the fight. I'm the only one who can now. The Order hasn't had a chance like this in centuries. No one has ever infiltrated the cult at this level, but the bond I've developed with Falkirk gave me the chance. I didn't want to go. I wanted to stay with you, but I had no choice. That's why I'm here. To do what needs to be done. But never doubt I'm on your side, my dearest Emily, and I always will be."

"Oh, Drake." She stared at him in tender loyalty.

He shook his head, comforted as always by her softness. "They had me cornered in that chamber. I had to say what they wanted to hear or they'd have shot me where I stood. I'm a former agent of the Order," he reminded her. "I've had to go above and beyond to make them believe they really succeeded in turning me. If they suspected it's a ruse or that I have regained my memory, they would force me to tell them everything I know. They'd torture me again to get it out of me, and this time, I know I'd break. Emily, I can't go through that again. I'm sorry if that makes me weak, but you have no idea . . ."

"It doesn't make you weak. I will not let them hurt you, either!" she whispered.

A pensive smile curved his lips at her protectiveness. "Well, that is why I couldn't tell you what was really going on. You are hardly the world's best liar, my dear. I feared you might give me away—unintentionally, of course—and then they'd kill us both. I'm doing all I know to keep us alive."

"Oh, Drake." She hugged him. "I knew it couldn't be true. I knew you'd never let them hurt me. You almost had me fooled, but I understand now why you had to lie. I won't give you away," she added, glancing up again to stare soberly into his eyes.

He was glad to see she had regained her composure. And then he noticed that he, too, suddenly felt a great weight lifted off him just by telling her the truth.

It felt wonderful to touch her and drink her in with his gaze. The fifteen minutes they'd been granted were moving much too fast.

When she reached up and caressed his cheek with an expression full of thoughtful care, he savored her soft touch. "I hate being separated from you," she whispered.

"I hate it, too."

"Wouldn't they let you come sooner?"

He shook his head. "They don't trust the two of us together. If I had known you were aware of their twisted plans, I would have found a way. You must have been terrified all this time, and here I thought you were all right."

"And I thought *you* were staying away because you were angry at me about the other night. I have to apologize, Drake. I shouldn't have tried to manipulate you," she whispered.

He shook his head. "It's all right."

"No, it was wrong of me to try to do that. I didn't realize till afterward how much you probably needed at least one person who wasn't trying to play games with your head."

"You were only trying to help me."

"I thought if I could persuade you with my kisses, then we could leave, just escape, the two of us—"

"Emily-girl, you could persuade the sun to fall out of the sky with *those* kisses," he told her, and smiled fondly as she blushed. "Not bad for a neophyte."

"Well, at least they were sincere."

"Mmm," he said.

"But I see now you can't leave," she continued, getting back to business, though her violet eyes shone with the same hungry attraction he was feeling at the reminder of that night on the balcony. "After what I overheard, I know why you need to stay here and defeat them. They are truly evil."

He nodded in full agreement.

"Now that I understand," she said sternly, "you have to let me help you. Don't argue with me," she added as she clutched the lapels of his jacket with both dainty hands.

She gazed up at him in earnest determination. "You will stop shutting me out. The time has come for us to work together. No more secrets, no more lies. You can't do this alone. There are too many of them for one man to handle—even you."

He gave her a rueful smile, taking her adorable insistence on helping him only halfheartedly. "You help me more than you know just by being here."

"I can contribute more than that, if you'd stop shielding me. Just tell me what to do!"

Regarding her with a skeptical eye, even though he frankly adored the chit, he began to wonder if she was right. Perhaps there was some assistance she could provide. True, he was accustomed to having battle-hardened warriors as allies, but God love her, this little slip of a girl had the heart of a she-wolf. She was going to have to do.

Besides, Drake saw that it would be cruel of him to continue insisting that she simply sit alone in her room and do nothing, just trust him. Anyone would go mad, knowing she was slated for a gruesome death, and being forbidden to do anything to try to save herself.

That was too much to ask, he conceded. He'd already put her through enough by lying to her. All she wanted was to help. She was a capable person, loyal and smart. Hell, back in their childhood days, she had beaten him at many a contest though he would deny it till the day he died.

"Very well. I can't think of anything at this very moment, but let me give it some thought, and as soon as I come up with something, I'll let you know."

"You promise?"

"Yes," he answered firmly.

"You'd better not forget about me," she warned.

He scoffed. "What man in his right mind could?"

"Yes, but this is you we're talking about, my dear lunatic."

"Right," he murmured, as they both began to laugh quietly. "Come here, you, cheeky." He pulled her into his arms and hugged her, still chuckling.

As Emily hugged him back, he couldn't remember the last time anyone had made him laugh.

"God bless you," he whispered, grateful to his very soul for the much-needed moment of levity. He gave her a kiss on the forehead. "I continue to doubt that there's a man worthy of you on this planet, you know."

"Well, there's one," she confided, then she pulled him down and kissed him.

Drake returned her kiss, pulling her into his arms. In the moment, as her satin lips caressed his with captivating warmth, he thrilled to her affection; at the same time, in the back of his mind, it dawned on him that she was an utterly amazing human being.

He couldn't believe she had followed him.

He couldn't believe anyone would ever love him so much. Throughout his life, people—usually other Order agents—had expressed being in awe of him, but now it was his turn. He was in awe of *her*, and it was his turn to feel humbled.

Emily ended their kiss, pulling back with a serene smile and a dreamy glow in her eyes. He could do nothing but stare breathlessly at her, feeling as though he were seeing her for the first time.

"Are you inspired yet with some way I can help?" she murmured.

A sudden, soft laugh escaped him. She was persistent, to be sure. "*That* helped tremendously. Perhaps another?"

"Drake," she chided.

He shook off the daze of pleasure she had left him in and ruefully brought himself back to the task at hand. "My main concern is that you're going to have to lie like you've never lied in your life. You can't let them see you're afraid or that you know what they have planned. Just play the oblivious female. That will help us avoid complications."

She eyed him dubiously. "Like those girls your mother wanted you to marry?"

He flashed an unexpected smile. "Exactly."

"How much time do we have before this ritual?"

"Ten days."

She winced. "Well, at least, it'll be over soon."

"It might not hurt if you could try to befriend your guards a bit in the meanwhile."

She nodded. "Good idea. I can see how that could be useful. I shall soon have them eating out of my hand!" she murmured with a crafty smile.

"Well, you don't have to go and make me jealous," he retorted playfully. "Honestly, though, do not be too obvious, or they'll wonder what you're up to. Just a sprinkle of your eccentric charm will go a long way, believe me."

She propped her fists on her waist. "Eccentric?"

"Hmm? What? I didn't hear anything."

Her response was a playful tap on his chest, the lightest of smacks. "At least I'm not a lunatic."

"I'm beginning to think you are," he whispered with a smile. Then he glanced at his fob watch. "They're going to order me out of here in a moment or two. Are you going to be all right?"

"I will, now. But first, there's something you should know." She glanced past him, keeping her voice down. "I didn't want to tell you this before, because I wasn't sure if you were one of them or not, but I wrote to your friend, Lord Rotherstone, from Munich, after I had followed you to the castle. I told him where you were."

"Did you?" he asked in surprise.

She nodded. "If they got the message, I should think they're likely on their way by now."

Drake absorbed this news with mixed emotions.

"That could be good for us, couldn't it?" she urged. "We could use more help."

"As long as they don't get caught, yes," he murmured. "But you do realize they have orders to kill me. Why would you tell them where I was?"

She gave an innocent shrug. "I was afraid when I finally caught up to you, I might find out I had got in over my head."

He gave her a wry look. "I am shocked to hear you admit such a thing is possible."

"Look who's talking." She chucked him lightly under the chin while her eyes sparkled with a sly twinkle. "You're the one who thinks he's indestructible."

He shrugged.

"Well, it's hard to say this, Drake, but if you had betrayed everything you once believed in, I realized . . . you were going to have to be stopped. And I knew I wouldn't be able to do it." She shook her head.

"You'd have been willing to have me killed for the sake of the Order?"

"I'm sorry. Is that wrong?" she whispered. "You believed in it all your life. I couldn't let you—"

He stopped her with another kiss. "Virgil should have recruited both of us," he answered very softly. "I can't think of anything finer or more noble that you could say to me."

She searched his eyes. "I prayed it wouldn't come to that."

"And it won't," he promised. "Thank you."

She stroked his hair, soothing tensions in him that he had barely noticed collecting. "We'll just have to figure out some way to let them know once they get here that you are still one of them."

He nodded wryly. "In the meanwhile, you should forget that I am. As far as you know, I'm a nasty Promethean convert, remember?"

"Right," she murmured, smiling at his warning. "Got it."

"Good." He took both her hands in his. It seemed so natural to be open with her that he could not imagine now why it had been so desperately important to him at first to shut her out. "We're going to make it through this, all right? I won't let you down."

"I know you won't, Drake. You never have."

"I think I have," he said wistfully. "I should have married you a long time ago."

She fell silent, holding his gaze.

The guards banged on the door at that moment, calling to him that the fifteen minutes was over. Drake glanced angrily over his shoulder, then looked at Emily again.

"I'll find a way for us to talk again soon," he murmured. "I'll speak to James, too, about letting you go outside. It's ridiculous for you to be locked up in here every day. You're not going to run away."

"Not as long as you're here."

He kissed her cheek. "I'll see what I can do. Are you going to be all right?"

She gave a firm nod, though she still held on to his hand. "Feeling braver already."

He smiled, mystified. "You really are a miracle, Emily."

"The miracle will be when we both get out of here safely. Promise me you'll be careful." She still wouldn't let go of his hand. "I know you're in pain, Drake, and that you don't really believe you'll ever be all right again, but once we've dealt with them, then we can be together, and I promise you, with all my heart, I'll help you find your way back to the sunlight. You *will* be whole and happy again, as you once were. You will find healing, all right? So, don't give up. You just need time and tender loving care, and I'll be with you every step of the way to make sure you get both."

He stared at her, wanting to believe, despite the edge of uneasiness her tender words aroused. He managed a nod and slid his hand from hers. "I'd better go."

"Be careful," she breathed, as he withdrew and walked toward the door.

"You, too. Stay strong, girl."

"I will. And Drake? Thank you for trusting me at last."

"No, Emily, thank you. For everything. Especially for not losing faith in me," he answered in a low tone that the guards would not hear.

"I never will."

He reached for the door handle.

"Um, Drake?"

He paused, glancing back in question.

Emily folded her arms across her chest with an irresistible, teasing smile. "I heard them force you into admitting you love me."

"Hmm," he said, rather on guard. "You heard that?"

She nodded, regarding him in amusement.

He looked at her for a long moment. "What makes you think they forced me?"

The joy that broke across her face was like the sun bursting out from behind the cold, formidable mountains.

Her smile beamed: He sent her a wink from the doorway, then he went out and closed the door behind him.

Her guards eyed him with a certain degree of suspicion when he stepped out into the hallway. No doubt they had never seen that expression on his face. How could they? What he felt just then hadn't been in his heart for two years.

Hope.

Still, he jerked his thumb sternly over his shoulder. "Watch her," he ordered in a dark tone.

"Yes, sir," they said, reassured again that he was still the hard bastard they all feared.

But when his back was to them as he walked off down the hallway, he couldn't chase the daft smile off his face.

France

Rotherstone's team had reached the thick forests of the Argonne, in the Champagne region of France, and there they made camp for the night. The nearby brook babbled in the darkness; the tethered horses drank and grazed around it, while the low bonfire crackled.

From across the flames, Max regarded his two fellow agents, each of them sitting on his bedroll unfurled on the forest floor. None of them had much to say.

Virgil was haunting all of them these days.

Leaning on his soft leather saddlebags, Max turned around to put the map away, having already familiarized himself with the next day's route.

So far, they had been making excellent time over the mostly flat ground, but that would change, given the extremely rugged terrain ahead.

From Calais, they had swept across the north of France, the Belgian-style windmills they passed reminding them that they were but a stone's throw from the Flemish border—and the fields of Waterloo. Max remembered that grim triumph all too well, but he did not linger over the memory, focused on leading his team onward to catch up with Drake at the castle in the Alps.

Passing to the north of Reims, they kept to the countryside, since, after all, they were Englishmen. The war was over, but grudges lived on in pockets of both countries here and there. They could not afford delays in needless conflict with the locals.

Tomorrow they would gain the oft-disputed territory of Alsace-Lorraine. It would probably take another three days to reach the next major landmark on their journey: the city of Strasbourg on the eastern edge of France. From there, it was upward into the Alps, a hundred miles over the mighty mountains to Stuttgart, then a trek south, to Augsburg and, at last, to Munich.

Then they would find this Waldfort Castle.

What they might encounter when they got there was anybody's guess. Studying his two teammates with a shrewd, assessing eye, Max mused that they'd have to be ready for anything. He had a feeling there was going to be one hell of a battle once they reached the German stronghold where the Prometheans had gathered.

Their barely mentioned grief over Virgil wasn't helping. None of them quite knew what to do with themselves since they had found their beloved Highlander murdered by his own son. Every one of them felt guilty, but it was too late now. Max hated himself for the anger that he felt toward Virgil, but damn it, the old man should have known better than to trust that son of a bitch.

He let out a sigh, missing Daphne's arms around him. She had a way about her that helped to calm him down.

All three men had sent their wives together to one of the Order's secure estates, just in case Drake had started giving up their names. That seemed unlikely, for if he hadn't done it so far, why would he start?

Still, none of them were willing to take any chances with the safety of the women who were everything to them. They hadn't told the wives, either, how serious the danger was this time. They'd explain the situation later.

If there was a later, Max thought dryly. In truth, Virgil's death made failure seem possible in a way that it never had before, for if the old Highlander, with all his decades of training and experience, could make a mistake that had cost him his life, it brought home the point that any of them could.

For that matter, Max couldn't begin to think how he was supposed to pull the trigger on his boyhood friend. He would never forgive himself for letting Drake escape. But how he could have anticipated that Drake would grab that poor, sweet Emily girl and use her as a hostage?

Ah, it was a bad business.

Then, as much as he wanted to lose himself in private daydreams of his bride, another weary glance across the fire at his friends reminded him that they were in as bad shape as he was over Virgil's death.

As team leader, it was up to him to boost morale.

The fire crackled, sending up a plume of sparks and a spiral of rising smoke. An owl hooted from somewhere in the surrounding black trees. Max sat up and casually rested his elbow across his bent left knee.

The fire's glow sculpted his friends' faces. He studied them, putting his own cares aside, and wondering what to say. Meanwhile, the orange flame of the bonfire in the midst of the three men reminded him of the color of Virgil's moustache years ago when the Highlander had come to the Rotherstone estate in his role as Seeker, and had recruited Max for the Order when he was but a pup. That Scotsman had been more of a father to him than his own sire, the wretched drunkard. If not for Virgil, Max was sure his life would have served no purpose. He'd have simply followed in his dissipated father's footsteps.

He glanced at Rohan, Virgil's favorite. Rohan's father,

the previous Duke of Warrington, had once been the leader, or Link, of Virgil's team when he, too, had been a field agent decades earlier.

The previous Duke of Warrington had fallen in his prime, but Virgil had always looked out for his comrade's son, and Rohan, in turn, had adored the rugged Scot. In terms of character, they were cut from the same cloth.

All Max knew was that Warrington had barely spoken a word since they reached the Continent. The duke was dangerous under ordinary circumstances, but ever since Niall had murdered their handler right under their noses—in the heart of their very headquarters—lethal intent had burned in the warrior's pale eyes.

As for Jordan, he shouldn't even be here, Max thought. Falconridge was still recovering from wounds sustained in his vicious battle against the Promethean assassin, Dresden Bloodwell. Jordan had felled the bastard in the end, but not before Bloodwell had stabbed him in the side and slashed him right across the chest. He had nearly died.

That had been about a month ago. Though Jordan insisted he was fine, Max still thought he probably should have stayed at home. Of course, he wouldn't hear of it. If they were going, so was he. Jordan might be more of a gentleman than Max and Warrington combined, but he wanted revenge on Virgil's killer as badly as they did.

So far, Jordan's healing wounds had not reopened, but their journey had not yet reached the far rougher ground ahead. The mountains might well prove too much for him.

In the meanwhile, he insisted that he wouldn't slow them down, and he hadn't. If it came to it, he could take lodgings along the way and wait for them to return.

Although Jordan was still recovering from physical wounds, Max was far more worried about Rohan.

Niall Banks had no idea of the fury coming after him. He was as good as dead already, he just didn't know it yet.

Jordan took a swig of whiskey to soothe away the pain, then passed the bottle to Max, who accepted it gladly. Rohan was smoking a cheroot and poking the fire with a stick—rather vengefully—now and then.

Finally, Max let out a low laugh. "Do you remember the time we painted his horse blue?"

Rohan smiled wistfully. "For his birthday."

"He was certainly surprised," Jordan drawled. "How about the glue we put on that blasted pointer stick he always used in geography class?"

"Priceless. He picked it up and whacked the map to show us bloody Magellan's route round the world, and then he couldn't put it down."

Max grinned at the memory and took another swig of whiskey before passing the bottle on to Rohan. "We used to torture him, poor devil. I don't know why he put up with us."

"Ah, he loved the sport of it as much as he bellowed about our bad behavior," Rohan murmured with a brooding smile.

"We did give him lots of trouble, all of us, at one time or another."

"I didn't," Jordan retorted.

"Oh, yes, you did. Two words. Mara Bryce."

"Well," he conceded with a shrug. "He used to torture us right back."

"Run the fells for two hour at noontime in July," Max reminded them.

"Climb up the side of a cliff in a thunderstorm. That was fun," Jordan added.

"Right, then the chess games after he made us stay up for forty-eight hours at a time."

"Well, he knew what he was doing."

"Suppose so. We're all still alive."

"So help me . . ." Rohan uttered. He didn't complete the thought aloud. He didn't need to.

Jordan sent Max a keen glance. "Rather complicates matters, knowing it's his son. Any part of you that thinks we ought to spare Niall out of respect for his bloodlines?"

"Hell, no! We're more sons to him than Niall Banks will ever be," Rohan murmured bitterly.

"You'll get your chance, man, just be patient," Max assured him.

"It never should have happened."

"You can't undo it." Max shook his head, concerned at his most aggressive friend's bottled wrath. "Remember what he used to say? 'Be glad when it's darkest, because it only means you're close.'"

"I guess we're pretty damned close, then," Rohan growled.

Jordan shook his head, his gaze downcast. "I don't know about you, but I can't stop feeling guilty. All the times I said I didn't want to turn out like him. I should be proud to resemble him in any way," he declared with a hint of anguish in his cultured voice.

"We know what you meant, Jord," Max assured him. "You had the clearest view of how cut off he was from everyone. And you were right. He never really even got to live. All of us had to feel sorry for him from time to time. This war was everything to him."

"*We* were everything to him," Rohan countered. "We were the only 'sons' he had in his life. And we let him down. When he needed us, none of us were there."

"I don't think that's true," Max ventured after a ponderous silence in the face of his rugged friend's grief. "The old man let his guard down for one reason— because Niall was his son. This one's not our fault."

Rohan shrugged and took another drag of his cheroot with the air of a killer patiently biding his time, waiting for his chance. Which, of course, was exactly what he was.

Jordan sighed and lay back on the ground, vaguely touching his bandaged chest. He stared up at the endless distance of the stars. "What is it in man's nature that makes some willing to go to any extremes to gain power over others? Enslave his fellows, even by deceit?"

"If you're trying to understand the Prometheans, you're wasting your time," Max murmured wearily. "Evil doesn't make any sense, that's how it gets so far. It does precisely what a sane man would never do."

"He's right. You can't reason with such people. You can only kill 'em."

"And then what?" said Jordan. "More rise to take their places."

"So you kill them, too. And you just keep on killin' 'em till they stay down."

"What if we fall first?"

"We'll make more like us," Rohan said. "And if they keep coming, then, by God, so will we."

"I don't want my son to have to do this," Max remarked.

A dry, quiet laugh escaped Jordan. "Maybe you'll have a daughter," he said cynically.

"Son or daughter, maybe they'll want to," Rohan pointed out.

"Who would want to?" Jordan murmured wistfully.

"I did," the duke replied without hesitation. "At least then your damned life matters. Otherwise, what? Balls at Almack's, cards at White's? Bloody meaningless."

"You know, it doesn't sound half-bad at the moment," Max drawled, and the other two succumbed to quiet laughter.

"I guess not," Rohan said with a snort.

"Get some sleep, lads," their trusty team leader ordered. "We've got another long ride tomorrow."

They grumbled at the reminder, but soon took his advice.

Max stayed up alone a little while longer, wondering who the Elders up in Scotland were ever going to find to fill the old man's shoes. Someone was going to have to be appointed as the new chief of their London headquarters.

He lifted the bottle in another private toast to his dead mentor. The thing about Virgil was that even when his boys had trouble of any kind, he never gave up on them.

There'll never be another like him.

Max glanced up to search the stars. Soon they'd be in Germany. At the moment, he couldn't help wondering if Virgil would have really given up on Drake.

Chapter 12

Bavaria

A few days later, Drake stepped out of the cool gray shadow of the castle and paused in the afternoon sunshine, gazing at his one little ally in this fight. Emily was picking wildflowers in a sunny meadow just beyond the gardens. As always, she remained under the watchful eyes of her guards, but Drake ignored them, a tender pang taking hold of his heart.

God's truth, ever since he had confided in her about the true nature of his self-appointed mission, he was no longer sure he was doing the right thing.

It had been easier not to question his plans when he had kept them bottled up inside himself alone. But sharing them with her had caused him to step back and check himself. Did his plan really make sense, or was he merely being driven by pain into some dark and twisted death wish?

He hadn't cared about the answer before, but now it seemed to matter.

The other day, he had deliberately not told Emily his scheme concerning the flammable gas leak inside the Promethean temple. He knew she would too quickly grasp that his chances of surviving the fireball were very slim, indeed. He didn't want her to worry.

But as much as he hated to question himself, he'd begun to wonder. Was his notion really for the best?

He did not doubt that it would work. He had only begun to wonder if he was thinking like a lunatic. Could it be that if everything he'd been through had him galloping headlong into self-destruction merely to escape facing up to it? Had he survived all that merely to throw his life away?

Maybe it didn't have to be that way.

Maybe his dearest, sweetest, most trusted friend could somehow give him a reason to go on.

As he strode across the terrace and down through the gardens, eager to join her in the field, he could not take his eyes off her—the warm beauty drenched in sunshine with an armful of flowers, the ribbons on her playful straw hat billowing on the breeze.

One thing was certain. Any hope that he had left in life centered around her. Their difference in rank no longer mattered a whit, if it ever had. He had the sense his life depended on her though of course he would never admit to it. But privately, he had noticed the change within himself ever since he had taken her into his confidence.

Prior to their talk, he had been filled with nothing but darkness and hate, rage and bitterness eating him up from within; but ever since he had let her in, her gentle words of hope and promises of healing echoed in his soul.

He had found himself oddly distracted since then, repeating her words over and over in his mind, until the one small ray of light left in him began to gather strength. Maybe she was right.

Maybe he could be saved. Maybe, somehow, he could be whole again . . . but that was a question for another day. First they somehow had to survive this deadly Promethean chess game. And that was chiefly up to him.

He'd kill all of them to protect her. But he put violence out of his mind when he reached the garden gate, his spirits lifting as he went through it, closing it behind him.

He began walking toward her.

Though she was still essentially a prisoner, he was glad at least to see her out in the fresh air where she belonged. He had spoken to James after his talk with Emily the other day, as promised, telling the old man it was not in her nature to remain indoors around the clock, especially when the weather was so fine.

James had warily agreed that she could spend an hour or two outside each day, as long as she did not wander away from her guards. For reasons of his own, the old man had also given Drake permission to visit her every day if he wished, for up to half an hour.

Of course, he was not allowed to touch her in any improper fashion, and the two of them would have to be at least informally chaperoned by her guards. They wanted their virgin sacrifice intact for the night of the eclipse. *Revolting.* Still, it was better than nothing, and the truth of the matter was, they would never get their hands on her. *Over my dead body.*

Just then, Emily glanced over and saw him coming. She straightened up at once, her load of flowers in one arm; she sent him a cheerful wave with the other.

He couldn't help but smile.

"Buon giorno, il mio amico!" she greeted him, much to the amusement of her current guards on duty, a pair of swarthy Sicilians from the cardinal's retinue.

"You're learning Italian now?" he replied indulgently as he walked over to her through the tall, breezy grasses.

"Sì, non è così difficile," she answered with a shrug.

He chuckled. "Now you're just showing off."

"No, if I really wanted to impress you, I'd demonstrate some of the curse words all my charming foreign bodyguards have been teaching me to help to pass the time."

"They're teaching you to curse?"

"Oh, yes. I now have at least two or three choice epithets in Italian, German, Spanish, French, and Russian."

"Charming."

"I know! Your mother would be so impressed." She threw a daisy at him.

He caught it and just stood there smiling like an idiot. Then she pointed at him and uttered a word at his expense to the Italians, who burst out laughing.

"Sì, bella!"

Drake rested his hands on his waist, attempting to scowl, but in truth, not even close to being annoyed by her cheeky taunts. He was the one who had told her to charm her guards. It appeared she had already checked that item off her list of things to do.

Having favored the Italians with a sunny grin, she turned back to Drake. "So," she said pertly. "There you are."

"Here I am." He pulled a petal off the daisy and threw it at her. "I thought I'd come and look in on you. I see you're enjoying the sunshine."

"Oh, yes, quite! Look at my bouquet!" With the guards so near, she was playing her role as the blithe girl, unaware of the danger, just as they had discussed.

But Drake saw the deeper shadows in the violet of her eyes and knew she was still afraid of what the future held.

"They're going to look so pretty in my room," she chattered on. "As I was just telling Giancarlo, I haven't seen any red Alpine flowers out here at all. Yellow, pink, white, blue, even orange. Loads of purple. But no red. Isn't that curious?"

"Hmm," said Drake. "I suppose it is."

The Italian shook his head, dismissing her girlish prattle with a knowing shrug and a worldly smile.

Drake returned it. "Give us a few minutes, would you?"

His colleague nodded warily, glancing toward the shade. "I'll be just over there. You know the rules, *Capitano*. Don't lose track of the time."

He gritted his teeth slightly at the reminder, did not reply. Instead, he turned and followed Emily, who had strolled on across the meadow. A few feet ahead, she bent gracefully, picking another colorful bloom and adding it to the bunch.

"How are you?" he murmured urgently to her once they were out of earshot of the guards.

"Very glad to be free of my chamber at last, I can tell you. Whatever you said to make them let me out, I cannot thank you enough. You've saved my sanity. How are you?" she countered. "You look terrible. Aren't you sleeping?"

He shrugged; lack of sleep was the least of his worries. "More of the Prometheans have been arriving. James is keeping me hopping to make sure everything runs smoothly. What about you? I see you've been making good progress on what we discussed."

"More than you know."

"What do you mean?"

She gave him a mysterious sideways smile. "Never you mind, love. Just help me pick some flowers."

He eyed her warily, noting the canny tone beneath her idle words. "You're up to something."

"Who, me?" She picked another blossom, inhaled its scent, then held it up to inspect its delicate structure. "Beautiful, aren't they? Some of these mountain flowers are quite new to me, but many of them are familiar to English meadows. It's like seeing my old friends. . . . Mountain laurel. This tall, handsome one is the Blue Thistle. This little white one, the Silverstar—the locals call it edelweiss. Isn't it charming? This yellow one is the Alpine auricula. We've got their cousins back in England. So, how many Prometheans would you say will be here at the castle once their number is complete?" she murmured in an idle tone.

He shrugged. Of course he'd seen the list. "About two hundred, including their bodyguards and entourage. "Why do you ask?"

"Hmm." She ignored the question, continuing her commentary on the flowers as she plucked another bloom. "This bold orange one is the *Arnica montana*. Makes a good poultice for cuts and bruises. Maybe I should gather extra," she added, shooting him a wry look askance.

He smiled at her, but now she had his full attention. She was definitely up to something . . .

"We've got a variety of marguerites. Here's Meadowrue." She gathered an airy mauve flower with a cloudlike plume. "And do you know what this stately, bluish purple spike is called?"

"No idea," he said, amused, as she picked it and added it to the bunch. "But it is the same color as your eyes."

"Is it?" She turned to him with a faint, mysterious smile, pausing. "It's known as monkshood. *Aconitum napellus.* The wicked cousin of the lowly buttercup." She turned away and walked on.

"Wicked?" Drake followed, furrowing his brow. "What do you mean?"

She glanced back to make sure her guards kept their distance. "If ingested, the poison of the monkshood is strong enough to stop a man's heart within minutes. Fifty stalks like this should easily be enough to kill two hundred men."

Drake's stare homed in on her in astonishment. "Should you be touching that?" he blurted out automatically.

"It's all right. It has to be taken internally. I don't want to collect too much of it at one time, though, in case they notice."

He somehow found his voice again as he followed her. "Are you sure about this?"

"Fairly. This species looks a little different than the one we have in England, but of the dozen or so subspecies known, all are highly toxic. All we have to do is figure out a way to put it into something they'll either eat or drink . . ."

Drake could not believe he was standing there with his innocent little Emily discussing mass murder.

And here he'd thought *he* was the dangerous one.

"If we run out, I've also seen some yellow wolf's bane growing around here. It's a cousin to the monkshood, just as deadly. I took a few stalks for added measure."

"And they're mixed in your bouquet?"

She nodded almost demurely, turning away. "You

always told me the best place to hide something is in plain sight."

Drake's heart pounded as he followed her, quickly picking a daisy to busy his hands. "So, what exactly do you propose? What's involved?"

"I must first reduce the plants to powder. That will make it easier to slip it into the food. By day, I'll dry the stalks out under my bed where they won't be noticed. By night, I'll hang them by the hearth fire to speed the drying process. Once they're dried, I'll crumble them into flakes and we'll find a way to slip it into something the Prometheans will consume. Either food or drink will do. It can even be cooked without diminishing the poison. That's why I wanted to know how many men you expect. I have to make sure I've got a sufficient dosage for them all."

"Does it have a taste?"

"No one's ever lived to say so. There is no antidote. There'll be no turning back."

"God, Emily. Are you sure about this?"

"I told you I could help."

"Promise me you'll be careful handling that stuff," he ordered.

"Don't worry, I'll wear gloves." She glanced down to show him she was wearing white gloves now like a dainty little lady—plotting mass death. "You look shocked."

"Because I am."

"Do you like my plan?"

"It's brilliant," he admitted. Indeed, he thought her plan was even better than his.

It had a much higher chance of success and would be easier to target. One thing was certain. The Prometheans would never see it coming, feeling themselves to be safe in the home of one of their most esteemed fellow conspirators. And yet they would be poisoned by the wildflowers growing all around them, concocted by the one person there whom they regarded as innocent and helpless.

Rather poetic justice, Drake mused.

"I hope you don't think badly of me for this," she said, her somber gaze full of adorable sincerity as she searched his eyes.

He gave her a tender half smile. "Of course I don't. Just remind me never to cross you."

She lowered her head. "I suppose it must sound rather diabolical."

"As only a woman could dream up," he agreed. "Emily."

"Yes?"

"If I let you do this, you have to know you'll never be the same. Killing one person can change a man who's trained for it, let alone two hundred, and you are just a girl. I'm not sure you can live with this. I'm not sure I can let you."

She considered his words, gazing off into the distance, then shook her head and glanced back at him with steel in her eyes. "All I care about is our future together beyond this place. I'd do anything for you, Drake, and these are the demons who hurt you so badly—I'm not even sure they deserve to be called people. Besides, it's us or them. Look at what they want to do to me! Let us take the action we must now and worry about it later. Why do you look at me like that?"

He shook his head ruefully. "Because you sound like me."

She gave him a wan smile. He saw the tension in her eyes.

"What do we do about Falkirk? Are you willing to let him die?"

Drake hesitated.

"I fear that sparing him would be too complicated," she warned. "Separating him from the others, we'd risk alerting them that something isn't right. We could try, if he means that much to you, but—"

"No. No, it's all right."

She studied him with a skeptical gaze.

Drake shook his head. "His willingness to hurt you destroyed whatever trust I might have had in him."

Her stare softened with compassion. "I'm sorry. I know you went through a lot with him. But you know he's not your friend. He got you out of the dungeon, but where was the sacrifice in that? It cost him nothing. He did it for himself. He's been using you all this time, as you well know."

"Yes." Staring at her, he knew that she was the only one here who really cared about him. Unlike James, she had risked everything to follow him there, a feat that had nearly cost her her life on more than one occasion.

As his gaze skimmed her gorgeous violet eyes and the rich temptation of her lips, he did not know how he held himself back from kissing her there and then.

But, of course, it was forbidden.

If he touched their so-called virgin sacrifice, they'd both pay for the sin with unspeakable torment.

He nodded slowly but could barely find his voice. "You're right," he managed at last. "James must die with the others. It is for the best."

"Then I'll keep gathering monkshood," she murmured in agreement. "I'll let you know the moment it's ready."

As they strolled on through the field, Drake picked another daisy and twined the stem around the one in his hand. Then he picked a third and added it, continuing with the fond thought of surprising her.

"How does the monkshood work?" he asked in a low tone. "Does it take long? Will they be able to fight?"

"No. That's why it's ideal. Their extremities will start to go numb several minutes after the poison enters the body. Some will die slower than others—depends on their size. If you leave my bow where I can quickly retrieve it, I can help you to finish off anyone who might linger long enough to cause us problems."

"How did you know about this?" he whispered as he added a fourth flower to the daisy chain he was making for her. She had not yet noticed.

"Monkshood? Oh, it's been known for ages. It's in my old apothecary books," she said casually, waving a honeybee away from her bouquet. "According to legend, the Druid shamans were the first to discover it. When their tribes went to war, they'd tip their arrows with it. Then the Romans used it for the same purpose—also, to execute criminals. Which is what we're doing here, isn't it?"

He nodded, more fascinated by her than ever.

But their time together was up.

"Capitan!"

He glanced back. The Italian guard held up his fob watch and pointed at it. Drake waved to acknowledge the summons, then he turned back to Emily. "It seems that I must leave you once again," he said with a weary sigh. "But first, take off your hat."

"Why?" she asked curiously, though she complied with his request. When she swept the wide-brimmed chip hat off, her long, light brown hair blew in the breeze.

"Because," he said with a foolish doting smile, "I made this for you." He tied off the final stem in the daisy chain and gently set it on her head, a crown. "Beautiful."

She beamed in delight, the white-and-yellow daisies starring her tresses, and it took all the discipline in Drake's warrior nature not to lean down and capture the smile on her lips with his kiss.

She was blushing, but he quite believed that the joy sparkling in her eyes was lovely enough to last him the rest of the mission.

"And with that," he said, "I bid you a fond farewell until our next tête-à-tête." He sketched a bow and turned to go, but then he felt her hand grasp his elbow.

"Wait."

He turned back to her with a questioning smile.

She searched his eyes heatedly. "I found a way out of the castle," she murmured. "Through the dungeon. There's a broken place in the wall just wide enough for someone to slip out."

He went motionless. "You're jesting."

"No. I found it the second day I was here. I'm not proposing that we escape by it," she added hastily. "We have our reasons for remaining. What I am trying to say is that—" She faltered, her blush deepening. "I can get out anytime to be with you."

He was not easy to shock. But his eyes widened slightly as her reckless words forged on.

"We both know we may never get out of here alive."

"Of course we will," he forced out.

She shook her head impatiently. "There's no need for pretty stories, not with me. You know how I feel, how I've always felt about you. What you're doing here is so valiant, so brave, it makes me love you all the more. The fact is we may never get the chance to be together in the future, and that means all we've really got is now." She swallowed hard. "I just have to slip past my guards. The watch changes at eleven."

"That's when I get off duty," he uttered, holding his

breath as he stared at her in amazement. *Is she propositioning me?*

"It shouldn't be too difficult for me to slip out. Then I could come to you."

"My room's the first place they'd look if they noticed that you were missing."

She shook her head. "I don't want to meet anywhere in the castle. This place is evil, and full of evil men."

"Where?" he whispered.

She glanced across the meadow, toward the trees, then she looked at him, squinting slightly in the sun. "In the forest. It suits us, doesn't it?"

He could barely speak. "Tonight?"

She nodded. "We've waited long enough . . . wasted too much time."

"You know it's dangerous."

"I realize that. But it's worth it, at least to me. One chance. One night with you."

Drake could hardly bear to look at her, the fierce passion warring with shy, trusting innocence in her eyes.

His heart was pounding; his whole being throbbed with the shock of her desire for him, the heady thrill of anticipation. He had wanted her for longer than he had allowed himself to acknowledge, and there she was offering herself to him, this very night?

How would he ever endure the night's watch ahead, knowing the prize that awaited him afterward?

He was already aroused, a fact that would soon be visible to her guards as well if he did not get ahold of himself. He tore his stare away from her, lowered his head, and though he was fairly panting, managed to bring his lustful response to the virginal Emily under control.

"Tonight, then," he forced out. "As soon after eleven

as we can both manage. Be careful," he added in warning, glancing at her again.

"Don't worry." She smiled serenely at him, with daisies in her hair. "I'll see you then." As she bit her lip on a shy smile, Drake nearly moaned.

He stared at her sweet mouth, already craving another taste of her. *Lord, it is going to be a long day.*

Somehow pulling himself together, he gave her a heated smile, nodded in farewell, then took leave of her. But he could feel her feminine gaze inspecting his body appreciatively as he walked away. His pulse continued pounding as he headed back to the castle, barely able to think. What man could, knowing tonight he would make love for the first time to the only woman who had ever held his heart? And it had all been her idea . . .

The rest of the day would be an agony, every dragging hour; the sun inched much too slowly toward the west. Moonrise was nothing but a dream. How he would manage to concentrate on his duties until then was beyond him. He'd waited all his life for this, and, at last, the time to claim her as his own was almost at hand. What if she changed her mind at the last moment?

But he knew she would not.

They were meant to be together, as she had always known though he had resisted. No matter. He was done fighting the truth.

Night could not come fast enough for him.

Scotland

A majestic sweep of sea and sky surrounded the hilltop cemetery where the Order's fallen warriors slumbered. Mossy stone angels and Celtic crosses battered by wind and weather marked the graves of the honored dead. They who had known only battle in life had finally found peace, and Virgil was joining them.

Standing beside the freshly dug grave, Beau couldn't help wondering how long it might be before he, too, found himself in a similar bed.

True to his word, he had escorted their beloved Highlander's body to the Order's headquarters in the wilds of Scotland. Virgil had known so many of his happiest years at the school training his boys it was no surprise that this was where he had wanted to be laid to rest.

Glancing over his shoulder, Beau had a fine view of the college compound: the central square clustered round with various buildings, a ring of green fields surrounding them, the lot enclosed by woods.

He could just hear the crack of gunfire from the shooting ranges where the lads were at target practice, and the military chants of those running drills on the training fields and scaffolding towers, being molded into the next generation of warriors. In the distance, the Abbey, with its crowning statue of St. Michael the Archangel, stood braced against the hill, like a bulwark against the evil ever churning in the world.

Three stately buildings flanked the square in front of it. Beau could have walked their corridors blindfolded, so well did he recall his own years in this place. Directly across from the Abbey was Salem Hall, the main school building, where classes were in session even now.

Beyond classical studies, languages, the sciences, and mathematics were courses ranging from navigation to battlefield medicine and the chemistry of explosives.

The other two buildings on the square were dormitories. Past these lay a scattering of smaller buildings: the teachers' residential halls, stables and storehouses, the old armory for indoor fencing practice, the guesthouse for visiting parents, the library, and, of course, the infirmary, where every boy ended up sooner or later. Nobody got through his entire education there without at least one broken bone. But one of the main lessons drilled into a lad in this place was that pain was insignificant.

In the surrounding athletic fields, many of them were working on that lesson now, battering each other at football and rugby, pugilism or other classical sports to hone skills they'd need later—footraces and sprints of various distances, wrestling, javelin throwing—all carried out under the watchful eyes of their trainers. The day was fine, but these ordeals were held in all kinds of weather.

Farther off, in the equestrian fields, the horse master had his young riders racing around jumps and assorted obstacles in agility drills.

At every turn throughout the Order's carefully planned program, the idea was to turn an ordinary boy into as perfect a warrior as he could become by the time he reached manhood, and the main lesson, always, was about surmounting fear.

Beau certainly drew on that training now. With Virgil dead, his own team missing, and Rotherstone's more experienced agents away on the quest to deal first with Niall, then with Drake, he was feeling quite alone in the task ahead. *How the hell am I supposed to fill Virgil's shoes until the Elders choose a replacement to run the London operations?*

He had a feeling they were going to choose one of the men from Rotherstone's team, probably the

Duke of Warrington, given his reputation. But at that moment, Rotherstone and company should be somewhere in the Alps.

Until they got back, he was on his own.

Turning away from Virgil's grave and heading back toward the compound and his horse, he made a mental note to check on his brother agents' wives, make sure everything was all right and that they had all they needed at the luxurious country estate, an Order safe house, where they had been secluded under the watchful eyes of the trusty Sergeant Parker and his men.

After being spirited off there with barely a moment's notice, the three fashionable ladies were probably rather annoyed to be missing out on the start of the Season.

But until the threat was cleared, they would have to remain there for their own protection, incommunicado with the outside world.

Meanwhile, back in London, this had posed a certain problem for Beau.

A problem called Miss Carissa Portland.

In leaving Town so quickly, Max's wife, Daphne, had not had time to explain to her adorable but feisty best friend where she was going.

Unfortunately for Beau, Miss Portland was one of that peculiar breed of female who needed to know everything. About everyone.

But you'd better not call her a gossip, he thought with a wry smile. She refused that title vehemently, because, she claimed, what she knew, she rarely told, except to her closest friends. She preferred to be called a *lady of information.*

Whatever she was, she amused the hell out of him.

For her part, Miss Portland never failed to greet Beau with a dubious lift of an eyebrow; he supposed her cynicism about him was wise, however, given his penchant for seduction. Perhaps she'd heard some gossip about one or more of his many dalliances.

All Beau knew was that, for him, a spy charged with keeping secrets, his attraction to the nosy little redhead was damned inconvenient.

He told himself a hundred times that she was not his type. Much too clever for a female.

Incurious women were so much easier to manage.

Carissa Portland, on the other hand, was sure to start asking questions soon. Questions Beau was not at liberty to answer. Like where the deuce her best friend had gone and why, and when she'd be coming back and why Daphne hadn't told her, herself. The mere thought of it gave him a headache. Alas, as charming as he found Carissa, Beau could not divulge the wives' location nor the reason for their sudden disappearance. She wasn't going to like it, but it wasn't *his* fault all her friends had married spies.

As an outsider, Carissa was not allowed to know the true nature of the Inferno Club, and as a *lady of information,* doubly so. It was not that they didn't trust *her.* They didn't trust anyone.

His one advantage was that the baffling chit seemed to have become allergic to him. Ever since that one enchanting waltz they had shared at a ball some weeks ago, she rushed off in the opposite direction whenever she saw him coming. He barely knew what to make of it. He was an excellent dancer and quite sure he hadn't stepped on her toes. Needless to say, it was not the reaction he normally got from the fair sex.

Given her tendency to flee him, he doubted she'd work up the nerve to confront him with her questions, but if she did, he intended to plead ignorance. Why should *he* know where Rotherstone's wife was, after all, or the other ladies in their set?

Of course, until everyone else in their circle of friends returned, that left only him and Carissa in London to make do with each other. It was a perfect chance to get to know her better . . . except that Max had already warned him of the fate he'd suffer if he fooled with Daphne's innocent companion.

Just then, Beau spotted someone coming across the green turf toward him—the tall, bony figure of an aged warrior with white hair and a long white beard.

He bowed in deep respect to the Grand Master of the Order as the venerable old relic approached. "Sir."

"I have news for you, Lord Beauchamp," the ancient knight rasped. "But I am afraid you're not going to like it."

"Sir?"

"Virgil's death has drawn the attention of the Home Office. I've been informed they wish to conduct their own formal inquiry into the matter."

Beau's eyes widened.

"As the most senior agent left in our London head-quarters at the moment, you will meet the panel and sit for their interrogations when you return to Town. It is important," he added, "that they see you as coop-erating."

He quickly masked his shock, nodding. "I understand, sir."

"Good. The sooner you answer their questions and let them have a look round and let them satisfy their curiosity within reason, the sooner it should be over. Then we can get on with our business."

Beau shook his head, mystified. "Pardon, sir, but the Home Office has never pried into our affairs before."

The Grand Master sighed. "Times are changing, Sebastian. Our ancient notions of chivalry seem quaint to these modern men of progress, and they are jealous of our power."

He nodded with reluctance though this assignment sounded rather like hell on earth. Playing nursemaid to government bureaucrats? "Very well, sir," he said grimly. "If they wish to come into Dante House to look over our shoulders, I shall be an accommodating host. Are they to be given access to the Pit?"

"You may allow one or two of their investigators in for a visit, but bring them in by the river gate to preserve the secrecy of the labyrinth."

"May I ask if there's been any specific complaint against the Order that brought this on? Anything I should know about?"

"Nothing specific, merely a general mistrust—to the best of my knowledge. If you hear otherwise, do let me know. Just be obliging and don't get the rest of us hanged," he drawled.

"Hanged, sir? We've done nothing to deserve the noose, I'm sure," Beau said with a smile.

"Do you think that matters to the politicians?" he countered wanly.

The shrewd warning in the old man's eyes sent a chill down Beau's spine.

"I reckon not," he conceded.

"Few words as possible, my boy. What is it?" he asked, noting Beau's frown.

"It's too bad Falconridge isn't here instead of somewhere in the Alps. He's got more tact and patience for this sort of bother than the rest of us put together."

"Don't worry, I have full confidence in your ability to see the matter through, Sebastian, and if Virgil were here right now, I'm sure he'd feel the same. Do what you do best," he added with a hint of roguery. "Charm 'em."

Beau flashed a rueful smile in answer. "Well, if you put it that way."

When the old man nodded his dismissal, Beau came to attention and gave him a salute.

A short while later, he rode off on his horse, leaving the Abbey to begin the long journey back to London. Nearly a week on the road would at least give him time to prepare himself for the ominous prospect that awaited him in London.

A Home Office probe? He shook his head to himself. It did not bode well.

Chapter

13

Bavaria

*T*hat night, Emily stood silently beside her chamber door as she listened for the changing of the guard.

In the moonlit room behind her, the lush bouquet of flowers she had picked that afternoon graced the table. Meanwhile, hidden away beneath the luxurious canopy bed, the blue-blossomed stalks of monkshood were drying. At the moment, however, her poisoning plot against Falkirk and his followers was the furthest thing from her mind.

All that mattered tonight was being with Drake. She was not prepared to take the chance of leaving this life without having poured out the fullness of her love upon him.

After she had given herself completely to him, then, if their quest failed, at least she could die fulfilled, knowing she was one of the lucky few in life who had tasted the sweetness of her heart's desire.

Her body already ached for him. The anguish of missing him was too sharp to endure. She wanted to be at one with him, defying all those who would seek to keep them apart.

It shouldn't be long.

The men outside her door exchanged a few low-toned words in German. She could not understand their words, but the annoyed impatience in their tone was unmistakable: The Spaniards due to relieve them at their post were late again.

Ever since Drake had told her to charm her guards a bit, she had taken note of their usual practices and had also noted the regional rivalries and prejudices they had about each other. The Germans liked the Austrians well enough but disapproved of the Spanish; they were all rather afraid of the towering blond Russians, but most despised the Italians for their cheerful air of assumed superiority. Meanwhile, the French merely rolled their eyes at the lot of them.

Emily glanced toward the mantel clock, squinting in the darkness to check the time. She could just make out the brass hands pointing to eleven o'clock on the nose.

Believing their charge—the helpless damsel—to be asleep, the German soldiers got disgusted with waiting for their more casual colleagues from the south and walked away, presumably to go and find them. Listening intently, Emily heard their footsteps begin moving away from her door. Right on schedule, their paces echoed slightly down the corridor.

Now!

Her pulse hammered in her ears, but her movements were silent as she opened her chamber door a crack.

A glance confirmed it: The way was clear.

The German guards turned the corner at the end of the hallway, where a tall pendulum clock began to strike the hour.

She slipped out without a sound and closed the door behind her. The Spaniards would be there in a heartbeat to start the third watch, which would last until dawn.

Immediately, she fled down the corridor in the opposite direction from which the men had gone. Gliding along the wall with practiced stealth, she was glad she had dressed in her forest clothes, for it was easier to move quickly in them than in some frilly gown.

Her heart pounded as she made her way through the deserted halls of the castle, keeping a leery eye out for any Prometheans or even the servants, who could not necessarily be trusted, either.

She reached a lonely corner stairwell, descending the stone-carved steps with speedy, silent footfalls, her brown cape flowing out behind her. At the bottom of the stairs, it was only a short dash down another corridor to the place where, days ago, she had found the entrance to the dungeon.

Pausing with her back to the wall until she had made sure no one was coming, she ran to the lower stairwell, whisking lightly down the other set of steps with her heart thumping.

When she reached the octagonal lower chamber, where the heavy door to the dungeon waited, she reached into her pocket and took out a candle stub that she had brought. With trembling hands, she lit it off the torch, then she carried it over to that formidable wooden door reinforced with iron. Summoning up her courage, she grasped the handle and hauled it open.

She stepped into the pitch-black darkness beyond,

held up her candle with a nervous gulp, then quickly pulled the door shut behind her. *There.* At least she had managed to make it that far without getting caught. She assured herself she would be in Drake's arms before she knew it.

Then she ventured carefully down the same dark stairs where, more than a week ago, she had followed the tabby cat. Back then, she had noticed the daylight permeating small chinks in the rock, but now the blackness of that subterranean prison engulfed her, weighing on her chest and making her feel almost as if she couldn't breathe.

The horrible place with all its eerie echoes of endless suffering reminded her afresh of all that Drake had been through; it steeled her resolve to fight this with him and for him, by any means necessary.

With that, she walked up to the break in the wall where the cat had slipped out. She lifted her candle and assessed the climb, all the while warding off the cold, instinctual terror that the hideous place inspired.

Needing both hands free, she set her candle aside, knowing she'd be unable to hold it and climb at the same time. Somewhere out there, Drake needed her, was counting on her. Her heart and body ached for him; nothing could stop her from going to him.

She grasped the cold, broken rocks in the castle's foundation, determined to get out, though it would call on all her forest-honed agility. The ultimate prize awaited out there in the woods.

Of course, just then, Drake was probably still extricating himself from his duties, giving his report to the captain of the third watch on any news from the night's patrols around the castle.

Emily took a few running steps, then vaulted up the side of the dirty dungeon wall, clamping her hands onto the break in the great foundation stones. Hanging there for a second to steady herself, she put out another heave of effort, launching herself up into the horizontal opening.

She lay there briefly, catching her breath; she was almost out. Sliding herself on her back, sideways, under the crushing menace of the stone that hung above her, she reached the exterior edge of the castle wall. Peering out, she saw it was a drop of some ten feet to the ground.

More importantly, a scan of the surroundings revealed no one nearby. It was possible there were guards posted on the wall far above her, but that was why the timing of this rendezvous was perfect. They had timed it to fall between the changing of the guards.

Without a minute to waste, she rolled her body to the edge of the great foundation stone that faced the outdoors. She lowered her body to hang by her hands, decreasing the distance for her drop.

She let go, falling to earth, and landing deftly, without so much as a stumble. Her pulse pounding, she turned around and oriented herself; as soon as she got her bearings, she began sprinting toward the woods.

This night had been so long in coming. She could barely wait to feel Drake in her arms. She could not wait to kiss him. They had both been good about their desire for each other for so long, resisting temptation since they had first become aware of each other as members of the opposite sex. They had obeyed their parents and kept their hands to themselves, no matter how badly both of them might have wanted to explore each other's bodies. But that night, there was nothing to hold them back.

As she fled across the meadow where they had met earlier under the watchful eyes of her guards, she was glad, in hindsight, that she *had* suppressed her attraction to him through all the years when he had been a young rakehell sowing his wild oats in London, earning his wicked reputation.

She had watched him, or rather, heard about how he was always discarding the women whose favors he had enjoyed too easily. One after another, he left them in the dust. But she had been too shrewd ever to let herself become one of them. And so she had remained in his life. In his confidence. She had maintained his respect and her own by resisting that unbearable temptation—at least, until they had been forced to share his room here at Waldfort Castle.

Then the truth had become too hard to hide, and Drake too hard to resist. That night on the balcony, the pleasures they had tasted had awakened needs in her she never knew existed. As she dashed toward the woods, her knees felt weak and shaky. A quiver of want fluttered low in her belly at the prospect of how it would be. Then she gained the cover of the woods, full of whispering, windy motion, but serene, a place of enchantment, all the branches silvered by moonlight.

Her chest heaving from her sprint to freedom and from a burgeoning sense of aliveness, she turned back and scanned the landscape to see if he was coming yet.

All the while, the pure joy of knowing he cared for her, too, sang in her heart; her very blood burned with her need for the man she had loved all her life.

That night, she would give herself to him completely.

They had waited long enough.

Though he could barely concentrate with his mind all caught up in Emily, Drake somehow finished giving his instructions to the French mercenary in charge of the third watch.

Then he nodded, taking leave of the men, but still he permitted no reaction to register on his face. His expression remained as cold and stern as ever.

His thoughts were anything but.

What they'd planned was madness under the circumstances, but her offer had been beyond his power to refuse. Deep down, he supposed he had always known he was hers for the taking. Perhaps she had finally figured that out herself.

Marching back into the castle, he crossed the Hall of Arms by his usual route, as though heading up to his room. But once he was out of sight of the other guards, he departed from his customary course, slipping down a small, dark corridor to the right and leaving the building again by a service door.

He stole out into the night, moving covertly through the castle grounds toward the woods beyond the meadow that she had indicated earlier. Glancing this way and that, he kept a watchful eye out for his fellow guards, ducking out of view when a pair of them sauntered by, high up on the narrow stone balcony that girded the nearest tower.

The pair stopped to scan the moonlit landscape from their high perch before moving on. Drake waited until they were gone, then he pressed on. Slipping silently out of an iron gate, he kept to the shadows until he reached the perimeter of the meadow where he had visited Emily earlier and found her gathering monkshood.

He was still astonished by her stroke of genius, coming up with that frankly sinister plan, but why was he surprised? Lately, he'd had no success at all predicting what she might do next. There were depths and layers to the grown-up Emily that he never could have guessed when she had been his childhood playmate.

He kept to the cover of the tree line as he rounded the field, entering the woods as soon as he came to a dirt path on the far end of the meadow. It led into the forest from between a neat break in the trees.

Drake ventured in, keeping his hand on his weapon in case of trouble as he scanned the darkness for Emily.

Suddenly, she stepped into view farther down the path and beckoned to him. He picked up his pace as he strode toward her, a surge of warmth flooding through his body in response to her.

When he joined her, she greeted him with a hug, throwing her arms around his neck. He wrapped his own around her waist. She felt wonderful in his arms though he suppressed a groan of want at the supple heat of her body against his.

"Did anyone see you?" he whispered as he held her.

"No. Did you have any trouble getting away?"

"No, but if I had, seeing you would be worth it." He captured her beaming face between his hands and bent his head to press a quick kiss to her lips. "Come on, let's get farther away from the castle."

With a nod, she slipped her hand in his and let him lead her down the path.

Slivers of moonlight penetrated the boughs, caressing her delicate face, as he longed to do. The darkness deepened as they walked hand in hand through the windy woods. The more they put distance between themselves and the castle, the better Drake could appreciate her wisdom in suggesting they meet out here. There was more to it than the practical need to avoid being discovered. Away from the enemy's foulness, the battle smoke of his secret mission cleared until he was able once more to glimpse the bright new vision of a future she had planted in his mind. Out here, it was easier to hope that one day it could be real.

All he knew was that the feel of her small, dainty hand in his meant more to him in this moment than all his years of loyal service to the Order.

At last, they came to what he instantly recognized as a fine spot for a seduction: an agreeable scattering of large rocks amid the trees, at a distance from the castle that he deemed safe enough. They were nowhere near the guards' posts and should be well out of earshot, even if they made some noise . . .

Emily glanced at him in question because he had stopped. He smiled ruefully at her, then nodded toward a large, flat boulder. "Want to sit down?"

She shrugged at him, wide-eyed.

He turned to her, his expression softening. She was obviously nervous about what they had come out here to do; with a somber stare, she watched his every move.

He took both of her hands in his own. "You trust me, don't you?"

"Completely."

"And I trust you. Don't be afraid," he whispered. "You don't have to do anything you don't want to do with me. You know that, right?"

"I know," she forced out, a fierce blush in her cheeks, while her voice trembled. "I've wanted this for a long time."

"So have I," he murmured hoarsely, then he rested his hands tenderly on her shoulders and bent to press another kiss of gentle reassurance to her lips.

A small moan escaped him as she parted his lips with the tip of her tongue and tasted of him freely, while her hand alighted on his chest, caressing him with innocent but barely restrained passion. *God, this girl.* Delight in her dissolved the darkness in his soul. He thrilled to her touch as her fingers tightened, clutching the lapel of his coat.

She paused, breaking their kiss, her chest heaving; Drake stared at her, wretched with desire, as her lashes swept upward. She gazed into his eyes in dreamy hunger.

"We might as well hurry," she murmured. "We might not have much time."

He flinched with pleasure as she backed out of his arms gracefully, unfastening her woolen cloak as she sauntered toward the rock. He could not take his eyes off her as she spread it over the stone like a coverlet and sat, waiting for him, leaning back to brace herself on her hands.

She cast him a roguish smile, the nymph. "So, what are you waiting for?"

He shook himself out of the trance. "Sorry," he forced out. "It's just you're the most beautiful thing I've ever seen."

"Why, thank you." She held out her hand to him.

He walked toward her, marveling, as though he were the virgin. No one in London would have believed that a former rakehell of his stature could have been rendered speechless by a milky-skinned beauty offering herself to him, heedless of the consequences.

But he was done resisting temptation. He went and sat down beside her, laying his hand on her knee for a moment, caressing her, holding himself back.

Staring hungrily into her eyes, he soon pulled her into his arms, then claimed her waiting mouth with hard, unbridled kisses. She returned them each with a soft moan, curling one hand sensuously behind his nape. The other hand skimmed down his chest once more. Then her dainty fingers began plucking at his neckcloth, loosening it. Unfastening the buttons of his shirt.

Her hand slipped inside his shirt; he groaned as

her trembling fingertips found and began to stroke his bare skin. Surely she could feel the thunder of his heart beating beneath that gentle touch he had so long craved. The need to be inside her stormed through him.

"Ah, Emily," he purred, when she finally released him. His voice sounded drunk in his own ears. "You could lead a saint astray."

"Fortunately, you're no saint," she whispered. Leaning back, she held his stare as she began unbuttoning her shirt. "Far from it."

He chuckled.

Then he watched her with a dark smile as she slipped her shirt over her head. " I could say the same for you."

"Which only goes to show how perfect we are for each other."

"It would seem so," he breathed, as she bared her breasts. His eyes glazed over with unbridled want at sight of her offering. With her lithe, athletic figure, her breasts were not large, but they were perfect in shape, each a perfect mouthful. Her pink nipples, swollen in the hint of the balmy night's breeze, teased him into a state of total, throbbing hardness. Her skin was white silk, her shoulders, alabaster elegance.

Even her stomach was beautiful, soft and slim, velvety-smooth. He reached out and caressed it by her navel, longing to make it round and heavy with his child.

Don't do it, his conscience begged him. *You're going to die before this is over and she's going to be left alone, ruined.*

But God forgive him, he could not hold back. He needed it too much.

He reached across her waiting body, planting his left hand by her hip, then he leaned down and accepted all that she wanted to give.

She closed her eyes and sighed with pleasure under his caresses. "Your hands are so warm. It's lovely."

His member swelled; his heart pounded. Then he paid homage to her breasts. She arched her back to thrust the hardened tip of her nipple more deeply into his mouth.

He sucked and fondled, shifting position, laying her back on the rock. It was easier that way to unfasten the rest of her clothes, especially the silly brown trousers that she actually thought made her look like a boy. Anyone who could look at her and mistake this luscious creature for a lad did not deserve, in his opinion, to be called a man. She was all girl, woman, wood nymph, princess . . .

Then he had unbuttoned the placket at the waist of her little trousers and slipped his hand inside to stroke her womanly flesh, his fingers lustfully clutching one slender, feminine hip. But then, his heart pounding with unbearable excitement, he trailed his fingertips toward the center of her body. The first damp touch of her dewy core, so eager for him, inspired him afresh with the blinding need to strip himself. He quickly began unbuttoning his waistcoat.

Emily curled upward to dote on him while he took off his coat. He paused to offer it to her as a blanket. She let it fall across her thigh, more interested in kissing his neck.

He all but forgot what he was doing, savoring the softness of her lips, so sweet and safe against his jugular. He gradually remembered what he was about and pulled his waistcoat off his shoulders.

She helped.

"I can't believe we're doing this," she whispered as she nibbled his earlobe.

Registering a moment's agonizing doubt, he went

motionless. Was this a warning that she was considering backing out?

But then he saw his worry was for naught. She reached down, uninvited, and squeezed his cock.

He nearly laughed in sheer happiness, relief. Thankfully, she didn't notice, preoccupied with exploring the instrument that would soon pleasure her.

"You're going to have to show me what to do," she panted.

"Don't you worry, sweet, I certainly will," he assured her in a husky murmur.

She pulled back a small space to smile mischievously at him. "Are you sure you haven't forgotten how?"

"If so, I'm sure I can figure it out."

She giggled.

She was just too adorable, he thought as he captured her face between his hands and kissed her for all he was worth. But he still had to take off his shirt. He wanted to feel her breasts against his bare chest.

He ended the kiss and got on with it, lifting his shirt off over his head. A slight breeze blew, but arousal had him much too hot to feel the coolness in the air.

Emily leaned closer, pressing her warm lips to his chest. He closed his eyes and let her do as she liked. He did not even flinch this time when she touched the ugly brand that she finally knew was not evidence of a betrayal on his part but a sign of just how far he was willing to go for the cause and the country that he loved, even to sacrifice his own body, his life. God knew he had already given up his sanity.

His heart, on the other hand, had always belonged to her.

She caressed his shoulders and his arms, while her lips lingered with silent sorrow at the place where they had seared their symbol into his flesh. The reminder of all that pain threatened to overwhelm him.

He captured her chin with his fingertips and lifted her face so he could consume her mouth again. He poured all his determination to forget what had happened to him into that kiss. The dark world spun around them.

Perhaps she felt it with him, or somehow carried a part of it for him, for he soon felt the tear that spilled from her eyes; it dripped hot and wet on his hand as he cupped her precious face in his palm. Already aware of the encroaching darkness, though he sought to focus only on her beauty, his heart, too, despaired.

Maybe there was no hope for them beyond this place, but at least they had this moment. If it all went wrong, no one could ever take this night away from them.

"I love you," she whispered.

The emotion was too tangled and too great. He couldn't even speak. His throat burned with the tears he was too well trained to shed. Instead, he shut his eyes and kissed her all the more rapturously, as he had dreamed of doing since he was seventeen. She put her arms around him and met his kiss measure for measure, as if she knew that, forget her apothecary cures, this was her best medicine, the one she'd give only to him.

Their kiss was a slow, soulful joining that deepened and quickened with escalating passion. It left them both trembling with want. He knew the time had come. She wanted him, needed him as much as he needed her.

When she touched him restlessly once more through his black leather riding breeches, he licked his lips with wild anticipation but made a private vow that he would take it slow. Except for that night on the balcony with her, he had not been with a woman since his capture, and she was a virgin.

He knew he mustn't scare her. Hell, he'd be hard-pressed not to scare himself with the violence of his hunger. His want of her shook him to the core. She could have asked him for the moon, and he'd have promised it to her if only she would give him what he craved.

He would never forgive himself if his control slipped, if his need ran away with him, and he got too rough. God knew he was out of practice and, worse, aflame with lust, but he swore, whatever happened, he would make it good for her. Vaguely he recalled that, long ago, he had once been an expert. He had no memory of the details, but he was aware that there had been an indecent number of women in his past. Now their faces blurred together, and their names, why, he had rarely bothered to learn them.

Why should he? he remembered thinking. They weren't Emily, so what the hell did he care? By contrast, every memory, every nuance of their years together since childhood remained vividly imprinted on his battle-scarred mind. His parents could have said she was not good enough for him until they were blue in the face, but he knew the truth. She was meant for him, and he loved her. Only her.

That was why they could not stand her, and why they did not dare send her away. Until that night, Emily and he had played by the rules. He had never dishonored her; she had never tempted him to try. Odd as she was, adorably so, she was a girl of sterling character. Always pure, always a lifeline to him.

So many times he had begun to lose his way. But whenever he needed to be set right again over the years, when the war began to get to him, he knew he could always go home and see her, and she would be there. Maybe not his wife, not his lover, but there for him, asking nothing in return . . . as if she knew deep down that she was the secret to how he kept going.

God, he thought as he held her, the girl had saved his life in more ways than he could tell her—and now he would take her on the forest floor like an animal? She deserved so much better than this. Nevertheless, the drive to completion had taken hold of him.

He could barely think, in a fog of desire. Excitement curled unbearably in the pit of his stomach, but he took pains to hold himself in check. He'd die if he overstepped his bounds, moved too fast, and frightened her. It was imperative to make sure she was truly ready. So he crept lower, mesmerized by her white skin, pearlescent in the moonlight as he inched lower, parted her thighs, skimming his lips across the smooth tops of them . . . and between.

If he had no words, no speech, she must surely have known how much he adored her by the way his tongue touched her, the way he worshipped her with his lips and hands. The taste of her nectar transported him. The graceful undulations of her body fascinated him until she panted, *"Oh, God, Drake, please."* He moved upward over her body until he covered her, resting his elbows on the unyielding rock beside her shoulders.

He gazed sweetly into her eyes as he caressed her hair. "The first time is not without pain," he whispered.

Her only answer was to pull him closer, and her kiss, so sure and true, spoke to his wounded heart more deeply than any words could have reached him.

He grasped her hip, kissing her face as he entered her, trembling with restraint; slowly, carefully, he moved, so as not to hurt her, even as he broke her maiden barrier with as gentle a thrust as he could manage.

Gaelen Foley

She groaned softly but seemed to welcome that particular pain, wrapping herself around him. She nestled her face into the crook of his neck, her arms draped around his shoulders. Drake was in a state of tantalizing bliss, buried deep inside her.

They both were silent . . . reverently so.

His heart slammed in his chest. He could feel her pulse pounding also. He held himself in check, kissing her, barely moving, until her body began to signal her acceptance of his taking. The tension gradually eased from her limbs. As he stroked her hair and kissed her cheeks and brow and eyelids, he felt her finally relax.

Her hands alighted on his bared hips, a shy invitation to him to move again. Her tentative hold tightened when he reached between their bodies and rested the pad of his thumb ever so lightly on her core. The soft touch stoked the fire of her pleasure, and soon, whatever pain she had experienced in her deflowering was forgotten. He fought back a fierce surge of triumph to know that she was his; he watched her yielding to their passion.

"Oh, Drake, it's so beautiful. You're beautiful," she blurted out in a ragged whisper.

His heart clenched at her innocent wonder.

And then he loved her until she glowed.

It seemed impossible that joy could be born in the midst of the darkness that surrounded them, but as they gave themselves to each other completely, it leaped to life like a small flame.

One light was all it took to illuminate the darkness. Surely the love that had never left them from their earliest years could defeat the evil that had engulfed them. He hushed her with fond, chiding urgency when her cries of pleasure grew louder.

"Easy," he whispered, pausing.

"Sorry," she mumbled, then added feverishly, "Don't stop."

He obliged her, but soon, he, too, was incapable of muffling his own heady groans as he came inside her. Pleasure racked his body that had known so much pain.

The all-consuming sweetness of release painted a new layer of memories, healing ones, on the dark canvas of his soul. He had known she cared for him, of course, but it was not until this moment that her pure love had pierced the cold stone walls around his heart until he could feel it, receive it, in his very core.

He shuddered in her arms, kissing her with mad abandon. She ran her fingers through his hair and returned his kiss in a manner that told him without a need for words that she was his for the taking whenever and wherever he had need of her.

It was possibly the best moment of his life. Certainly the calmest that he had known in years.

She held him for a long time afterward in silence, until, quite out of the blue, she remarked: "This rock is digging into my back." She chuckled wearily. "I've only just now noticed."

He moved aside so she could sit up. He glanced down at himself in the moonlight and noted the slightly darker smears of her maiden blood on him. It brought the precariousness of their situation back sharply to his mind.

He picked up his discarded waistcoat and pulled his fob watch out of the small front pocket. It was just past 1:00 A.M. He was in no hurry to return.

Meanwhile, beside him, Emily let out a sigh of deep feminine satisfaction and rose with a languid movement to dress. He eyed her naked body in open admiration. She was lithe and lean, and her sensual stretch inspired thoughts of a second round already.

He knew perfectly well there was little chance his lewd notion would meet with her approval. The ex-virgin would want a little recovery time.

Still, a man could dream.

When she moved like that, he wanted her all over again. "You're very beautiful," he remarked as he hitched up his breeches and fastened them, determined to be a good boy.

Having just finished putting on her shirt, she cast him a shy, startled smile, and flipped her long tresses free of the collar. "Am I?"

"Very," he said.

"Well, thank you. You know," she said thoughtfully as she tucked her shirt into her trousers, "I'll be glad to give those Promethean bastards the monkshood."

He raised an eyebrow. "Indeed?"

"I could kill anyone who was ever cruel to you," she said coolly, a glint of ferocity in those violet eyes.

He looked at her in amusement. "You're even starting to sound like me."

"How can you stand to be here? To look at them? I don't know how you can bear it."

He shrugged, lowering his gaze. "I don't know, either. I just do."

She paused. He looked up again, sensing her gaze. She smiled tenderly at him, then walked to him where he still sat on the rock. She stepped between his sprawled thighs and captured his face between her hands, leaning down to press a warm kiss to his lips.

It chased away the pain that her questions had brought, while her long hair fell forward, veiling the two of them in their own little world. She smiled at him, gliding her thumb over his cheekbone. Then she kissed his nose and gave him a grin. "So, that's what they didn't want us doing together all those years," she mused aloud.

"I'm glad we did."

"I'm glad, too," she whispered, and kissed him again.

"Emily?" he murmured.

She pulled back a couple of inches and serenely lifted her eyebrows at him in question.

He took her hands in his. "I'm so sorry I didn't battle my parents and marry you when I should have, years ago, before all this. When I had the chance."

She smiled fondly, tilting her head.

He shrugged. "I wasn't ready for marriage . . . and I thought you'd always be there," he admitted, lowering his head. "I'm ashamed of myself for being so cavalier. I took you for granted."

"But I'm guilty, too. I hid my feelings because I was afraid if you knew how I felt, you'd stay away. Besides, I didn't want to put any added pressure on you. You had enough to worry about." She sifted her fingers through his hair. Her touch lifted his gaze until he met hers once again. "Anyway, there's no point dredging up the past."

He shook his head, refusing her tender excuses on his behalf. "I was selfish. You deserved better than that from me—and now, even worse, I've dragged you into this—"

"You didn't drag me; I came of my own free will."

He let out a sigh. "I fear I'm bad for you."

She grinned and punched him lightly in the shoulder. "Probably so, but still somehow I cannot stay away from you—my lord," she added in jaunty sarcasm.

He looked at her in dismay.

"Oh, come, if you were half the villain you believe, you wouldn't care what effect you have on me." She stepped closer, hugging him.

With him seated and her standing, her breasts were practically in his face, and that was a prospect that would have cheered up any man.

"You're not selfish or anything else you said. You are my Drake and I adore you and that's the end of it." She released him and started to turn away, but she had made him smile. He caught hold of her wrist and tugged her back, tumbling her onto his lap.

Her soft derriere pressed the top of his thigh. "So, you're blind to my faults, eh?"

"Hardly!" she snorted. "No, I see them just as clearly as you see mine. But strangely enough, I love you all the more for them."

He raised an eyebrow. "Oh, really?"

"Of course. If you weren't broody and growly and secretive, you wouldn't be my Drake. But fortunately, you know how to make me laugh—at least you used to. This covers up a multitude of sins."

He bounced her on his leg for her impertinence. "Well, as honored as I am to serve as milady's jester, we'd better get back inside before we're missed."

"Really?" she uttered plaintively. "Can't we just run away?"

"You just said you can hardly wait to poison them," he reminded her. "But if you really do want to escape, I can help you get away—"

"No! I'm not going anywhere without you. Don't be daft," she cut him off, then looked away. "You're right, we should be getting back." She rose from his lap and reached for her cloak.

"Emily."

"It's all right, Drake. I understand you've got to see this through, and I intend to help. You can't talk me out of it any more than I can you. So let's get back inside and finish this."

Drake didn't know what to say.

They walked through the woods side by side, heading back to the castle. He took her hand in his as they continued down the path, but neither spoke, both lost in their thoughts.

At the end of the path, they kept to the tree line rounding the meadow to avoid being spotted in the open. Before long, they were going silently through the wrought-iron gate around the gardens, stealing through the grassy walks. Nearing the building, Drake left her hiding behind a mound of boxwood and went ahead, stealthily slipping back into the castle by the same door on the ground level through which he'd left. He made sure the way was clear before beckoning her over, then he closed the door silently behind her.

When she was beside him once again, they exchanged a wordless glance, slightly tense, but resolute.

Their plan was simple. They'd take separate routes up to the third floor, where the bedrooms were located. She'd stay out of sight while he went into the upper hallway and used his authority to summon her guards away from the door of her chamber. He would distract them with some small task as an excuse; this would give her an opportunity to sneak back into her room. The Prometheans would be none the wiser. But the time had come to part ways once again.

He drew her into his arms and held her for a moment as the shadows of a distant torch danced across the stone walls of the corridor.

"Thank you for tonight," he murmured at length, pulling back to look deep into her eyes. "Thank you for all you've done for me."

"You don't have to thank me," she whispered with a shrug. "I love you. I would do anything for you."

"And I you," he forced out, moved by her artless simplicity. He lowered his head and kissed her, gathering her near. It would be so hard tonight to let her go.

But he had no choice.

"Be careful going up," he whispered.

"You too." She smiled. "I'll dream of you tonight."

"You're sure you know the way?"

She nodded, stepping back from him. "I'll let you know when the monkshood's ready. Good night."

"Good night, Emily."

She smiled and turned around, heading into the darkness.

"Emily?" he called after her in a low tone.

She stopped and glanced back.

He stared at her. "You've always had my heart."

Her violet eyes lit up. She ran back to kiss him one more time, throwing her arms around him.

"Go to bed," he scolded in a warm whisper after a moment, smiling. She gave him a final, stubborn kiss on the cheek as he playfully pried her away from him.

"I wish you were coming with me."

"So do I. Someday," he said.

She gave him a skeptical smile, then blew him a little kiss as she backed away from him. Then she pivoted with her cloak billowing out behind her, and, heading for the stairwell, she stole off into the shadows alone.

Drake let out a smitten sigh when she had gone. Then he sauntered off in the other direction, taking a roundabout course to the third floor to give her time to get into place.

A few minutes later, he was in the hallway around the corner from her room. He took a deep breath, chased any sign of lovesickness off his face, leaving only his usual cold-hard-bastard expression.

Thus armored up, he stepped into view around the corner. "Guards! You men there." He beckoned to them with a stern look. "Come and give me a hand checking these corridors. I thought I heard something."

"We can't leave the door, sir."

"You bloody well can and will if I give you an order. Now get over here!" he commanded.

And so they did, following him as he sent them on a fool's errand in opposite directions.

Emily waited until the guards had stepped away. Then she slipped around the corner and dashed down the hallway, ducking into her room without a sound.

She shut the door and locked it, then leaned against it, mouthing a silent yawp of triumph.

Heavenly Lord! She had just been deflowered by Drake Parry, the Earl of Westwood. The man of her dreams—!

She floated rather than walked over to the bed and cast herself down onto it, dreamily smiling at the ceiling.

You've always had my heart, he had said.

I knew it! I just knew he loved me all this time. She hadn't dared to hope, but in her heart, she had known that it was true. She shut her eyes and let out a sigh of pure weary delight, slightly sore from her deflowering and exhausted from the nerve-racking tension of all this stealthy sneaking around.

Even so, she'd probably be awake to see the sunrise in a few hours. Who could sleep when one was madly, utterly in love?

Chapter

14

Somewhere in the Alps

blood red sunrise filtered through the trees and lit the winding road ahead. But Niall Banks was heartily sick of magnificent mountain scenery and sweeping rustic views. When all this was over, he decided, he was going to Paris for a month or more to play. He did not want to see another tree or cow pasture for a very long time. For the present, unfortunately, another day of grueling travel waited.

As reluctant as he was to subject his already aching body to another long day's rugged travel, he dared not linger. Not with an unknown number of Order agents on his trail.

Tying his bedroll onto the back of his saddle, he shrugged off vague premonitions of doom and made sure his two horses were securely tethered to each other.

The animals were as sick of the journey as he was, no doubt, but at least he was able to keep up his pace by alternating between them. He swung up into the saddle, then paused with an angry wince to rub the shoulder that James Falkirk's pet demon had dislocated for him.

The shoulder had improved, but the rigors of his journey had it aching, along with the rest of his body. Then again, perhaps he had grown too comfortable in life, he mused as he kicked his horse into a canter. Raised under princely conditions, accustomed to having an army of henchmen and servants at his command, he was not accustomed to being left to his own devices.

Perhaps this experience was good for him. After all, he was destined to become the future leader of the Prometheans, as Malcolm Banks's son. The post was virtually guaranteed to be *his.* There was no question in Niall's mind that he was entitled to it. His father had been grooming him for it for years.

My father . . . Is he really?

As he gritted his teeth against the annoying clamor of morning birdsong, his mind strayed back to the same gnawing question that had haunted him ever since he had first come face-to-face with Virgil Banks— supposedly, his uncle—or so he had been told. So he had grown up believing.

But Niall found he no longer knew what to think.

It was an intensely uncomfortable realization, facing the fact that Malcolm might not really be his father. Might have been lying to him all his life. He had placed the utmost trust in Malcolm's authority, protection, and power. More than that, he had considered his father to be his closest friend. What did it mean if their entire bond was based on lies? Who, then, was he supposed to trust?

He wanted reassurance that Virgil had been lying,

but he found that he was afraid to question his father on the subject. He did not want to rouse Malcolm's wrath by asking for the truth even though he had a right to know.

Ah, but what did it matter now? He'd made his choice. Virgil was dead, by *his* hands.

He tried to tell himself that the towering red-haired Order agent's claim that they were father and son had been a lie aimed at trying to confuse him. The Order had probably hoped that if they could turn him, they could use him as an informant.

Unfortunately, there was no denying the evidence in the mirror. He looked a hell of a lot more like his late uncle Virgil than he resembled Malcolm Banks. But how could it possibly be true? How could Malcolm lie to him like this?

If Niall was a real Promethean, would he even care?

What if he was supposed to have been with the Order all this time?

Niall was bewildered. Resentment such as he had never known was churning in his soul against the smaller, blond, spiky-haired man he had always believed was his sire. Just if, hypothetically, it was true, then what the hell had happened?

How had he ended up in the wrong home? *On the wrong side?* If Virgil was his father, then why had Malcolm raised him as his son?

The answer to that one came readily enough. *To hurt Virgil.*

Whatever their relation, the Malcolm Banks he knew was fully capable of that. When he hated someone, he could be very creative in how to torture them in mind and soul if he could not get to them in body.

Well, then, what about my mother? Niall wondered, as the horses clip-clopped on, up the dusty road.

He didn't even remember her. She had died when he was two years old. He'd been told it was a fever, but he had never quite believed it. If she had been caught somehow between the two warrior brothers, between the two sides, there was no telling what her real fate might have been.

With so many questions swirling in his mind, Niall knew he'd have the chance to ask them soon. He had sent the message to Malcolm to meet him at Waldfort Castle with his men. He would be there before long. But what was the point in asking, especially if he wanted to keep his ambitions about succeeding Malcolm as the head of the Council? At the moment, he did not even trust the man to give him an honest answer. The only one who had seemed to be telling the truth, painfully forcing out his gruff confession . . . was Virgil.

Niall saw that if he had not killed him, he might have had the truth at last. But it was too late now.

He had murdered the man, aye, with his own hands, and like so much in life, he thought with an uneasy glance over his shoulder, sensing the forces of vengeance behind him, it could not be undone.

Bavaria

That morning, Emily put on the light blue muslin gown her gracious hosts had given her to wear, buttoning the three-quarter sleeves, straightening the neck, smoothing the skirts, and staring into the mirror with the grim resolve of one dressing for battle.

After giving her virginity to Drake, there was no turning back. They had become one. She knew it as surely as she breathed, and as surely as she saw that the Prometheans had to be stopped.

The fight was part of Drake's family heritage from the time of the Crusades, and through him, it had come to her. She had never truly hated anyone before, but now she relished the thought of making them pay for what they had done to him. In short, having made herself his woman, she was fully committed to him, and to their sinister plan, as it was the only way to secure their future together.

To that end, she lifted her chin, took a deep breath, and squared her shoulders, then she turned on her heel, left her chamber, went in search of opportunities for how, precisely, to poison them.

The monkshood would be ready soon. She needed to find the right sort of food in which to put it. Something that the leaders and their bodyguards would eat, but the servants wouldn't touch . . .

They all stopped talking when she appeared in the doorway of the elegant breakfast room.

Ever since she had been transferred to the luxurious bedchamber and treated as an honored guest, she had been invited from time to time to join them for their meals.

She had never dared accept their invitation before, much too terrified to sit down among a roomful of high-ranking demons who intended to kill her.

They looked at her in surprise, and to her astonishment, a few of the rich and powerful men rose and bowed to her.

Quite the high treatment for the woodsman's daughter, she thought, her heart pounding at her own, ruthless intent. To them, of course, she was an object of veneration for the moment, their sacrificial lamb. They studied her in morbid fascination as she smiled politely.

Then she ventured over to peruse the lavish offerings on the sideboard. After accepting a warmed plate from the footman, she quickly scanned the selection for items of food or drink into which she might easily slip the poison when the time came. Her previous status as a servant had given her access to the kitchens.

Perhaps she could stir it into the waffle batter or grind it into the sausage mix. They'd never notice it amid the grains of coarse black pepper.

She jumped when James Falkirk suddenly appeared by her elbow. "Well, this all looks delicious, doesn't it?"

"Indeed," she forced out, recovering quickly. At once, she veiled her murderous musings behind a demure smile like those she had often seen on the highbred belles that Lady Westwood used to approve of for her son. "Good morning, sir."

"Good morning, Miss Harper. I hope you've been enjoying your new room."

"To be sure, sir, it's fit for a princess."

"Jam?"

"Please." The dark color of the strawberry preserves would hide the monkshood well, she mused, as he passed the little, crystal serving dish to her.

Unfortunately, not all the men had partaken of it.

Falkirk watched her put a glob of jam on her toast with a speculative smile, his pewter gray eyes assessing her. "There's something different about you," he said.

"Really?" She turned to him as if she had nothing to hide, but her heart was pounding.

He studied her. "I don't know. I can't quite put my finger on it."

She glanced down at the pretty muslin gown they had given her to wear. "I'm not used to dressing in such finery," she confessed. "And I think the sun has lightened my hair as well. We are so much nearer its rays on this mountaintop."

"Hmm, yes. Perhaps that's it," he said, sounding un-convinced.

She gave him a guileless smile, but the old man was far too perceptive. He eyed her skeptically as she turned away and added a sausage to her break-fast plate. In truth, she had just lost her appetite in her sudden dread that he could somehow see into her mind. Sense the murderous scheme she had planned. Or tell somehow that she was no longer a virgin.

Nonsense! That was just his way, she told herself. It was the same eerie mannerism that he had used to ma-nipulate Drake.

Still, her fears whispered that she was about to be exposed. Perhaps the Prometheans had found out somehow what she and Drake had been doing out in the woods. If it came down to it, she knew she did not have the skill to fool a master liar like James Falkirk.

She went and sat down in a chair by the window, keeping to herself as she attempted to take a few bites of the food. But the presence of so much evil in the room made her rather queasy. Her mouth was so dry with fear that she could barely swallow.

As quickly as she could manage it without drawing further attention to herself, she put her plate aside and fled the breakfast room.

"Have a pleasant day, Miss Harper," Falkirk called after her.

"Thank you, sir—you do the same," she blurted out, glancing back.

He narrowed his eyes and searched hers with an un-nerving stare. Her heart leaped into her throat when she saw the suspicion on his face. Moreover, she real-ized in that moment why he unsettled her so. When you looked deeply enough into his eyes, she thought, you did not see a soul inside. He was as empty as dead,

dry bones. Which explained his fascination with prey-
ing on others who were yet full of life, like Drake and
her.

Emily lowered her gaze, sketched a curtsy, and hurried away, but truly, she could kill him for what he had
done to Drake. Warping his mind, making him believe
that he was safe in order to use him, making a mockery
of compassion. The old man deserved to burn in Hell.
And soon he would. So would they all. Her certainty
on that point helped to calm her down after Falkirk's
stare had rattled her.

Unfortunately, her reassurance was short-lived, for
when she stepped into the upper hallway to return to
her chamber, she stopped cold.

The maids were in her chamber. Cleaning her room.

The blood instantly drained from her face. Her pulse
pounded so hard in her ears she could barely hear herself think. If the monkshood was discovered, she was
doomed, and probably Drake along with her.

Somehow, she checked the wild impulse to run into
her chamber and shoo them out with a hasty smile.
Any such reaction on her part would only rouse their
suspicion.

Oh, God, how could she have failed to foresee the
staff's intrusion? But she was only the woodsman's
daughter. No one had ever cleaned her room for her
in her life!

She was not used to being treated like some sort of
princess, and besides, she had been distracted, leaving
her room a while ago as she faced the nerve-racking
prospect of going down to breakfast with the elite Promethean conspirators.

Heart pounding, she marched resolutely down the
corridor. Perhaps not all was lost. Maybe the maids
hadn't found it yet, and even if they had, these women

had become her friends since her arrival, more or less—at least casual acquaintances. Even if the monkshood were discovered, they need not immediately conclude she was hatching a secret murder plot against the owner of the castle and his cronies. Not unless she went in there behaving like she had something to hide.

Just be calm. Act normal, she ordered herself. *If they get too close to finding it, distract them.*

Right. Taking a steadying breath, she proceeded on to her chamber, somehow restraining herself to a sedate walk though she was shaking. *They probably won't find it anyway.* But the moment she stepped into the doorway, the blood drained from her face.

They already had.

The maids seemed more amused than suspicious as she tried to explain her "project" in a mix of gestures and halting German: She had hoped to dry the pretty purple wildflowers to make perfume.

They laughed at her naïveté and gave her to understand that, first of all, the proper way to dry flowers was to hang them upside down before the window. Didn't everyone know that?

She pretended embarrassment, laughing sheepishly at herself, but the older woman, Helga, wagged a finger at her, warning her not to touch this particular kind of wildflower again, for, in fact, it was *giftig!*

Poisonous.

The younger maid comically pantomimed a choking death to help drive home the older woman's point.

Emily feigned horrified shock at this news.

Trembling from head to toe, she thanked them for the warning, but was too rattled to think of any credible protest as the efficient pair began sweeping up the monkshood and throwing it away, tossing the deadly stalks into their dustbin.

Heart pounding, she could only watch helplessly, terrified that if she dared argue, they might become suspicious.

Before long, the maids had finished with her room. Still chuckling over her foolishness, they collected their rags and brooms and cleaning brushes, then rolled their cart on to the next chamber.

She thanked them in a hollow tone, then shut her door and leaned heavily on it, closing her eyes with a silent curse. That had nearly been a catastrophe.

It still might be if the droll women mentioned her silly "mistake" to anyone else on the staff. There were those in the castle who might not buy her simple tale of drying flowers quite so easily.

James Falkirk, for example. He might recognize the monkshood flower from the meadows of England and realize exactly what she had been up to. Given his peculiar role in life, he probably knew a thing or two about poisons.

To be sure, she wasn't out of the woods yet.

More to the point, the monkshood was gone. Their plan was foiled. She had already picked all the monkshood growing around the castle. *What are we going to do now?*

With knots in her stomach, she realized she had to tell Drake immediately. She hoped he would not be furious at her for allowing the poisonous plants to be discovered; but in case more trouble came of it, she had better warn him without delay. She left her chamber, her jaw clenched, anger at herself thudding in her temples.

When she found him in the lower courtyard, as before, engaged in his morning combat practice against the other guards, the sight of him helped to soothe her nerves.

It seemed strange that a man who was obviously so dangerous should have made her feel so safe. But just being there, where he could see her, made her feel protected. One look at him, and her courage was renewed.

Drake would not let anything happen to her. He had promised. Her faith in him was total, especially now that she knew he was still himself. As long as they were together, she had a strange, childlike faith that nothing could touch them.

The Prometheans might believe in their dark occult superstitions, but love gave Drake and her a magic of their own, one more powerful than all of the enemy's evil.

Then she smiled in amusement, watching as her beloved warrior stumbled, caught his balance, and spun around to slam his elbow into the jaw of the opponent coming up behind him.

Nicely done, my dear.

The match was won. Drake slapped the fellow on the shoulder as if to say no hard feelings. The guard wiped a trickle of blood off his lip, looked at it, then scowled harmlessly at Drake.

Drake shrugged and turned away with a roguish grin, and when Emily saw it, her heart soared. She hadn't seen him smile like that since before his capture, and she knew then that he was truly healing.

He glanced up just then and saw her on the balcony above. Another sort of smile immediately softened his rugged features. An intimate glow stole into his dark eyes.

He placed his hand lightly over his heart and sketched a bow to her. Delight like champagne bubbles tingled through her body at his playful gallantry, but more than that, in his knightly gesture, she recognized a flash of the old Drake she'd always known.

The rogue. The hellion. The irresistible charmer.

My God, she thought, *he's going to be all right.*

It might take time, but he was on the mend. Blinking away a sudden mist of grateful tears, she stuck to her purpose and rested her chin on her hand, thus sending him their agreed-upon signal that she needed to see him.

At once, the flicker in his dark wary eyes acknowledged his receipt of the message. But he turned away with a casual air and took a swig of water from his canteen. One of the men asked him a question in a language she didn't speak. Drake answered him in kind, but Emily took this as her cue to withdraw.

As much as she loved gazing at him, it would not do to draw too much attention to herself. She abandoned the balcony, intent on arranging herself in a place where Drake could reach her without too much trouble. To that end, she took a book out to the garden and sat in the shade.

One of her bodyguards followed, standing at a respectful distance on the other side of the terrace. She looked at him and sighed, slightly vexed. Being a prisoner, even one well treated, was so very tiresome.

Fortunately, the more everyone at the castle got used to her, the less carefully they watched her. She hoped that remained the case after the maids' discovery this morning.

Leaning back against the bench, Emily opened her book, but concentration proved impossible. The truth was, she was scared. Her restless gaze drifted off to the snowy peaks far across the valley. For now, she could only wait for Drake to come to her. Then they could figure out their next move. She just hoped he wouldn't take too long.

Drake bided his time, waiting to steal the chance to go to Emily. He wondered what she wanted. For his part, he'd been thinking of her constantly since they had parted ways the night before. Their rendez-vous in the woods had been so exquisite that he half feared it was a dream. But the blood, her maiden blood, that he had washed off his body upon returning to his room afterward had confirmed that it was real. And he had awakened with his heart lighter, happier, than he could ever remember feeling.

He savored the prospect of a few minutes in her company, but in the meanwhile, closer to hand, he had become aware of an interesting situation.

Apparently the rumor had gone round among the French mercenaries about what the rich men intended to do to the girl. To Drake's wry amusement, he had overheard Jacques and his fellow soldiers murmuring among themselves about doing something to stop this unspeakable thing from happening. Drake did not let on that he had heard them, but it was useful to know that Emily had won an inkling of sympathy from someone besides him.

A short while later, as soon as his duties permitted, he went in search of her and soon found her sitting in the garden. "Miss Harper." A fond warmth stole through him as he sat down beside her.

Her welcoming smile filled him with tender protectiveness. Just gazing at her beauty gave him nearly as much pleasure as her touch. He smiled back, scanning the tortoiseshell combs with which she had pinned up her hair in ladylike fashion.

He was not used to seeing her like that, dressed up in pretty gowns. She looked . . . why, she looked exactly like his future countess, he mused with a knowing smile. "You wanted to see me, my lady?"

She started to reach for his hand, but then glanced over furtively at her guard and stopped herself. "I'm afraid it's not good news," she murmured.

High above them, an eagle circling in the sky screeched.

"What's the matter?" Every muscle suddenly tensed. "Did someone notice you were gone last night?"

She shook her head discreetly, worry in her eyes. "The maids came this morning and found the monkshood while they were cleaning my chamber."

He froze.

"I don't think they suspect anything. I told them I was drying flowers to make perfume for my own enjoyment, a hobby. They believed me, but they warned me it was poisonous. I told them I didn't know. I do think I convinced them—they had a good laugh over it. But I had no choice, I had to let them throw it out."

He stared at her with his pulse pounding. A heartbeat behind his horror came utter fury at himself for allowing this to happen in the first place. She shouldn't even be here.

"I'm so sorry," she whispered. "Our plan is ruined, and it's all my fault."

"Don't worry," he said automatically. "It will be all right."

"How?"

He considered the question, avoiding her anxious stare as his face darkened. "Which maids?" he asked in a hard tone.

"W-why?"

He just looked at her.

"Drake, no! You can't. They're innocent women."

"If they tell anyone, you're dead. I don't care. Whatever I have to do to keep you safe."

"No," she ordered, dropping her voice to a whisper. "For heaven's sake, you can't just go around killing anyone who gets in our way!"

"Why not? I'm a Promethean, after all," he added in an acid tone.

"Drake."

"Fine, I'll bribe them, then. To leave."

"Don't you think their sudden disappearance would make the others talk? It might already be too late. If they've mentioned it to anyone . . . oh." She didn't finish the sentence, only sighed and put her head in her hands.

Reining in his rage, Drake put himself in check and tried to clear his head. Perhaps his offer to execute the women was a bit extreme. But any thought of a threat to Emily had somehow taken on a whole new meaning. "How did this happen?" he asked in a hard tone. "Why did you let them in?"

"I wasn't there. I left the room to go down to breakfast to try to figure out what food I might be able to slip the poison into." She shrugged. "So much for that."

He eyed her fiercely. "Tell me you were careful."

"I was careful—though your James makes my skin crawl." She shuddered and shook her head. "What are we going to do?"

"What, indeed?" he murmured, drumming his fingers on his leg. *This,* he thought, *is a fucking catastrophe.*

Gossip was one of the only forms of entertainment the servants had, and the comical tale of the English girl nearly poisoning herself with wildflowers would circulate quickly. It wouldn't be long before word made its way back to James, and what, then? Were he and Emily to sit passively waiting on tenterhooks for one of the German peasant women in mere good humor to put a wrong word in the right ear? The axe could fall at any time—or not.

It was intolerable.

More to the point, it suddenly wasn't worth it.

It wasn't worth her life. And maybe it wasn't worth his, either. All of a sudden, Drake was done with this mission.

The scales fell away from his eyes. Good God, he must have been mad ever to have thought of it, let alone attempted to do this thing.

"Drake?"

He turned and looked at her. "We're leaving here," he said to her. "Tonight."

Her eyes widened.

"The hell with this. To hell with all of them." His low snarl brimmed with anger. "I'm getting you out of here. You're going to have to sneak out of your room again, just like you did last night. Can you do that?"

"Well, yes, but what about the Prometheans?"

"I don't give a damn about them or any of this anymore!" he whispered. "The Order, the Prometheans—they both can go to hell! All I care about is you."

Her violet eyes were incredulous; her lips parted, but no sound came out. She stared at him in amazement.

"It's one thing to risk my life. I won't risk yours. This was a fool's errand, anyway. Their war has been going on for centuries. Who the hell am I to think I could end it single-handledly? I came here wanting to die, Emily. It seemed the only way to make the pain stop. But I don't want that anymore. You've given me hope. You and I have a chance to be happy. We've been denied so much." He took her hand regardless of her guard's wary scrutiny from the far end of the terrace. "I knew when I survived the attack that killed my team that God must have spared my life for a reason. But maybe it wasn't for this. Maybe it has to do with you."

Tears rushed into her eyes. She squeezed his hand more tightly. "I love you."

"Never stop. You are air and light and water to me," he whispered.

"What shall I do? Tell me how to help."

"Take a nap today. Get as much rest as you can. Tonight, sneak away from your room again at the changing of the guards, eleven o'clock, just like last night. I'll meet you in the same spot, and we'll set out from there. I'll leave one of the gates poorly guarded so we can more easily get out. I'll bring supplies for us, as well."

"Can you get my bow and my bag of remedies?"

He nodded. "Dress for the journey, my little tracker."

"What, not in this?" she asked, summoning up a brave smile that he knew was just for him.

He trailed an admiring glance over her. "You look sweet enough to eat in one bite," he murmured, "but we've got a long journey ahead. Before you leave your room, arrange the pillows in your bed to look like you're still there if anyone glances in on you before morning. It could buy us a little extra time, and every minute will be precious. We've got to get as far ahead of them as we can before they even realize we're gone."

"Where will we go? Back to England?"

He mulled the question. "That's what they'd expect . . . for us to speed down to Munich. From there, the fastest way out of the region is by river. The second obvious choice would be due south, to the Gulf of Venice, eluding them by sea."

"I've always wanted to see Venice," she said eagerly.

He tapped her on the nose. "I'll take you there—some other time. It's rough ground through the Dolomites, then we'd have to outrun them." He shook his head. "We'll head in the least likely direction they'd expect us to go, northeast, into Bohemia."

"How romantic," she breathed.

He glanced at her in amusement. "There's an Order safe house in Prague. They'll take us in."

"No, they won't. Have you forgotten you have the Initiate's Brand on your chest? Drake, the Order is not going to help you anymore. Word's gone out that any agent who finds you is authorized to kill you. That's why I wrote specifically to Lord Rotherstone. At least we know he is your friend. I believe he'll do all he can to save you. Maybe there's some way we could meet him on the road."

He shook his head. "I don't want to drag him and his team into this. Don't worry, I'll give myself up peacefully to the agents in Prague. They can write to Virgil; he'll vouch for me."

"You're sure you want to do this?" she asked softly, searching his eyes, as if she could not believe he would ever choose her over his duty.

He nodded. "I should have listened to you from the start. Damn it, I can't bear not to kiss you," he added in a whisper.

"Soon you'll be able to kiss me all you like," she promised. "Be careful today."

"You do the same, and I'll see you tonight." He rose, holding her smoldering gaze in heated anticipation of the freedom they'd soon share. He gave her a slight bow, then started to walk away, when another thought occurred to him.

He turned back and looked at her for a moment, this angel he had loved all his life.

"What is it?" she asked, worry flaring in her face.

He took a step toward her, keeping his voice down. "I do have one condition you must agree to if we're going to do this plan."

"What's that?" she asked, as earnest and wide-eyed as ever.

"As soon as we get out of this, you marry me," he whispered.

A pink, glowing smile spread across her face like sunrise breaking over the mountains, her violet eyes full of warm, hazy light.

"Done," she choked out ever so tenderly.

It took all his strength not to catch her up high in his arms and swing her around in a jubilant circle; but then he'd have to do something nasty, like cut her guard's throat, and that would rather spoil the day.

She stared at him in utter adoration.

He restrained himself to a sly, doting wink as a farewell, then went on about his business.

Emily took Drake's advice and rested through the day, but sleep proved impossible. Her heart was in too great a tumult, soaring on the heights of joy at his proposal and crashing to the depths of fear after the discovery of the monkshood. It was exhausting.

All she had to do was get through one last day, then they'd be leaving.

She made her preparations and was ready to go, waiting in her room, before the clock struck ten, let alone eleven.

She sat by the window, staring out anxiously at the night, arguing against the pessimistic half of her that was certain something would go wrong.

Dressed in her forest clothes, she sat by the window, taking a last, long look at the panorama of the mountain range from the castle's elevation.

Her sojourn here was surely the strangest thing that had ever happened to her. She hoped she and Drake were doing the right thing leaving without completing the mission. She supposed he had a plan, perhaps to alert the Order where the Prometheans were so that all the agents in the region could descend on them and finish them off.

She shrugged to herself. At the moment, she didn't know. He had never been the sort of man who told her everything.

The weather looked promising for their escape, she noted, scanning the landscape. It was a beautiful night, clear and fine. The silver moonlight turned the distant snowy peaks to pearl beyond the indigo forests.

Then, through the trees, down on the southward road from Munich, she noticed tiny lights some miles from the castle. She wondered what they were, but they disappeared, and she brushed off the question. Probably just a farmhouse or a roadside inn that she had never noticed before.

Whatever it was, Drake and she would be traveling in the opposite direction.

It was nearly eleven . . . almost time to go.

Silently leaving the window, she made her final preparations for fleeing Waldfort Castle. She had packed all
her belongings into her knapsack, at least those that
the Prometheans had let her keep in the room. Next,
leaning over the bed, she arranged the extra pillows
under the blanket to make it look like she was still
sleeping there, as Drake had instructed. This done, she
padded across her chamber and listened by the door.

Given the night's importance, she was not taking any
chances about the guards' leaving early. If the two Germans had been aggravated last night at the Spaniards
arriving late, she had made sure to repeat that situation by setting the tall pendulum clock in the hallway
five minutes fast. When it began to toll eleven—five
minutes early, unbeknownst to them—and the next
pair of guards still did not appear for duty, the dutiful
Germans had had enough.

Once more, thinking her asleep, they reasoned
with each other in low, angry tones. She covered her
mouth to hold back nervous laughter. They sounded
so offended at being inconvenienced yet again by their
fellow guards that they abandoned their posts, marching off to find the charming Spaniards and teach them
a lesson.

Emily listened at the door, her heart pounding. As
soon as the stern rhythm of their footfalls died away,
she opened the door a crack and peered out.

They were gone. At once, she slipped out, closed the
door silently behind her, then fled down the hallway, as
before. The castle's interior was quite black at that hour.
Feeble spheres of light at long intervals barely warded
off the gloom. She darted from one safe cover to the
next, repeating her route from the night before exactly.

In short order, she was gliding down the stone steps
into the octagonal room, lighting another candle stub

by the fire there. Then she crossed to the waiting door.

No one had ever opened the dungeon door with so light a heart, she thought, but for her it was the portal to her freedom. She walked through it boldly, and went to meet her destiny.

Drake could not put his finger on it, but something felt . . . off.

His watch ended uneventfully, and the night was calm, but he was still unable to shake the uneasiness that had dogged him for hours.

He did his best to set it aside, eager as hell to get out of there. He had everything ready to go out in the woods. Supplies. Weapons and ammunition for him, Emily's bow and arrows. Maps, as well as a few bits of incriminating evidence to give to the Order as a token of his sincerity.

And so, as much as it went against his nature to abandon a mission or desert his post, as soon as he finished handing over authority for the third watch, he did just that.

The breeze riffled through his hair as he walked ever so calmly, casually, toward the gardens. He ducked out the door with a final glance over his shoulder. Then he slipped out into the night.

As he stole across the grounds, his heart pounding, he ignored an illogical twinge of guilt over what would become of James. He scowled at the thought. There were others who'd protect him.

James might view his escape as betrayal, but Drake hoped that if the old man cared for him at all, as he claimed, he'd understand and just let him go. Let him have a chance at a real life, not this enslavement. At any rate, it was Emily who needed his protection far more than the new head of the Council.

Drake did not know if it would ever be possible to take her back to England; but wherever they ended up, even if it meant living under an assumed name somewhere, at least they'd be together, man and wife, and that was all that mattered to him. He had given so much in service to his country, and what had it got him? Nothing but pain.

Stealing through the darkness, he reached the woods where they had met last night, turned in at the dirt path, and jogged up silently to meet her.

She beckoned to him from the path ahead; her face shining, she welcomed him with an embrace. He caught up her close in his arms and gave her a hearty kiss in greeting.

"Hullo to you, too, my lord," she whispered with a breathless smile when he finally released her.

"Are you ready?" he murmured.

"More than ready." She slid her hands down his arm and threaded her fingers through his.

They stared into each other's eyes for a moment. Any hesitation in him fled. Just being with her shored up any doubt in him that this decision was correct.

Then he nodded, squeezed her shoulders fondly, and set her aside. "Wait here." He went to pick up their things, which he had hidden earlier under an old brown tarpaulin behind the rock where they had made love.

Two knapsacks stocked with food for the journey, two large canteens filled with water, and two dark-hooded cloaks that would help conceal their faces in the woods.

Emily grinned when he gave her back her favorite forest knife, along with her bow and quiver of arrows. She immediately pulled them on, hanging them over her shoulders, then buckling the knife belt around her waist.

Drake already had all his weapons on from the night's guard duty. "Now, then. I followed this path earlier today to see where it went. It'll take us to the smallest gate on the castle's outer walls. That's our way out. The small gate is meant for people on foot or on horseback, not for carriages like the front gate, with the drawbridge. The reason I'm telling you this now is because we won't be speaking a word once we get near there. Guards are posted at the gate. I'll take care of them," he murmured. "When we get close, you'll hide. I'll deal with them and get the gate open, then I'll signal for you."

She nodded, absorbing every word.

"As soon as we're through the gate, we've got to cover as much ground as we can before morning. The next watch comes on at seven o'clock. We've got to put as many miles as we can between us and the castle before then. Questions?"

He saw one in her eyes. *Are you really going to kill the guards up there? They're your men. They know you.* But she opted not to ask it, and he was grateful. She already knew the answer. They both did.

Nice, tame fellows were not chosen for the Order.

She gave him the only response he could have desired, lightly capturing his face in her hand and pulling him down to kiss her. He cooperated gladly, but though his blood heated with renewed hunger for her, there was no time for delay.

He ended the kiss and looked into her eyes with a degree of resolve more savage than she probably had any idea that he was capable of. "Let's go."

She nodded, her belief in him shining in her eyes.

He kissed her forehead, then tenderly pulled the hood of her cloak up to hide her sweet face in shadow. Laying his finger over his lips to signal her to silence, he took her hand and led her toward the gate.

$\mathcal{D}$rake was impressed with her ability to keep up with him—but then, he always had been. Emily shadowed him as he stalked up the dark path toward the gate. When the castle wall came into view ahead through the tunnel of the trees, he glanced at her to make sure she was still all right.

She gave him a somber nod; he smiled fondly.

She made his heart dance like a star.

They continued on a little farther. About fifty yards away from the gate, he halted her with a touch on her arm. Then he guided her to the side of the road and found a wide old tree for her to hide behind. Turning to her, he laid his finger over his lips again, warning her to be silent. They were in earshot of the guards; anything more than the softest whisper might be overheard.

He scanned the wall and saw the pair of sentries at their usual posts.

When he glanced at her again, he read the apprehension in her eyes. He lowered his lips to breathe in her ear the softest reassurance. "Don't worry. I just need a few minutes."

"Be careful," she mouthed the words at him.

He leaned down and kissed her, restraining the primal ferocity rising up inside him for the task ahead. She laid her hand on his chest and closed her eyes, visibly offering up a silent prayer. He didn't want her to worry. Their final separation would only be a brief one.

He was glad when she opened her eyes again and sent him off with a cheerful little salute. It made it easier to leave her there alone. In truth, walking away from her in that moment was harder than he expected. But he promised himself he'd be right back to collect her when he'd cleared the way and opened the gate for their escape.

Steely-eyed, he strode toward the wall, approaching stealthily, mentally planning his attack. He scanned the top of the wall above the gate and picked out the two men stationed in the darkness.

It was too dark to tell which two were on duty. He didn't want to have to kill them, but if it came to it, he would. He would gain access to the gatehouse as a trusted ally, then reveal his true intentions when it was too late for them to react.

As Drake walked toward the wall, he noticed that both men had come to attention, looking outward into the woods. He could hear their terse exchange in French.

"Did you see something?"

"I thought I heard something in the woods . . ."

"Who's there?" one demanded, but not in his direction.

Drake shook his head, thinking they had been confused by the sound. Just as he drew breath to call out to them to make his presence known, a curious cry suddenly tore from the man above.

The sentry fell off the wall, toppling onto the forest floor nearly at Drake's feet—an arrow in his throat. The second man above was hit in the chest while the first was still gurgling for air. Drake looked up, shocked, as an all-too-familiar sound clanked softly in the darkness: the metallic ring of a grappling hook biting into stone.

His first thought was of Rotherstone. *Bloody hell! Max?* It had to be the Order, right on schedule.

Drake pressed back into the cover of the trees, well aware that his former friends were under orders to kill him on sight. This would surely test the bonds of loyalty, especially since he had let them believe he had turned traitor so they would not try to follow him.

A sinewy masked man all in black appeared on the top of the wall. *Warrington?* Drake wondered. Immediately, the intruder stepped over the second dead guard to open the gate for his fellow agents.

Drake leaned against a tree in the darkness and scowled, wondering how many men Max might have brought along for the task. Two, three? Against a whole castle full of Prometheans?

But of course. Those were the kinds of odds the members of the Inferno Club liked.

Drake watched in rueful affection, waiting for the right moment to call out to his former colleagues without getting himself killed. But as he watched them, the smile faded from his face.

The number of riders who streamed in through the narrow gate in single file, each ducking as his horse cantered through the low opening, made him understand that this was not the Order.

Two, three, five. Ten. Twenty . . .

There was no way Max could have assembled twenty agents that quickly. The castle was under attack, and there he was, James's head of security, on his way out, deserting his post for a woman. *What the hell is going on?*

He did not know, but he stayed out of sight and prayed Emily did the same behind the great old tree where he had left her.

Near the end of the riders' column, the moonlight gleamed on the spiky, white-blond hair of a fit, middle-aged man who seemed to be their leader.

He moved to the side of the road, barking commands as they rode past him: "Remember your orders! Hunt down every member of the Council that you find here and kill him! They are traitors! Fifty gold coins for the man who brings me Falkirk's head!"

Drake stared in horror from the shadows.

Malcolm Banks.

How had he found out about the gathering? Drake was baffled, but there was no time to solve it. He had to get back to Emily.

As soon as he joined her, she clutched him.

"What's happening? Who are these men?"

"It's Malcolm Banks. James's worst enemy, and the Order's. He's Virgil's evil brother."

"Drake!" She seized his lapels when he stared after the intruders. "You cannot be thinking of going after them!"

When he glanced at her, he saw the terror in her eyes. And she saw the uncertainty in his. *Who will protect James?*

"No! Don't leave me!" she fairly wailed in answer to his hesitation—and her despair convinced him.

"I'll never leave you," he reminded her, as well as himself, covering her hands with his own to comfort her. He knew in the pit of his stomach that James would die tonight, but he had made his choice. He put the old man out of his mind and glanced toward the gate. "The distraction will make it all the easier for us to slip away unnoticed. Let's go."

"Oh, thank you," she breathed. "I thought you'd—"

"Shh, quiet. Now come on." He kissed her trembling hand and drew her warily toward the gate.

Behind them, closer to the castle and all around the walls, the sounds of battle now rang out as the castle's defenders realized they were under attack.

No doubt they were wondering where he was.

Drake struggled to ignore the pull *toward* the fight. A lifetime of training for just such events, to go toward the sound of the guns, not away from it, made his every step feel like he was slogging through deep mud. He could not bear to think of how frail James was and what Malcolm would do to him, now that he'd probably found out it was James who had been responsible for handing his son, Niall, over to the Order.

James had never really been his friend, he reminded himself, though it had felt like it. He had only been using him. And James had been willing to use Emily for the sacrifice of dearest blood, and that he could never forgive. Drake shoved the prospect of Malcolm's revenge out of his mind as the gate came into view through the trees.

He felt Emily tense as she huddled near him, for they saw that Malcolm had posted two horsemen by the gate, presumably to keep any of his intended victims from escaping.

But this was a boon. "I'll kill them, and we'll take their horses," he breathed, his lips grazing her hair, a bit of an evil glint in his eye.

He was glad of the chance for violence. He needed to get rid of some of his rage.

"I want you over there." He nodded at another large tree closer to the wall. "Get out of the line of fire and stay down."

She nodded, not daring to question him when he was in that this state; she stole away from him, slipping behind the other tree as he had commanded.

Crouching down, he pulled his rifle off his back, planted his knee in the sod, and brought the gun up to his shoulder. He assessed the targets' position; the closer one was an easier shot.

He narrowed his eyes, lining up his sights on the horseman's chest. Then he squeezed the trigger, and the man fell dead off his horse.

The other man yelled out in surprise while the horse spooked, swerving to the side with an angry whinny. The dead rider slumped and fell but dangled, his foot caught in the stirrup. The second guard had already drawn his cavalry saber and was charging in Drake's direction, drawn by the rifle's flare.

Drake's practiced hands required only thirty seconds to reload, but the powder's flash had left his vision slightly dazzled. Rather than trust his aim, he stepped out from the cloud of drifting gun smoke and came around the tree with his sword and dagger at the ready.

Despite the rider's furious kicking, the horse slowed its pace leaving the trail, minding its footing in the darker woods. Drake braced himself for the onslaught.

From the corner of his eye, he saw Emily leave her hiding place to capture the spooked horse. The dead man's foot was still caught in the stirrup, and the horse was panicked, dragging the corpse about as it tried to flee the awkward burden. Skilled as she was with animals, he knew she would have the horse under control in short order.

He turned his attention back to the rider bearing down on him. Then the horseman was upon him, using the advantage of his mount's height to swing and slash at Drake. Drake parried the blows, circling as the horse swung its hind end around. Its massive weight clumsy in the underbrush, it tossed its head, rearing up a bit when it sidled into a mound of brambles.

The rider slashed at him again. Drake blocked the ringing blow on his sword and struck back with his dagger, gashing the man's thigh. The rider bellowed and changed position, coming at him from another angle. Again he parried, absorbing the force of the blow on his blade, deflecting it with practiced skill.

Then the horse joined the battle, trying to bite him, ears flattened against its head. Drake saw those bared ivory teeth coming at him in the darkness and was just in time to swat the horse's head away, barking a rebuke.

The rider reeled his horse about, reaching for his pistol. Drake reacted automatically, smacking the horse in its barrel chest; it reared up as the man fired, throwing off the rider's aim. Drake ducked; the bullet bit into the tree trunk behind him. As soon as the horse's front hooves touched back to earth, Drake moved in and grabbed the rider, hauling him out of the saddle.

He threw the man to the ground and fell upon him viciously. They both were nearly trampled as they brawled.

Drake barely felt the blows he took to the face and the body; he was too absorbed in landing the ones he dealt out. Everything was slow and crisp and clear, his heart thudding in his ears like cannon fire. The next thing he knew, Drake was down on one knee with his knife to the Promethean's throat. Without the slightest hesitation, he dispatched him. The man's struggles ceased.

His chest heaving, he dropped the corpse forward, avoiding getting himself covered in any more blood. He rose, wove unsteadily on his feet just for a second, gained his balance, and took a deep breath. *There. I'm all right.*

He took a step back from the dead man, spared a second to check if he was hurt at all, and saw he was still in one piece. Just as he reached to capture the ill-tempered horse, he heard a high-pitched scream.

Emily? He drew his breath in and looked over.

When he saw her running up the path on foot, another Promethean rider chasing her, the already black night turned to nightmare.

"Emily!"

In the next second, he swung up onto the horse of the man he had just killed and gathered the reins, tearing out onto the path after them.

When he spotted the corpse of the Promethean guard he'd shot lying beside the path ahead, he realized she must have succeeded in calming the spooked horse and freeing the dead man's foot from the stirrup. But in chasing the animal out into the open, she must have let herself be seen.

"Don't touch her!" he bellowed at the cruelly laughing rider, who was even then bending down out of the saddle at a canter. With one arm, the large man scooped her up and threw her across his lap.

Emily screamed and fought him, and Drake urged his horse into a full-out gallop, vowing that what he had just done to those other two was nothing compared to what her captor would get.

The rider was heading back to the castle, where the blazing torches revealed a full-pitched battle under way. When the man glanced over his shoulder and saw Drake in hot pursuit, he spurred his mount on, galloping around the bend into the courtyard, where Drake normally practiced with his men.

The courtyard was a seething cauldron of violence, a shocking difference from their controlled martial exercises.

He knew that Emily must have been as furious as he was to end up there again, when escape had been so close. Then, as he prodded his horse on through the melee, trying to catch the rider who had taken Emily, his gaze fixed on her, he saw her reach under her cloak for something.

Only three or four lengths behind them, he had an excellent view of what happened when she suddenly pulled out her forest knife, whipped her arm behind her, and stabbed the brawny rider in the side.

"Bitch!" he exploded, throwing her out of the saddle; she went tumbling to the ground, but rolled clear of Drake's horse as he veered past.

"Get out of here!" he yelled at her, but the wounded rider blocked her escape, circling back with vengeance in his eyes. The man pulled out a pistol and aimed it at her while she was still getting up from the ground.

Drake charged, leaping off his horse onto the man before he could pull the trigger. They both crashed to earth, each struggling to get control of the gun.

When it went off, it was pointing at the Promethean. He quit fighting, screaming as part of his skull burst open. The bloodcurdling cry ended abruptly even as Drake jumped to his feet and scanned the courtyard for Emily.

"Capitaine!" a familiar voice cried.

He glanced over and saw Jacques embattled. *Damn it.* "Drake!"

Emily ran to him. "Get on the horse and go!" he ordered, catching the animal's reins again.

Wide-eyed, she gave him a shaky nod, and Drake dashed off to help Jacques, he barely knew why. Hell, it was one thing to steal away in the night when all was quiet, but it was beyond his power to turn his back on an ally under siege. Besides, whether he knew it or not, the French sergeant and his band of mercenaries had won Drake's respect and a measure of his trust when he had overheard their murmurs about doing something to save Emily.

While Drake ran to assist Jacques against several opponents, the ill-tempered horse on which he had told Emily to ride away started acting up again.

From the corner of his eye, he saw the bay rear up and nearly kick her in the face when she tried to mount it—a delay that only succeeded in drawing to her the attention of more of Malcolm's men.

To Drake's utter fury, more of them went after her again. While he blocked and hacked his way through one soldier after another, he saw Emily run into the castle, her cloak flowing out behind her.

Good enough, he told himself. *She'll hide.*

She was familiar with the ground floor's maze of dark corridors and stone chambers. Malcolm's men were not. Skilled in stealth as she was, he trusted she could stay out of sight until he could come to her.

Then he threw another opponent to the ground and introduced him to Saint Peter, a savage sort of ecstasy pounding in his veins.

Once Jacques and his men began to get the courtyard under control, Drake abandoned the fight, sprinting into the castle to find Emily.

He ran into the ground floor of the castle and saw more fights in progress but ignored them, looking everywhere to find her.

"Emily?" he yelled into one hallway and the next.

Where the hell is she?

At last, through the clash, he heard her answer faintly. "Drake! Upstairs!"

He followed the sound of her voice, dashing up the steps two at a time, his bloody sword in hand. But when he reached the top of the stairs, she nearly shot him with an arrow.

He threw up his free hand. "Don't, it's me!"

Her eyes were wide and stark with terror. He saw that she'd been backed into a corner. Then he glanced down at three dead men on the floor before her, all with arrows sticking out of them.

He lifted his gaze to hers again in astonishment, while the skirmish raged on in the great hall not far off.

He realized she was in shock and took a cautious step toward her. "Are you hurt?" he asked softly.

"N-no. You?"

"No."

"Drake, I killed them," she whispered.

"You had no choice," he said, reaching out his hand, but she wouldn't take it.

"This is my last arrow."

"You don't need it. I'll protect you. Come on. Let's get you out of here."

She just stared at him, paralyzed by the violence all around her, not moving from where she stood, her bow and arrow at the ready.

As Drake wondered how to calm her down, he was suddenly distracted by the bloody spectacle unfolding in the great hall.

He could see in through the wide-open doors as one of Malcolm's men hacked down Septimus Glasse as he tried to run away. Another skewered the cowering cardinal. The Russian writer was already dead on the floor.

My God, Malcolm is doing the Order's work for us.

The French marquis made a bold stand before the fireplace, until their bullets raked him.

Malcolm Banks himself went striding past the doorway into view, commanding his men. "Drag that old bastard here to me! You can have the gold—I'll cut off the traitor's head myself. Bring me Falkirk!"

"Unhand me, you cur!" He could hear James's voice, and was barely aware of moving toward it, until Emily suddenly shouted, "Don't go!"

He glanced back at her, his heart pounding.

"Please. It's my last arrow."

He walked over without a word and handed her his loaded pistol. "I'll be right back," he promised in a low, deadly tone, gazing into her eyes.

"He isn't worth it," she pleaded.

He did not try to explain. Leaving her with adequate protection, he ran to try to save the old man's life.

Entering the great hall, he flung himself heartily into the fray, ignoring the fact that he could feel the darkness taking hold of him. At last, he was free from the self-restraint of practice, free to disgorge his hatred on them. He no longer cared that Emily was watching. In that moment, he barely knew her name. For all he knew, he might still be in the dungeon in reality; this, a madman's futile dream, and she no more than a wisp of light in the all-consuming darkness. Only the savage rage inside him tasted real. Pain, death, blood, these were real.

He sent a man's head flying with a most effective strike. Time slowed; sound distorted; he blindly stabbed at anything that got in his way. His pulse booming in his ears, his hands tingling with the battle fury, he slit another enemy open and tossed him aside, deaf to the screams, only reveling that tonight at last they had given him a reason.

Slash, slice, thrust, block. He was in his own world, a terrible place that seethed with bloody fantasies of vengeance. Perhaps the Prometheans had won if they could take a knight of the Order and turn him into this, a last, sane part of him observed.

Fuck the Order, thought Drake as he twisted the knife in another man's chest. Tonight was not for them or even James.

It was for him.

The Prometheans had turned him into this by what they'd done to him, so let them pay for it.

"Drake!"

Dimly, he heard James calling. He paused in his killing and looked through swimming rage for the old man.

James was backing away from Malcolm, but when Drake spotted him, James pointed toward the distant corner.

"Go to Emily!"

He whirled around and through the open doorway saw her under attack. He drew his arm back with his dagger and hurled his knife without a second's hesitation.

It seemed to take forever as it flew across the corridor.

Those precious seconds, watching it, reopened a narrow window back to sanity and wedged it open.

Then the blade struck home in the man's back.

Emily threw him off her, ashen-faced, not injured, though her shirt was torn. From across the room, she looked into his eyes and spoke words that he heard more in his soul than with his ears.

Come back to me.

He knew she did not mean literally, to her side.

She had seen what he'd been doing. She meant, *Come back from Hell.*

But didn't she understand that Hell was where he belonged?

A garbled cry suddenly sounded from a few feet behind him. Drake whirled around to find James impaled on Malcolm's sword.

"You traitor." Virgil's brother sneered as he drove the blade in deeper.

Drake vaulted over the couch and hurled himself at Malcolm, though he already knew deep down it was too late for James. Malcolm hollered for his bodyguards as Drake seized him, but Drake had already killed most of those nearby. Others harkened to his shout from around the castle and came running, but they stopped when they saw Drake's blade at Malcolm's throat.

"Call off your men," Drake growled at his ear.

"Halt," Malcolm told them grudgingly.

They stopped.

"Put your weapons on the ground!" Drake ordered.

No one complied. He pressed the edge of his sword a bit more insistently against Malcolm's neck, nicking him just enough to draw blood.

"You heard him!"

Malcolm's black-clad men glanced around uncertainly at each other, then slowly disarmed themselves, setting their weapons on the floor and straightening up again.

Jacques arrived just then. He and his mercenaries quickly surrounded them.

"I suggest you take your hands off me if you want to live. I don't think you realize who I am," Malcolm said haughtily.

"Of I course I do." Then he lowered his voice to a whisper, so only Malcolm Banks could hear: *Tell the devil that St. Michael sends his regards."*

With that—treacherously—he cut his throat.

Malcolm's men gasped.

Drake dropped their master's body with a dark smile. Then he murmured to Jacques, "Take them outside and get rid of them. Burn the bodies."

Jacques looked at him in surprise: Malcolm's men had put down their weapons, as directed.

Drake shook his head before the Frenchman could bother asking if they ought to be spared. "Save your breath. They'd have done the same to you."

Jacques absorbed this with an uneasy look, then shrugged and nodded in trepidation, as if to say, *It's on your head, then, not mine.*

I can live with that. Drake gazed back at him serenely.

As the mercenaries marched their prisoners out, Emily came running into the great hall; she paused, visibly shocked by the litter of corpses, but she picked her way around them, taking her medicine bag off her shoulder. She ran to kneel by James.

Drake joined her. She must have decided that if the old man was worth saving in his eyes, then she would help, too, with her medicinal skills.

Fearing he had failed, that James was already dead, Drake braced himself, watching her uncertainly.

She pressed her fingertips to the old man's throat, feeling for a pulse. Then she turned to him, wide-eyed. "He's alive!"

Chapter
17

$\mathcal{E}$mily flexed her fingers, trying to stop their shaking. How was she to work on the old man with her hands trembling so? She doubted there was any number of stitches that could save Falkirk, but she had to try. She knew how much he meant to Drake, in the illogic of the human heart.

She might personally abhor the head of the Council, but she had to try to save him, or Drake would only end up suffering more torment in the future, from the guilt of having failed him.

She followed at a brisk pace as Drake carried Falkirk into the parlor and placed him gently on the divan.

He was in and out of consciousness.

She set down her medicine bag and opened it, shoving aside a thought of monkshood as she glanced at her collection of apothecary herbs. "Get him a blanket. I'll need more bandages, as well. Can you bring him whiskey or something for the pain? I can also use the liquor to clean the wound."

Drake nodded and sped to get all three.

Falkirk seemed so small and frail lying there that, as Emily glanced at him, getting out her scissors and tweezers, she could scarcely believe she had ever been afraid of him. She was not looking forward to the prospect of sewing his abdomen back together, but it had to be done.

As she attempted to lift the torn, bloodied part of his vest away with the tweezers so she could clean the wound, she suddenly noticed him staring steadily at her, his gray eyes glazed with pain.

"You never cease to surprise me, Emily Harper." His cultured baritone had gone weak and raspy.

"Pardon?" she echoed, taken off guard.

"I know you despise me," he said in a dry tone. "And yet you'd work to save my life—even though you know it is impossible."

"Well, it is true I think you're a villain. But this isn't for you. It's for Drake."

He let out a wan laugh. "Clever girl."

Emily frowned. Though clearly in pain, the old man did not seem much perturbed by his imminent death, a fact she found even more unsettling than his seeping wound.

"How long do I have?" he asked with a wince.

"I don't know for certain. You might pull through, it just depends—"

"Miss Harper, the time for lies is past. How long?" he repeated.

She shrugged in dismay. "Perhaps an hour. Maybe less."

"Then I must act swiftly. Send in Drake at once," he forced out. "I wish to speak to him alone."

She hesitated.

"Oh, bother, there are greater matters at stake than

the life of one miserable old man!" he snapped. "Go, girl! Get me Drake at once."

Far be it from her to deny a man his dying wish.

She did not know what he was about, but she could see in his eyes that his mind was made up. She rose, adjusted the pillow behind his head in spite of herself, then stepped out to summon his distraught bodyguard.

Drake had all the requested items in his arms and was on his way back to the parlor, giving instructions to his underlings on his way. His face darkened when he saw her waiting. Emily folded her arms across her chest, chilled by the memory of his ruthless capability. Mainly, however, she was furious at herself. They had been so close to escape!

If only she hadn't let herself be seen trying to catch that stupid horse. She shook her head.

Drake dismissed his men and marched over to her, bracing himself for the worst. "How is he?"

She searched his eyes before answering, praying that the terrible night would not set him back too badly. He had been doing so well. "He is dying," she admitted.

Drake flinched and looked away.

"He's asking for you." She gestured toward the room. "He wants to talk to you privately."

"Very well," he said with a nod. Then he paused. "Are you all right?"

She closed her eyes and shook her head with a sigh. "Don't ask me that."

He lowered his gaze, took a deep breath, and squared his broad shoulders. Then he went in to see James.

"Good God, don't look so gloomy," James said wryly when he walked in. "Everyone's got to die sometime. I'm old. And, frankly, I'm surprised I lasted this long.

We both know I rather had it coming for quite a long time."

Drake sat down heavily on the chair beside the divan. He shook his head. "This is all my fault," he said in a taut voice. "If I had not turned away—"

"Then Emily would be dead."

"You knew I could only save one of you." He studied him. "You gave your life for her."

"Well, as I said, I'm old. She's young . . . and probably carrying your child already."

Drake looked at him in surprise. "Am I so obvious?"

"I have eyes, boy. I'm not a fool."

Drake shook his head, still torn by his choices in the thick of the fight, playing it over in his head, trying to find the mistake. "If I had been faster—"

"Please. You have already saved my life three times. You pulled me out of the path of an Order agent's bullet back in London. The second time, you kept me from drowning when our ship sank in the North Sea."

"If it weren't for that Waterguard vessel, we'd both have frozen," Drake murmured.

"Then at the Pulteney Hotel you saved me from Niall Banks. Unpleasant fellow. If you hadn't come along when you did, he would have strangled me and taken the Alchemist's Scrolls."

"You really can't stay out of trouble, can you?" he said with a fond half smile in spite of their dire situation.

"Well, I'm afraid it's caught up to me this time." Though James smiled weakly, the bandage he held to his middle was turning red.

"I failed you."

"It does not signify. It was bound to end like this for me sooner or later. If you play with fire, and all that. No more glum talk. There is a reason I wanted to speak to you privately, while we still have time."

"Yes, sir?"

"It's about the girl . . ."

"Emily?"

"Yes. I have been watching the two of you since she arrived. To be honest, I've never seen anything like it."

"Like what?" he murmured uneasily.

"Her love for you." James searched his face. "Everyone professes to love something or someone, but they are few, those who would carry it out to the end of the line, unto death. She is not afraid to die for you."

"Nor I for her."

"But you are a warrior. You have the training. All she has is her heart." He shook his head. "We are both undone by her, in our separate ways."

Drake eyed him warily. "I don't understand."

"Ah, my boy, I have defied priests, philosophers, indeed, the laws of justice all my life for what I deluded myself into believing was the love of Mankind. Our Promethean vision . . . bringing all the earth under the rule of one benevolent power . . . no more wars. Universal brotherhood . . . it sounds so inspiring, doesn't it? And yet look at the means we use to try to achieve those ends."

He shook his head. Drake stared at him.

"And here is little Emily, with her perfect willingness to give up her own life. Asking nothing for herself. Pure, unselfish humility . . . Her innocent devotion to you is the genuine article. That is love. She has shown up all our high-minded notions for what they truly are, a sham. You must understand, in my eagerness to do good, I never intended to hurt anyone . . . but it's too late for excuses. All is folly. The truth is, I have sunk into evil."

"James—"

He shook his head, silencing him. "What I wore as

virtue was a fine cloak over a monstrosity—and now I must go and face whatever lies beyond the veil. If anything is left of the man I once was, long ago, then I must act now, with my last breath, to try to reverse the consequences of my actions."

"What are you saying?" Drake whispered.

"I was wrong. My whole life has been wrong." He groaned, looking away. "You must know I did not give a damn about you when I first had you removed from that dungeon."

Drake stiffened, but, of course, he knew.

"I have not given a damn for anyone since I let them kill my son." James shook his head with a fierce, inward stare. "He was eleven when I sent him to the altar. Dearest blood. He'd have been about your age by now. You must not let them do this to Emily."

"I never meant to," Drake informed him slowly.

James turned to him at last with an odd, weary smile. "I thought not. Yes . . . I see you clearly now, Lord Westwood. The Initiate's Brand may have marked your body, but the Order's seal is on your soul."

Drake held his stare.

"That is why it all depends on you now. You must finish this."

He looked at James in question.

"Finish what we both know you came here to do. I can help you destroy this bloody death cult once and for all. I can put you into position, but it's up to you to carry it through to the end of the line. Will you do this?"

"Yes."

The old man grasped his hand with a clawlike hold, staring feverishly at him. It was the only time Drake had ever seen his control slip. "Promise me," he rasped.

Drake's heart pounded. "I promise."

"Destroy them all," James whispered. "And then may my son be avenged."

Emily had moved among the rooms in the castle's main floor, helping the injured. The question of which side they were on at the moment seemed irrelevant. They were human beings, and there were more of them in desperate need of aid than the guards' surgeon could handle alone.

Still, as she followed the sounds of their groans, it was difficult to walk past the place where the dead men lay on the floor with her arrows sticking out of them.

She could not stand to look at them even though it was they who had attacked her, and if she had not defended herself, they would have killed her. They had laughed at her. None of them had thought she'd really shoot.

She hurried into the great hall, a place of carnage. The rug in front of the fireplace was hopelessly ruined, along with most of the upholstered furniture. Lord knew her plan to use the monkshood would have been a great deal tidier.

She picked her way around the bodies and their pools of blood to assist the surgeon with another bleeding lord of the Promethean Council.

She mused on how Lord Rotherstone and the other Order agents would have relished this sight, their enemies laid low. She wondered where he was, if he had even received her letter.

As she and the surgeon helped their patient, one of Jacques's men gain his feet—he was not too badly injured—she saw the parlor door open down the corridor.

Drake stepped out. He must have finished saying his private good-byes to Falkirk. His grim expression was hard to read from that distance, but he called all the survivors in to hear some words from James.

The dying head of the Council wished to speak to all the survivors right away.

The many Prometheans who had come to the castle from all over Europe began shuffling in to hear what he had to say. Emily drifted in surreptitiously, keeping to the outskirts of the room. She wanted to know what was going on. She hoped no one noticed her.

Meanwhile, Drake returned to Falkirk's side. She watched him, still not quite able to believe some of the things she had seen him do that night.

When all the survivors of the attack had assembled, she sensed fear in the hush that fell over them as they gathered around their stricken leader.

"Gentlemen," Falkirk began in a weak voice, "as you've heard by now, I shall be leaving this world shortly. No, it's all right," he assured those who let out sounds of protest. "The important thing is that Malcolm Banks has left it, too—thanks to Drake."

His voice quavered weakly when he spoke again. He cleared his throat.

"Unfortunately, this leaves you all without a leader.

"Losses on the Council have been heavy. Nevertheless, the light always breaks in the darkest hour. I have called you together because I believe that tonight, the moment of our destiny has arrived."

Emily looked at Drake. His hard, beautiful face was inscrutable. He looked like he was carved from stone as he stood by James's side, his arms folded across his chest. Remote, cold, intimidating. His coal black eyes were ominous, his clothes streaked with blood.

He barely looked like the same man, the same tender lover, who had caressed her so passionately the night before.

A silence had fallen over the room.

"There are many secrets hidden in the Alchemist's Scrolls, but one . . . whose time, I feel, has come. I had told the Council earlier . . ." His speech was growing more labored. "But now the time has come for me to reveal it to the rest of you, as well. I think you will agree."

"What is this secret, my lord?" one of the men near the front spoke up.

"Valerian's greatest prophecy, telling of how our ultimate victory would come . . ."

They leaned closer; Emily stared.

"The Alchemist recorded a vision of a knight who would forsake the Order of St. Michael and join our ranks. A warrior-prince who would rise to the apex of our creed and lead our armies to the victory we have so long sought.

"Gentlemen," Falkirk whispered, "I give you Drake Parry, the Earl of Westwood. You saw his performance this night. It was he who killed Malcolm. He is the one we have awaited for an age."

Emily held her breath, immobilized as her blood ran cold.

"He is one of us now. He knows the enemy's ways. Listen to me," James insisted, as their shocked whispers flew around the room. "We were defeated under Malcolm, a corrupt financier concerned only with lining his own pockets. He was bound to fail, and for myself, I am just a humble scholar, old and weak. But Drake is a warrior. He is what we need right now. Look at him! Strong, fearless. Unbreakable, though our torturers did their best. He proved his loyalty tonight with his sword, and I tell you, he is the key. Now, my brothers, I urge you with the lifeblood I have left to accept this man who has saved my life three times as your new head of the Council, and the fulfillment of Valerian's greatest dream."

Emily was horrified, but Drake appeared blackly serene.

"What say you?" Falkirk urged, scanning them.

"A-are you willing, Lord Westwood?"

Drake turned, expressionless, to stare at the man who had asked the question. "I am willing."

"Well, I'm not!" Emily cried, pushing away from the wall and shoving through the crowd so he could see her. "Are you truly mad?"

"What is she doing in here?" someone protested.

"Who let her in?" another huffed.

"You cannot do this. I will not let you!"

They ignored her.

"Mind you, this girl is no longer an acceptable sacrifice for the night of the eclipse," Falkirk told them sharply. "She killed three men tonight."

"She did?" someone muttered in shock.

"This disqualifies her as an innocent. Miss Harper, please leave."

"I will not!"

"Emily, go," Drake ordered.

She stared helplessly at him, but was forgotten again before she could decide whether she was inclined to obey.

"You must put it to a vote among yourselves. Quickly, now," Falkirk urged the others. "I have told you my will. My strength is nearly gone."

"James, is this really the counsel you would give us? To make this creature of the enemy our ruler?"

"He is no enemy! I swear by dearest blood that what Valerian recorded centuries ago has come to pass. Drake is the only one who can bring our great struggle to a victorious end, at last."

Somber glances were exchanged. Grim nods.

"Very well, then. Let the brethren vote."

"So be it."

"All in favor?"

Emily watched, shaking her head and overwhelmed at this calamity, as bloodied hands were raised, one by one, around the room.

"It is unanimous, old friend," a distinguished gentlemen near the front informed James. "Your successor has been chosen."

Drake nodded in acceptance of their lauds and raised his chin. They pledged their loyalty to him.

Falkirk eased back against the divan, tension easing from his ashen face, as though he had just accomplished some great feat.

Then the frightened, wounded men began asking Drake's instructions on a dozen matters all at once; but Emily, who had still refused to leave, could only stare at him in disbelief. She could not wrap her mind around it. This *had* to be a ruse, though she did not see how.

So much for taking him home safely.

Her beloved Drake had just been made the terrifying new leader of the Prometheans.

Chapter
18

$\mathcal{J}$ames was dead, his body burned in accordance with the creed. Malcolm's followers had also been disposed of, and the eclipse was just three nights away.

Bizarre as it was to find himself in that position, Drake knew he had to act like a proper ruler of the Prometheans. And somehow he found this alarmingly easy to do.

No sweeter revenge could have been offered up to him than to be given total power over his enemies. He loved more than he cared to admit having them bow and scrape to him. None of them dared cross him.

Those who had tortured him in mind and body now found themselves at his mercy. With a word, he could order everything done to them that had once been done to him, and worse.

He enjoyed seeing them quake when he walked into the room. They tripped over themselves to grovel to him, and the fear he read in their eyes when he spoke to any of them was highly gratifying.

After all, their fear of him was key to his security, and Emily's.

Likewise, it was only Drake's fear of what Emily would say that stopped him from using his delicious new power as he might have wanted to.

But God knew he was tempted . . .

Strange that after James had undergone a deathbed conversion to the light, his own views were trending darker.

Head of the Prometheans . . . What would his old friends in the Order think of him now?

He was well aware that he was playing a game more dangerous than any Order agent before him had ever attempted. The Promethean secrets open to him were wider and farther-reaching than any agent had ever gained access to, as well.

Sitting at a large oak desk in the study that very afternoon, he had before him a full list of the Promethean safe houses throughout Europe, the locations and suppliers of their ammunitions stores, the names of their agents embedded in foreign governments and universities, and, most importantly, the information James had been waiting for—the far-flung bank accounts where Malcolm had stashed the fortune the Prometheans had amassed through their deviltry in the stock exchange.

He was leaning on his elbow, musing on all the secrets exposed to him, when Emily came in.

He looked over. Despite everything on his mind, he was glad to see her. Unfortunately, there was no missing the uneasy look in her violet eyes. It had been there ever since the battle in the great hall. They had not really discussed the events of that night. What was he to say after what she had seen? He did not know how to account for himself.

She had known, at least intellectually, that he was trained to kill. Now she had seen it for herself, and she had killed, as well.

He had never wanted her to experience such a thing, but she had done what she had had to do. It was a curse she had brought upon herself by following him there.

As she sauntered toward him, in any case, they were doing their best to carry on with some shred of normality.

Drake was just happy there was no more sickening talk of her as the sacrifice. He was now the Promethean leader, and she was his woman, his concubine. She was safe in this position. They both were, for the moment.

But three nights from now came the ritual of the eclipse, and when they all were gathered in the mountain temple, then what?

Emily drifted over to stand beside his chair, put her arm around his shoulders, and bent to kiss him lightly on the head. He loved her smell, breathing her in as she leaned near. Her wholesome beauty pleased him. Her ivory muslin gown with a charming print of muted purple flowers hugged her lush, alluring curves. He closed his eyes, absorbing the guileless love that she poured out on him so lavishly.

James's words from their final conversation haunted him. *I have never seen anything like it, her unselfish love for you.*

Drake wondered what he could do if she ever figured out he didn't deserve it. But for the moment, she was still his, and the light caress of her lips eased the tension from his brow.

"How are you today?" she whispered. "You seem so burdened."

"Hmm," was all he could reply as she straightened up again and withdrew to lean against the window near the desk. He shrugged away the question. "How are *you*?"

She shrugged in return; he wondered if she knew the gauzy muslin of her gown turned just a little bit transparent in the sunshine streaming in.

At least it looked that way from where he sat in shadow.

"More men just arrived out in the courtyard," she informed him. "I think they are from Denmark."

"Then our number is almost complete."

" 'Our'?"

" 'Their' number is almost complete," he muttered, correcting himself.

She studied him warily.

"I wish you wouldn't look so frightened," he said, irked by the uncertainty in her eyes. "I've kept you safe thus far."

"I just can't believe we're still here. That you of all people have been chosen as the leader of the Prometheans. It is, to say the least, a bit ironic."

He couldn't argue that.

She shook her head and looked out the window, sunlight glimmering along her delicate profile. "We were so close to escaping! Just when we almost got away, the evil of this place reeled us in again, and now we're trapped. I don't think we're ever getting out of here."

"Why do you say that?"

Her shoulders lifted. "Just a gut feeling."

He gazed at her for a long moment. "At least we still have each other."

She glanced over and met his gaze. "Do we?"

"I'm right here, aren't I?" He dropped his gaze to the ledger book for the secret accounts laid out before him, the words on the tip of his tongue pushing to get out, though he barely dared admit what he was thinking . . .

Millions sterling at his disposal.

Houses around the world.

An army at his beck and call.

Influence in nearly every government on earth.

He looked up calmly from the ledger and met her gaze. "Perhaps it's not so bad."

His soft words sent an icy chill down her spine.

Indeed, if the dark stranger sitting there before her had not been her childhood companion, Emily would have been scared to death of him.

Outwardly, he looked the same, for the most part. He was dressed in the all-black clothes he usually wore, an ominous yet striking outfit, with his black hair and brooding, jet-black eyes.

He seemed larger somehow, she wasn't sure why. He couldn't have grown taller in the past few days, but perhaps he'd added muscle.

His black coat lay snug and sleek across his broad shoulders. His mother would have said he needed a haircut, she thought, her gaze following the length of glossy sable locks curling over the back of his collar. But for herself, Emily found his wilder look appealing.

If only he weren't so distant. He'd been so remote for the past two days, keeping his thoughts to himself. But she saw the new, stony hardness in his eyes, a ruthlessness he no longer bothered hiding and no longer tried to fight.

She feared that the battle in the great hall had affected him worse than he let on. He was not hurt in body, warrior that he was. But inwardly, he seemed to have ranged into a dark territory where she could not follow.

"What's wrong, for God's sake?" he murmured in annoyance. "Why are you staring at me like that?"

"I am worried about you," she confessed.

She saw that he hated the words as soon as she spoke them. He looked away with a scowl, flames of defiance flickering in his eyes. Nevertheless, she could not help herself. "Why won't you talk to me? I know that you are suffering—"

"Don't start that again! I'm fine."

"But James—"

"Is dead. So be it."

She shook her head and stared beseechingly at him. "This was not supposed to happen. We were going to get away."

"We have to play the hand we're dealt," he answered in a softer tone.

"What are we going to do?"

"Leave it to me. You do still trust me, don't you?"

"Yes, of course, but—"

"Come here, sweet." He held out his hand to her.

A thrill ran through her body as she noticed the smolder in his eyes. Reluctantly, she left her perch by the window and accepted his invitation. He pushed his chair back from the desk and drew her onto his lap.

She closed her eyes when he kissed her temple. "You smell like flowers," he breathed against her hair. "Don't be afraid. You know I'm not going to let anything happen to you, don't you, darling?" He nuzzled her cheek, cuddling her. "Everything's going to be all right."

"I'd feel better if I knew what was going on in that head of yours."

He was silent for a long moment, stroking her hair. "Do you really want to know?"

She nodded.

"Very well . . . I've been thinking . . . what if it could be turned to good somehow?"

"What do you mean?" she murmured.

"The Prometheans. They've already got the machinery in place to make an impact on the world. Perhaps in the right hands, it could be used for good . . ." His words trailed off when she turned and looked at him in cold horror.

"What?" he asked, stiffening.

"Listen to yourself," she breathed, appalled. "You don't know what you're saying."

"No, actually, I do. It's all right here in these books and papers. I can do whatever I want with it. They're prepared to follow my orders—"

She shot up off his lap and walked away.

"Where are you going?"

She stopped and turned around slowly. "I can't be a part of this. I won't. You must not contemplate this. If you do, you're on your own."

He glowered at her.

"Drake, if you have ever listened to anything that I have ever said, heed me now. Do not be tempted by this power they've placed in your hands. It will destroy you."

His lips twisted bitterly. "Tempted? Who wouldn't be? You can hardly think me a saint after the things you've seen."

"No, not a saint. But a knight of the Order. It's all you've wanted to be since you were a little boy. And now you are actually considering accepting this role? As head of the Promethean Council? Your archenemies?"

He shrugged, watching her, his chiseled face a mask of cold amusement. "A boy doesn't always grasp the way of the world, love."

She shook her head, at a loss. "Do not say such things. You must not even think them!"

"Why not?" He stood abruptly. "Open your mind! Of course I'd have to be careful. But what if I could use this power somehow to stop the sort of thing that happened to me from ever happening to anyone else again?"

"Oh, Drake."

"You can't stop me."

She swallowed hard. "I'll leave you."

"No, you won't." With a dark, devilish smile, he rounded the desk and slowly stalked toward her. "You couldn't bear to. Look at the lengths you've gone to to be with me. We both know you'll follow where I lead . . . even into darkness."

She swallowed hard, her heart pounding, but refused to admit to herself or to him that he could be right.

He came to stand before her. "We all have our price, my angel. Even you." He cupped her cheek, a storm of tender passion raging in his onyx eyes. "If I choose to rule them, you'll be by my side. You are mine, and you always have been, just as I have always been yours, no matter who has tried to keep us apart."

She quivered as he caressed her, her senses beginning to reel at his nearness. If Drake could be corrupted by the hunger to hold total power over those who had tormented him, perhaps she could be corrupted, too, by her sheer, mad love of this man.

He was her obsession. Her fatal flaw. Why else would she be here, risking her life for a madman? If he were not her greatest weakness, she would have married some country yeoman years ago rather than holding out hope that she, a commoner, could someday win the earl.

But her want of him had nothing to do with his title or even his deadly male beauty. She needed him like he was the other half of herself.

Even so, she knew that she could not allow this. If he really did accept Promethean corruption, he would be much too dangerous . . . to the Order . . . and the world.

She lifted her chin, meeting his gaze with whatever courage she had left. "I'll kill you myself before I'll let you betray yourself and all you once believed in."

"Would you now?" he purred. "I'd like to see you try." He called her bluff with a knowing half smile.

"Then I will leave you," she forced out, issuing her second warning. "You'll be left alone."

"My angel, you know I could never allow that." He tilted his head and kissed her, his hand lightly cupping the back of her head so she could not pull away.

Emily tensed, though his lips were silky-warm, all too enticing. He felt her resistance, and his mouth curved against hers in a wolfish smile.

Drake ended the kiss, but as leaned his forehead against hers, she could feel the heat in his touch and knew he wanted her. "You know what the poet said, darling. Better to reign in Hell." He stroked her cheeks with his thumbs. "You need to trust me. I'll keep us alive."

She shut her eyes, trembling. "I want to go home," she said in a small voice.

"Do you know what I want?" he breathed as his fingertips glided sensuously down the sides of her neck. He leaned closer and kissed the corner of her mouth. His lips skimmed her cheek, her brow, her eyelids. "It's you, Emily. You're all I really need."

"Drake—"

"Shh, it's all right." He lowered his head and kissed her neck. Emily's toes curled in her light kid slippers.

She hated herself for being completely unable to protest. Better to reign in Hell, indeed. Better to serve as Drake's harlot than anyone else's wife. As his warm, luxurious kiss descended to the crook of her shoulder, she knew that she had made her choice years ago. The only way she could stop loving him would be for her to die.

In spite of everything, she felt herself melting under his expert ministrations. He moved closer, drawing her to his chest. His arms wrapped around her. He enfolded her in his seduction, kissing away her fears as his deft fingers plucked the pins out of her hair, bringing it tumbling down around her shoulders. He raked his fingers through it as he nibbled on her lower lip with a soft, heady groan.

He left her swaying on her feet, enthralled, when he went to lock the door. In a haze of need, she turned absently, her chest heaving, and watched him with a glazed stare.

Twisting the key in the study door, he turned around again with flames in his eyes. He took off his black jacket and cast it aside as he came to her, lifting off his shirt.

Her hands alighted on the hot, hard wall of his chest as his lips swooped down to claim hers. The next thing she knew, she was locked in his arms, overwhelmed by the ardent incursion of his tongue in her mouth.

Her hands tingled as she clung to his broad shoulders. His bare chest heaved against her bosom, maddening her with the desire to be free of her chafing clothes. He drove her back almost roughly a few steps, kissing her all the while until her senses were inflamed. When she felt the solid oak desk behind her, she leaned her hips against it.

But he pressed her down to lie on it, licking her lips and sucking lightly on her tongue while his practiced hands untied the ribbons of her bodice, parting her gown.

His lips moved lower, down her neck to her chest as though irresistibly drawn; Emily tilted her head back as he lay atop her. A delicious tremor raced through her entire body a moment later as her nipples received the benefit of his full attention. Nothing else mattered anymore.

Doom might be irrevocably closing in on them, but in that moment, they were lovers, bent on enjoying each other to the utmost in whatever time they still had left.

Raking her fingers through the ebony silk of his hair, she thrilled to the feel of his fingertips skimming past her knee, lifting her skirts.

Flushed and panting, he tore himself away from her breasts to apply his kisses lower. Emily gasped in shocked delight as his mouth boldly claimed her throbbing center.

He was absorbed in the task of pleasuring her, and he was not a man who did anything by half measures. Her senses flew, wild and crazed, like a Congreve rocket, out of control. He left her, cruelly, writhing with his kisses and hovering on the brink of release, when he stopped and rose, his sculpted lips shining with her dew. He dried his chin with a rough pass of his forearm, staring at her like he would never get enough though he had already devoured her.

His creature entirely, she stared at him in near-mindless lust as he freed his towering erection and leaned down, planting his hands on the desk on either side of her.

She grasped his taut, muscled hips as he stood between her legs at the edge of the desk. He took her, guiding his pulsating member into her core. Her body received him with ease, still dripping with arousal from his kisses.

The fierce glide of his fevered rhythm soon put her in a trance. He drove into her with total male dominance.

She was all-yielding, all-quivering acquiescence, putty in his hands. Every heaving breath that left her lips bore a wanton echo of her wild desire for this man. His unbridled passion stoked her hunger to a state of sheer wantonness.

She arched beneath him with each silken thrust, his iron length buried deep inside her. He, too, was in the flow of rapturous instinct, having his way with her completely.

"You are too delicious," he uttered drunkenly, fondling her thighs. He lifted her heel to his shoulder to deepen his penetration and kissed her ankle in dreamy sensuality as he made love to her.

Time ceased to have any meaning. Emily was absorbed in him. She watched him flinch with pleasure and thrilled to the groans of heated ecstasy on his lips. He held her stare; she read the raw emotion in his night black eyes as he brought her to the brink of surrender. Indeed, she was in his thrall, eager for his every walloping stroke as he clutched her waist and whispered harshly in her ear for her to come. She could do nothing but obey, letting out a light, breathless scream. He growled, he grunted, slamming into her, exhausting her with the hurtling collision of his lovemaking, freed of all restraint. She bit her lip against a small whimper of pleasure-pain as the inferno of his ravishment swept over her in delicious, fevered violence.

His fingers gripped the soft flesh of her buttocks as Drake surrendered all control. He bit her shoulder hard enough to leave a lover's mark. Her heart was still pounding after his big, heavy body had gone still, leaden atop her. She could feel his heart pounding against her chest.

Panting, he shifted his weight to keep from crushing her, then he ran his hands down her sides gently, lovingly, caressing her. He wrapped his arms around her waist. "I needed that," he breathed.

"Me, too."

He was silent for a moment, holding her. "If I had to choose between your threats, Em, I'd rather have you kill me than ever leave me."

Leave you? I'd sell my soul for you, she thought as she lifted her hand weakly to curl her fingers into his hair.

"Hell, I'd load the gun for you myself," he murmured, his lips nuzzling her ear. "Just . . . never go away."

She hugged him. "I'm sorry, darling. I shouldn't have said those things," she whispered, closing her eyes and pressing a reverent kiss to his sweat-dampened brow. "You know I'd never hurt you. I was just scared."

"I know."

"Don't talk like that anymore," she chided in a whisper, but the reminder had brought back the grim reality of their situation.

"Whatever happens, you must know I'll keep you safe," he murmured, slipping his arm around her.

"But they're evil, Drake." She winced as he pulled out of her body with a soul-deep sigh.

"Well, we're all a bit evil, aren't we?" he answered, straightening up and fastening his trousers.

She sat up and studied him warily as she began righting her clothes, as well. "Some more than others," she said, wondering if he had just done all that to her in part to gain her compliance.

He was, after all, a trained spy. Among other things.

"Let me do this my way. I can rein them in. Trust me," he ordered in a velvet whisper, leaning down to capture her face between his hands, and giving her a frank kiss on the mouth.

Like a seal of ownership.

She did not protest.

Just then, a knock at the door diverted their attention from each other.

"Who's there?" Drake demanded with a glance over his shoulder.

"It's Galtür, my lord."

"Just a moment!" Drake called back.

Emily sent him a curious glance.

"Count Galtür, of Austria," he whispered. "One of the Hundred." Then he offered her his hand with a smile.

His coal black eyes, heavy-lidded with sated pleasure, could have seduced her all over again. But she warded off the fresh surge of temptation and accepted his assistance, hopping down off the desk. He steadied her with a possessive half embrace. "Ready?"

She made sure her dress was buttoned though the mirror above the fireplace revealed her general state of dishevelment. She let out a rueful sigh. "I suppose."

He sent her a roguish wink, then went and unlocked the door.

Emily saw their visitor—an obese Continental nobleman in a flamboyant purple full-dress coat, with a high, starched neckcloth in the dandyish style.

"Pardon the intrusion, Lord Westwood, but I've brought someone very special to meet you," Count Galtür said. Because of his high, restrictive cravat, he had to bend from his massive waist to see the small child by his side. "Come along, lad." He gave the child a nudge into the room.

Emily was just about to sit down, but when she saw the boy, she stopped.

Drake had also gone very still. "What's this?"

"This is our special guest. His name is Stefan."

The Bavarian shepherd boy wore traditional peasant garb, a short neat jacket providing a glimpse of the brightly embroidered suspenders holding up his brown *lederhosen*. He had eyes of Alpine blue and tousled golden curls like a cherub.

About six years old, he literally looked like an angel that had fallen out of the sky. All he lacked was harp and wings.

As Count Galtür shooed him in, Stefan looked all around him at the room, wide-eyed, and clearly rather scared, as though even he could sense something wrong in this place, that maybe he shouldn't have come here or trusted these strangers.

"What is he doing here?" Drake inquired, folding his arms across his chest.

"He has come to see the castle. He is to visit with us for the next few days and learn how to be a knight, then he will be our special guest on the night of the, er, feast."

Emily felt the blood drain her face.

She had forgotten about the Prometheans' need for a sacrificial innocent ever since Falkirk had declared *her* no longer suitable for that hideous role.

Staring at the little boy, apparently her replacement, she felt sick. It took everything in her not to run over, grab the child, and put herself between them and him.

"We found him well outside the nearest village," Galtür said meaningfully, while he dabbed the greasy sweat off his bloated face with a handkerchief. "He told us he was watching his family's flock when one of the lambs strayed. He followed it, but a wolf came, and he says he is very ashamed, but he ran away to escape the beast. The wolf took the lamb, alas, and now our poor Stefan is afraid to go home because his parents will be angry."

Emily was repulsed by the fat man's cloying tone.

"So, I asked him if he would like to come with us and see the castle," Galtür said, smiling brightly at the lad. "I told him he could learn to be a knight, or even pretend to be a prince."

"Indeed," Drake murmured. She knew him well enough to sense his rage in that one word though he hid it from the others.

She watched with her heart in her throat as he bent down slowly to the boy's eye level. "What do you think of the castle so far, Stefan?"

He repeated the question in German since the boy did not understand.

"Sehr groß." Very big.

Drake smiled at the boy in calming reassurance, then Emily's own progress in the language carried her through the rest of their exchange.

"Don't you worry about that wolf. I will personally hunt it down and kill it. I will give your father money for the lamb and tell him that this was not your fault."

"You will?"

"Ja."

"Thank you, sir." Stefan tilted his head, studying Drake. "Are you the king of this castle?"

He laughed quietly. "No. I'm just Drake."

Emily realized at his answer that he had just made up his mind in regard to his earlier temptation.

Stefan's arrival had done more than she ever could to remind him and persuade him that Promethean evil was not to be trifled with. It had to be destroyed.

He offered the boy his hand, and Stefan shook it. Then he straightened up to his full height once more. "Now, if you need anything, you let me know," he instructed his new little friend.

"Thank you, Herr Drake."

"Come along, Stefan. We have a fine chamber set aside just for you." Count Galtür gave Drake a questioning look; he accepted their new sacrifice with a grim, subtle nod.

The fat man nodded to him, then grinned down at their oblivious victim. "Come along, my lad! Let us see if we can't find something to eat to restore us after all that walking. Our cook has just made pastries. Are you hungry?"

"Oh, yes, sir!"

Galtür pulled the door shut, leading the boy off to get a snack and continue their tour of the castle.

As soon as they had gone, Emily turned to Drake, speechless—her horrified demand needed no words.

He turned to the window, closing his eyes. He locked his fingers as in prayer and brought his hands up to his mouth with a stricken look and a barely audible utterance. *"God help me."*

Chapter
19

Bavaria

$\mathcal{R}$otherstone's team had picked up Niall Banks's trail along the way to Munich, but they had not yet caught up to him or located him precisely enough to corner the bastard and carry out their revenge.

Leading his comrades northward out of the quaint Bavarian capital, Max recalled the particulars from Emily Harper's letter, and knew they should also be getting close to Waldfort Castle. The Promethean stronghold was nestled somewhere in the rugged country they now traversed.

Meanwhile, perhaps the tedium of the long, monotonous journey had worn a bit of the edge off their watchfulness that day.

All seemed quiet. The thick primeval woods showed no signs of human habitation. The thin, dry air made them weary as the endless, dusty road spiraled up the mountain.

But then, all of a sudden, as they came around a bend, gray towers burst into view above the trees, just a few miles ahead.

"Shit, is that the place?" Jordan muttered, reining in.

"Bloody hell!" Rohan immediately reached over his shoulder for his rifle. "Come on! We've got to catch up to Niall and stop him before he gets there!"

"Keep it quiet, though. Hold your fire until you've got a clear shot," Max ordered. "Let's not alert the whole damned place we're here."

"Do you think Malcolm's up there with an army?" Jordan asked with a trace of worry.

Max nodded. "Likely." More importantly, Drake was in the castle, as Emily's letter had advised.

They hoped he had not moved on.

"We'll kill Niall quietly out here in the woods, then move in closer to see if we can get a look inside those walls."

His fellow agents nodded.

"Let's go."

They urged their horses into a gallop though the animals strained against the steep incline.

Max's heart pounded as they rode. That was the first time they had isolated Niall within a finite space.

In the Alpine wilderness, the escape routes open to him were nearly limitless. But they finally had him pinned down to a stretch of ground somewhere between their current location on the road and the castle gates ahead.

The only mistake they could make at this point would be to pass him.

Or to miss the shot, he amended.

Or rouse the attention of the countless Promethean foot soldiers surely guarding the castle . . .

"There!" The eagle-eyed Jordan reined in suddenly, pointing into the forest.

Max looked over and spotted their quarry: Niall had pulled off the road to let his horse drink from a stream.

He looked as shocked to see them as they had been at suddenly spotting the castle.

Indeed, he had dismounted. On foot, he held his horse's reins, but as soon as he saw them, he reached to get back onto his horse.

Max looked down the rifle's sights and took a shot. It grazed the horse's rump. The animal screamed and ripped away from Niall, carrying with it the musket strapped to the saddle.

Still armed with pistols and dagger, Niall turned to flee. He splashed across the stream and bolted deeper into the woods.

The chase was on.

Unfortunately, once they left the road, the terrain in the steeply sloping woods was too difficult for the horses, the turf too soft and loose, too many stones and roots.

"Jordan, keep the horses!" Max ordered their injured friend as he and Rohan jumped down from the saddle. "Shoot him if he comes back out on the road."

"Yes, go!" he said impatiently, capturing the reins of their mounts. They left him and their horses behind, racing off into the forest to hunt the man who had killed their handler.

Max cursed at the difficult sprint over angled ground, his pulse hammering. An earthy smell of rich soil rose from his every running stride. He pressed off the solid surface of fixed stones when he could find them in his path. But the seconds seemed to drag as he and Rohan raced through the same woods where, unbeknownst to them, Emily had first been captured weeks ago.

Rohan suddenly fell to on one knee, bringing his gun up to his shoulder. "I've got the shot."

"Take it."

Boom!

His bullet flew just as, in his haste, Niall tripped—fatefully—on a root.

"Shit!" Rohan hissed, though he *had* hit his target—in the shoulder. They heard Niall's brief, low cry. Rohan was already reloading. "Shoot him, Max!"

But Niall returned fire: Max ducked behind a tree for cover, then, glaring with fury, he advanced, his rifle at the ready.

Rohan was a couple of yards behind him to his right as Max reached the stream where Niall had been watering his horse. Its babbling lull was the only sound; the birds had gone silent.

With a bead of sweat running down his face, Max scanned the forest, his finger on the trigger. He wanted a clear shot, but at the moment, Niall was just a blur of motion as he fled through the leafy trees.

Max had to glance down to watch his footing as he crossed the quick, rushing stream. The rocks were treacherous, slippery with moss and pristine Alpine water. When he glanced up again halfway through the current, Niall had disappeared. Max splashed on the rest of the way through the brook, with Rohan right behind him.

Niall was enraged—and in a lot of pain.

The bullet had torn through the same shoulder that had so recently healed after being dislocated by James Falkirk's mad bodyguard. Still, he was glad to have the flesh wound compared to what he would've got if he hadn't tripped.

He had recovered his pace, though, pounding uphill through the forest toward the gates of Waldfort Castle. He knew that as soon as he reached them, he could send some of his father's men out to deal with these bastards on his tail.

He did not doubt that, by then, Malcolm had taken the castle, that Falkirk and his fellow traitors had been put to death. Either way, Niall had no doubt that his place as future leader of the Prometheans was securely restored.

All he had to do was get inside the castle gates.

He came barreling out of the woods onto the drawbridge, and instantly, the sentries' guns were aimed at him.

"Halt! Who goes there?" they roared, clearly rattled by the shots they'd heard fired.

"I'm Niall Banks! Let me in, you fools! I've got three Order agents on my tail, and one of the bastards just shot me! Move, now—or you will answer to my father!"

Nothing happened.

The two Frenchmen looked at each other skeptically.

"Open the damned gates now!" he screamed, punching the metal portcullis. "I'm already shot! Do you want them to kill me? I said *move!*"

The older one shrugged at his comrade. The other begrudgingly went and began to raise the portcullis.

Niall snarled under his breath, glancing behind him as it inched upward much too slowly.

His heart pounded. He could feel the Order agents nearly breathing down his neck. They were just behind him somewhere in the woods.

He did not wait for the portcullis to open all the way but rolled through the narrow opening.

Jumping to his feet, he laid hold of the first guard he got his hands on. He threw the man against the stone wall, out of the way of any incoming bullets his pursuers might happen to fire.

"When I give you an order, I expect to be obeyed!" he roared in the man's face. More guards approached while the portcullis groaned shut behind him. "My father will hear about this! You! Let the surgeon know that I shall need him shortly. You two, take me to my father."

The men exchanged an odd, wary look.

"You wish to see the head of the Council?" the older, leathery-faced Frenchman asked.

"That's what I just said," Niall snapped.

The Frenchman shrugged. "Very well, monsieur. We shall show you to the great hall."

"About bloody time," he muttered, marching ahead of them. The two useless sentries flanked him. "Where's Falkirk?" he demanded.

"Dead, monsieur."

He snorted in satisfaction. "Good. Just as I thought." It sounded like everything had gone according to plan.

Then he stepped into the great hall and realized he was wrong.

Very wrong.

For they did not take him to see his father or uncle or whatever Malcolm was to him.

Instead, they made him wait in a reception room for several minutes like a peon. A chill was already creeping down his spine when he was taken into the great hall . . . And brought to stand before none other than Falkirk's lunatic bodyguard.

"Well, well. If it isn't my old friend," Drake said, relishing this moment. He folded his arms across his chest, studying Niall Banks in amusement. "I see you've had more trouble with that shoulder."

The red-haired giant had gone utterly pale. "What are you doing here?"

Drake raised his eyebrows politely, lounging at his ease on the lordly wooden chair at the head of the great hall. "I might ask the same of you."

"I was told James is dead. So how is it that you, his bodyguard, are still alive?"

"Dumb luck," he replied with an insolent shrug.

Niall turned to the others in the room, incensed. "What is going on here? He is not one of us! This madman attacked me in London. He handed me over to the Order!"

"You were lucky I didn't cut your throat," Drake said serenely. "It was James who stopped me, you'll recall—even though you tried to kill him."

"James Falkirk was a traitor—as are you! Are you people blind?" Niall demanded. "This man is an Order agent!"

"No, he is the current head of the Council," Emily spoke up, standing by his chair, her hand on his shoulder. "And if you want to live, you'll give him your allegiance."

Niall glanced around, turning pale. "Head of the Council? Where is my father?"

Drake drummed his fingers in the silence. "Let's just say he's not here."

"Did he come?"

"Oh, yes, we had a charming visit. At least now I have an inkling of how he found out about our location. From you, wasn't it? Tell me, how did you escape the Order's custody?"

Niall narrowed his eyes at him in hatred. "I took the old man off guard. Virgil Banks. He'd dead, for your information. I strangled him. Took his keys, and let myself out."

Drake went perfectly still, masking his horror.

Virgil's dead? His throat closed.

It could be a lie, he told himself at once. But he dared not let his shock show on his face. Everyone was watching. Emily's steadying touch on his shoulder brought him back to the present though his heart was pounding.

Niall looked at him with a cold smile as if he knew exactly the effect his news had had. "Now tell me where my father is."

"Certainly," Drake answered, recovering in the next heartbeat, though he knew not how. "He was standing right about there, where you are now, when I cut his throat."

Niall lost his mind. Jacques and his men rushed in to control the red-haired giant when he let out a roar and tried to rush at Drake. *"You killed my father?"*

"I did," he clipped out matter-of-factly, rising from his chair. "If you don't respect my authority, you are more than welcome to join him." He drew his knife as he walked toward them. "Hold him for me."

"Wait!" Niall got control of himself when he saw his reflection in Drake's blade, inches from his face.

"What?" Drake growled. Thinking of Virgil's possibly being dead, he was half-tempted to cut the bastard's nose off.

Then in the morning, he could blind him in one eye, and the day after that . . .

"There are three Order agents in the forest," Niall panted nervously, as though he could read Drake's murderous intentions in his face. And perhaps he had also recalled the broken bone he'd received the last time they'd met.

"Talk."

"They've been hunting me all the way from London." He swallowed hard. "If you're really one of us, then send your men out to kill them," the brawny young Scot challenged.

"Kill them?" Drake drawled. "What a fool you are, Niall. The eclipse is tomorrow night. We take them alive," he told the others. "Then I will gut them on the altar as offerings to Father Lucifer, before I kill the child."

Then he threw Niall to the surgeon, who had just walked in. "Put him in the tower room and keep him under guard," Drake ordered Jacques, gesturing to the surgeon to tend him. "One wrong move," he warned his prisoner.

Niall glared at him but kept his head down as they led him out at the point of a gun.

The only reason he had not tossed Niall into the dungeon was that he did not wish to test the Prometheans' loyalty. They had transferred their allegiance to him easily enough, thanks to James's backing; but their sympathies might shift again if he appeared to treat Niall with undue disrespect.

After all, most of the men present had long expected Niall to become the next leader of the Prometheans after Malcolm Banks. Drake could not afford the outbreak of another battle between factions with the ceremony of the eclipse so near. Somehow, he had to hold this wild group together just long enough to herd every last one of them into that vile temple.

And then it would be over.

"Sir, will you be riding out with us?" one asked.

He nodded. "To your horses!" he commanded the guards, flashing a bold smile. "Order agents in the forest! This is good sport! We bring them in alive. They're more useful that way."

"Drake, be careful," Emily whispered from a short space behind him. He wasn't aware she had followed him down off the dais, but when he turned to her, her forceful stare was a pointed reminder that his former colleagues were under orders to kill him if they got the chance.

He smiled darkly, recalling especially Warrington's reputation as an assassin. But for appearances' sake, it was vital that he go personally and lead his Promethean henchmen on this chase.

It was the only way he could think of to make sure the reckless bastards got away.

He kissed her hand with a look that told her not to worry, then marched out.

As soon as Max and Rohan had burst back out of the woods onto the road, Jordan brought the horses to them.

"Did you kill him?" he asked, as they swung up into their saddles.

"Missed," growled the big duke.

"We have to get out of here," said Max. "Niall made it into the castle. They'll be out here looking for us shortly."

"What about Drake?"

"We can worry about him later. Fall back!"

They reeled their horses around and cantered down the mountain road to seek a more secure position.

In moments, they could hear the expected riders pounding after them in the distance.

"We need to get off the road," Max said tautly. "They'll be upon us in a moment."

Rohan nodded, scanning the landscape. "Let's try to get above them. There!"

The hill he pointed to looked a little easier for the

horses to negotiate than much of the rough terrain that surrounded them. Wasting no time, they veered off the dusty, winding road up into the wooded high ground.

They were barely out of sight when the pack of men from the castle rode into view.

"It's Drake!" Max whispered.

Jordan stared at their former colleague, shaking his head. "He's not just one of them, he's giving orders."

"Must have considerable status as Falkirk's body-guard."

Rohan took aim.

"Warrington, no!" Max shoved the barrel of his rifle skyward just as Rohan squeezed the trigger.

The duke turned on him in fury. "What the hell are you doing? I had the shot!"

Max stared hard at him. "No. There's got to be an-other way."

"Er, gentlemen," Jordan murmured as Drake's men pointed toward the forest, trying to determine the location the single shot had come from. "Argue later. There are thirty men down there, and personally, I'm in no shape for ten-to-one odds today. That only makes it worse for you two, so I suggest we make a timely egress."

Rohan glowered down the hill at the enemy. "Damn it, Max, you should have let me kill him."

"Did it ever occur to you he might know what he's doing?" Max retorted.

Jordan ignored them both. "The farmers we talked to yesterday told me about a cart path to the west. It's not on the map, but I wager it's going to be our best way out of here. Follow me!" He kicked his horse into motion; Rohan followed, still scowling.

Max, however, turned his horse in the opposite di-rection, his pulse pounding.

"What are you doing?" Jordan cried, glancing over his shoulder.

"I'm going to let them catch me."

"The hell you are!"

"I know what I'm doing! You two get out of here!"

"Have you lost your mind?" the duke demanded.

Max shook his head impatiently. "I know it's a risk, but I cannot believe Drake would ever betray us. That means he's got a plan, and I intend to help him. I've got a better chance of doing that if I can at least get in there and talk to him."

"You're mad," Jordan marveled.

"It's my own affair if I am! Now, go! I'm sorry, but I have to do this," he said impatiently when his friends refused to leave. "He's our brother. I can't leave him behind. If I don't come back, tell Daphne I love her."

"Bloody hell!" Rohan said.

"If you're going to let them capture you, maybe we should join you. The more the merrier?" Jordan offered grimly.

"No," Max clipped out. "I need you on the outside. Be ready to give me some cover when I drag him out of there—and the girl, Emily, too, if she got this far. Now go. Take that cart path, but try to find some way to watch the castle from a safer location."

"You're sure about this, Max?"

"Entirely. I'm responsible. I'm the one who let Drake escape my custody."

"You're the one who's going to have to kill him if it turns out you're wrong, and he really is a traitor," Rohan warned. "No more excuses."

"If I am wrong, then, yes, I will. You have my word," Max agreed. "Now go, please." He kicked his horse into motion again, riding east through the woods while they went west. With any luck, he could draw the enemy to him so his friends could get away.

He urged his horse on over the treacherous ground, trying to find a spot where he could pretend to make a stand and get captured without getting himself killed.

The bullet that had streaked just above Drake's head, close enough for its breeze to riffle his hair, only added authenticity of his present claim of loyalty to the Prometheans.

He had a feeling he had Warrington to thank for this further proof of the Order's enmity. Although his private goal was to let them get away, he had no choice but to let his men tear off in the direction from which the shot had come. They began to search the woods.

"This way!"

"No, down there!"

"Split up!" Drake ordered, motioning some of his men toward the cloud of dust that had appeared on the faint westward road down below. Whoever had kicked it up had already disappeared around the curve of the hill, but it was no great mystery who had likely produced it.

Meanwhile, others had caught the trail of a third rider spotted among the trees. Uneasiness rippled through him. Why would they split up when they were so badly outnumbered? Drake followed the pack in deepening concern.

Then the men were hollering, their threats and curses echoing through the woods.

"Put your hands up! Weapons down!"

Bloody hell. When Drake arrived, he hid an inward stab of dread behind his cold expression.

They had Max surrounded, on the ground. They had pulled the marquess off his horse and had taken a few choice swings at him, along with a kick in the gut.

"We got one, sir!"

"So you have." Drake stared fiercely at Max. *What the hell do you think you're doing?*

The men were thrilled—an active Order agent for the sacrifice, one of the Archangel's own knights!

But if they had known the sly bastard half as well as he did, they would not have been so quick to congratulate themselves.

Indeed, they would have realized that an agent of Rotherstone's capability did not just happen to get himself caught.

You cocky bastard, Drake thought as he realized Max had contrived to surrender himself. But why? To get into the castle? Or did he think Drake couldn't handle things alone? He shook his head at his boyhood friend. *Misguided fool.*

"Bind his hands. You're losing your touch, old boy," Drake remarked.

Max merely smirked.

Drake jumped down from the saddle and sauntered over to Max. "Where are the others going?"

"What others?" Max replied in polite boredom.

Drake punched him in the stomach for his insolence.

The marquess doubled over a bit with the blow, but surely knew that Drake had to make it look like they were really enemies. "Nice seeing you again, too," he forced out.

"What are you doing here?" Drake asked.

"I'm afraid I came to kill you."

"Ah." Drake nodded. "Doesn't seem to have worked out for you very well."

"Not yet, no." Max straightened up with a slight cough, catching his breath. Despite half a dozen rifles pointed at him, his silvery eyes glinted with steely confidence even as one of Drake's men yanked his arms behind him, shackling his hands behind his back. "Tell me, Drake, how's dear old Falkirk these days?"

"Dead, I'm sorry to say. But you might be interested to know he made me the new head of the Council before he died."

Amazement flickered through Max's eyes, but he quickly hid it behind his bravado. "Well, I always knew you'd go far in life, my friend."

He laughed darkly. "I'm not your friend, Max. You and the rest of the Order left me for dead, remember? The lot of you can go to Hell for all I care. In fact, I will personally make sure you do. Put him back up on his horse."

Drake's men did his bidding—none too gently. When the Promethean guards had shoved their captive up into the saddle, Drake personally took the reins and led Max's horse behind his own, heading back to the castle.

When they rode into the courtyard, Drake found Emily outside, anxiously waiting for him to return. He saw the relief in her face as she realized he was back, quite unscathed.

Then her gaze moved to Max on the horse that Drake led behind his own, and a chill of fear crept into her eyes.

Until that moment, Drake had been unsure of how exactly to play his hand. The fact was, he was worried. With the ritual of the eclipse taking place tomorrow night, he had barely slept in days, on the very knife-edge of suspense. Rotherstone's arrival was sure to heighten the Prometheans' suspicions. As if keeping Emily and little Stefan safe were not enough to worry about, now he had to keep Max alive, as well.

Drake felt close to overwhelmed with the momentous task ahead. But the instant he looked at Emily standing in the sunlight, the idea suddenly crystal-lized in his mind.

Perfect.

The break in the dungeon wall through which she had slipped out of the castle to meet him in the woods . . .

Hiding his distraction, Drake lowered his gaze as he reined his horse to a halt and swung down off the saddle.

All he had to do was find a reason to lock her up below along with Max. He winced at the thought of her in some dungeon cell, but he saw no other way.

She was just going to have to trust him.

Emily watched in trepidation as his men got Max down from his horse. "What's going on?" she whis-pered to Drake as he stalked past her, leading the way into the castle.

He ignored her—or at least, made a show of doing so.

Visibly appalled, she stared at Max as the guards marched him past her, his wrists shackled behind him; the marquess gave her a warning look in answer.

She kept her mouth shut, but followed the men as their party tromped into the great hall. The surviving Prometheans crowded around to get a look at the cap-tured Order agent.

Drake was all too familiar with the creeping sensa-tion their scrutiny must have sent down Max's spine right about then, with a crowd of twisted occultists gawking at him. But unlike Drake, who preferred to keep his hatred to himself, their stares provoked the proud marquess to a flash of his famous sarcasm.

"Good God, what a stench is in this place!" Max glanced around at the Prometheans. "Now I see why. It's full of human excrement—complete with buzzing flies," he added, nodding scornfully at Drake.

Drake turned to him, smiled, and sighed. He had no choice. He hauled back and punched him in the face.

Emily gasped. "Drake!" She came running over in protest. "What are you doing?" she cried.

He ignored her yet again. "Throw this blackguard in the dungeon," he ordered Jacques.

Emily turned to Max in confusion. He was glaring at Drake. "Are you all right, my lord?"

Before Max could answer, Drake clasped her elbow and turned her away from their prisoner. "Don't you talk to him!"

"You didn't have to hit him!" she exclaimed.

He leaned toward her, glowering. "Are you questioning me?"

She blinked.

"You know, I'm getting very tired of your presumption on my favor. I don't tolerate any disrespect from them—" He gestured to the roomful of people around them. "The same goes for you. So you'd better mind your tongue, my girl. Don't forget, you can easily be replaced in my bed."

She gasped in shock. "How dare you?"

"I can do as I please," he said. "Oh, I'm sorry, did you think you were in charge around here? You seem to need reminding about your proper place. Perhaps a night in the dungeon will help refresh your memory."

"*What?*"

"Jacques, do we have an extra cell available down there?"

"*Oui, Capitaine,*" the Frenchman said uneasily.

"Good. Then take this haughty little bitch away. By morning, maybe she'll think twice about challenging me."

"Drake!" she burst out, aghast.

He nodded for her removal, playing well the sinister part of the top Promethean chief.

She stared at him in utter confusion, her eyes big, blue, fragile saucers.

Trust me.

Two guards grasped her by the arms and began dragging her off to the dungeon. *"Drake!"*

"Silence!" he roared back. "Don't whine to me! You brought this on yourself, you cheeky wench! Get her out of here."

"Oui, Capitaine. Come, *mademoiselle."*

"Drake, please! What did I do wrong? Let me go! Drake, don't do this to me! *Drake!"*

As the men led her and Rotherstone away, he steeled himself against her echoing pleas, knowing he could not give in to pity.

The time to explain would come soon enough.

He turned away, returning to his throne-like chair in the great hall, his face a mask of dark, hard indifference. "Good riddance," he drawled. "I was growing bored of her, anyway. Now, then, what is the next order of business?"

$\mathcal{E}$mily spent the remainder of the day and the whole night in a dungeon cell, angry, wounded, and bewildered.

What the hell is going on?

Drake had never spoken to her like that before in her life. Another blasted ruse? It had better be. Oh, yes, he had better have a damned good explanation, she thought in unabated fury, even though she gathered that her favorite blackguard had some new trick up his sleeve.

Some of the things he had snarled at her in the great hall had cued her in to the fact that—as usual—there was more to his behavior than met the eye. He usually knew what he was doing. Still, how dare he call her a bitch?

Ruse or not, she was still stung, after all she had done for him. No woman had ever given so much and been so put upon, she thought, feeling justified in sulking in her cell. She wanted to wring his bloody neck.

Thankfully, the presence of Lord Rotherstone two cells down and across the aisle from her helped keep her courage up against the encroaching darkness of this horrible dungeon.

When the guards withdrew, they were able to exchange some basic information in hushed tones. She confirmed that the Prometheans had indeed chosen Drake as their new leader and explained how it all had unfolded on the night Malcolm Banks had invaded the castle with his private army.

She also described the prophecy Falkirk had found in the Alchemist's Scrolls, but for fear of being overheard, she did not even whisper to the marquess that Drake had fully regained his memory and their incarceration was probably just a ruse.

The very walls had ears.

Besides, her own faith on that point was wavering, frankly, after Drake had admitted two days ago that he was tempted to embrace his new role in life.

She wanted to believe he had put that wicked notion out of his mind—but he was not acting like himself.

Ah, she was so weary of it all . . .

She leaned back against the clammy stone wall, staring into the inky gloom of the subterranean prison and battling moment by moment a wave of irrational fear.

Even if it was a ruse, how could he do this to her? Didn't he know being trapped down here in the darkness would plunge her back into the awful memories of her ordeal when she was seventeen?

If it were not for the nearby marquess, she'd have given in to panic hours ago and would have probably been reduced to wild screaming, just like she had been for days in the pit of that well, where she had thought she was going to die.

But Drake had rescued her, she reminded herself,

shivering. She hugged herself around the waist, trying to ward off the chill. He had not done this to hurt her, she promised her bruised heart. He had to have a reason.

Nevertheless, the darker it got through the long, cold night, and the longer she remained a prisoner, the harder it got to stay brave and hold on to hope.

If there was one benefit to be gained from the experience, however, it was that it brought her closer to Drake in a strange way. At last she had a firsthand glimpse of what he must have gone through. All those months of being trapped down here. It was hard to stay angry at him when she pondered all he'd suffered.

Tasting the horror of it for herself, she was left wondering if anyone ever really could come back from that, as she had assured him that he could.

Maybe she had been wrong. Maybe he *would* be permanently scarred in his soul, just like they had left their mark upon his body. All the love she had to give might not be enough to truly heal him. Maybe, without telling her, he had made up his mind to quit fighting it and had already given in to darkness . . .

Just then, she heard male voices down the corridor.

Someone was coming. She rose quickly and crossed her cell, grasping the rusty bars as she peered through them, waiting to see who it was. Had Drake finally come to his senses and ordered her release?

The brisk rhythm of bootheels ringing out over the flagstone echoed down the torchlit corridor.

Emily drew in her breath as Drake himself suddenly appeared, marching out of the shadows.

She stared, shocked to see him in this godforsaken pit where he'd endured hell on earth. She could not imagine what it cost him to come down personally and face the place again, when he could have easily sent one of his countless henchmen. Instead, he had come alone.

He stopped outside her cell and immediately began unlocking it with his key; still upset with him, she didn't know what to say.

For that matter, she didn't know what to expect, either—a reprieve or more trouble?

Warily, she studied the stark look on his angular face, but he was closed within himself once more, utterly guarded, mysterious, impossible to read.

In truth, she was so disoriented from being locked up, she wasn't even sure if it was night or day.

He slid the door open and gave her a curt nod. "Come out."

Emily was all too glad to leave her cell, but she darted past, eyeing him in suspicion. "You mind telling me what's going on?" she demanded.

He shut the door behind her. "You and Max are leaving the castle, now."

Her eyes widened. "We are?"

"You'll use that break in the wall where you slipped out to meet me in the woods. It's almost dawn. I want you out of here before the sun rises."

"What about you?"

"I'll follow when I can. It's a bit more complicated. I'll have to bring the boy."

"Right," she murmured, eyeing him mistrustfully.

"Wait here for a moment." He gestured to the guard's empty stool by the wall, beneath a hanging lantern. "I need a private word with Max before you two set out."

"You're not going to hurt him, are you?"

He turned and looked at her in dismay. "No, Emily."

She shrugged, sending him a pointed look of reproach.

His mouth tilted ruefully. "We hit each other harder than that in training."

"Humph."

He looked at her for a long moment. "You're angry at me."

"Oh, how unfair of me! I can't imagine why!"

"I'm sorry, but I had to make it look convincing," he whispered impatiently.

"You fooled me," she said with a snort, folding her arms across her chest as she sat down beneath the light. "Honestly. That's your apology?"

"But surely you knew it was just a ruse!" he exclaimed in a low tone.

She sighed and shook her head. "Oh, Drake, I am so heartily sick of ruses."

He frowned. "Stay here, I'll be right back," he muttered. Then he stalked off once again into the shadows.

Drake took leave of her and went to free his boyhood friend. His fists were clenched. With every step, he had to keep his mind fixed on the task at hand because being down in this place was too horrible.

If returning to Waldfort Castle was not bad enough in itself, never had he dreamed he would ever come down to the dungeon of his own free will.

He'd had no choice. He had to get them out of there, Emily and Max. All he could do was ignore the volcanic rage and pain coursing through him at the memories, struggling on to do what had to be done.

When he came to Max's cell, the marquess glared at him. "You've really turned into quite a bastard in your old age, haven't you?"

"I know," Drake forced out in a droll tone as he opened the cell door. "Come out."

Max eyed him in suspicion.

"Hurry up! We haven't got much time."

Max took the invitation gladly, leaving the cell with

a few swift strides, pausing to glance up and down the dark corridor.

"Sorry about all this," Drake mumbled.

Max turned to him. "What the hell is going on?"

"You're getting out of here, and you're taking Emily with you. I have a plan."

"Really?" he drawled. "And to think, I was beginning to worry."

"Well, don't. By tomorrow, the Prometheans will be no more than a dark legend. Gone."

Max's face instantly sobered. "How? My team's not far. What do you need us to do?"

Drake told him what he had in mind.

When he had explained, Max stared at him. "You're sure?"

He nodded in grim resolve. "It's the only way."

Max studied him, then shook his head. Abruptly, Max hugged his friend. "Go with God, brother."

"Just take care of my girl. If she should be with child, forge the papers for a marriage, will you?"

"It's as good as done." Max grasped both his shoulders and stared imploringly at him. "Are you sure there's no way you can get out of this?"

Drake considered, then shook his head. "There's a slim chance I could get out unscathed, but I don't want you to give Emily false hope," he whispered. "Believe me, I've tried to come up with something else, but this is our last option. I'm confident I can get the boy behind the blast door. Myself, I can't guarantee that I'll be fast enough."

"We'll wait."

"Just make sure the three of you kill any of them who might escape."

"Don't you worry about that," Max assured him with a gleam in his silvery eyes.

"And make sure you collect Stefan from the tunnel as

soon as you can afterward. Try to get in there quickly. He's going to be terrified."

"I'll make sure he's safe."

"And take him back to his family."

"We will."

Drake paused, lowering his gaze. "Don't tell Emily what's really going on until you're well away from here. Otherwise, she'll likely do something rash. She'll end up ruining everything."

Max gave him a pensive smile. "She's a good woman, Drake. First-rate. Your parents were wrong to forbid her to you."

Well, it's too late now, he thought, clearing his throat against the lump that briefly constricted it. "Come on," he said, nodding toward the corridor. "You two need to get out of here before it's light."

"I won't argue that," Max muttered.

Drake walked back to Emily, dreading this moment, hoping he could hide his heartbreak. It was time to say good-bye.

"All right, then," Drake greeted her. "You both have got your jobs."

She stood up hopefully as he returned with Lord Rotherstone.

"Emily, you're going to show Max the way out. He's got his team outside the walls. You'll join them. We've got a few schemes up our sleeves. Max will explain more about it once you're clear. Show us that break. Better hurry," he added, glancing back in case his men were wondering how much longer he'd be gone.

She nodded and sped ahead of them toward the fissure in the foundation wall. Beckoning them toward it, she explained the drop that Lord Rotherstone would come to on the other side.

The tall, lean agent nodded and vaulted up into the break, sliding in horizontally between the heavy stones. "Don't take too long," he warned.

"I'm right behind you," she whispered with a nod.

Then he disappeared into the predawn twilight.

She turned to Drake. "You're coming soon?"

He nodded. "I'll be along as soon as I've got the boy. Sometime later today."

"Be careful, and hurry." Having decided to discard her anger at him for locking her up in the dungeon all day, now that she knew his reasons, she pressed up onto her tiptoes and kissed him on the cheek. "See you soon."

He grasped her forearm gently. "Wait," he whispered as she started to move toward the opening.

She turned to him in question. "What is it?"

He stared into her eyes. "I've got a favor to ask of you."

"Anything," she said at once.

"There will come a moment where Max is going to ask you to fire an arrow. You have to do it—for me."

She furrowed her brow with a curious smile. "That's all? Fire an arrow?"

"Yes. It's crucial to the plan. Will you do it?"

She shrugged. "Of course."

"Promise me, Emily, that you will not fail."

She took his hand and placed it on her chest, over her heart. "I promise you, dear Westwood, I will shoot whatever blasted arrow you want as long as we're getting out of here." Then she paused, a bit puzzled. "Surely one of your fellow agents is a better shot than I am."

"Not with a bow and arrow. Besides," he said, "I want it to be you."

"Then I will do it, and my aim will be true."

"Thank you." He looked tenderly into her eyes. "I can always count on you, can't I?"

She smiled ruefully at him. "You know you can."

He cupped her face between his hands and kissed her with quiet, soul-searing passion.

She trembled, eager to be free of this place at last. The sooner she left, the sooner their new lives together could begin.

"Let me go," she whispered. He had drawn her into his arms, and even now refused to release her, though she tried to push him away with a doting smile.

"I'm so sorry about yesterday," he whispered. "I didn't mean to hurt you. I did it—"

"For the same reason you do everything," she interrupted. "To protect me. I know." She caressed his cheek. "It's all right, my love. I forgive you, I suppose."

He turned his face to kiss her palm. "You are all that is good in the world to me," he breathed. Then he captured her hand and kissed it, and sent her on her way. "Now go. And do as Max tells you in the meanwhile. You can trust him as you'd trust me."

"Hurry," she shot back. "I'll miss you. And don't scare Stefan. Keep him smiling as best you can, all right? Just pretend it's a game."

He nodded.

Then she climbed up toward the break in the wall; he steadied her as she crawled toward freedom.

Emily glanced back, holding on to his hand a moment longer through the stones. "I love you!" she whispered.

"I love you, too, sweetheart. I always will."

His soft words made her beam and blush and smile from ear to ear. "See you soon?"

* * *

He nodded mutely, unable to speak. *Someday, my love.* She sent him a kiss, then her fingertips slid out of his grasp, and she was gone, vanishing through the wall.

The emptiness in that stone crypt without her was profound. All the light seemed to go out of the world. But Drake warded off the temptation to despair.

His work that day had only just begun.

He filled his lungs slowly with a deep breath, lifted his head, squared his shoulders, and headed for the stairs.

Stopping to blow out the lantern nearby, the better to conceal the fact that his "prisoners" were no longer in their cells, he paused, suddenly realizing that he was standing near the entrance to the torture chamber.

Icy loathing arrowed down his spine. Instinctual terror choked him, making his heart pound. He stood very still for a long moment, but then he knew he had to face it one last time . . . before the end.

Slowly, by inching, agonized degrees, he made himself walk over to it and peer through the open doorway into that dark place. The chamber where they had taken a hardened agent who had once, as a lad, aspired to be the Order's greatest hero and turned him into a ruined, cringing wretch to get their information. Every name of every agent that he knew. But they had failed.

He had never broken.

Somehow, near the border of all that his body and soul could take, his mind had performed a sleight-of-hand trick that had left even *him* fooled, folding in on itself, as it were, leaving him a blank slate who could remember nothing.

And then James had made them stop, fearing they'd kill him, and the information would be lost.

Dear old James, that master manipulator, had taken a man born an earl and turned him into a slave.

And so he would have remained if it were not for Emily. She had rescued him as he had once rescued her.

Fully restored by her love to what he truly was, he had to fulfill his destiny—not the Alchemist's foolish prophecy. The one Virgil had prepared him for.

But it would cost him . . . everything. And after their brief taste of love in this dark place, it was a price he did not want to pay.

He would have given up anything to stay with her, even his soul, his sense of right and wrong, and so, yes, he had wavered in the face of temptation; but she was gone, and he would be an Order agent to the end.

He would go into the temple and die tonight killing the enemy, as he brought his well-played ruse to its close.

It was the only way. He could finish this war for all of them, forever. The Prometheans en masse would meet their fiery reward, and his own suffering would end.

Peace filled him at last as he finally accepted the inevitable. This was his destiny.

He knew that Max and his team would take care of Emily for him. He did not have to worry anymore about keeping her safe. She would be devastated when she realized the truth, but this was how it had to be.

She'd heal in time, he told himself, and, someday, she would find a way to be happy without him. For himself, he was grateful for the time they had had together. At least they had had a taste of the love that could have been.

Drake reached in and pulled the door to the torture chamber shut. He locked it, then slid the key under the door, where no one would ever be able to find it.

They'd never be able to open that hellish compartment to terrorize anyone else.

With that, he pivoted on his heel and marched resolutely toward his fate.

At the end of the corridor, he began climbing the stone staircase that led back up into the castle.

Still lost in his wistful thoughts of Emily, he opened the heavy door at the top of the stairs, stepped out into the octagonal antechamber—and was suddenly grabbed from behind. Niall Banks jerked him off-balance, slipped behind him, and thrust a pistol against the back of his head.

"Don't move."

*N*iall was gratified when Westwood froze for a second, taken off guard, but the current leader of the Prometheans recovered his composure—and his sarcasm—rather quickly.

"Gracious, Niall, a guest in this castle, and this is how you behave?"

Niall wrenched his arm for his insolence. "Mind your manners, or I'll blow your fucking head off."

"Easy—"

"Shut the hell up." Niall's heart pounded.

While the surgeon had tended the gunshot wound to his shoulder up in the tower room, a few of the Prometheans who had once been loyal to Malcolm had slipped in to see him, defying Westwood's orders.

In hushed tones, they had told him all that had transpired at the castle, and having heard it, Niall vowed it would not stand.

His entire being churned with hate, rage, confusion, and loss. But he focused all his fury on this lying upstart, the interloper, who had killed the only man he'd ever thought of as his father.

Now he'd never know if Malcolm or Virgil had really been his sire, and therefore, would never know who he really was.

It was all Westwood's doing, and yet the bastard had the nerve to stand there and mock him—even after stealing *his* rightful place?

It was time to take back control.

Niall knew, however, that he couldn't just kill Westwood in cold blood and simply expect the others to recognize him as leader.

He was well aware that some of them did not respect him as they should, believing he had received his prominence in their organization merely because he was Malcolm's son, not because he'd earned it.

He had to show them once and for all that he deserved to be the next head of the Prometheans, and he realized he could do so by exposing Westwood as a fraud.

Somehow, he had to make the earl admit that he was lying.

Niall had found some supporters to back him up—men who were also unsure if Westwood could be trusted, but feared the black-eyed Englishman too much to stand up to him without someone like Niall to lead the charge.

They, as well as men loyal to Drake, had come rushing into the cramped octagonal chamber.

Hostility filled the room.

"We're going to have the truth now. Watch his face, all of you!" Niall barked at them. "You'll see it in his eyes if you look hard enough. That's right. Take a good look at your so-called leader," he instructed over the buzz of their low, worried murmurs. "He got to James somehow and tricked you all, but there is no doubt in my mind this man is still working for the Order!"

"Oh, really?" Westwood countered in a bored tone, sounding not the least impressed with their insurrection nor concerned about the gun to his head. "And have you got proof of that? Because I'm really beginning to find your accusations rather tedious."

"We both know you're just trying to distract attention away from your own incompetence. You led those Order agents straight to us by allowing yourself to be followed. Your father would be so disappointed."

The pain of his father's death still fresh, Niall tensed at the reminder. "Don't you dare speak of him, you lying bastard."

"Niall, it's plain that grief is clouding your judgment. We all know you are a man ruled by emotion. But you need to stop and think about what you're doing here," he advised calmly. "Otherwise, you're going to end up just like Malcolm. Dead."

Niall shook his head with a low laugh at the impudent warning, checking his outrage. He thrust his pistol harder to the back of Westwood's skull. "You're in no position to be making threats, you cocky son of a bitch. I know why you're here. To deceive us all, just like Virgil taught you to, under deep cover. But it's over, Westwood, you filthy Order spy. You're not going to get away with this deception anymore. Not with me. I'm not James."

Drake was counting the seconds.

He had already raised his hands in a token surrender, but his true purpose in doing so was merely to keep them high enough to strike more easily when his moment came. He'd have to be damned fast about it, too, or things could go nastily awry.

Meanwhile, the fact that so many of the guards had left their posts, drawn to watch the confrontation, would give Max and Emily a few more precious seconds to get away.

"Now, Westwood, if you want to save yourself a great deal of pain, I suggest you start talking. You can begin by admitting in front of all of us what you're really doing here. Or shall we go down to the torture room and have a more serious talk, alone?"

A slight shudder ran through him at that threat though he knew it wasn't going to happen. He could not let them go down to the dungeon, for they'd see that Max and Emily were gone.

Drake strove for patience, planning his attack. He had to draw this out a little longer to give her and Max a few more minutes to speed farther away from the castle. He decided to distract his foe by goading him to anger.

"Niall, Niall," he said with a casual sigh. "You don't seem to grasp how your situation's changed. I realize you're jealous of me. That you think you're entitled to lead this organization. But the brethren learned the hard way they couldn't trust your father; and as you've been riding Malcolm's coattails all your life—"

Niall muttered a choice expletive at him.

"Nobody has any reason to trust you, either.

"You lack experience, discretion," Drake continued. "You can't control your temper. Hardly anyone takes you seriously."

"Is that a fact?" he asked through gritted teeth.

He could sense Niall's fury building. *Perfect.* "The

fact is, you don't have what it takes. You know it, and so does every man here. That's why they chose me instead of you to be their leader."

"Well, that's a mistake that I intend to correct," he ground out in a tone that said he'd had enough, and he pulled the gun back a few short inches to get a cleaner shot.

Now!

With lightning speed, Drake dropped his body and drove his hands upward, shoving Niall's arm high; he spun in a flash, steadied himself with a slight step to the left, and delivered a massive round kick to the outside of Niall's knee.

Niall lost his balance with an oath, and Drake lunged for the gun; in the next heartbeat, he had stepped behind the red-haired giant, wrenching his arm up behind him. But Niall still clutched the pistol.

"Drop it," Drake ordered, panting.

Niall hesitated.

Drake wrenched the pistol; Niall cursed again, his finger tangled in the trigger.

"Drop it now, or I'll tear your goddamned finger off," Drake snarled.

"Relax," Niall rasped, and slowly let go of the gun.

As soon as Drake pried it out of his grasp, Niall suddenly rammed his elbow straight back into Drake's midsection.

Drake bent forward with a low woof of pain, but quickly blocked the upright fist that came hurtling toward his jaw.

Immediately, Niall stepped away, and, reaching for his blade, he spun to face Drake.

The dagger came slashing toward him. Drake grabbed Niall's arm and pulled as he took a deft step to the side, using his enemy's own momentum to throw him off-balance.

Having deflected Niall's attack, Drake retaliated with a sharp chop of his hand into the crook of the man's neck.

At the blow to the sensitive nerves there, Niall went rigid and let out a gasp of pain, automatically dropping the knife. But, recovering quickly, he bent to try to retrieve his weapon; Drake kneed him in the gut.

Niall stumbled backward, the air knocked from him. Drake pursued and sent him sprawling with an explosive uppercut to his jaw.

Toppling onto his back, Niall winced as he banged his head on the stone floor.

Drake kicked him in the ribs for good measure, then, looming over him, pointed Niall's own pistol at him.

"Go on, beg," he taunted in a low tone. The darkness rose in him, eager for revenge.

"You won't shoot me! You can't," Niall gasped out rather desperately, his chest heaving. "I know what you are! The Order's code won't allow you to kill an unarmed man!"

The chap had balls, to try a bluff like that, Drake admitted to himself. He'd give him that. But then his eyes narrowed as he saw Niall's hand creeping toward another small knife discreetly hidden in his boot.

He smiled, much to the consternation of the men watching, who hadn't noticed the weapon.

"You're right," Drake said softly, "except for one small point. I don't work for the Order anymore."

He pulled the trigger.

The others jumped at the bang.

Niall crumpled onto his back, dead, a bullet to the heart.

His few supporters started forward in surprise, but they froze when Drake glanced over at them.

The watching French guards, loyal to him, exchanged startled glances.

Satisfied, Drake threw the empty pistol onto Niall's body. Then he surveyed the men, lightly dusting off his hands. "Are we through here, or would anyone else like to question my authority?"

They shrank back from him with murmurs of denial, terror stamped across their faces.

"Good. Then get back to your duties, and stay away from my prisoners." He sent a meaningful glance over his shoulder at the closed dungeon door. "A few hours in solitary will make them more amenable. And bury this idiot," he added in a lower tone, stepping over Niall's body on his way out.

After that, Drake thought his own mother would have believed he had indeed become the true leader of the Prometheans. He'd half convinced himself.

When he returned upstairs to his chamber, he braced his hands against the chest of drawers and stared into the mirror, his heart still pounding after that near miss.

He had looked into Niall's eyes before he killed him and realized the man had truly been on the brink of exposing him. Still, it had been harder to pull the trigger than he had expected because the red-haired bastard had looked so much like Virgil.

Drake let out a long exhalation and lowered his head, still leaning on the chest of drawers. He told himself he only had to keep the charade going for a few more hours and it would all be over.

In the meanwhile, his old beloved handler was avenged.

A sound from the doorway jolted him, still in his heightened battle state. He turned, ready to fight, then quickly reined in the instant wrath of his warrior response.

It was just the little boy.

The sight of him reminded Drake bitterly of the Prometheans' hypocrisy. For all their talk, none of them had volunteered some loved one of their own for the sacrifice of "dearest blood." Instead, they had kidnapped an unsuspecting child in broad daylight.

He nodded to the boy. "What are you doing, Stefan?" he asked, forcing his voice to sound calm.

"I heard a bang," he said. "It woke me up."

That's because I just killed someone. The deed seemed even darker in light of the child's innocence.

Drake rubbed his eyebrow. "Very well, you might as well come in for a moment. There's something I have to talk to you about—privately. Shut the door, eh?"

Stefan did so, and Drake slapped the surface of the chest of drawers and stood next to it, one fist on his waist.

The boy hopped up to sit on it, which brought him closer to Drake's eye level so they could talk, man-to-man.

"Now, then. Do you still want to be a knight, or have you changed your mind?"

Stefan's eyes brightened. "I still want to!"

"You're sure? It's a very dangerous job. You have to be very brave. You're sure you haven't lost your nerve?"

"I can do it! Well—are there any wolves?"

"No," Drake answered. "No wolves."

He looked relieved. "I know I can do it, then!"

"Very well. Now, let me tell you something." He sent a conspiratorial glance over his shoulder. "I don't go around telling everyone this, but I actually *am* a knight myself."

"Really?"

"Shh." Drake signaled his little accomplice with a finger to his own lips. "No one but you and I must know. Now, knights, you know, we always have adventures. That's why I wanted to talk to you. I actually have one planned for tonight, but the truth is, I could use a little help," he confessed rather ruefully. "Perhaps you would come along to help out, as my page?"

"I don't want to be a page boy, I want to be a knight!" Stefan declared firmly.

Drake rolled his eyes. "Very well, you can be a knight, then, but you have to do exactly as I say, no matter what. Do you agree to these terms? I will not tolerate disobedience. This is only your first mission, after all. You have to listen to me."

"All right," Stefan said, wide-eyed.

"No, it's 'yes, sir.' And salute." He showed him.

"Yes, sir!" the boy said brightly, his flattened hand zinging from his brow.

Drake smiled in spite of himself. "There you are. Not half-bad. Remember, tell no one. Secrecy."

"And be brave," Stefan repeated.

"Right. Now, our mission will take place this evening. I'll tell you more later, if you're good. You're going to have to wait the whole day until I come and get you, all right?"

"The whole day?" he whined.

"Knights do not complain, Sir Stefan," he informed him. "Come on. I'll walk you back to your room. You should stay out of sight to avoid Count Galtür."

"He smells like onions!" Stefan said with a grin.

"Yes, I've noticed."

"Do we get to wear armor for this?" the boy asked a moment later as they walked down the hallway toward the boy's chamber.

Drake suppressed a laugh. "We won't need it for this job."

"Maybe next time?"

"Sure, next time," Drake murmured grimly, depositing him in his room with an affectionate slap on the back. "Off you go."

After locking the boy in for his own protection, Drake turned, took a deep breath, then went in search of Jacques.

He intended to settle his account with the French mercenaries and send them on their way before he unleashed Armageddon. If anyone asked, he would simply tell the Prometheans that he had given his hired soldiers forty-eight hours' leave, to make sure they kept their noses out of the cult's private business.

But the Frenchmen wouldn't be back, and the Prometheans would never have the chance to realize it had been a lie. In the meanwhile, he had final preparations to make for the eclipse ritual that night.

It was going to be a long day.

The whole day had absolutely dragged, and still, there was no sign of Drake.

Emily waited with the others in the forest a few miles from the castle walls, her back braced against a tree, her bow in her hands. She couldn't believe he hadn't joined them yet. She scanned the dappled woods constantly, watching for Drake, waiting for him.

Where in the world is he? What is keeping him? Has something gone wrong? Oh, he'll probably be here any minute. Just be patient.

It was just that she had been patient for so long.

Lord Rotherstone and she had escaped the castle walls easily before sunrise, and by midmorning had met up with his two fellow agents in the forest.

Drake had told Rotherstone about the secret entrance to the Prometheans' subterranean temple. They had set out directly for the place.

The three agents were in there doing something, she knew not what, ahead of the midnight ceremony.

But all Emily could think about was Drake.

How much longer before he comes?

Every minute of the day crawled. She knew it would not be easy for him to slip away unnoticed, especially since he had to bring the boy. She hated being separated from him.

All she could think about was getting away from Germany, departing the whole blasted Continent. She wanted to go home. When she was back on English soil, she swore she'd kneel down and kiss the ground.

Inside the rock-hewn temple, Max and his mates strained their muscles, prying the great wooden cap off the old mine shaft.

At last it came free, and he nodded to them. "Let's move it out of sight so they won't notice it."

Rohan hefted the thick wooden circle up onto its side, and Jordan helped him roll it toward a back section of the cave.

"Come on," Max urged, hurrying them along though they all were fascinated by the place. "Watch your step."

It was getting darker by the minute, but they did not dare light a lantern as the firedamp fumes from the depths of the mine shaft began drifting out to permeate the temple.

"We'd better get out of here."

They headed for the long, curving staircase hewn into the cave's stone wall.

Rohan eyed the pair of statues there darkly. "This

looks a lot like that place Kate and I found in the Orkneys—the Alchemist's Tomb."

"Wished I could've seen it," Jordan murmured.

"Aye, you would've loved it," the duke said with a grin. "Instead, you had to content yourself with translating the Alchemist's Scrolls."

Jordan nodded with a mysterious twinkle in his eyes.

Then they walked in single file under the arch formed by the figures' joined hands: a heroic male figure and a giant, devilish Prometheus, a large torch between them at the apex.

As they began climbing the stairs, Max paused, pointing toward the sky doors that Drake had described. "It's closed now, but there's the shaft that Emily will need to aim for."

Rohan sent him a skeptical glance. "Can she really do this?"

Max shrugged. "Drake has no doubt she's skilled enough."

"But will she?" Jordan murmured.

"He made her promise." He looked from one to the other and shook his head. "We'll see. Come on, march. Let's get out of here."

"Right."

They bounded the rest of the way back up the long, carved steps, then slipped back out into the woods, rejoining Emily.

Max warned them all to keep quiet, then they moved through the woods, seeking a higher vantage point from where they could watch all that would be happening down there that night. He wanted to see the full parade of the robed Prometheans approaching for their bizarre moon ritual.

More importantly, Max mused, glancing at Emily in private foreboding, they needed a good position from which their fair archer would be able to make her shot into the temple's open sky doors at the moment of total eclipse.

$\mathscr{D}$rake could scarcely fathom how his life had come to this . . . The night of the gathering.

The night of the eclipse.

Darkness had descended over the forest, and a huge full moon had crept up over the jagged peaks.

Robed figures, scores of them, faceless in their hooded cloaks, made their solemn trek through the indigo night in silence, snaking up the road from the castle and disappearing into the lightless opening in the mountain.

No lights were lit so that their eyes could adjust fully to the darkness, the better to view the celestial ballet of the stars and the bright moon and the earth's black shadow.

Drake, clad in the same dark flowing garment as they, oversaw them all, standing by the entrance. His hood pushed back, his face was expressionless as he watched them warily, accepting their bows to him as leader as they streamed past.

Beneath his cloak, he was heavily armed in case anything went badly.

Meanwhile, his little assistant "knight," Sir Stefan, waited safely behind the iron door in the underground tunnel that James had made Drake check for wild animals. That was where the sacrificial victims were normally kept until it was time for them to be brought in. Since Drake appeared to be following all the proper protocols, no one seemed to realize yet that anything was wrong.

Inwardly, Drake supposed that half of him was terrified, the other half, oddly serene. He had more or less made peace with his own death, which was imminent, but given the need to focus, he ignored all the churning emotion inside himself and, with cold control, fixed his mind and all his will on the task at hand.

All that mattered on this surreal night was ending this war for good and making sure the boy got out alive.

The Prometheans kept coming in their solemn parade across the moonlit field. It was a beautiful, clear night, but dashed eerie. Drake glanced around, discreetly scanning the tree line. Max and his team should be hiding somewhere in range, with Emily under their protection.

Meanwhile, from inside the cave, an ever-growing chorus of deep male voices made the macabre stone vault resonate with the Prometheans' ancient chants.

The great wooden sky doors sealing the stone shaft remained closed, waiting for all the men to gather. The longer they stayed shut, the better, Drake knew. Opening them would be a high point of the ceremony as the believers turned their attention to the night sky.

Nodding to the last of the men to arrive, again Drake mentally rehearsed the lines he had to say in praise of a force at odds with the beauty that surrounded them. The very shape of these majestic mountains proclaimed the mighty power of their Maker, but the Prometheans were pledged to the rebel angels' side, the sworn enemies of God.

He wrapped his hand around the hilt of the dagger under his robe and reminded himself of the motto of the Order of St. Michael the Archangel, savoring every word. *"He makes His angels winds, and His servants flames of fire."*

When the last Promethean had entered the temple, Drake personally pulled the great stone door shut and made sure it was locked.

No one would be getting out alive.

Then he pulled up his hood, his eyes gleaming in the darkness, and began walking slowly down the rock-hewn steps. He could detect no smell of the fumes that had been building up all day in the temple provided Max had done his part.

Because the explosive gas was odorless, Drake had no evidence to put his mind at ease. He could only pray that his fellow agents had opened the old mine shaft.

There was no remedy now but blind faith to hope that this plan was going to work.

It had to. The Order had never in all its centuries-long history had a chance like this. For him, that left no choice but to trust his four allies with his life.

His shoulders squared, Drake walked under the arch with its towering satanic figures. The brethren cleared a path for him, their chosen leader, as he crossed toward the altar.

Ah, James, if you could see me now, he thought wryly.

After mounting the dais by the sacrificial altar, Drake lifted his hand: The chanting stopped.

As its echoes died away, he gestured toward the men stationed by the crankshaft: "Let the doors be opened to the sky!" he ordered.

Fear of death could make even the most seasoned warrior's heart pound. A bead of cold sweat rolled down Drake's face. But it was already too late for him to turn back. Nor would he.

Emily, my love, he thought as the heavy wooden sky doors slowly rolled back, exposing the huge, golden orb of the moon. *May your aim be true.*

Lord Rotherstone had led them to a position farther up the mountain, hidden by the forest. Emily stood with them on a rocky outcropping where a break in the trees afforded them a clear view of the strange activity in the field below.

They had seen the line of robed figures streaming into the mountain. Now they heard a ponderous creaking sound coming out of the hill.

"What is that?" Emily whispered. For her part, she was worried. She could not understand why Drake had not yet come. How far was he going to take this before he slipped away?

She had thought he would have joined them hours ago. By that time, they should've already started the long journey home. But perhaps he had run into problems trying to get away. She had asked the men about it. Their responses had been vague.

Below them, the creaking sound ended with a deep-toned slam. She glanced at the marquess in question.

"Doors opening, see?" he whispered. "The cave is now exposed."

His friends exchanged a glance.

Emily squinted in the darkness and could just make out a rounded opening that had been closed before.

"Let's just hope it works," muttered Lord Falconridge, the elegant agent she had once smashed in the head with a potato back in London—to keep him from shooting Drake, naturally. To her relief, the agreeable blond earl wasn't the sort to hold a grudge.

"What do you mean, you hope it works? What is going on?" Emily demanded in a whisper. "Where's Drake? How much longer till he comes?"

All three men looked at her.

"What?"

Lord Rotherstone stared at her, then he slowly dropped his gaze. She glanced at the other two. "What's going on?" she repeated, but these, too, looked away. "Is something wrong?"

"Emily, Drake's not coming," Lord Rotherstone forced out abruptly. "But he left instructions for you. Remember?"

"Wait—what—not coming? I don't understand. He said he would join us."

"He lied, Miss Harper," the large, gruff Duke of Warrington tersely informed her.

She turned to him in confusion.

"He made his choice," Rotherstone whispered, laying a hand on her shoulder to steady her near the low cliff where they stood. "He's going to finish this."

"What are you talking about?" she breathed. Horror was spiraling inside her, making her head reel.

"Take out your bow, Emily," Falconridge murmured.

She did as he said, but she still didn't, wouldn't, understand.

Rotherstone nodded to Warrington, who took out a handkerchief and a flask of whiskey and proceeded to douse the one with the other.

"Give him an arrow, Emily," Falconridge said softly, nodding toward the duke.

Her hands were shaking as she reached over her shoulder and quickly took an arrow from her quiver.

She gave it to Warrington, and he began wrapping the liquor-soaked cloth tightly around the arrowhead, tying it in place.

"I don't understand," she said again.

"You see that opening in the rock below," Rotherstone murmured, nodding toward it. "Drake wants you to fire your arrow into there. You told him you'd do it, remember? You said you wouldn't miss. It won't be long now. We'll set this arrow afire when the moment comes. Then you'll shoot, and you can't afford to miss."

"Why? What will happen? Tell me!"

"There will be an explosion," Rotherstone admitted grimly. "The cave where those devils all have gathered is filled with a flammable gas seeping up from an old mine shaft."

"But Drake's in there!" she forced out.

Lord Rotherstone gazed at her calmly, sadly. "Yes, he is."

"But . . . he could die!"

The three warriors stared at her.

"Oh, God, no!" she whispered. "No."

"Emily, he is counting on you. Do not fail him. Drake's whole life has built toward this moment. This is what he wants. And as he told you, he needs you to play your part."

"I can't! I cannot possibly do this. I love him! No, this is madness. You cannot ask me to kill the man I love."

"I'm not the one who's asking."

"No." She shook her head. "I won't do it! You all are lunatics. I love him, I want him with me."

"And he wants you, too, but this is his destiny, just as loving him was yours. Do you love him enough to fulfill his final wish?"

"Oh, God." She turned toward the field, dragging her hand through her hair. She stared toward the hidden temple, furiously addressing her cruel, inscrutable lover in her thoughts. *You can't be serious. You cannot really want this. You lied to me! You said we'd be together. You can't ask me to kill you!*

But she could see his smiling face in her mind's eye, the kiss he'd given her back in the dungeon, the promise he had coaxed her to make. Shoot the arrow when the moment came.

And now she realized that had been a kiss good-bye.

She shook her head, unable to absorb it.

She had failed. Her warrior had chosen death and glory over life and love. She had failed to save him.

Failed utterly.

She remembered then the first time he had found her in these woods, when he had cornered her and she had begged him to run away without her. She had tried to take him captive, tried to force him to come with her by threatening him with her pistol. Smiling cynically, he had gazed at her in such misery in his dark eyes. He had told her to do it, shoot him.

Better that it should be you, he had said.

He had known even then that he would never make it out of there alive, she realized, shaking.

She had almost changed his mind the night they had tried to run away; but this "destiny" of his had stopped him from leaving in the form of Malcolm Banks's attack.

She shut her eyes. Love and fury filled her at the memory of that night, like oil poured on fire. Fury built to rage. They had taken him from her. This hateful, secret war, these evil worshippers. She wanted them dead, too, for what they'd done to him. *I'd kill them all for you if I ever got the chance,* she had told him once.

He had smiled cryptically at the time.

She had been prepared to do it with the monkshood, but that plan had fallen apart.

Now a second chance to fulfill her vow had arrived. *But how . . . ?* She shook her head, tears plunging down her cheeks as a dark dragon in the clouds opened its jaws and began to swallow the moon. *I can't. This is all impossible.*

But her whole life with Drake had been impossible . . . a beautiful dream. The earl's son and the woodsman's daughter.

Well, she had failed in her dream, but if this was what he truly wanted—and indeed, he had looked her in the eyes and said so just a few hours ago—then she vowed that at least he could have his. Even if it killed her.

They were one. If he chose to die, then so must she.

Life wasn't worth the living without him.

"Give me the arrow," she said in a strangled voice, putting out her hand.

Falconridge carefully handed the thing to her.

She gripped it, nocked it, stepped up to the cliff's edge, and lifted her bow to assess the shot. Except for the veil of darkness, there was nothing particularly difficult about it. Nothing difficult, but the fact that it meant killing Drake. The end of his life; the end of hers.

God give me strength.

She closed her eyes and lowered her weapon, for the moment had not yet come.

The shadow spread across the moon.

Drake hauled open the heavy iron door to the tunnel and left it open. He summoned the lad from the darkness. Stefan emerged, dressed in a white robe like a choirboy.

The Prometheans watched, riveted, as Drake led him up the few steps to the dais.

Stefan kept his eyes on Drake, following his every move. He was obviously scared, but he seemed determined to hold on firmly to his courage and trust in his fellow "knight." Drake had told him how everything would happen, to play along, and that everything would be all right.

He gestured to the boy to lie down. Stefan hopped up onto the stone slab, paused, and glanced around uncertainly at the dark cavern filled with men, but he did as he was told, lying on his back.

Drake had told him not to worry about the men, but to keep looking up at the moon. He'd have a fine view of the eclipse, and focusing his attention skyward would help distract the boy from his fear.

Stefan clasped his hands across his belly as he relaxed on the stone altar, where God only knew how many innocents had been slaughtered over the past hundred years.

It ends tonight.

Stefan tossed him a roguish grin, having this fine view of the eclipse, and Drake thanked God the boy still had no idea of what was going on.

He would give his awaited speech in English so the German-speaking child would not understand the foul things that he was charged to say. James had written the speech before his deathbed change of heart.

Then Drake lifted his arms in priestly fashion and began. "Infernal Father, ruler of this world, we come to your temple in the deep and gather as one to praise you on this sacred night!"

"All hail, Prometheus!" the chant returned from the cavern all around him, echoing eerily.

"Great Prince," he continued, "through folly we were

deceived on the brink of victory by our foul Enemy, the Tyrant. We have suffered our losses and seen the crumbling of our plans. But as your true sons, we will not surrender," he declared in a loud, firm voice. "We have punished those among us who have failed you, Dark Father. We hold this gathering tonight to vow that we shall rise again and work with all our strength to establish your black kingdom on the earth."

"Unholy ruler, guide us," the followers rejoined on cue.

"We come to you this night to ask you for the strength to begin our fight anew, and we offer you the sacrifice of this unblemished lamb." Drake unsheathed the jeweled ceremonial dagger and held it high, the blade pointing skyward. "Great Lucifer, light-bringer, Prometheus, stealer of fire from the gods, friend of man, and guide of our true carnal nature, hear us now!"

The shadow of the earth had nearly blotted out the moon.

Stefan stared at him in trepidation but kept still while the Prometheans watched Drake turn the blade downward toward the boy, though he still held the knife high.

"By the sign of the moon turned to black, by your fire, the hatred in our hearts, by the lies on our tongues in service to you, Infernal Father, accept this gift of innocent blood."

The moon was blotted out; the darkness was profound.

The moment of the eclipse was at hand.

The signal for Emily to shoot.

Drake held his pose, but his glance skimmed the black sky. *Come on, come on, where are you?*

She won't do it! he thought in sudden panic. Then what the hell was he supposed to do? He had no secondary plan. If she refused it, he was lost. He couldn't kill the boy—but they would. And they'd kill him, too. They'd realize Niall had been right: He was still working for the Order and had been all along.

Then he spotted it.

One tiny, distant flame arcing into sight against the black hole of the sky, hurled from the heavens, where the moon was but a silvery rim. Relief filled him. Gratitude at the girl's breathtaking loyalty.

Emily's flaming arrow was coming in fast.

Drake discarded the knife, grabbed the boy off the stone slab into his arms, and with every ounce of speed he possessed, dove toward the iron door to the tunnel.

Emily fell to her knees as soon as the arrow left her bow.

She didn't breathe, watching the tiny flame disappear into the mountain's hole, but she screamed a second later when the explosion followed.

The fireball from the mighty blast inside the mountain left her temporarily blinded. The warriors, Drake's colleagues, had turned away to shield their eyes. In the reeling seconds that followed, Emily fell onto all fours, sobbing her heart out and retching with what she had just done; but the men were all business, drawing their weapons and leaving their vantage point, advancing toward the place, for they were charged with killing any survivors.

There could be none, she thought, hearing the horrifying screams coming from the distance.

Oh, God, she couldn't stop thinking over and over again. _He's gone. He's gone. I killed him._

Maddened by grief, she staggered to her feet and stumbled away from the stony outcropping, running down to the field. She did not follow the men, but began wildly searching the edge of the tree line for one last flower of monkshood.

In the pale light of the moon slowly struggling out from underneath the shadow, she spotted one small stalk.

She recognized the place where she'd harvested it before. She must have missed that one, or the hardy weed had already grown back.

She ran to get it, stumbling, clumsy, fell to her knees before the low stalk. *I don't want to live without him.*

There was no reason to.

She tore a piece of the plant away. The leaves and stems were as deadly as the blossoms. She lifted it toward her lips, pausing to stare at it by the glow of the distant fire, already flaming out.

Her arrow had done its work. The men inside the temple were naught but charred ruins, burned alive from the second the air around them had ignited, setting fire to their robes. The Prometheans were dead. All of them.

She could see the agents waiting with their swords and pistols drawn, ready to cut down anyone who made it out alive, but they just waited. No one could survive that.

She looked over her shoulder with tears in her eyes, but oddly, into her grief came pride . . . in her hero. His courage. His cunning. His heartbreaking sacrifice.

You did it, Drake. You killed them all. You are the Order's greatest knight, just like you always said you'd be.

I love you, she told him silently. And now, in a few minutes, she would join him. Why wouldn't she?

Coming here, she had proved she would follow him anywhere. It was time to follow him again.

She brought her hand up to her mouth to eat the deadly plant when someone suddenly grabbed her arm.

Emily looked over angrily. Bloody spies and all their stealth! Wrapped up in grief, she hadn't even heard him approaching—Falconridge.

"Leave me alone," she wrenched out. "I did my duty to him. Now let me die."

But he grasped her chin firmly and turned her head toward the field. "Look!" he ordered, pointing toward the fire.

Through her tears, Emily peered in the direction the earl indicated.

And saw.

The outline of a small, skinny boy silhouetted against the flames. And, holding him by the hand, leading him away from the billows of smoke, a man.

She caught her breath on a ragged gasp and threw the deadly plant away.

Drake did not know if his hearing would ever come back after that deafening explosion. But since he had managed to survive and had saved the boy, as well, he was not about to complain.

Stefan had covered his ears the second Drake had picked him up, just like they had planned. He thought it a wonder he hadn't crushed the boy under him when he had leaped off the altar, pulled the iron door shut, then sheltered the child with his own body.

He could still feel the echo of that great blast reverberating through him, like being on a gunner's crew beside the cannon.

As they walked out into freedom, he was dimly aware of the little knight chattering away, giving him a chirpy recounting of their adventure, as if he had not been there himself. Drake couldn't hear more than a high, muffled singsong.

Then, as he and his wee pageboy crossed the field, through the smoke, he saw Emily racing toward them, crying.

He let go of the boy's hand as she came barreling into his arms. He caught her up around her waist and held her to him, trying to comfort her.

He could not imagine what she must have been feeling. "Shh, shhh," he said. "I'm sorry." Overcome with guilt, he dimly sensed her muffled voice but could not make out the words.

It hardly mattered. Nothing had ever felt as wonderful as her body in his embrace in that moment. He squeezed his eyes shut and buried his face against her neck, loving the silk of her skin, inhaling the smell of her, faint flowers, through the heavy, acrid sting of smoke that clung to him.

She was hope incarnate to him. Living, breathing love, and, God, she had proved her loyalty now as never before.

His eyes stung with fierce tears of love as he set her down and stared at her. "I can't hear a word you are saying," he enunciated carefully, watching her lips move.

She stopped, frowning.

Then he spotted Max, Jordan, and Rohan joining them.

Emily turned to them, and apparently informed them he couldn't hear.

Max said something to her; she left the men to confer with Drake for a moment and went to have a word with little Stefan, lowering herself to one knee before him a short distance away.

Drake could not take his eyes off her. He saw her check the boy for any injuries.

Drake felt a tap on his arm and turned to Max in question. "You'll have to speak up," he said loudly, pointing to his ear. "I've ruptured an eardrum."

Max pointed toward the mountain. "You did it."

Drake watched his lips, then gave him a rueful look in answer. "Close call, that." Then he shook hands with Max and accepted his congratulatory bear hug.

Warrington did likewise. From the giant duke's hug, there was no escape. "Man, I am in awe of you. And to think, I wanted to blow your head off!" He clapped Drake on the back and released him. "Virgil would be proud."

Drake smiled ruefully.

Falconridge then turned Drake by his shoulder, glancing him over from head to foot, checking for any broken bones. A man in such situations, after all, was frequently not aware of his own wounds until later.

Finding no additional signs of injury, the earl who had once put a gun in his face now offered him his hand. "Well done, Westwood."

Drake shook his hand in gratitude. "I have a question for you, Falconridge."

"Aye?"

"You translated the Alchemist's Scrolls for the Order before trading them to James."

"Yes."

"You had them in your possession for quite some time."

"A few weeks," he conceded, one side of his mouth already crooking upward. "Why do you ask?"

"Oh, you wouldn't have taken it upon yourself to add anything to the text, now, would you?"

"Who, me? Like what?" he asked innocently.

"Like a prophecy . . . a very useful one, at that."

"I have no idea what you mean," their scholar-knight answered with a placid smile.

Drake snorted, unsure what to make of his reply. Then he turned to the others with a sober look. "Niall's dead," he informed them.

"Good," Warrington growled.

"So are the rest of them," Max added, nodding toward the mountain.

All four agents turned and stared at the ruin of their enemies, then they exchanged grim glances.

"Well, it would seem the Inferno Club has certainly lived up to its name," Drake remarked.

The others started laughing, elated with their victory, but every last one of them was weary to his very soul of this dark work.

Then Emily led Stefan back over to them.

"Have you gentlemen met my fellow knight?" Drake asked his colleagues. "Allow me to present the young Sir Stefan."

"There was a dragon in there!" the boy announced in German. "We blew him up!"

"There certainly was!"

"He lived under the floor, and he ate all the bad people!"

"Yes, that is exactly how it happened," Drake confirmed, tousling the boy's hair. "Why don't you go have a word with these fellows?" he suggested. "They're knights, too."

"I want to hear more about this dragon," Warrington said to the child in his rusty German.

They drifted off while Stefan regaled them further, and soon launched into the tale of his recent battle with the wolf.

When they had withdrawn to leave the two of them

alone for a few moments, Emily turned to Drake, gazing at him like she would never let him out of her sight again.

Thankfully, his shock from the blast was wearing off, the thunder in his head growing still, so he could somewhat hear again. Drake took her hands in his and drew her to him. They could not stop staring at each other.

She shook her head in awe at him. "You did it."

"No, *we* did. Perfect aim. I knew I could count on you."

"I can't believe you made me do that."

"I'm sorry," he whispered.

"You lied to me!" He watched her lips. "I could throttle you!"

"I had no choice," he answered, wincing with regret. "I knew if I explained, you'd never go along with it."

"You're damned right I wouldn't!" she cried. But searching his eyes, she furrowed her brow, apparently realized this was not a point worth arguing anymore, and pulled him into her arms.

He wrapped his around her waist and held her for a long moment, resting his head in the crook of her neck, accepting her shelter for once. A ragged breath moved through him as he realized he was finally free.

The Prometheans were gone. The Order no longer needed him. He could devote himself fully to their future together. It was the fulfillment of a dream. He pulled back slightly, took her face between his hands, and kissed her in fervent amazement.

Running her hands over his arms, she returned his kiss with trembling devotion—but only for a moment before she stopped him.

"Tell me we will always be together from now on," she choked out. "No more secrets. No more lies."

He gazed at her in soul-deep sincerity. "Yes." He nodded slowly. "You have my word this time." He kissed her hand while the moon grew brighter, struggling free of the shadow. "You will still marry me?" he added, staring at her with some concern about her answer after what he'd put her through.

But a radiant smile broke across her face. "Of course I will," she whispered in a tone of tremulous joy. "If it's the only way to keep you out of trouble."

He smiled ruefully. They both knew it was true.

Then, with fresh tears in her eyes, she threw her arms around him once more and covered his sweaty, dirty face in kisses. He cupped the back of her head after a moment, gazed at her, and shook his head rather dazedly. "I love you so much," he whispered.

"I love you, too. Drake, you are my life."

He trembled in awe at the love that poured from her very fingertips as she caressed his face, wiping away a smudge of soot. Her touch was healing, her kiss sheer heaven. He claimed her lips again.

When the kiss ended, he gazed at his soon-to-be bride for a long moment, marveling at the woman that little Emily Harper had become—her courage, her beauty, so unique. Nothing common about his future countess. He admired her otherworldly violet eyes, brilliant in the restored illumination of the moon.

"What are you staring at?" she teased in a whisper.

"My future."

She smiled. "Will you take me home now, beloved?" she asked him softly. The same question she had been asking from the start. Indeed, the only thing she had ever asked of him.

He swallowed hard, nodding with a pang for all he'd put her through. Then he drew her protectively into his embrace, pressing a kiss to her forehead. Holding her, he made her a silent vow that, from this night forward, she had only to ask; he'd give her anything she wanted.

From the time they were children, Emily Harper had given her all for him. It would be his privilege to do the same for her, tonight and forever.

"Yes, my angel," he answered at last in a husky whisper. "*Now* we can go home."

London

A brisk morning rain pounded his umbrella as Beau hurried down Whitehall with long, swift strides. In one of those countless stuffy rooms in Parliament, the panel of investigators from the Home Office was waiting to grill him. He was on edge, dreading the day ahead and very nearly running late.

He had been up most of the night rehearsing short, efficient answers to the questions he expected—but he suddenly stopped in his tracks when the petite, elegant figure of a young lady stepped into his path ahead.

"Lord Beauchamp!" she called in a firm tone that would brook no denial.

His first reaction at the sight of Miss Carissa Portland was mad delight. His second was, *Oh, God. Not now.*

The charming gossip—no, "lady of information"— stared at him, all business, as if she, too, wished to interrogate him this morning. The pert look of expectancy on her delicate face warned him in a glance that Miss Portland wanted answers.

He already had a fair idea of what she wanted to know. Not that he blamed her. For a chit who had the dirt on all the latest scandals, it must be killing her not to know where her best friend had gone—namely, Max's wife, Daphne, Lady Rotherstone.

Still, Beau's grin thinned to a more guarded smile, and he slowed his pace, approaching her. Hang it, he did not have time for this at present.

Fortunately, he well remembered that, so far, flirting with her had proved the quickest way to make her run.

"My dear Miss Portland! What an unexpected pleasure," he greeted her with a bit of a purr in his voice. Strolling toward her, he let his gaze roam over her slim, fetching figure. "What on earth brings so fair a flower out in such inclement weather?"

Her coral pink lips fairly pursed with disapproval at his blaze of charm. "I came to speak to you, my lord."

"Indeed? Walk with me?" He gestured toward the pavement ahead. "I'm afraid I'm awfully busy. I have an appointment."

"Then I will be brief." She turned to walk beside him but declined the arm he offered, peering at him suspiciously from beneath the brim of her dark velvet bonnet.

"So, what can I do for you?" he asked, keeping his expression carefully neutral.

"*Where* is Lady Rotherstone?" she demanded at once. Her voice was hushed, as though they were discussing foreign espionage. "I know you must know something."

He strove not to smile, matching her serious expression. "Mmm. Why do you think that?"

"Because you and Lord Rotherstone are fellow members of that dreadful Inferno Club!" she shot back with a nervous glance around. Decent girls did not mention that supposed den of iniquity, not in broad daylight. "I know you two are friends. He must have told you something!"

"Rotherstone went off on a hunting trip to Switzerland or something," he said with a shrug. "You would know better than I where his wife might be. I would assume she's taking some time to herself at one of their country estates."

"No! That's the problem! I've already written to all of them to check. The staff wrote back. She isn't there! Daphne's nowhere to be found, and Kate, the Duchess of Warrington, seems to have disappeared as well!"

"Do you think they've gone off somewhere together? Paris, maybe? Shopping or something?"

"But why wouldn't they invite me?" she asked rather plaintively, almost moving Beau to pity. But she quickly hid whatever small hurt she might have felt. "This isn't like them. They should be in London, especially Daphne, now that the Season's started. She hasn't missed the opening day at Ascot since our debut. I tell you, something's wrong! What if they're in danger? Please, if you know anything, my lord, I am beside myself with worry!"

"Worry?" He stopped walking and turned to her, holding his umbrella over both of them to help protect her from the elements. "My dear, I'm sure there is no need to fret—"

"Lord Beauchamp, do not patronize me! If you know something about this, you'd better tell me what it is!"

"Or what?" he asked mildly, trying to calm her down with a playful smile.

Carissa didn't smile back. "Or—" she said, edging closer and narrowing her fiery green eyes. "I will tell Society that you are under investigation in Parliament *again*."

Beau went motionless.

"That's where you're headed now, isn't it?"

Cunning little minx. But he saw the look in her eyes, a look that said, Don't you dare trifle with me. And he realized this was not the time to lie. He swallowed a curse. "How did you know?"

"My uncle is the Earl of Denbury. I am his ward. I live with his family, you know. He's quite political. He and his friends in the House of Lords keep each other apprised of what's going on in each other's committees. Well . . ." She lifted her chin a bit defensively. "I sneaked into his study at home and glanced over his papers."

Beau lifted his eyebrows, gazing at the impudent hoyden with a whole new appreciation. Lady of information, indeed!

"What did you do this time, anyway?" she prodded him. "Another duel?"

He frowned. "How did you know about that?"

She just looked at him.

"That was years ago!" He snorted. "I was cleared of all charges, anyway."

"Humph." She assessed him with a skeptical eye.

He turned away, scowling. "If you will excuse me, Miss Portland, I must go."

The impertinent chit had the nerve to grab the crook of his arm as he stepped away. "You're not going anywhere until you tell me where Daphne is!"

Beau turned around and glared at her. "I can't."

She arched one slender auburn eyebrow in warning.

He growled, but did not dare trust the clever gleam in her emerald eyes. "Daphne's fine! Kate's with her, and they're both perfectly safe, so stop worrying," he whispered in reproach.

Though he was thoroughly irked by the feeling she

had bested him in this, he could not afford to have the little gossip spreading news all over London about the Home Office's probe into the Inferno Club.

Besides, he could see that her worry about her friend was genuine, and he could sympathize all too well, with his own teammates, Nick and Trevor, missing now for months. Oh, yes, he knew exactly how she must be feeling. "I'll tell Lady Rotherstone to write to you to confirm that she's all right."

"Well, where are they? What's going on? Why can't I see them—"

"That's all you need to know! Now, I mean it, keep your mouth shut about this investigation."

"Or what?" she retorted, throwing his own breezy challenge of a moment ago back at him.

Beau stared at her.

"Or this," he whispered. Then he reached out and grasped her nape, pulling her to him and kissing her hard, while using his umbrella to shield them from view.

His heart thundered, right along with the teeming gray skies. Carissa Portland held perfectly still as he ravished her mouth in forceful abandon.

She seemed to be in shock.

He didn't care.

He'd been dying to taste the girl since the first night he'd laid eyes on her. Of course, as he devoured her satin lips, he knew full well that Max's team was going to thrash him for this if they found out.

Daphne herself had noticed Beau's interest in Carissa; but he was not to touch her. He had been *warned*. The alluring little redhead was an innocent.

So everyone assumed.

Beau had his doubts.

Familiar as he was with the ways of women, he

sensed a certain dormant passion hiding underneath her prim demeanor, and he was rather sure that given a little time, he could coax it out.

Which was why Daphne had informed her formidable husband Max about the way that he, the unrepentant libertine Beauchamp, eyed up young Carissa. Beau was quite sure, no matter what she said, that Carissa rather liked it.

But shortly after that, he'd been advised by Max and Jordan and, most worrisome, by Rohan, of exactly what would happen to him if he laid a finger on Daphne's little friend.

If they had known him better, they would have realized this would only add fuel to his fire.

Tasting her forbidden lips at last, he was happy to take whatever beating followed. The kiss he stole was worth it.

Extravagantly so.

He made the most of the experience, savoring her tongue in a most indecent fashion. God, he'd known it—he could feel the passionate woman in her holding herself back with everything she had.

At last, the little would-be blackmailer recovered her wits enough to push her palms hard against his chest.

Beau released her, his heart thumping, victory in his eyes.

He smiled at her matter-of-factly and braced himself for a slap.

It didn't come.

Snapping out of her daze all of a sudden, she backed away, red-faced and sputtering. "Why you, you—how dare you!" She looked him up and down like he was an evil genie who had just popped out of a bottle.

Beau slipped her a crooked smile. "Let's do that again, sometime soon."

Prim once more, she sucked in a gasp, whirled around, and fled.

He stood in the street and laughed aloud, his blood pumping, his heart light with merriment—until he suddenly remembered the waiting panel of bloody bureaucrats.

He pulled out his fob watch and glanced at it with a curse, dashing off.

Then he ran the rest of the way to Parliament.

Also available from Piatkus

MORE THAN
A MISTRESS

Mary Balogh

When Jane Ingleby interrupts a duel in London's Hyde
Park, Jocelyn Dudley, Duke of Tresham, gets shot,
and Jane, late for work at a milliner's workshop, loses her
job. She is angry enough to demand a new job of Jocelyn,
and he is angry enough to hire her – as his nurse. Her blue
eyes are the sort a man could drown in – if it wasn't for
her imprudence. She questions his every move, breaches
his secrets and touches his soul and soon the dangerous
duke is offering her a different job – as his mistress.

Jane tries to keep it strictly business, an arrangement
she is forced to accept in order to conceal a treacherous
secret. Surely there is nothing more perilous than being
he lover of such a man. Yet as she sees through his devilish
facade and glimpses the noble heart within, she knows
the greatest jeopardy of all is the rising passion that could
tempt her to risk everything . . .

978-0-7499-4217-5

Do you love historical fiction?

Want the chance to hear news about your favourite authors (and the chance to win free books)?

Mary Balogh

Charlotte Betts

Jessica Blair

Frances Brody

Gaelen Foley

Elizabeth Hoyt

Eloisa James

Lisa Kleypas

Stephanie Laurens

Claire Lorrimer

Amanda Quick

Julia Quinn

Then visit the Piatkus website and blog

www.piatkus.co.uk | www.piatkusbooks.net

And follow us on Facebook and Twitter

www.facebook.com/piatkusfiction | www.twitter.com/piatkusbooks

piatkus